TREASON OF HAWKS

THE SHADOW: BOOK FOUR

LILA BOWEN

orbit

www.orbitbooks.net

ORBIT

First published in Great Britain in 2018 by Orbit

1 3 5 7 9 10 8 6 4 2

Copyright © 2018 by D. S. Dawson

Map by Tim Paul

Excerpt from *Strange Practice* by Vivian Shaw
Copyright © 2017 by Vivian Shaw

The moral right of the author has been asserted.

A CIP catalogue record for this book
is available from the British Library.

ISBN 978-0-356-50945-7

Printed and bound by CPI Group (UK) Ltd, Croydon, CR0 4YY

Papers used by Orbit are from well-managed forests
and other responsible sources.

MIX
Paper from
responsible sources
FSC® C104740

Orbit
An imprint of
Little, Brown Book Group
Carmelite House
50 Victoria Embankment
London EC4Y 0DZ

An Hachette UK Company
www.hachette.co.uk

www.orbitbooks.net

For Kate.
This grasshopper thanks you for all you did to get me here.

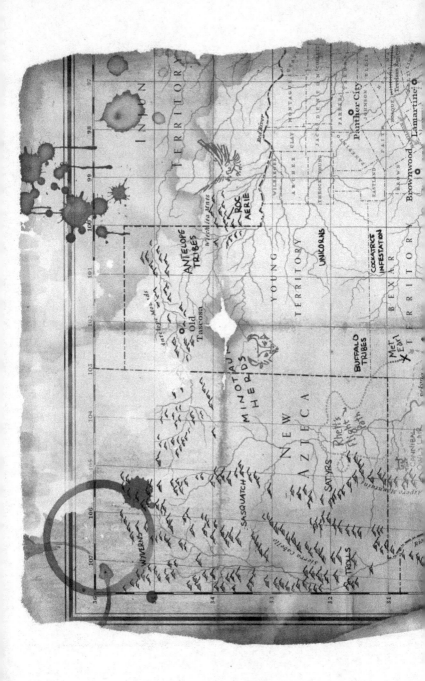

© Tim Paul 2018

CHAPTER 1

Sam Hennessy was dying on the sand, and Rhett Walker wanted to die, too. Watching the blood burble up out of Sam's belly hurt more than a knife in his own chest ever could. Even worse, Dan put his hand on Rhett's shoulder and squeezed like they were already at a funeral.

"I'm sorry, Rhett," he said, real sorrowful, and that was all it took.

Leaping to his feet, Rhett asked, "How long can he last?"

Inés tilted her head toward Cora, who hovered nearby, her arm around Meimei and her eyes full of tears. "Not long," Cora said, and Inés nodded in agreement.

"A day?"

Cora put a hand to her belly in sympathy. "Yes, but he'll be in pain."

"You keep him alive. You hear me? You keep him alive."

Rhett knelt to kiss Sam's bloody lips, gentle as a goddamn butterfly. "Hold on, Sam. I'm gonna save you."

"You can't," Sam protested, a bare whisper.

"Don't tell me what I can't do. You just keep breathing."

Rhett was already running for Ragdoll by the time Dan found his preacher voice.

"Shadow, what are you doing?"

Without stopping, without answering, Rhett slung himself into the saddle and kicked his little appaloosa mare harder than he ever had before. They tore across the prairie, Rhett laid low on her bristly neck and the rangy mare running like hell itself had lit her tail. Rhett didn't have to look back over his shoulder to know what was happening behind him. Inés would be holding Sam's hand, saying comforting, nun-type things. Healer or no, Cora would've lost interest in the dying human boy to focus on her returned sister. And Dan would be watching Rhett's trail of dust rise into the hard blue sky, frowning, hands on his naked hips.

Because what Rhett was gonna do? He already knew Dan would hate it.

It had taken two hours, maybe, for Rhett and Inés to accompany the wagon from San Anton's finest hotel to the homestead of the rich fools who'd accidentally adopted a murderous alchemist in the guise of a child. But now, unencumbered by idiots, Rhett and Ragdoll skidded into town in what felt like forever but was most likely just an hour. It wasn't hard to find what he needed, but he had to wait longer than he would've liked, and the price in promised gold was higher than he would've preferred. At that point, Rhett would've given any damn thing to save Sam, even his first taste of real wealth or the promise of other earthly comforts.

It was dusk, and Ragdoll was asleep standing up, the sweat dried in whorls on her spotted back, but she ran like the devil when Rhett was back in the saddle and kicking her again, even considering the new burden she carried. That's why he'd chosen this mare, so long ago. Like him, she wasn't big or pretty, but she had a heart as wide and wild as Durango, and if anybody could get him back to Sam in time, it was Ragdoll. If they managed to save Sam, he promised he'd shower his pony with carrots and oats and sugar cubes for the rest of her life.

Every hoofbeat pounded in time with Rhett's heart, the orange dust of the prairie strolling by with what felt like infinite slowness, purple shadows creeping along as the evening sky went dark and exhaled sprinkles of starlight. Normally, Rhett loved few things in life as much as a good gallop, but now all he felt was panic and terror and something he thought he'd left behind: the sensation of being powerless. What did it matter that he was the Shadow and nigh invincible if he lost Sam? What was the point of life if a feller lost the thing he wanted most right when he finally got it all settled?

At least he knew which way he was headed, even if it was too dark for him to see. The Shadow's tug pulled him, desperately ripping him across the prairie. Funny, that—the Shadow had never much cared about a human before. Well, except for when the Captain was dying. Dan had once—well, several times—told Rhett that the Shadow was supposed to be a sort of savior for monsters, but Rhett figured there was more at play than Dan had always assumed.

At least it was easy, this time, to do as the Shadow commanded.

Soon he saw the black wood skeleton of Herbert and Josephina's ranch house rising up against the indigo sky. Even closer, and he saw the cluster of his friends, waiting for him, watching him gallop and skid to a stop. He could almost feel Dan's disapproval, but Dan could shove his goddamn disapproval down his smug gullet. At least, judging by the way they were all there, circled up, Sam had to still be alive.

"How's he doing?" Rhett asked, sliding out of the saddle to land on numb feet.

Dan stepped forward, white teeth shining by starlight. "He's still alive, but barely. What is that?"

3

"I think you mean *who* is that, and her name is Emily. Right?"

He turned to the girl still sitting on Ragdoll's rump, her frothy skirts flecked with horse hair and sweat. He figured a gentleman would help her down, but he wasn't much of a gentleman and was just fine with that. She nodded once, regal and wary, and slid down off the horse like any farm girl in Durango would've.

"And Emily is a vampire," Dan continued.

"Well, I reckon you're a goddamn genius, Dan. Now get out of the way and let her fix Sam."

But Dan stepped in front of Sam, legs spread and teeth bared, naked and unafraid. The feller had come here as a coyote and was therefore without clothes, but he wasn't going to let that stop him from being vexful. "She won't fix him, Rhett. She can't. No one can. She'll kill him and turn him into an undead monster that can live only by feeding on human blood."

"Same thing."

"Rhett, would Sam want this?" Inés sat on the ground, Sam's head in her lap. Even through her nun's veil, Rhett could feel the disgust and judgment rolling off her, the black habit subtly writhing in a way that suggested her gorgon head-snakes were unhappy.

"I know he doesn't want to die," he shot back.

The night went so still that Rhett could hear a tortoise, somewhere nearby, toiling over the rocky soil with a dry, determined rasp.

Inés pressed on. "He said he wouldn't want to stay alive thanks to necromancy. Is this not similar, but with the added requirement that he would have to kill in order to live?"

"You don't speak for him, goddammit, Inés! You don't even know him!"

Emily stepped forward, hands up in a peaceful-type gesture. For all that she looked like a plump farmer's daughter, her hair the color of hay and her eyes the color of manure, there was a grace and power to the vampire whore that Rhett found fascinating in about the same way he found scorpions fascinating—he'd watch from afar but didn't much want to get within stinging distance when they were riled. Or hungry.

"We don't have to kill," she said, lightly lisping around her fangs. "It only takes a sip or two a night to keep us going. And cow blood'll do in a pinch, if he's not a picky sort."

"And what do you get out of this…arrangement?" Dan asked.

Emily shrugged soft, white shoulders. "I don't drink deep too often. Part of changing him over means I get to drink him about dry. And I could use the gold."

Dan's eyes shot to Rhett, who shrugged.

"I told her she could have my share of the herd money."

Rubbing his eyes, Dan shook his head. "I don't care about the money, Rhett. I care about watching you turn a fellow Ranger into the kind of monster he's dedicated his life to fighting. I care about you disregarding Sam's dying wish. Most of all, I care about the fact that even after all this time, your selfishness is going to prove the ruination of the best of us."

"Maybe it'll be the savior of the best of us, Dan. Did you ever think of that?"

"He won't thank you."

"He won't thank me if he dies, either, as dead fellers can't talk. I'm willing to make that choice, Dan."

"Of course you are! You always are! That's the problem!"

Rhett walked past Dan, banging his shoulder when Dan wouldn't budge. Looking down at Sam in the darkness, he could barely see the feller breathing. Sam's fine blue eyes were closed, his sweet lips speckled with dried blood. There was a waxy look to Sam's skin and a powerful stink about him, but Rhett didn't care.

"Do it, Emily," he said, low and deadly.

The girl moved to walk around Dan, but he intercepted her, blocking her path. That was the thing about Dan—he could be standing in the middle of the desert stark naked and still look like a preacher when he threatened a vampire. Emily stopped, but not like she was scared.

"What if he changes?" Dan asked, but soft this time. "What if he's a different person? Think about it, Rhett. Sam is a man of sunlight, of kindness and good cheer. How will he feel, waking up a creature of the night? He'll never see another sunrise again. Did you consider that?"

His hands were in fists, his teeth clenched, and Rhett couldn't take it any longer. He turned and shoved Dan as hard as he could, a year's worth of rage launching the man into the dust on his ass.

"Do it, Emily. Now. And as for what I've considered Dan, I suggest you stop trying to know my mind. I'm beyond your teaching, beyond your preaching. This is what I am, pigheadedness and all. I'm the goddamn Shadow and I'm a Ranger Captain and I already made this decision before I ever kissed Sam's dying body on the lips and galloped away. So it's on me, and you can go on with your stiff spine and judging eyes, knowing you might be right, but that don't mean I'm wrong."

Dan rose, slow but wary, more animal than man for all that he hadn't gone over coyote.

"You're damn right it's on you," he said, each word deadly heavy. "And I hope you tell Sam I fought you every step of the way. I hope you're happy with your grand folly."

Moving like a wraith in the starlight, Emily kneeled by

Sam's side. "He's so close," she said, softly. Inés, still supporting Sam's head, said nothing, but her veil inclined just the tiniest bit in agreement.

Rhett's fingernails dug moons in his palms. "Do it, girl."

"This is wrong," the nun said softly, her fingers feathering Sam's hair as if he were a sleeping child.

"Wrong is a silly thing," Emily murmured as she pulled down Sam's collar and settled into position, tender as a lover. "I remember what the preacher used to say on Sunday morning, all that business about sin. I thought I was a bad girl because my pa told me so, and then the preacher told me so, and then the old man they married me off to at fourteen told me so, too." She looked back at Dan, fangs sparking with moonlight. "I'm a person. I ain't bad. I'm just different from you. I reckon you know what it feels like to be different. This boy might feel different when he wakes up from it, but in his heart, he'll still be mostly the same."

She winked at Rhett and bit into Sam's neck with a soft crunch that made Rhett wince. Concern and jealousy reared up in his heart, and he kneeled on Sam's other side and took his cold, limp hand.

"You know that if you mess this up, I'll kill you, right?" he asked, voice rasping.

Emily moaned and gulped softly as she drank, but she didn't respond with words. She just lifted the middle finger of one hand and kept on.

"I can't watch this," Dan said. He walked away, but not far, and paced in an annoying sort of fashion.

As for Cora, she stepped closer, arm still around Meimei, who cowered against her sister's side. "Fascinating." Cora leaned in, cocking her head in that doctor way she had. "I've never seen this process before."

Rhett stroked Sam's waxen cheek. "It ain't pretty."

Inés had gone so still and quiet that Rhett had forgotten she was there at all. "That word: mostly," she mused. "Did you even notice it, in your haste? The girl said Sam would be *mostly* the same."

"I'm mostly the same as I used to be," Rhett shot back. "Folks change. They got a right to change. I reckon nearly dying changes a man."

"You lost an eye. He'll lose his humanity."

"Better than his life."

"What about his soul, Rhett?"

Before he could say something cruel or clever, Emily pulled away with a soft pop, her eyes all pupil and her lips red and kiss-swollen. Her milk-white skin had a rosy flush, and she swayed in place a little like she heard music on the night breeze.

Sam's hand was beyond cold now, and Rhett barked, "Well, girl? Get on with the next bit!"

Emily nodded as if suddenly remembering where she was and what she was doing. Holding her wrist up to her mouth, she bit it open and held the wound to Sam's lips. After a few long moments of nothing happening, Rhett was getting ready to snap the girl's goddamn neck and stab her in the heart. His first kill flashed in his head, the monster in Pap's barn that had started his life as a cowpoke, as a man, as a Ranger, as the Shadow. The twig had sunk into that wicked vampire's heart like a knife in butter, and Rhett reckoned it would be about the same with Emily, especially considering she was currently dumb as a blood-fat tick.

"Is it working?" he asked, heart in his throat, his rage collapsing into terror as Sam continued to refuse the girl's blood.

"I...I don't know," Emily murmured. Fear flashed in her

eyes as she squeezed her arm, a squirt of fresh blood painting Sam's still chin. "I never done this before."

"What do you mean, you've never done this before?" Rhett roared, hand on his knife.

Dan walked to them and stood over Sam like the graven angel on a tombstone.

"Maybe it's for the best," he said, soft as anything.

Rhett had never wanted to throttle Dan so badly, to shove those words back down his faithless throat. "It's gonna work, Dan. He's gonna be fine. It *has* to work."

Dan sighed in that way that he had, the one that suggested Rhett was a naughty child who would never, ever learn. A child who would burn his hand at the stove, again and again, until he was just a big ol' mess of scar tissue and regret.

A hand landed on Rhett's shoulder, and he ignored the instinct to sink his teeth into Dan's fingers as the man said, "Even the Shadow can't change destiny, Rhett."

Rhett's head fell forward.

The only thing he hated more than admitting Dan was right was admitting Dan was right about this.

Sam wasn't waking up.

CHAPTER 2

Rhett had pretty much given up when Sam's body convulsed, twitching like a bug that wouldn't die. His cold fingers jumped in Rhett's hand, and his blue eyes popped open and fastened on Emily's face. She smiled a sweet and almost motherly smile as Sam pulled his hand out of Rhett's and clamped it down on the girl's wrist, holding it to his lips as his throat began to work, swallow after swallow.

"Sam?" Rhett rasped.

Blue eyes sprang to his face, latched onto his own eye. Sam's golden eyebrows raised in confused question, but he didn't stop drinking.

Rhett's heart leaped like a kid goat, joyful and filled to the brim with hope. He wanted to say a hundred honeyed things, call Sam darling and sugar and sweet petunia and tell him how it had seemed to him for a minute there like life wasn't worth living, not without Sam. But he wasn't a man of words and sweetness, and all that came out was, "You still in there?"

Sam grunted but made no comment.

"How long's this going to keep going on?" Rhett asked, for although he couldn't deny his happiness that his plan was working, he was having doubts about the method. Sam wasn't looking at him with adoration and gratefulness and love; he was looking at Emily like a starveling dog looks at a piece of raw meat, and it made Rhett feel all hollow inside and a little jealous. Sam had never looked at a girl like that, not ever. But his lips were red and plump against the girl's skin, his cheeks flushed and his eyes wide and soft like when he and Rhett had been in Buck's bar, or in the hayloft, or...

"Goddammit, Sam! Let go of her!"

But when he reached for Emily's arm, she swatted him away with more strength than he expected. "He has to finish," the girl said. "Don't risk it."

"Risk? What if he doesn't finish?"

She gave a bosomy little shrug. "Don't know. Never asked."

Since Sam had already let go of his hand, Rhett stood and paced along with Dan. But he had to carefully avoid looking at Dan's face, because the feller was looking sad and smug at the same time, and the possibility of an I-told-you-so-idjit didn't bode well for Rhett's temper.

"Where'd the humans go?" Rhett asked Cora, just for something to take his mind off of Sam's mouth making love to the vampire whore's arm wound.

"They took the wagon back to town." Her voice was oddly formal now, as if they'd never shared anything at all. "Dan said they would most likely send the sheriff here tomorrow. Or that at least they'd try. Their story will be difficult to believe. Still, it would be best if we were...elsewhere." She looked around the plat, nose wrinkling in disgust at the half-built ranch house. "The fools. Such a waste. I hate it here. I can't wait to get back."

Rhett did a double take. "You mean back to San Anton, or back to your wagon?"

Cora stood tall, and her face went over cold. "Back to Calafia.

I told you: I'm taking Meimei back to our family, where she'll be safe."

"I can't believe I'm hearing this," Rhett muttered. "I don't got time to take you to Calafia, girl. I got business in Durango. And the Shadow doesn't want to go there, neither."

"I never said I wanted *you* to go to Calafia, Rhett."

The way she said it, stern but kind of sad, made Rhett want to shoot a cactus full of holes. He glanced at Sam, who was still drinking, still not looking at Rhett. His eye went to Dan next, finding the man standing over Sam, arms crossed, mouth grim. Inés was just a shape in black and white, witnessing Sam's transformation, as still as one of her statues. The night suddenly seemed a very empty, cold, hard thing, sharp as stone. Rhett's hand went to the small leather bag he wore around his neck, shifting the contents in his palm. So many people had left him, and all that remained of them hung heavy against his tightly bound chest. Monty, Chuck, Chicken, the Captain, Earl. Everybody was leaving him.

"You can't go," he said, and he was ashamed at the sound of it, the cowardice of it. The selfishness of it. The pleading in it.

"I can go, and I will. Not tonight. Not tomorrow. But soon. I can hitch the wagon by myself now, or we can take a stage, if Winifred wants to keep the wagon for her child." Her small smile was no comfort. "You'll be fine, Red-Eye Ned. We are safe. You did your duty. The necromancer is gone."

"But I ain't gone."

She shook her head sadly. "Neither is the Shadow, and it never will be. That's the problem. I am not a cart you can drag around. I have my own destiny, and it is in the west." Her hand cupped his cheek, soft and warm and dainty, so unlike the feel of Sam's big, broad fingers. "Some things are not meant to be. Some things never were."

Meimei's round face peered up at him from under Cora's arm, solemn as an owl. To think: He'd gone to all this trouble to free Cora's baby sister from an alchemist's whim. But that was a lie, wasn't it? He hadn't killed Trevisan for Meimei, nor for Cora. He'd done it because it needed to be done, because the Shadow demanded it. And now that the tug to save Sam had relaxed, the Shadow was already pulling him somewhere else. Back to San Anton, sure, but it would take him in another direction after that. He was only seventeen, but his life stretched before him like a mountain he'd never finish climbing. Hell, he couldn't even really take a rest to enjoy the view. His hands would tear and bruise, his muscles would ache and cramp, and he'd just have to keep climbing until the day he fell.

"Goddammit," he murmured, turning away from Cora before she could see him cry.

But there weren't many safe directions to look, just then. Instead of Cora, now he saw Dan's damning eyes and the distasteful scene of Sam sucking off a girl's arm like he'd die if she made him stop. And that, Rhett quickly realized, was exactly what the girl was trying to do. She'd given Sam her right wrist, and he had her arm trapped in his big hands. Now she was tugging away from him, rocked up onto her heels, her fangs bared in frustration and her left hand shoving his cheek, nails dug in.

"Make him stop!" she mewled. "He's gonna kill me!"

Rhett looked to Dan with alarm, and Dan gave him a cold glare.

"This is your shindig, Rhett. You break it up."

"Hellfire," Rhett muttered, hurrying to kneel on Sam's other side to try to pry him off the girl.

Inés scrambled out from under Sam's head and stood some bit away, hands holding down her veil like she wasn't taking any more chances today—or like she wanted to be able to lift it quickly, should the situation call for a sudden end. Cora and Meimei were already out of range of the struggle. Watching everybody else find somewhere else to be, Rhett realized he was the only person willing to tussle with two vampires for Sam's life—which was gonna be a hell of a tricky thing since he'd stab himself in the foot before he caused Sam a lick of pain. That was his self-appointed job: stand between Sam and danger. But Sam wasn't human anymore, was he? And Rhett had to make sure it had worked, that Sam was what the girl said he would be. That he was fixed and nowhere close to dying. He stopped trying to pry up Sam's fingers and flipped up the cowpoke's shirt to show a smooth belly rusty with stains that looked black by moonlight. The knife wound was gone, leaving only rippling white muscles and spare hipbones that Rhett longed to trace in a quiet moment, worshipping Sam like he'd dreamed about for years and finally gotten to do for a few short weeks.

Fine, then. It had worked. Which meant Rhett couldn't let Sam kill his savior.

Sam wasn't even aware of him, not really. He was still latched onto the girl's arm, his eyes gone fiery and furious.

"Aw, hell," Rhett said.

Pulling out one of his revolvers, he pistol-whipped Sam Hennessy, clocking him hard enough across the temple to lay a human man out cold for a full day if not scramble his wits permanently. Apparently vampires could also go unconscious, because that's exactly what Sam did. His hands fell away from Emily's arm, his wild blond hair flopping back into the dust. Emily cried out and staggered to her feet holding her arm like she'd been snakebit. She had lost the dreamy, rosy look and was white and panicked now.

"Take me back to San Anton," she hissed. "I don't want to be here anymore."

Hands on his hips, Rhett considered their present situation. Three horses, an unconscious vampire, a scared vampire, an angry coyote, a gorgon, a dragon, and a traumatized human child, and he had to get them all to San Anton safely before the sun rose. Because Sam was a vampire now, wasn't he? And if Sam didn't get back inside by the time those first golden rays peeked over the horizon, something horrible would happen.

A new kind of terror kicked in, and the Shadow did what he always did. He led, whether he wanted to or not.

"Inés, if you'd please take Meimei behind you on the chestnut. I'll drape Sam over Ragdoll's saddle and ride behind; that prancing gelding of his'll break his damn teakettle. Dan can take Emily behind him on Sam's gelding. Cora, you turn into a dragon and fly. I don't care if y'all approve. We're heading out. Now."

Ragdoll waited just a few steps away, cropping at the scant greenery, and she didn't complain when Rhett took her reins and led her over to Sam's unconscious body. But she hadn't complained about Emily, had she? Either horses couldn't smell monsters, or the filly knew she had nothing to fear.

"I know you're mad at me, Dan, but I'd appreciate your help getting Sam up here."

With a sigh of great frustration, Dan helped Rhett drape Sam over Ragdoll's saddle. It was an awkward thing, swinging up on the little mare's rump with deadweight spread out before him, and she danced a little and snorted to show her annoyance. Dan's chestnut trotted over at his whistle, and he held the reins while Inés swung up into the saddle and settled her habit. Crooking a finger at Meimei, Dan gave her a smile he'd never shown Rhett, sweet and open.

"Come here, little one. Let's get you ready for a ride," he said, his voice kind and gentle. Cora murmured something to Meimei in their language and Dan swung her up behind Inés, who spoke to the child in tiny, sad kindnesses, reminding Rhett that the nun had once been a mother herself. Meimei's bitty fingers curled over the edge of the saddle, her eyes never leaving her sister. Cora went a bit away, but not too far, and rippled into her fearsome dragon form. Watching her, Meimei's face lit up with a joy that made Rhett's heart ache.

Dan and Emily worked out their own riding arrangement, their voices too low for Rhett to hear. Of course, he just assumed they were all complaining about him, but he'd never let that stop him before. At least Emily was accustomed to naked fellers acting peculiar, considering she lived her life above a saloon. As soon as everybody looked ready enough, Rhett gave Ragdoll a gentle squeeze and set her walking back toward town, steering her according to the Shadow's whims. Not that he needed to; she knew well enough where she was going, and she stepped gentle as if sensing Sam could use all the help he could get. Or maybe, Rhett considered, recognizing that a predator was splayed over her meaty muscles and she'd do well not to disturb him from his rest.

Rhett was out in front, the others following along at their own pace. Inés kept up her conversation with Meimei, too low for Rhett to hear what passed between them, but he figured it was something nunnish or instructive, or—oh, hell, who knew? Meimei didn't speak, but Rhett assumed she was probably pretty shook up, having had Trevisan inside her for so long, the poor little critter. Dan and Emily, too, shared their whispers as Cora's wings beat lazily overhead, sounding like flaps of tarp billowing in a storm.

"Chatty old hens, the lot of 'em," Rhett grumbled to Sam's back. It was a nice back; he'd always thought so. It seemed rude to stare at Sam's rump while the feller was sacked out, but a pleasant back and broad shoulders could be appreciated without it being unseemly. "I wish you was awake, Sam. Wish it was just another boring night on the trail. Not that our nights were boring, mind. I just wish nothing terrible was happening. My best nights were the ones nothing happened at all. You'd shoot a little deer or a prairie chicken, ride back with a big ol' grin. We'd all eat around the fire. Donkey Boy would have plenty to say, of course. Mostly complaints. Hellfire, Sam. You wouldn't think I'd miss him, but I do. I can't explain it. It's like having a pebble in your boot, but you get used to it, and when you dump it out, there's a pebble-shaped hole in your foot that feels even worse."

Sam had nothing to say on this topic because he was still unconscious. The bruise where Rhett had clocked him had faded, at least. It was nice, having one less thing to feel bad about, Rhett reckoned. He hated to see Sam in pain, hated to see any cuts and bruises mar that suntanned human skin.

But Sam wasn't human anymore. He was paler now, and a monster, like Rhett.

Well, not exactly like Rhett. Sam didn't turn into a harmless bird. He was a vampire, for now and always. On one hand, that meant Sam would be harder to kill. On the other hand, that meant a whole lot of possibly bad things that Rhett didn't want to admit Dan was right about. But as far as Rhett saw it, the only other choice would've left him riding back to San Anton behind a corpse. As it was, Sam was, at least, breathing. Rhett knew this because he checked every ten seconds.

He'd considered finding a Lobo to change Sam over, but he knew for a goddamn fact that all Lobos were bad. All Lobos *went* bad. Even nice fellers couldn't stay nice, after a Lobo bit 'em. Sam would've had the sunlight and regular food, but he also would've been an evil goddamn werewolf, and then Rhett would've had to kill him, and hellfire! All this because of one piddly little knife thrown by an asshole.

"I'm sorry I let you down, Sam," he said, almost a whisper, checking to see if any of the others were close enough to hear him. Didn't look like it, so he might as well pour his heart out.

"I wasn't fast enough. I wasn't focused. I thought you'd have the good sense to stay the hell away, like we'd talked about. Cover me with the Henry, that's what I told you. But you had to get into the thick of things, didn't you?"

"I did it to save you, dumbass," Sam mumbled sleepily.

Rhett tried to hide his startlement with a solemn nod that Sam couldn't see. "Well, sure you did, Sam."

"Stop this goddamn horse and let me ride like a man. I'm no sack of oats."

Sam sounded the same, but something about him was different, and Rhett couldn't put his finger on it. Was it how Sam moved, how he smelled, how his skin was cold and even whiter than usual? The Shadow's belly wasn't flipping to make his trigger finger itchy, at least, but Rhett had to admit that Sam had lost his fragility and gained something else, a sharpness that set Rhett on edge in a way that he never thought he could be around Sam Hennessy.

But he did what Sam asked, reining Ragdoll to a stop and muttering, "Never would've taken you for a sack of oats, Sam."

As if he hadn't been stabbed and nearly dead just a short while ago, Sam slid off the saddle, and Rhett hopped from the pony's rump and into the saddle, which should've been warm from Sam's body but...wasn't. Sam put his foot in the stirrup and hopped right back up behind Rhett, right as rain on Ragdoll's rump and twice as plucky.

"Never thought I'd see the day when you let me ride Ragdoll," Sam observed.

"It ain't exactly day, Sam."

The night was silent but for the creaking of the saddle and the clop of hooves. Rhett felt a right fool, bringing up something as awkward as suddenly finding oneself a vampire.

"You're a good horseman, Sam. You could've rode her anytime you pleased, but I know the kind of mounts you favor: leggy and headstrong and peculiar-looking."

Sam's hand settled on Rhett's thigh.

"Leggy, headstrong, and peculiar is my particular brand of poison, I reckon. But I look for heart, too."

Rhett turned to look back, and their eyes met, and Rhett had to look away first.

"Seems your mounts also share a tendency to make bad decisions. Almost like they're looking for trouble. If any horse is gonna find a gopher hole, it's gonna be yours."

Sam's hand fluttered away, and Rhett missed that small point of connection, but it was right challenging to touch a man riding behind you in the saddle. All tentative, Rhett reached back, blindly, and their fingers intertwined in a crooked sort of way.

"Let's not dance, Rhett. Whatever's happened to me, I'm still me, and I know my mind. And I ain't mad, I don't think."

Rhett felt a lift in his heart, and his fingers tightened on Sam's. "You're not?"

Sam let out a great sigh that shook the stars. "Dying ain't fun. I was scared, Rhett, scared beyond my bones. I always figured when my time came, I'd smile up and God would smile back down, and I'd drift off somewhere with pretty boy angels playing harps. But it wasn't like that. It hurt, and it was confusing and jumbled, and God didn't show his face, and I found myself begging anybody as would listen to a prayer to let me live. But God didn't answer my prayer, Rhett. You did."

"I couldn't lose you, Sam."

"Hell, I know that. Wasn't like I wanted to be lost. I bet Dan had a fit."

"Having a fit is Dan's particular brand of poison."

"Then aside from Dan's temper, I guess it worked out okay. I'm here, and Trevisan's dead? And Meimei's right in the head? She's herself?"

Rhett's shoulders rose in a shrug that felt like admitting to failure. "Yes, he's dead, and maybe. Who knows what's in that child's head? But she talked to Cora quite a bit, and she smiled at Dan, and those are two things I haven't yet mastered, so I reckon she's on her way."

That earned Sam's first real chuckle, which made Rhett laugh, and soon they were cackling like roosters. Their outburst went on so long that Dan had to holler at them to shut up, but that only made them laugh harder. All too soon, the shared madness passed, and their guffaws fell off to manly coughs. It felt like they were alone in the great wide prairie, the others far behind, offering the kindness of much-needed space. Rhett realized that sleep hadn't been his friend recently. He'd had quite a few shocks, and he hadn't eaten, and his body felt as light as a goddamn feather, his head full of fluff and his heart pushed to the brink. He was worn thin, and maybe that's why he said what he said next, for Rhett was a man who couldn't abide rudeness, and even as he said it, he recognized it was about the rudest thing he'd ever said.

"So you're not evil now, are you?"

Sam's posture changed, his fingers disengaging from Rhett's. His breathing went stiff, and a new chasm of space opened between them, and Rhett could well imagine Sam's jaw was working, too, his Adam's apple bobbing up and down as he considered his next words. Rhett almost felt shame for asking such a thing, but shame seemed to him like a stupid emotion, so he just let Sam have his silence.

"Of course I'm not evil, Rhett."

"But... but if you were evil, you'd say that, too."

"Don't make me slide off this horse."

"I got to ask, Sam. It's my job. It's what I am. And the Shadow doesn't wanna hurt you, but I don't know how to feel."

"I don't know how to feel, either. This has never happened to me before." Sam paused a moment, considering his words in a way Rhett never did. "Do you think *you're* evil?"

"Hell no."

Sam's voice went quiet and deep. "You've killed a hell of a lot more folks than I ever have, and you were only with the Rangers a few months. I reckon plenty of folks would tally your books and see you as the real monster." Rhett drew a breath to speak, but Sam's hand landed on his back and shut him up. "Not me, Rhett. Not me, ever. I'm on your side, always. No matter... what I am. I'm just saying... well, I'm what you are now. A sort of weapon. You don't have to worry about me no more. I can run into battle by your side, always have your back. I'd think you'd be happy."

"I am happy, Sam!"

There was a cough somewhere behind them, and Dan's muttered "Bullshit" rode the wind.

"You're happy I'm alive, Rhett, but maybe you're not so happy with what I am now."

"You're what I made you!"

"That don't change the taste of beans, and you know it. I can feel you, holding yourself apart. Your back's stiff, and when you hold my hand, it's like you're searching for warmth that ain't there. I know I feel cold now. Like a chunk of goddamn wax. But you feel warm enough to me."

Against his better judgment, Rhett leaned back, his head falling on Sam's shoulder, his nose turned into Sam's neck, breathing in that good, Sam smell. But now it was overlaid with old blood, leaked shit, and the cold-dirt musk of a different kind of predator. Rhett realized he didn't care.

Sam stiffened at first, but then he sighed and wrapped his arms around Rhett's middle, nuzzling the top of his head.

"I love you, monster or no," Rhett promised.

"Same," Sam said. "Same."

But Rhett's disquiet, like Sam's smell, didn't go away.

CHAPTER 3

When they were near enough to San Anton to smell the city's stink, they stopped and redistributed their people. Dan, being naked, turned himself back into a coyote. Inés and Meimei continued on the chestnut, the child's tiny arms around the nun's waist, and Emily stayed on Sam's leggy roan, alone. The gelding seemed less dancey than usual, whether because Emily was a calmer rider or because the horse didn't want to get sucked dry and was trying to be polite, Rhett couldn't say. Rhett was worried, for just a moment, that Sam would choose to ride behind his vampire mama, but he didn't budge from Ragdoll's rump, and Rhett realized he'd been holding his breath.

They skipped the fancy hotel where they'd met Herbert and Josephina, assuming their paid muscle would be waiting to intercept the devious nun and her Ranger escort, even if the sheriff found the rich fools' story as implausible as it sounded. Instead, they headed for Mr. Marko's hostelry, where Winifred met them out front, arms crossed over her dressing gown and her shawl brushing the dirt for all that it was after midnight.

"Is it done?" she asked.

"Done enough," Rhett answered, feeling testy.

Mr. Marko stumbled out in a nightshirt to help with the

horses, which gave the crew an excuse to be quiet and let their exhaustion sink in. Once the hostler went back to bed, grumbling good-naturedly in German about morning pastries, folks split up to seek their rest. Dan paid Emily in gold pieces, and after a whispered conversation with Sam, she gave a polite nod and left. Dan and Winifred went to their room at the inn attached to the stables; Inés, Cora, and Meimei took Sam's old room there; and that left Rhett and Sam to stand alone in the quiet barn, wrapped in the comforting warmth of tranquil beasts.

"She said I needed to find someplace dark to sleep during the day. Emily, I mean. When the sun goes up, I'll be compelled to sleep, and if the sun should touch me, I'll burn. A little sun'll be like touching a hot stove, but full sun'll turn me to ash." Sam dug his boot toe into the hay. "I reckon we can build a box into the wagon. Make it look like a steamer trunk, but put the lock on the inside. Funny how all this time you been worried about me running off into battle, but now I can be killed by a little sunshine."

"You're not gonna get killed, Sam," Rhett said, low and husky.

"Well, I don't intend to, fool. That's why we're gonna need a box. But it'll be morning soon. I'll sleep in the wagon in the barn today, covered up in your buffalo robe. That should keep the sun out."

They were close enough to touch, just then, but not yet touching. Sam looked up, gave Rhett a look of naked longing. But not like he wanted to mess around. Like he needed nearness, reassurance. Deep in his belly, something—not the Shadow—suggested Rhett shouldn't touch a vampire, much less curl up next to one in a dark, private space.

Rhett told that cowardly part of himself to get fucked.

More tentative than he'd been in a while, he reached out to cup Sam's cheek. It felt the same in all ways save that it was cold and clammy, no longer warm and heating to Rhett's touch. Rhett wouldn't let himself recoil. Instead, he closed the distance and ever so gently went in for a kiss, giving Sam plenty of time to turn away, if that wasn't what he wanted. But Sam didn't resist; he just stood there, eyes closed, mouth opening, hands in fists at his sides like he was as scared to touch Rhett as Rhett was to touch him.

Their lips brushed, and something inside Rhett seemed to die. It was Sam—he knew that—but Sam's lips were cold, cold as a corpse in the rain. When Sam's tongue touched his, it was like being stroked by a snail, by some slimy thing that lived in the bottom of a well. Until Sam started kissing him for real, and then it was like being swallowed up by a wave. Sam's body warmed to his, his hands gripping Rhett's face like iron wrapped in velvet. Electricity jumped between them, and Rhett found himself consumed with hunger and also, maybe, just a tiny bit frightened of Sam's new strength and power. Soon they were dragging each other into the wagon, pawing at clothes and growling. Sam's teeth fastened on his shoulder, and Rhett went still for a moment, waiting to see if Sam's fangs would break skin. But they didn't, so he relaxed, and as always, accepted with open arms whatever Sam gave him.

Some time after, they lay curled together as spoons, naked and slick, the warmth trapped under the buffalo robe allowing Rhett to pretend that Sam was still human. Normally, Sam went to sleep first, and Rhett enjoyed the few moments before he followed him into oblivion, matching his breaths to Sam's and savoring the sight of the feller's bare body, splayed unconscious and sweet.

But this time, he could feel himself slipping away, his body giving in to exhaustion as Sam curled around him, steady and strong and alert.

"Go to sleep, fool," Sam whispered in his ear, his breath as cool as a breeze from the springhouse.

"You first," Rhett murmured.

Sam shook his head against Rhett's neck. "Not anymore. Give in, Rhett. Let me take care of you, for once."

"Ain't you tired?"

Sam took a few breaths to ponder it. "No. I've never felt more alive."

Something about that didn't sit well with Rhett, but he couldn't hold out any longer. He fell asleep, curled into himself, a vampire wrapped around him, strangely entwined in a new sort of darkness that still, somehow, felt like home.

Rhett slept all through the next day and didn't stir until Sam went rigid and alert, startling him awake.

"It's sunset," Sam said softly, nuzzling the back of Rhett's neck.

Rhett shifted comfortably against him. "How d'you know?"

"Same way you know things. I just do."

A bridle jingled nearby, and it was Rhett's turn to go rigid and alert. His fingers inched for the gun on the floor in his discarded holster. Behind him, Sam sniffed audibly and relaxed. "It's just Dan. Can't you smell 'im?"

Rhett took a deep breath, considering. "No, but I reckon the Shadow can, now that you mention it." Then, a little louder: "How's it going, Dan?"

The response from the barn beyond was typical Dan, blunt and to the point and ignoring pleasantries. "Mr. Marko is paid, and we need to move quickly. The sheriff is riding out to the homestead tomorrow to investigate Herbert's claims, so we need to run in the opposite direction."

Rhett sat up and rubbed the sleep from his eyes, feeling an ache in his every bone. "Anybody ever tell you you're a right friendly feller? Cheerful as a bluebird at sunrise."

Dan snorted a laugh. "No, but I've been told I have my uses."

The sounds outside suggested that Dan was hooking Samson up to the wagon, backing the big bay draft gelding into his place. The wagon shuddered, and peace fled. With a sorely aggrieved sigh, Rhett sifted through the mess on the wagon floor, hunting in the darkness for his clothes.

"Here." Sam nudged a bundle into his hands.

"You can see? In a closed wagon in a closed barn at dusk?"

Rhett allowed himself a small smile when he correctly identified the sound of Sam shrugging.

"Sure. My eyes are pretty good in the dark now. Not that I want you to get dressed, but..."

"But there are witnesses, and time is scarce," Dan finished tersely from outside.

Rhett fumbled with his clothes, hurrying to tie his binder on and get his shirt buttons right. Nearby, close enough to nudge elbows and knees every now and then, Sam did the same, but with far less fumbling.

"Let me," he said as Rhett struggled with his buttons, and Sam's clever fingers made quick work of the task that was proving a bit much for a man standing in a pitch-black closet with one eye and a headache the size of Durango.

"Don't take this the wrong way, but you look like hell," Sam whispered.

"Well, mother hen, it was a bit of a day. Days. Hellfire. I just want some coffee and eggs and some of that bark Inés keeps hid back here that dulls pain. Everything I've got hurts."

Sam opened the door and hopped down into the straw.

"Not me! I feel fit as a fiddle. Ready for the saddle. And a new set of duds. This shirt is ruined."

"Being stabbed in the guts'll do that to a garment," Dan observed. "You're just lucky you didn't shit yourself, too."

"Cheerful as a goddamn bluebird." Rhett groaned and hopped down after Sam, dreading what would happen when a sunbeam hit his brain.

But he'd forgotten: It was dusk. Sam wouldn't be awake otherwise. Headache-piercing sunbeams, at least, wouldn't be a problem for the next leg of travel. Sam searched his saddlebags for clothes he hadn't recently died in, disappeared for a bit, and came back smelling much better. The rest of the party showed up, packing bundles into saddlebags and cinching up girths. Cora and Meimei kept to themselves, and Inés greeted Samson with a scritch behind the ears and muttered at Rhett, "Yes, I know. The bark. You look like hell."

"That's what I like about this bunch. Everybody's complimentary."

Soon they were clopping out of Mr. Marko's barn in a line, the hostler himself waving them cheerfully off, beer mug already in hand. Dan and Winifred led the way on their ponies, with Inés and Meimei on the wagon seat and the spare horses all following along like ducklings. Cora flew overhead, and Rhett watched her belly scales flash in the moonlight and got the sense she was avoiding him. He also got the sense that he didn't mind that, as the kind of conversations she'd want to have right now weren't exactly pleasant ones. As for him and Sam, for once, they rode in back behind the wagon, their horses quietly clip-clopping in the night.

It might've been peaceful, but Rhett now recognized a different sort of worry for Sam than he'd had before. Sure, it was barely nightfall, but what if the sun rose early? What if Sam wasn't out of the way when it did? Rhett was the smaller feller; could he shield Sam with his body? It was clear Sam felt right safe, grinning at the constellations and patting his leggy roan, but Rhett had suddenly realized that twelve hours out of every day were not only unavailable to Sam but downright murderous.

"You seem relaxed," he said.

Sam nodded and grinned. "I feel relaxed. Powerful. Like nothin' can get me. It's nice. I always figured this must be what it felt like to be you, Rhett."

Rhett shook his head and spit into the dirt. "Oh, hell no, Sam. I feel like a sore spot all the time. Like a target. Ain't nothing relaxing at all about being me."

"But it's so hard to kill me now."

Rhett pointed to his gone eye. "Shit still hurts, though. Some of it's permanent. And just like before, you don't get to choose what happens to you. Sometimes the luck doesn't go your way. Sometimes they're gunning for you. Sometimes you got to have a silver bullet plucked out of your buttmeat with a tweezer. That'll knock a feller down a peg, for sure. And when I think about you getting caught outside at sunup—"

"Hellfire, Rhett. The sun's a predictable thing. No point in worrying about something like that. My instincts tell me when it's safe."

"Then I beg you to follow your instincts." A sudden inspiration caught Rhett. "And maybe you could wear one of these rigs." He thumped the saddlebag that held his pie plate and bible, making it jingle. "Hell, maybe we all should. If you only got one place where a bullet can kill you, it's just good sense to cover it the hell up."

"You sure got a way of bringing down a feller's mood," Sam

said darkly. "I tell you how good I feel, and you tell me how weak I am?"

"It's only because I care, Sam."

"I know. But it still rankles."

They rode in quiet for a while, and Rhett tried to enjoy the sensations of a calm night after all the struggle of the last week. Ragdoll was warm and quick below him, and the wagon creaked comfortably up ahead. He was accustomed by now to the sound of Cora's wings beating, to how she disappeared and reappeared, doing lazy circles and scouting ahead and behind like a good soldier doing necessary work. Or maybe she just got bored, going at the speed of Samson's plate-sized hooves, steadily clomping along while she could ride the breeze in that way that Rhett loved. Part of him itched to shuck his clothes and take to the sky as a bird beside the great dragon, but the rest of him knew where his loyalties lay, and it was in the saddle beside Sam. Plus, if Cora was in a bad mood, she might aim her fiery breath at him and singe his feathers.

The abandoned mission where Inés kept her library of monster lore was only a day or so outside of San Anton, even at this speed, but the Shadow was restless. It pulled him west, which he knew was the right direction to go, but something was amiss, and he couldn't quite put his finger on it. Was it drawing him away from San Anton—and the consequences of riding out into the desert with two rich white fools only to steal their adopted child, who had bitten off a finger each as thanks? Or was it drawing him toward his next responsibility? It was urgent, is what it was, and he knew he had little choice but to follow it.

Rhett sighed heavily, considering. Ever since that night on Mam and Pap's so-called ranch, when he'd been a scared little girl named Nettie Lonesome and he'd stabbed his first monster in the heart, he'd felt the Shadow's power. Even before he understood what it was, even before his dreams had given it a name, it pulled him this way, pushed him that. He didn't always understand what he was meant to do, at first, but he knew the tug wouldn't relent until he'd accomplished the Shadow's task. There was generally a momentary sense of triumph and release, when he'd killed whatever needed killing or saved whatever required saving. And then, sure as shit, a new tug would tremble in his belly and yank on his heart.

The Shadow's destiny spread out like a road that stretched in either direction, never ending, never finding any real destination. Every night, he would go to sleep knowing there was work to do come morning. Every morning, he would wake up, knowing that his work would never be done.

Or, well, shit. If he switched around his days and nights to be with Sam, he wouldn't even get mornings, would he?

The best possible future he could imagine was a dark, grim thing of little release, a life lived out of the sun.

What would it be like, he thought, to rest? To laze? To languish?

To have a simple life of simple duties, to wake up without fear or remorse or the heavy weight of expectation? To be like Mr. Marko the hostler, and arise looking forward to breakfast instead of dreading another fight?

Rhett shook his head. Above all, he was a practical feller, and it didn't do to dwell on shit that would never happen. Nothing about life suggested that comfort was to be expected. Life was hard work and a passel of worry and then you died, hopefully not too early, if you were lucky. Still, he had once dreamed of Sam Hennessy as something far away and impossible, and now Sam was one of the few constants in his life. He should stop thinking about what he couldn't have and start appreciating what he had...and before Dan preached at him to do so.

"Beautiful night," he said, eyes on Sam.

Sam gave him a smile Rhett had once considered sunny but now saw as a glimmer in the dark.

"That it is, Rhett. I smell rain somewhere in our future, but rain never hurt nobody. You reckon you'll be able to rest a few days, once we get back to the mission?"

The skin on the back of Rhett's neck prickled. "Sam, you can't read minds, can you? Because you're a . . ." He trailed off, uncertain of whether it was rude to point it out.

"Vampires can't read minds, silly." Sam gave him a fond and doting smile. "Or else I reckon we'd be in trouble. We being you and me, not all the other vampires. It'd be right useful, as a species, to have that gift, but Emily said that was just an old wives' tale. I can just read you, that's all. I know you. And you're unsettled."

"I'm always unsettled."

"True enough. But you been on this quest for a while, and you finally got rid of Trevisan. It would make sense for you to feel a bit peculiar. To not know what happens next." He paused and gave Rhett a wide-eyed, mother hen gander. "Or do you know? Is something tugging on your gut already?"

Rhett gave a huge yawn and let his shoulders slump. "It's tugging me back to the mission, and that's all I know."

"A few days' rest will do us good. Or nights of rest, I guess." Sam shook his head. "It's right confusing, having to rethink something so simple as day and night all the time."

The look Rhett gave him was wry as hell. "Tell me about it."

Sam's laugh was still bright and sweet to Rhett's ears, so he joined in. What he wanted most in the world just then was to kick his mare and gallop across the prairie, feel the wind in his hair and greet that sense of flying he so loved. But he knew well enough that folks who ran their ponies across unfamiliar territory in the dead of night for no good reason often ended up putting down perfectly good horseflesh due to snapped legs, and Rhett wouldn't hurt Ragdoll for anything. Maybe he'd stay up a bit after dawn, go for a ride by his lonesome to think about things. Or was that betraying Sam? Did Sam expect him to keep the same hours now, or was it understood that Rhett would straddle day and night as needed? He rubbed his eyes. Too much thinking on an empty belly.

"We stopping for food?" he hollered up ahead. "And didn't Inés mention some of that magic bark?"

"We'll stop when we get to the mission," Dan barked back. "I'm not interested in being questioned by the sheriff, and neither are you. It won't be long. You've lived through worse rides."

That got Rhett's dander right up. The only thing he hated worse than being told what to do was being treated like a goddamn child. Kicking Ragdoll into a canter, he passed the wagon and skidded to a walk even with Dan and Winifred.

"It ain't a measure of worse, Dan. But I had a hell of a fight yesterday, and I reckon I'd appreciate a strip of jerky for my trouble."

Dan reached into his saddlebag without a word and gave Rhett a strip of jerky and a look that suggested Rhett behave.

"I'll behave if I goddamn please," Rhett mumbled. "You got a strip for Sam, too, or are you feeling particularly stingy this morning—I mean night?"

At that, Dan's face did a peculiar thing, which was to show pity. Rhett didn't like it a bit.

"Sam can't eat jerky now, Rhett," he said softly.

Rhett mumbled, "I know that, idjit," before turning his horse to gallop right back to his place behind the wagon. But before he'd gotten Ragdoll's head around, a wave of nausea hit him like a punch to the teeth. It was as if the bottom of his belly had fallen out and a rope had slithered around his spine, yanking him forward hard enough to bruise. He dropped his jerky and pulled his gun as he spun his mare in a circle and took off galloping up a little rise just ahead.

"What is it, Shadow?" Dan hollered in his wake.

"I don't know," he hollered back, "but it's got to die, and I need to kill it!"

Hoofbeats and hollers sounded off behind him, but he wasn't about to turn back around to see who was joining him on the ride toward the fight. Whatever was happening was close and angry and immediate as shit, and the Shadow wanted it gone. It pulled him straight west into the darkness, and he was so et up with fury and worry that he didn't even get to enjoy his dang gallop.

"Don't step in a gopher hole," he begged to his little mare. "Just keep on going."

Sam and Dan and Winifred were soon running with him, and he heard the cold flap of leathery wings overhead. Nobody dared to ask him any other fool questions, for which he was grateful.

"Draw your guns," he warned. "Whatever it is, it's bad."

A high scream pierced the night, and then they were among another band of horseflesh and men. Or so he thought. The Shadow was on high alert, his belly flip-flopping everywhere, and a shot winged past his ear. He shot back, and the first enemy had turned to glittering sand before he understood what they were up against.

Chupacabras.

Their dry, musky scent was everywhere, their bulging eyes glaring and their toothy maws hissing. His people were all mixed up in the chupa gang, guns going off every which way, and as Rhett popped another chupa to gray sand, he wished like hell he'd made everybody buy a pie plate and a bible back in town, because just now, in close quarters with definite enemies in the darkness, none of them were safe. Any shot could kill an enemy—or a friend.

Hissing and screaming everywhere. Guns blasting, nothing but quick flashes in the night. Screeching horses engulfed in puffs of sand. Rhett didn't know what was happening, what he was doing, only that he had to kill as many of the chupas as possible. Because that was one thing he knew for sure about chupas: No matter how good a man might be, the moment he became a chupacabra, he became a monster, body and soul. That transformation, at least, he'd seen with his own eyes.

Something swooped out of the sky, a brush of wind and leather, and one of the chupas fell to the ground under a thrashing horse. Another body lurched nearby, and it was Sam, his fangs out and bloody and his eyes feral as hell, ripping out a chupa's neck with clawed fingers.

"The heart, Sam! You got to shoot him!" Rhett squawked.

"I know that, fool," Sam lisped around his fangs, whipping out his knife and turning the lizard-feller into dust. He brushed the sand off his shirt and added, "I did the first one with my teeth. They taste awful. Worse than raw snake."

Rhett spent a little too long watching Sam wipe off his mouth, and a hot bullet punched into his side. Turning in the saddle, he aimed for the feller who'd shot him and found it was a woman. Well, that wasn't gonna stop him from doing the right thing. He shot her a couple times until he finally hit her heart before turning to the next chupa still in the saddle. Scared, riderless horses were bumping into everything, bugling and snorting, and Ragdoll had to fight her way free, kicking and squealing and bucking. Rhett's crew kept on shooting every chupa they could see, while the chupas mostly just made a damn mess, hissing and spitting and raising hell.

It felt like hours but could only have been minutes before there was nothing left but a dozen milling horses and one chupa feller on the ground, wriggling under Cora's huge claws.

"Hold him down, Cora," Rhett hollered, slipping off Ragdoll's back and rubbing the tight, itchy spot where he'd been shot. "I got questions."

Cora did the best she could in dragon form, keeping the chupacabra in place until Rhett could get to him. The dragon backed off, and the chupa feller scrambled to his feet, going into a protective crouch. It was hard to get a good look at him in the dark, but Rhett knew their type well, having nearly been killed by one at close range when he'd been nothing more than a junior cowpoke at the Double TK Ranch.

A chupa looked a bit like the man he'd once been, and to the outside world—the world of Herberts and Josephinas, the world of humans who'd never killed a monster—they looked like normal folks. But what Rhett saw now and what he'd seen when Chuck had gone for his throat so long ago was a feller halfway to being a murderous lizard. Bulging eyes, slit nose, wide and lipless mouth full of razor-sharp teeth. Their legs and arms were skinny like a lizard's and strong as iron, their frames loose and full of hateful energy. This feller was like every other chupacabra Rhett had ever seen, which had been one before tonight, and he was looking forward to ending him.

"Why'd you attack us?" Rhett asked, once the rest of his folks had surrounded the chupa and the feller knew he was good and stuck. For an extra dose of incentive, Rhett put his revolver against the feller's heart.

"Attack you? You attacked us!" the chupa hissed, and Rhett was surprised to see cunning in the bulging eyes. He'd not known chupas could be clever, and he wasn't pleased to discover it now.

"Sorry, no. You were gunning for us, boy," he growled, pressing in his gun. "Your men shot first. Why?"

When the chupacabra didn't immediately answer, Rhett cocked his gun to hurry the feller along.

"Because you're trouble," the chupacabra spat, his voice tinged with an Aztecan accent.

"I'm only trouble to the troublesome. And why the hell would you care? If you stuck to the usual chupa lands out west, I'd just leave you the hell alone."

The chupacabra's smile had a cruel glint to it. "You can't hold us back anymore, Shadow. Can't put us in our place. We know the Rangers are gone from here—and we know why. We're watching you."

Rhett hid the twang of fear jolting down his spine behind clenched teeth. "Why should I care?"

"Because everyone has a weakness."

Rhett snorted a laugh.

"Yeah, and I know just what yours is, asshole."

He pulled the trigger, and the chupacabra exploded into gray sand.

The enemy was gone, but something about the whole ordeal didn't feel right. Chupacabras never came this far east—it wasn't how chupas worked. And how the hell would they know what had happened to the Rangers? If this was a scouting party pushing east, how many more chupas waited in some foul nest out west, over the line into Azteca?

As they rounded up the horses, Rhett noted that they were all well-trained beasts. And they all wore a brand, a stylized ER.

None of it made sense, but what rankled the most was the thought of somebody watching him. So who was it? And who the hell was ER?

CHAPTER 4

The night was suddenly quiet, but Rhett's heart and mind certainly were not.

"And what in the fresh hell was that?" he asked no one in particular.

"Goddamn chupacabras," Sam muttered. "Shot me in the side."

Rhett's heart sped up as he holstered his gun and ran to Sam, but halfway there, he remembered: Sam was no longer human. He hitched into a walk, trying to make it more of a saunter.

"They got me, too. But it's the first time you been shot since…" He trailed off and cleared his throat. "Tickles, don't it?"

Sam snorted, poking his finger through the hole in his shirt. "I reckon it's gonna be less a mortal problem and more of a laundry problem from here on out. But yeah, after it stops burning, it does tickle a bit. Anybody else hit?"

"I took one in the arm," Winifred said softly.

Dan's response to his sister's wound was similar to Rhett's response to Sam's, although Dan didn't affect a mosey halfway there. He hurried to her side, a hand on her horse's flank as if he knew touching his sister might get him shot, too. Even Kachina danced away from his touch, looking a bit insulted at his concern.

"Don't fuss," Winifred said, plucking the bullet from her arm as it emerged and tossing it on the ground with a sniff.

"I begin to worry for the child." Dan stepped back. "I assume it's immortal, or partly so. But we should consider keeping you farther away from the action."

"We should, should we?" she said tartly. "I don't think so. My instinct is to run into the fight, just like you. When my instinct urges me to stay away, I'll do that." Her glare settled on Rhett, and he struggled not to squirm. "You have anything to add on the topic?"

He shook his head. "Your body, your business. I'll never turn away a good fighter."

"There. See?" Winifred grinned triumphantly at her brother. "He's the Captain, not to mention the prickliest person I've ever met, and he has no quarrel. Neither should you."

Dan threw up his hands and muttered something in his own language as he returned to his chestnut and swung up into the saddle.

"We're all good, then. We'd best get back to Inés and Mei-mei and see how they fared." Rhett suddenly realized something was missing and looked around, but Cora was notably absent, in dragon or human form.

"Lord. Did Cora get shot? Did anybody see?"

Everyone cast about, but all they could see were milling horses, spilled clothes, and sand.

"Shit. Let's hurry back now and make sure she's good."

Hopping on Ragdoll, he considered the horseflesh left behind by the dead chupas. "These are good mounts. Dan, can you . . . ?"

Dan nodded. "Of course I'll round them up. You see to the women."

Ragdoll cantered off, and Sam and Winifred kicked their horses even with the ragged little appaloosa. The Shadow didn't have anything particular to say at the moment, just a general worried yearning westward, so Rhett did his best to navigate back to where they'd been when his gut had urged him to attack the oncoming chupacabra band. The wagon had stopped, but no one was visible outside. Samson was still between the traces, at least, stomping his big feet in an impatient but gentle sort of way, as if sleepily reminding everyone there was work to do.

"Inés? Meimei? Cora?" Rhett called, his eye darting everywhere in the low light as his chest went tight. "Sam, can you see them? Were they attacked?"

"I don't see anybody, Rhett," Sam said, drawing his gun.

Rhett drew, too. The Shadow told him nothing was wrong, but his heart told him everything was.

"We're here."

Cora hopped out of the wagon's back door and helped Meimei down beside her, while Inés took her seat in the wagon box, her veil, as always, hiding her feelings. Rhett sighed in relief and shoved his gun home in his holster but didn't relax.

"Is all well? Were you hurt?"

Cora stepped forward, her face solemn and her eyes huge and dark in the moonlight. She held Meimei against her hip, one arm wrapped around the tiny girl. Meimei looked at the ground. For a long moment, no one said anything, and Rhett would've preferred fighting two dozen chupacabras with his bare hands to waiting for Cora to speak her mind just then.

"We are leaving. I have decided. It is too dangerous here for my sister."

"Too dangerous in San Anton? Because—"

She put up a hand to silence him.

"Too dangerous near you, Rhett."

"But—"

"Whatever you say will not matter. My sister's safety is my utmost concern. I told you that we would return to Calafia, and the time has come. We will take a stagecoach from San Anton. I beg you: Stay far away from us. If she is hurt again, I will never forgive you."

Rhett realized he was holding his breath and sucked in air, his mind fighting for the right words to turn the girl's heart. Sam stepped up beside him, put a cold hand on his shoulder, and Dan and Winifred joined the circle.

"But you can't just leave. We need you." Even as he said it, Rhett knew how pathetic it sounded.

Cora's smile was gentle and sad. "You have a destiny you must obey. I do not. And I will find my own path. I will make sure that my sister is alive and whole and free to choose her own path, too. Humans don't do so well in your orbit, Shadow."

Sam's hand tightened on Rhett's shoulder, and Rhett flinched.

"Something brought us together, Cora. Don't that count for something?"

She shook her head. "There is no grand tally. You cannot see the future. Perhaps you were brought into my life to free us, and that is good. But you also got my grandfather killed. So many people die in your path. For Meimei, it is not a question of if, but of when. I have helped you in my way, and you have helped me, and there is nothing owed. Inés has given me enough money to get us where we're going, and we're going now. The coach, I hear, leaves at dawn."

Rhett's head hung. First Earl, now Cora—both by choice.

His posse was disappearing, and he didn't like it. He didn't want her to go. For all that they'd once been, for all they might've been, for all that they currently were not and would never be—well, he still liked having her around. She kept him honest. And having a dragon on a feller's side in a fight was a handy thing, not to mention having a sawbones around for after the fight.

Still, her body wasn't his business, any more than Winifred's was.

He sighed and looked up, hating his chin for quivering. "We brought back a small herd, if you'd like to choose a pony from the chupas' mounts. I reckon the bay has a kind eye, but I'd like to check his hooves before you-all head back to town."

At that, Cora smiled her old smile, the one that managed to be mischievous and sweet and kind, all at the same time.

"Thank you, Red-Eye Ned. I would appreciate that."

It was like a punch to the gut, every time she called him by the nickname he'd earned in the train camp, the name she'd whispered when they shared the same pillow, side by side.

But she wouldn't call him that anymore, would she? Because she was leaving.

Cora waited, imperious as a queen, and Rhett turned to seek the bay he'd picked out for her. The chupa horses were busy meeting the rest of the herd, but Rhett was able to pull out the short, thick gelding and check his hooves and his soundness and attitude under saddle. It gave him something to do, at least, instead of letting himself feel the swell of loss overwhelming him. He hadn't even gotten used to the new Sam, and now Cora was leaving. Unsatisfied with the bay's manners, he settled on a brown pony and tightened the chupa's saddle to help Cora up.

"You reckon you're gonna be okay on horseback together?" he asked. "I know it's not...that you're not so good with..."

"We can make it back to the city." Cora gently brushed his hand away from where he held out the stirrup for her and mounted by herself.

Rhett picked up Meimei under her arms and plunked her down on the gelding's rump, watching close to make sure that the dappled brown critter didn't take it amiss. He couldn't help thinking about everything that could go wrong for a beautiful woman and a child alone on the Durango prairie, and then it hit him: That's how scared Cora was to stay with him.

She was willing to risk it—the snakes, the scorpions, the chupas, getting lost, Lobos, all that—just to get away from the influence of the Shadow.

"You-all need food? Supplies?" he asked, roughly, looking at the ground as his eyes pricked.

"It's only a few hours, and I'm sure Frau Kloos will be glad to feed us and that Mr. Marko will buy the horse for a good price. But thank you. For everything." So quick, her knuckles grazed his face, and then she turned the horse, headed in the opposite direction.

"Ain't you even gonna say good-bye to the others?" he called, feeling desperate.

"I already did," Cora called over her shoulder. "They understand."

Rhett watched her go, short hair swinging black as ink in the moonlight, a lonesome figure headed out into the unknown with a little bundle clinging to her waist, eyes filled with trust. Nobody had ever looked at Rhett like Meimei looked at Cora, not once in his life.

He turned to Winifred. "So you knew?"

Winifred shrugged, her response to so many things, as if she'd grown tired of caring too much. "Of course. She told you from the start that she would leave. She told me that, too. The difference is that I understand why, and I think it's the right thing for her to do."

"But won't you miss her?"

Winifred snorted and redid her braid, her fingers making quick work of the fight-mussed strands. "Of course I will. But what I am supposed to do—keep her against her will? Nobody thanks you for forcing their hand. She's a wild thing, like me and like you. Like all of us. Only difference is that she has someone who needs her more than you do."

It was Rhett's turn to snort. "I never meant to need nobody."

Sam's arm landed around his waist. "Well, surprise. You need us. And I reckon we need you, too."

The scruff of Sam's neck rubbed over Rhett's forehead, and Rhett turned away from Cora's departing shadow.

"So what now?" he asked. "We just keep going? Anybody else want to leave? Inés?"

"We're headed toward my mission," the nun called. "I'm just going home."

"But are you leaving me? Leaving us?"

Her laughter carried in the night. "No. It is good to be useful again. I am glad of the destiny you brought me. Every monster I kill makes up for one of the statues that stands in my chapel."

"Dan? You plan on striking out on your own?"

Dan gave him a preacher look, arms crossed. "For good or ill, I'm stuck with you, Shadow. Even if it's only to act as your conscience."

"I like you more when you're acting as my deputy. Conscience can't shoot a chupacabra in the heart, and you're damn good at that."

Dan nodded once and walked to his chestnut, swinging into the saddle with great gravitas.

"And that's another thing we must discuss, Shadow. That last chupa standing said that someone was watching, that they know the Rangers are gone. That means Durango is vulnerable. If the Shadow isn't pulling you anywhere else, we need to consider how to protect the Las Moras region's borders."

Rhett landed in his own saddle, frowning. "Well, I figured we'd send a letter to the main office of Rangers with our bona fides, tell 'em we want to start up a new outpost. Not at Las Moras proper, of course, but the work needs to be done, and I'm still holding the Captain's badge. We got our duty."

Dan took a moment to tighten up the herd as Sam and Winifred mounted up, but then he turned his horse to face Rhett, looking halfway incredulous and halfway amused.

"Let me get this straight. You want to write to the main Ranger office and tell them what, Rhett? That we killed every Ranger we could find, stole their herd and guns, and burned down the old outpost, and now we'd like to try again on our own, thank you very much?"

Rhett's cheeks went over hot, but he refused to look down. "No, not in those exact words."

"Then what?"

"You're the one who's good with words, Dan. Not me."

"Well perhaps I don't have words foolish and suicidal enough for this task."

Rhett swore under his breath as he kicked Ragdoll ahead of the new herd and took up the Shadow's tug drawing them toward Inés's mission. "We're still Rangers. Just because what happened happened don't mean we're not Rangers." He looked to Sam. "You get it, don't you, Sam?"

But Sam didn't quite meet his eye. "I don't reckon there's

ever been a vampire Ranger before, Rhett. They always told us vampires was as bad as Lobos and chupas, that once a feller got turned, it was a kindness to kill him. Even though I know that's not true now, I don't think they'd believe me. Or welcome me."

"Anybody in their right mind would welcome you!" Rhett hollered, making a few of the new horses snort and skitter. The old horses, of course, were used to his fits.

"Did you even think about Haskell, Rhett?" Winifred asked. "Remember: He was selected by the main office. He was commended, given a promotion. That's the kind of man they want. And he likely has nothing pleasant to say about you."

The anger was thrumming up in Rhett now, as he considered how the world was currently arrayed against him. He strongly felt—hell, maybe the Shadow strongly felt—that the right thing to do was to set up a new Ranger outpost and go back to fighting the bad guys who needed killing. But for that, he needed permission, and as much as he hated to admit it, Winifred was right. Any feller who'd hire Eugene Haskell, the bigoted son of a bitch in charge of the Lamartine Ranger Outpost and Haskell's Rascals, was not someone Rhett could appeal to.

"So we write 'em anyway, tell 'em about the chupacabras coming this far east? Warn 'em?"

"Rhett, come on," Dan said, just frachetty as hell. "Can you imagine some outlaw sending the Captain a letter saying that he was going to just start playing rogue Ranger, taking out whatever threats he personally deemed dangerous? That some mysterious, mythical signal in his gut told him it was the right thing to do? It's never a good idea, asking permission for stealing power. Or claiming the gods gave you power already."

Rain started spluttering, and Rhett huddled down under his hat and shivered. For once, he was downright miserable, even while he was in the saddle and riding toward a bit of rest. It seemed like these problems might be at least a little easier to swallow in the sunshine rather than the cold November rain at midnight. He had to holler to be heard amid all the pattering drops.

"So, what? We just set up at the mission and take off our badges and kill stuff?"

Despite the incessant downpour, Rhett could almost hear Dan tiredly rubbing the space between his eyebrows. "Something like that, yes. We have a base of operations. We have money. We have a herd. We set ourselves up as a cattle outfit, maybe. Nothing that smacks of vigilante justice. We say we're raiding over the border for horses and cattle to sell like every other rancher in these parts. And if some chupacabras or Lobos die along the way, who could complain? They generally do the attacking, so we'd merely be defending ourselves. And it's not like it leaves any evidence."

Rhett had been prepared to get all ornery regarding whatever Dan said, but for once, the cantankerous coot made good sense. He thought about it while the squall worked itself out and started talking as soon as he could make himself heard.

"Well, shit, Dan. I could see that. Nice little cattle outfit like me and Sam—I mean, like we all could work at regular. It's not like we need orders from the main office to find monsters, anyway. So we take care of what needs killing and make it look like an accident or coincidence. Hell, by the time anything gets known back east, we'll already have the chupacabra problem taken care of. They want a fight, we'll bring it to 'em. And all their horses, too. I like the look of that spotted gray in the chupa herd, if we're calling."

"A cattle company, huh?" Sam asked, trotting up close enough to rub knees. "I do like the sound of that."

"And if we stay at the mission, you can sleep in the basement. Not a single dang sunbeam will ever reach you down there." Rhett grinned, warming to the idea.

"You're forgetting so many things." Winifred joined them, close up on Rhett's other side. "The mission is pretty far from the border, which means it's far from the chupacabra herds you're salivating over. And you haven't even asked Inés yet whether you can take it over. She might not want to host an outfit of rowdy cowpokes permanently, and you boys aren't exactly easy on a place."

"So maybe we'll start out at the mission and try to find a new outpost near the border. South a bit from Las Moras, I reckon. That's near chupas enough."

"There was this town called Gloomy Bluebird," Sam offered. "Small but steady, and it's already got a general store and a saloon. We could probably find a place around there. I seem to recall a brokedown ranch that the town drunk might be ready to sell, if it ain't burned down yet."

Every hair on Rhett's body stood up as he fought down panic.

Gloomy Bluebird was the place he'd run away from, never looking back.

That brokedown ranch was Pap's ranch, the one where he'd grown up.

And the town drunk? Well, that was Pap.

The Double TK was near there, too, and Rhett couldn't stand to see it again and remember those few fine days when he was a ranch hand just breaking broncs and joshing with the men, sitting on the white board fence with Monty and Poke and Chuck. Before Chuck turned into a chupacabra. Before Monty died in Rhett's arms.

Hell, there might even be Wanted posters up in that area

with Rhett's face on 'em. For all Rhett knew, Boss Kimble had decided that the new cowpoke named Nat had killed his good men and run away.

"I'd like to find something a bit north of there," Rhett said, trying to make his voice sound bored and unconcerned. "Up near Juan de Blanco's land."

"You know ol' Juan de Blanco?" Sam asked, looking at him in surprise.

Rhett looked away, rubbing his head under his hat. "I heard tell of 'im. Some feller told me sometime it weren't too hard to steal a herd off the old bastard."

Sam nodded. "That's true enough, right there. I seem to recall another little town, maybe halfway between Las Moras and Gloomy Bluebird. Right near a pleasant river. Darling, it was called."

"Darling, Durango. That's a pretty good name for a town."

"When you two are done dreaming, I could use some help with this damn herd," Dan barked.

Rhett looked up. Sure enough, some of the chupa horses were causing problems, especially a stallion who still had a man's pants plastered to his wet saddle. The rain was letting up, but everything felt cold and clammy and wretched, and Rhett was overcome with the desire to crawl into some warm, dry burrow and sleep until spring.

"Here's why the horses are acting up," he said, pointing down. "Move the herd a bit ahead."

They'd reached the site of the fight with the chupacabras, and Rhett reckoned it had to be pretty awkward for a horse to walk over what was left of its former rider, including his checkered shirt and underpants. Dan whistled and drove the horses ahead on their path, and Rhett stopped Ragdoll and slid out of the wet saddle, his pants clinging to his legs and his boots slurping in the sucking sand. Piece by piece, he picked up the discarded belongings, shirts and pants and boots and gun belts that had until recently belonged to a posse of goatsuckers. He walked them over to Inés's wagon, which wasn't too far behind, stuffing them into the back door in a sad pile.

"Never can use too many clothes and guns, I reckon," he said, but Inés only groaned, knowing all too well who'd be left washing everything once they were safely home.

As he delivered the last batch, his arms aching from the weight of sodden cloth and leather, the nun beckoned him close.

"Did you ask me if you could stay?"

"What?"

"I hear you talking. But no one has asked if you could stay at my mission. Are you becoming the sort of man who doesn't ask permission?"

"No." He almost finished with *ma'am*, but he wasn't going to give her that much power.

"Then ask."

"Ask what?"

Inés sighed, very much like Dan.

"Ask if you can stay."

Rhett sighed now, but more like a child who hasn't gotten their way.

"Señora Inés, could we please stay at your mission a bit while we try to get on our feet near the border?"

He couldn't see Inés smile—had never seen the gorgon smile—but he could sense that she was doing it, smug as a cat.

"You may. For a while. But you will fix the fences and take off your boots at the door. And I'd like a new coat of paint in the kitchen."

"Well, if that's the price we pay."

"It is."

"Then I reckon we struck a deal."

He tipped his hat to her, tossing off about a gallon of rainwater, and went back to where Ragdoll slept, head down and one hoof cocked, dripping wet. Everyone else was mounted and waiting.

Waiting for him.

Because even if they weren't Rangers anymore, even if they would never be Rangers again, he was still their Captain. It was a startling understanding, and a baffling one, but it felt natural, too.

"Let's head on out," he said, aiming for that perfect mixture of power and nonchalance that the old Captain had always managed.

They had their next steps in place. But Rhett's posse now consisted of a coyote, a vampire, a breeding woman, and a nun.

He had to find some new blood if he wanted to take on the chupas.

Finding allies was going to be a hell of a lot harder than finding monsters to kill.

CHAPTER
5

Just before sunup, Sam reined in his horse, muttered, "Oh!" in surprise, and trotted to the back of the wagon.

"I got to hurry, Rhett," he called over his shoulder, and Rhett realized he was being summoned and joined him.

As far as Rhett could tell, it was still night, but he reckoned this wasn't a point on which to challenge Sam, who surely knew and trusted his own body's needs to not catch on fire. If Sam said it was time, it was goddamn time.

"What do you want me to do?" Rhett asked.

Sam dismounted and loosened his girth before handing Rhett the blue roan's reins. Without being asked, Inés pulled Samson to a stop, and the wagon creaked to stillness.

"Put the buffalo robe over me and don't let me get uncovered so long as the sun's visible. Go on riding as far as you want this morning, I reckon, but please unsaddle my pony when you stop to rest." He climbed up into the open wagon door, his forehead all wrinkled up in consternation. "I never done this before, really. Never been this helpless. Just...just keep me safe, okay?" He looked down at his hands, turning them over as if expecting to see claws there. "I'll...well, I'll admit to feeling some fear."

The others had stopped their horses, too, and the herd milled in an annoyed fashion that suggested they were right ready for some rest of their own. Rhett looked ahead and behind to make sure everyone was safe and steady before hooking both sets of reins over a nail and following Sam into the wagon.

"I reckon we can hit Inés's mission by lunch, if we press on. If it'll make you feel better, I'll curl up in here with you, protect you with my body if it comes to that. Tomorrow night, we'll make up some bunks in the mission basement, and we'll get to making you a sleeping box for when we travel again."

Sam lay on his back on the floor and tried to tug over the buffalo robe, but it was caught on something and being stubborn, so Rhett yanked it off and draped it over Sam. For a moment, it looked uncomfortably like he was covering up a corpse, so he scuttled around to where Sam's head was and rolled back the robe to kiss his forehead.

"It'll be fine, Sam. I promise."

Sam's eyes cut sideways, all guilty. "I don't think we should make promises like that, Rhett. Nobody can promise that everything will be fine. Even when things are fine, well, they're always changing, aren't they? If you'd told me last week what I'd be today, I would not have called that fine. Some moments, I'm still not that sure."

In a fit of pique, Rhett spun around to straddle Sam over the waist and look deep into his eyes.

"You're alive, and you're here, and you're whole, and that's goddamn fine enough for me." And even if Rhett wasn't completely sure that that was how he felt, that was what Sam needed to hear.

A jaw-cracking yawn left Sam looking half-asleep. "I hope it's enough for me."

Before Rhett could argue the point further, for both of

them, Sam's eyes fluttered closed, the golden-white lashes sweeping down over pale cheeks. Rhett kissed his cold lips and covered him back up. Standing, he looked around the wagon, hands on hips, scanning for any spots where the dastardly sunshine might attempt to pierce the canvas. There were no holes in the oiled cotton canopy, thank goodness, but there were some places around the edge, where the canvas was tied down to the box, that looked suspicious. Growling to himself, he used books and cauldrons and all the peculiar baubles left from the old witch, Prospera, to block out all potential light. By the time he was done, he was soaked through with old rain and new sweat and the morning sun lit the inside of the wagon a lurid orange. If Sam thrashed in his sleep, he might expose some part of himself, and Rhett didn't like that a bit. But there wasn't much he could do. He had folks to lead. If only Cora had made the right decision and come along, it would've been a good job for Meimei, keeping watch over Sam from the safety of the wagon.

"Goddammit," Rhett muttered to himself.

He rigged up a crusty old horse blanket, tying it to the wagon's ribs just a few inches over the buffalo rug, hoping to give Sam one more layer of protection that he couldn't provide himself.

When Rhett hopped down from the wagon, everyone pretended not to look at him, but he'd learned that that's what being a leader meant: awkward stares. Everyone looked to him whenever they weren't sure what to do and glared at him while chewing his hide when things got tough. He tied Sam's roan to the wagon and hopped into Ragdoll's saddle.

"Well, come on," he said, all testy, kicking the mare into a lope that took him out ahead of the wagon. Dan and Winifred, back behind with the growing herd, said nothing, but Rhett assumed they exchanged glances passing judgment on him.

"Damn you, coyotes," he grumbled to himself.

It was lonesome as hell, leading his posse and herd through the middle of nowhere, aiming for Inés's old mission, which would always wear rusty splashes of dead monks' blood under the whitewashing. Rhett felt the weight of loss settle on his shoulders, heavier than the buffalo robe draped over Sam. He should've been heading back to the Las Moras Outpost of the Durango Rangers. Should've been ready to belly up to a table surrounded by his fellow fighting men and get served a sloppy bowl of Conchita's beans and tamales. Should've been looking forward to fighting the good fight and maybe earning the rare nod of appreciation from his Captain.

All that was left of that place he'd briefly called home? Ashes. And by his own hand.

He should've felt triumphant after killing Trevisan, but all he felt was loss.

Even stumbling up to the mission with a bellyful of jerky and regret didn't feel like much of a relief. The cluster of buildings sat there, stark and lonely on the prairie, nothing alive to see nearby but Inés's old donkey, which trotted out honking his fool head off, a sentiment returned by old Blue the mule, who'd been with Rhett since his days on Pap and Mam's farm, outside of a few weeks of Rhett's frantic meandering in the desert. Trundling along with the herd, the swaybacked critter had somehow managed the entire trip, hollering at every new horse they met along the way.

"Shut your holes," he grumbled, not quite meaning it.

He couldn't even grumble properly.

Inés parked the wagon close to the crumbling white wall on the afternoon shadow side of the mission, clever thing that she was, and Rhett felt his heart calm a little, knowing that Sam would be in the shade until nightfall. He slid off Ragdoll and peeked in the wagon, even felt under the buffalo robe to make sure Sam was still in one piece and breathing, which he was. Only then could he go about his usual business, unsaddling Ragdoll and Sam's blue roan and unhitching Samson and trying to get the expanded herd into Inés's ramshackle cow paddock with Dan's stoic glare catching him, now and then, weighing him.

"You got something to say, Preacher?" Rhett asked.

For all that he was vexful, Dan was a good hand with the beasts, and he remained tight-lipped as they wired the gate shut and got the new horses unburdened of their tack. The two men walked up and down the row of saddles, blankets, and bridles, and without a word, they started sorting them into two piles on which they mostly agreed, one for items of fine make and usability, and one for rangy old things that were of little value. Inés's mission had a smallish adobe barn, nothing special, just something big enough to hold grain and a stall for a colicky or birthing horse, and they carried the good tack in, shoving the saddles onto their pegs and hanging nice bridles from rusted nails.

Nearby, Winifred went to the door of the wagon. "This safe to open?" she asked.

"I reckon," Rhett said, on high alert. "But you'd best be careful."

She gave him a nod that suggested he was a fool and went about unpacking all the clothes and guns they'd taken off the chupacabras, spreading them out in the sun to dry and determine what was useful, what had been permanently marred by chupacabra spit and blood, and what guns they might add to their arsenal. It was a good thing to do, Rhett reckoned, and he appreciated that she was being cautious about Sam. With Cora gone and the two women no longer sharing a bed and secret smiles, he found it easier to think kindly of Winifred.

Dan, on the other hand...

Dan kept his gob shut as they filled the troughs with water from the well and pulled out some of the skinnier and older ponies for a handful of grain. Being among the horses made Rhett calmer, but Dan was all pent up, and the moment he couldn't stand it anymore, he cut his eye to Dan.

"Just get it out, man," he finally said, exasperated as all get-out.

Dan stopped working, hands on his hips.

"You could be starting a war," he said, quietly.

"I thought it was your idea, Dan? I was the one who wanted to go on being Rangers."

"Not with the white men, although I assume your continued existence would feel like a war to any of them who could properly appreciate your powers. No, Shadow. I mean with the chupacabras. The more you dream on it, the less you think about the Lobos and the other creatures that plague humankind. You want to take out these chupas because one chupa threatened you. Tell, me, Rhett: How many times have the Rangers gone after the chupas?"

Rhett shrugged. "Plenty? Wasn't Sam in a fight with 'em, once?"

Dan shook his head. "Wrong. Sam was caught up in a raid by the chupas, back when he was a ranch hand, before he'd ever met a Ranger. Thing is, there's this peculiar sort of unspoken truce. If the chupas don't venture too far into Durango, the Rangers pretend they don't exist. As long as they stay in Azteca and what they do can be written off as cattle rustling from Juan de Blanco or suchlike, it's ignored. Now why do you think that is?"

Fully exasperated now, Rhett threw up his hands. "If I knew, would you shut up?"

"I think it's because someone, somewhere made a deal. I don't know who or why that might be, but in all my time with the Las Moras Rangers, we never went after chupas. Captain rarely spoke of 'em. None of the men, not even Jiddy, wore chupa teeth among their tallies. For all the Lobos and shifters and cockatrices we went after, we left the chupas alone."

Rhett needed something to do with his hands to take his mind off his annoyance, so he went about fortifying Inés's old fence, putting fallen, weathered boards into place and pushing posts back to square. He struggled for the right thing to say as he looked for and found his favorites in the herd, checking their state: Ragdoll, Blue, Sam's blue roan, Samson, BB the gelded unicorn, and the little gray he'd picked out, the one he was thinking about training up and calling Squirrel. After the chupa attack, they were up to about three dozen horses now, a respectable herd again. He turned to Dan, eye blazing.

"They started the war, Dan. Them. The chupacabras. They came too far over the border. They came after us. They shot at us. At me, in particular. They had a message. They said they've been watching us. So don't you think I'm starting it. But I'll tell you this: I'll goddamn end it."

Dan put his head in his hands before shouting at the sky, "Why am I shackled to the biggest fool alive?"

"Your sister?" Rhett said, feigning innocence. "Well, she does give a good haircut."

To Rhett's great surprise, Dan did the last thing he expected: He punched Rhett right in the face.

His head rocked back on his neck and pain bloomed behind his eye and his brain rattled around in his skull. He fell on his ass in the dust, and both Blue the mule and Inés's little donkey took to braying like it was the funniest thing they'd ever seen.

Normally, Rhett would've seen red and leaped up to beat the ever-loving shit out of Dan, but he was mostly just impressed.

"All the times you could've killed me, and now it's fisticuffs in the dirt," he said, a hand to his aching jaw.

Dan put down a hand to help him up, and Rhett looked at it like it was a snake poised to strike.

"Take it, fool," Dan said, grinning. "I feel so much better now. I believe I see your point of view. Sometimes, punching a feller in the teeth is the only way to go."

Rhett spit a gob of blood into the dirt as his loose teeth tightened back into his jaw, yet another benefit of being what everyone else might call a monster.

"It does tend to lighten the mood," he admitted. Then, "You really think it's the wrong move, going after the chupacabras? Even if I'm beginning to think that's what the Shadow wants to do?"

"You don't know for sure what the Shadow wants, Rhett. You know direction, but that's all." Dan paused and cocked his head. "Or do you know, at that? Is it getting clearer now?"

Rhett shrugged, not enjoying the other feller's keen eyes on him, not wanting to look too deep but doing it anyway. What did the Shadow sense? While Rhett had worried over Sam, trying so hard to get used to being that close to a vampire, what had his gut been trying to tell him?

"I do see a little clearer, maybe. It's out west for sure, whatever's next. Tastes like chupacabra. Sitting on the border like thunder waiting to strike."

"Thunder doesn't strike. Only lightning can do that."

"Then it's like a storm, maybe, and the lightning ain't yet begun, but now that I'm listening, there's one hell of a rumble, out west."

Dan snorted. "Well, that's a dark goddamn portent. Can we maybe get some stew going and get some rest before we give in to it? We're not going after it tonight, at any rate."

Rhett looked over the herd, frowning. "No time to fetch a cow, and we both know there's no game out here. I reckon that old mare'll do. Overgrown hooves, teeth rubbed down to nothing. She'll be tough, but it'd almost be a kindness, wouldn't it? Goddamn chupacabras, riding a thirty-five-year-old horse with bloodied spurs."

Dan nodded grimly. "I was going to say the same thing. Life's getting a bit peculiar, if you and I agree on so many things."

Wading into the herd, Dan made a beeline for the scraggly old black mare and led her out by a wisp of tangled mane. Seeing her mince through the gate, gentle and tripping thanks to white-blind eyes and hooves that curled up like fern fronds, Rhett was right glad the chupa who'd burdened her old bones was dead. They walked side by side, leading her away to a quiet spot on the other side of the barn, where her herd wouldn't have to see her fall. One shot to the forehead and she quivered and collapsed where she stood, graceful as a queen. Rhett's heart stuttered in his chest, and his eyes pricked. He would've sworn at himself for being such a girl if a tear hadn't fallen down Dan's cheek. It was an awful thing, watching the light leave a horse's eyes. When she was on the ground and gone still, Dan said something over her, and Rhett didn't know what it was, but he reckoned it was probably some sort of prayer, wishing her well wherever she'd gone.

"Poor old girl," Rhett murmured.

"It was a mercy," Dan confirmed.

That didn't make butchering her any more fun, but that was life in Durango. If a feller wanted to eat, he ate whatever meat there was, from spitting possums to hissing snakes to horses so old they didn't know they were dead on the hoof. His anger at Dan faded away as they undertook their grim work, neither man complaining nor shirking. Rhett went off to fetch the old pot from the cold, empty kitchen as Dan took out his knife and set to it. It would be a rangy stew, but Inés knew well enough how to make anything taste better than hunger.

As he plunked the pot in the dust and pulled out his Bowie knife to pitch in, Rhett found himself smiling. His destiny still hung over his head, and Cora had abandoned him, and the chupacabras did indeed feel like a dark, oppressive thunder-head threatening him from farther west, but for now, all was well. They were on safe land, with a structure that would keep Sam safe, and they had plenty of gold and a herd of decent enough horses. Even the spare saddles and bridles would be worth something, or they could keep them around for the cat-tle outfit they'd somehow decided to start up. For at least a few days or weeks, maybe, Rhett could play at cowpoke, get his hands dirty with horse sweat and good Durango dirt instead of blood and sand.

"So you know anything about buying land or building a ranch, Dan?" he asked.

But before Dan could answer, all the hair went stiff up the back of Rhett's neck, and his stomach flipped, and he bolted to his feet and whipped out his gun. Something was coming from the north, and it wasn't human.

"What is it?" Dan murmured, quietly placing the knife and meat into the pot, wiping his bloodied hands off on his pants, and drawing his own revolver.

"I don't rightly. But it's a monster, sure enough."

"A bad monster?"

Rhett scanned the endless prairie up ahead, squinting to see what was on the way. It wasn't coming fast—he could tell that much. It was limping. It was hurt. And yet that didn't mean it was safe.

"A hurt monster."

"Do we go find it or wait for it to attack?"

Rhett rubbed his forehead, which ached. Reaching out with his Shadow sense like that was wearing, and Dan's punch hadn't yet quit throbbing inside his skull, for all the good of his fast healing.

"It's coming slow. We don't have enough time to saddle up, but we could ride out bareback to meet it. Keep it from getting anywhere close to Sam." After a beat that he knew Dan would notice, he added, "And the women."

Dan threw him a sour look, shoved his gun home, and fetched his favorite chestnut out of the pen. It took Rhett a moment longer, as he needed a halter, at least, to ride, whereas Dan could ride a naked horse—well, while naked. But soon they were loping out toward the horizon, crossing long shadows as Rhett fought to keep his seat and scowled at Dan's ability to ride firm without a lick of tack.

Dan pulled ahead, and Rhett let him, and when Dan drew his gun and fired, Rhett was downright surprised to find that whatever he'd hit didn't up and bust into a puff of smoke. It just yowled in an indignant sort of way.

"Goddammit, Dan. Do I got to finish everything?" he muttered, laying low over his skinny mare's neck and kicking her into a full-on gallop.

By the time he reached Dan, the thing on the ground was writhing in pain, and Dan hadn't yet killed it, and Rhett's belly was just flip-flopping every which way. Much to his surprise, it was something he'd never seen before: a great golden cat with a reddish mane around its noble head.

"Well, are you gonna kill it or not?" he muttered.

Dan gave him a preacher look. "It didn't attack me, Rhett. It still hasn't attacked. My bullet popped out, and it's just staring at me, yowling."

Rhett hopped off his horse, gun drawn, and walked a wide circle around the cat. Its piss-yellow eyes followed him, shining with pain, and it opened a mouth chock-full of knife teeth and let out a horrible, babyish yowl.

"What the hell do you want?" he asked it.

In response, the cat yowled and worried at its chest with its nose and paw, where he noticed a blossom of slick red.

"Why ain't that bullet popped out?"

"It's very near his heart," Dan said. "And probably silver."

"Well of course it's goddamn silver. But why won't the cat change over and talk to us? It's obviously some kind of shifter." He squatted some distance off and looked real close. "*He's* obviously some kind of shifter."

Dan looked back to the mission and sighed.

"We'd best pull out the bullet and ask him ourselves."

Rhett wished he'd thought to say that, but he hadn't, so he just shrugged and muttered, "Then get me the goddamn tweezer."

CHAPTER 6

The cat was too big to move, and nobody in their right mind wanted to be trapped inside a small, sturdy building with a giant beast—or the monster feller who surely lurked within—so they fetched what was left of Cora's doctoring kit from the wagon and carried it out into the cool of a Durango afternoon. Inés and Winifred wanted to come along and help, and Rhett argued that they shouldn't, and then they both ganged up on him until he felt quite put upon and threw his hands in the air and suggested they were welcome to toss themselves at whatever murderous monsters they so chose and he would respect their right to die.

As Rhett dug through Cora's neatly kept box, searching for the large, metal tweezer she'd had plenty of chances to use on him, it finally came home for him how desperate the girl had been to get away. This box was—well, if not her life, her calling. She was a healer, through and through, and knew more than any sawbones Rhett had ever heard of. And yet she'd taken off with her little sister without a single thought for her box of tools. That was how scared she was to be near him, and her a dragon to boot.

"Here we go," he muttered, pulling out the shining tweezer. Everything in the box was clean, he noted, and for once, he figured he'd try to keep it that way. That's how Cora would want it. And maybe there was something important to doctoring that had to do with cleanliness, for all that Rhett personally reckoned washing was overrated.

All this time, the cat had lain on its side, great tail twitching as it made growls and a rumbly sort of purr and stared at Rhett with a disturbing intelligence. But it hadn't once swiped at anyone, and he reckoned that meant the feller behind the golden eyes didn't mean them too much harm. The eyes were familiar somehow, but he couldn't quite place why.

"You gonna hold still for me, puss, or do I got to tie you down?"

In response, the cat rolled a bit to expose his chest and let his head fall back to the ground.

"He's a lion, you know," Inés said. "All the way from Africa. I've only ever seen them in books."

"The bird I turn into is from Africa, too," Rhett told the cat. The lion. "So let's be pals while I prod the big bloody hole in your chest. Deal?"

The cat sucked in a big breath and rumbled at him in an obliging way.

"Here I go. Sorry in advance if it hurts a bit. This ain't usually my job. Our healer up and left, and she was the one with clever fingers and kind ways. I'm good with a horse, decent with a cow, and downright rude to a donkey, mind, but I'm pretty rough on everything else, if I'm honest."

At that, the lion's head jerked up, and he pinned Rhett with an alarmed and damning glare while growling, one giant paw crossed over his chest. Rhett held up his hands and leaned away from those claws.

"You want somebody else to do it, then? Somebody with steadier hands, maybe?"

The lion's head dipped once.

Rhett shrugged.

"Fair enough. I wouldn't want me digging around near my heartmeat, either. Who's got the daintiest hands?"

If he was honest about it and looking only at the physical, he did, but he tried to forget that most of the time.

"Oh, shove over," Winifred said, snatching the tweezer from him and kneeling at the lion's side. "As long as you're not a cat shaman, I'll do it. I'm a good bit gentler than Rhett, at least." She fluttered her fingers at Rhett, dismissing him, so he stood and stepped back to give her plenty of room. He did keep his hand on his gun, however; no way to know what kind of man was waiting under that fur, only to arise with all his faculties once the mortal danger was past.

The cat blinked solemnly at Winifred and settled back down, his great paws held helpfully out of the way. The girl had to curl over her little belly, Rhett noticed, to reach the beast. The afternoon sun was long, and the bullet was apparently in a tricky place, but after several long moments of prodding and cussing, Winifred withdrew a splat of silver from the lion's chest. Rhett half expected the critter to fold inward in a puff of sand, knowing how easy a little scrape on a monster's heart could end it, bullet or no. But as he watched, the wound healed, the buff fur smoothing out over the great cat's chest and the bright red blood going rusty and dry.

The beast rippled, and to Rhett's great surprise, became someone he actually liked—and had thought to never see again.

"Digby Freeman?" he whooped, holding out a hand to help the feller up.

"Barely," Digby acknowledged, wiping a sheen of sweat from his deep brown face. "That bullet was a hair too close for comfort, if you catch my drift." He took Rhett's hand and stood, naked and easy, and shined his bright white grin on Winifred. "And I thank you, Miss, for your gentle way. I reckon Ned here would've scrambled my innards with that big ol' needle of his, given half a chance."

Winifred grinned at him, as they already agreed on one of the main points of life. "You're welcome. And please, call me Winifred."

Dan stepped forward wearing the blank, stark face that suggested naked fellers shouldn't grin at his sister like that for too long if they didn't want another bullet for their trouble. "And I'm her brother, Dan."

Digby cocked an eyebrow at Dan before holding out a dusty hand, which Dan took in the sort of punishing handshake that made them both grit their teeth as their forearms went tight as iron girders. "Name's Digby Freeman, as Ned said. Formerly a foreman at the Trevisan Railroad, not that it's a role I'm proud of." He withdrew from the handshake and held up his right hand, wiggling it to show his missing pinkie. "Us former employees are easy to identify, considering we're all nines now when some of us were born a perfect ten."

As he laughed at his own joke, his voice rich and warm in the cool of November, a wash of thankfulness spread over Rhett like a cozy blanket. He didn't care for many people in the world, but he liked Digby Freeman quite a bit. He reckoned he'd like him even more now that the feller wasn't forced to lord over him and lock him in a freezing train car every night.

"Well, Digby, now you know everybody but Inés here. And Sam's asleep, but you'll see him tonight. And I guess I got to come clean with you: My name ain't Ned. It's Rhett. I gave a false name at the railroad."

Digby cocked his head and barked a laugh. "Didn't I tell you? First time I met you, I said you didn't look like a Ned. I figure a lot of us made up new names, once we realized we were gonna be held captive. I wasn't born a Freeman, you understand; had to claim that one myself. More dignified of a moniker, don't you think? But what happened to your eye? It was red, but it's not red anymore, is it?"

Rhett shook his head. "Well, no. Not now. I was using a kind of magic to hide... to make me..."

He glanced at Dan with some desperation, unsure how much of his own truth to reveal, but Dan just shrugged and said, "You get to choose your friends and your enemies, Rhett. Sometimes you only get one chance. Choose wisely."

Digby's eyebrows rose expectantly as he waited. Rhett chewed his lip with a furious energy. He didn't usually tell folks about his destiny until he was sure they were on his team and gonna stick around, but folks hadn't been sticking around much lately, had they? Still, if he didn't tell Digby just now, Digby would have cause to doubt him. No point in riling up a good feller, especially not a strong and friendly one who could turn into a goddamn lion.

"I got this destiny, see?" he said, almost pleading. "I'm this thing they call the Shadow. I get called to kill things that need to be killed—most of 'em other monsters, whether the magical type or the Trevisan type. Being the Shadow means folks can't tell I'm a monster, most of the time. My eye isn't red, I don't give you that flip down in your belly. It helps me hunt. So while I was in the railroad camp, I had to use a witch's magic powder to make my monsterness show on the outside, is the best way to say it. So I could get hired. I wasn't hiding who I was from you-all so much as hiding my..."

"Dastardly potential?" Digby ventured. "From that bastard Trevisan? Suits me fine. Hell, son. You killed him. Set us all free. You can have all the magical destinies you want as long as I don't have to shit in those railroad trenches in the rain anymore." He looked around and added, "Say, anybody got any pants?"

Rhett slapped his forehead. "Yeah, I reckon if I was gonna meet a posse, I'd like to be dressed for it. Follow me on over to our general store, if you don't mind the smell of chupacabras too much."

The women headed back indoors, and Rhett led Digby over to where they'd laid out the chupa duds and swept an arm out like he thought a fancy waiter would. "Help yourself, friend. We took out a whole crew of them little lizard bastards, so we got plenty to choose from. And if you're picky, you can wash 'em off in the trough over there. If you wanna spend the afternoon as a cat, nobody here'd complain. We're all...something else."

"And we find Rhett less vexing when we're something else," Dan added, as he'd moseyed along in their wake, arms crossed as if he were still forming his opinions on Digby Freeman.

"I'll stay as I am for now, but many thanks for the option."

Digby didn't seem conscious of his nekkidness at all as he inspected the various garments strewn out in the dirt, picking things up and comparing them to his stocky, muscled frame before discarding them. He finally settled on a pair of pants he reckoned would fit and found a shirt that didn't have too many holes in the front from the chupa's acid blood and the bullets that had spilled it. He took up some socks, not minding that they were mismatched, and shoved his feet into a pair of nicely worn-in boots. For a cat, he didn't seem too persnickety. Rhett considered him and reckoned Digby made a fine enough cowpoke, and that the brighter colors suited him better than the uniform charcoal gray that had dominated everything back at the railroad camp.

"Well, and if I haven't wandered into a land of plenty," Digby said with his broadest grin, thumbs on his waistband as he surveyed the mission. "A veritable Arcadia. You got a sweet little setup here, Rhett. What's your business?" But he didn't say it in a wheedling sort of way, more in the way one wealthy man might speak to another, and Rhett understood that wherever he was, whatever his situation, Digby would have a sort of regal confidence to him that Rhett himself had never felt.

"So far, we're squatting at Inés's mission, but I reckon she'll want us gone, long term. We just got back from ending Trevisan permanently." Digby's face lit up in surprise, and Rhett wiped his hand through the air. "Long story. I had to kill him twice. Tell you later. Point being, we need something to do. Me and Dan and Sam used to be Durango Rangers, but our outpost...well, it met a bad end. Now I got this destiny telling me to hunt monsters, but no posse to do it with. So we figured we'd head closer to the border, try to clean up some of these chupacabra nests and sell their horses. You ever fought a chupacabra?"

"A chupa-what-a?"

"You'll learn soon enough. All's you need to know for now is they're all nasty, but they like stealing horses. So we're gonna set up a base, act like a cattle outfit, and hunt them ourselves. And other monsters that need killing, too."

"Although some of us have our doubts about this plan," Dan added.

"Yeah, well, it was pretty much your goddamn idea. You just have doubts about me." Rhett turned to Digby. "Dan has had doubts about all of my plans, but they've worked out so far."

"Not for Earl."

"Goddammit, Dan. You're a Ranger. You know as well as I do that not every man has what it takes. Earl didn't. But there are some men out there who do." He rolled his eye toward Digby.

As for Dan, he made that little grunt that meant maybe Rhett was right, and maybe he wasn't, but Dan didn't approve either way.

Digby dug around in his pockets, looking carefully out at the horizon. "Huh. A cattle outfit, and killing monsters. That does sound like a piece of work. Hard work. For just three men, you say? Sounds like you're gonna need some fellers you can trust. Fellers who have what it takes. Fellers with, say, experience killing things."

Rhett looked at the same horizon as he stood at Digby's side. "I reckon that's the truth."

This time, Dan didn't grunt.

Digby pulled a coin out of the chupa's pocket and shined it on his shirt. "Now, you might have to teach these fellers some things they shoulda learned when they were little but didn't—for reasons not of their own choosing. How to rope a cow, say. Or shoot a gun."

Rhett nodded. "Those are easy enough things to practice on the trail. Hell, I had to get taught how to stab a man, a while back. If a feller's got an itch to learn, no reason not to teach him."

"And I can be a patient teacher, when my student isn't of a childish mind," Dan said.

Rhett shot him a dirty look. "Point being, Digby, if you

71

should like what you see of us, you might consider traveling along. Whether it's a good fit for all concerned or not, a feller's got to know how to rope a cow and shoot a gun in Durango, and we got lariats and guns enough to share. Ain't that right, Dan?"

Dan nodded slowly. "Right enough, and I appreciate you showing an unusual level of caution, Rhett." He turned to Digby. "I like what I see of you so far, Digby. Rhett told us you were kind to him and fairer than expected in that hellhole. But I think, before we move on, we need to ask: How did you come to be dragging yourself to our doorstep with a silver bullet scraping the meat of your heart?"

With a snort, Rhett realized that this was a goddamn important question, but he'd been so glad to see a comforting and competent face that he hadn't thought to ask it. As far as he knew, the only folks who worked with silver bullets were the Rangers, and the only Rangers within a week's ride were those in the employ of one Eugene Haskell.

Digby looked down, his brows knitting like he wasn't used to being confused and coming up empty. Since he was already staring in that direction, he moseyed over to one of the many piles of chupacabra garments and selected a fine hat, which he worked in his hands as he found the right words. It was an action Rhett understood intimately. It was good to have something in your hands when you had nothing but empty answers to give.

"I don't know who it was that shot me, and that's the truth. Me and a couple of the boys from camp were doing okay—you saw us take off, and we had some supplies. Ol' Buzzard knew how to live off the land here, and he taught us how to get along. I ain't from around here, as you might've guessed. We weren't bothering nobody, and we kept far away from towns, knowing full well that we'd look like trouble to anybody who wanted to roughhouse a little without repercussions. That's another word I've always liked—repercussions. Thick and rich, like a good stew, ain't it? But I didn't want any repercussions of my own, if you catch my drift. No use running away from one wicked white man just to drop yourself into the hands of another when you're missing your papers.

"So things were going good, and we were headed over toward Azteca, where we figured life was a little more friendly to folks who weren't the color of milk, and then one night, two fellers rode up toward our fire. We tried to look harmless and act hospitable, but I reckon maybe that just made us look guilty of something? I didn't see any badges, but the way they acted, all high and mighty and smug as a cat in the cream, suggested they were lawmen of some type. Said we looked like trouble, and that a posse of brown folk had been harrying some local town, and we'd best turn ourselves in."

Here, Digby snorted and looked down, a sheen of sweat on his face despite the fact that it wasn't all that hot, considering.

"I reckon you can understand why a man once enslaved and now free ain't about to turn himself over to a lawman he knows is lying—not of his own free will. We only had one gun and two knives, taken off the foremen at the camp. And we were out of bullets. But we knew well enough what we were, under our skin, and there was a good chance those other fellers didn't. I told everyone to turn, and it was right hilarious for a few minutes there, a camp all run over with critters nobody in Durango'd ever seen before."

"I'd have liked to see that," Rhett admitted with half a grin.

"Me, too." Digby's voice had gone grim. "But I was part of it, and I remember what it felt like, stepping on a burning log as I tried to run away. Well, those fellers knew what was up, weren't scared a bit, and they took to shooting us like ducks in a barrel. Which normally isn't such a problem, but these bullets hurt like the dickens. And they killed my friends."

"Silver," Dan said. "We know it well."

Digby held up the silver slug Winifred had pulled out of him. He'd clutched it in his left hand all along, like he couldn't quite let it go.

"To think just a little change in metal can take it from tickling to burning like hell itself and worming its way into you. I could tell I was an inch away from letting that damn thing hit my heart, so I didn't change back. I was too afraid it would jump an inch to the left and leave me sand. So I ran and ran, and when I couldn't run anymore, I crawled. Couldn't find food, couldn't find water. Just knew I had to go this way, sure as a fish on a line." He tapped his temple. "You know how it is, when you're in your other skin. You got some sense, some parts of yourself, but not a lot. I don't know why I came here, but it was the only thing that made sense." Then his broad grin split his face again, like he'd forgotten that bit about nearly dying alone in the desert. "And it was the right thing, too, because didn't y'all know what to do?"

Dan's eyes were narrowed in that way that made Rhett nervous, and therefore Rhett was not surprised when Dan said, "It's the Shadow. It's Rhett. His destiny. It tends to...call things."

"Call things?"

"Mostly bad things, before now," Rhett admitted.

Dan barked a laugh. "I'm bad, am I? I saved you when you were lost in more ways than one. And then Winifred came. And then Earl. Each of us has done you a good turn that you're yet to personally repay. Whether something pulls you to it or you pull it to you, it seems to play into the puzzle of your life in a way that benefits you the most."

"Goddammit, Dan," Rhett growled. "How many times do I have to tell you I didn't ask for this? I'd much rather just stay home and break broncs. None of this is my doing."

Rhett wanted to punch Dan's smug smile as he shook his head. "And yet here we are. And you've called another person to you. I wonder what your use will be to the Shadow, Digby."

Digby exhaled and shrugged. "Hell, brother. As long as the food's good and it doesn't involve chains and breaking rocks with a pickax, I don't know if I'll complain."

They all stood there for a moment, sort of staring off into the desert in a manly and thoughtful fashion, and Rhett tried to hide his rage. Dan knew him well enough to know he was angry—hellfire, Dan had goaded him there just for fun. But Rhett didn't want to embarrass his damn self in front of Digby by doing something stupid, like the old Rhett would've done, punching Dan in the face or shouting something he would later regret. Seemed like if he did that, somehow, Dan would win. And the only thing Rhett wanted more than the feel of his knuckles peeling back against Dan's teeth was not letting Dan triumph this round—especially in front of a witness. Maybe that was growing up, he reckoned: learning when to shut the hell up and not kill anybody, even when you really wanted to.

"Let's do something useful instead of standing around here chewing lips," Rhett finally said, hoping to take back some control. "Put all these duds up, unless you reckon any more fellers are currently dragging themselves across the sand to find me while nekkid."

Dan scooped up a pile of clothes and headed for the barn,

his arms full. "Naked, Rhett. Although I reckon with you, they're always nekkid."

Rhett picked up a pile of shirts, skin crawling when he thought about the leathery gray skin of the chupacabras who'd worn them most recently. "I reckon you're right, Dan. If they crawl here of their own volition, they're naked." The word tasted strange on his tongue. "I save nekkid for my private time."

"What's that about nekkid?"

Rhett looked up and dropped his armload of clothes when he heard Sam's voice. Sure enough, the sun was headed down, painting the shadows a vibrant blue against the stark orange dirt as the temperature dropped to shivery.

Rhett jogged toward the wagon, the clothes forgotten on the ground. "Don't come out yet, Sam! Sun's still in the sky!"

But when he got around the barn, the wagon was still all closed up, thank goodness.

"I know," Sam hollered. "I'm awake, but I can tell it's not time yet. I'll stay in the wagon a few moments more, if you want to join me."

His voice was as inviting as a hot pie on the sill, but Rhett glanced back to where Digby and Dan had stopped their work to watch him.

"We'll catch up," he called, flapping a hand at them. He could already tell that Dan was gonna give Digby an earful of gossip about Rhett's many faults and proclivities, and he didn't care a bit. He showed Dan his middle finger for good measure.

And then he was tucking himself through the little door at the back of the wagon. The scent of Sam enveloped him, overlaid with the dust of the buffalo robe and the remaining herbal tinge of the wagon's original owner. Sam was sitting on the small bed, and Rhett was glad to see that the sun couldn't penetrate the canvas, thanks to the shadow of the barn.

"We got to get you a bed in the mission," Rhett said, touching Sam's face in the near dark as if reassuring himself that Sam hadn't turned into ash.

"I know," Sam said. "I was twitchy, going down this morning, but it ain't your usual kind of sleep. Like falling in a hole you didn't expect. You know how a feller wakes up a little, sometimes, whether to take a piss or roll over? I don't do that, now. I just sleep, heavy and deep. And when I wake, I'm on alert. I wonder if I'll ever feel sleepy again."

"I'll feel sleepy for you," Rhett said, yawning as if on cue, his jaw cracking.

"You didn't rest today? At all?" Sam asked, worried as a mother hen.

Rhett shook his head, knowing Sam's vampire eyes could see the motion, even in the falling dark.

"Too much to do. Traveling, butchering, sorting goods. And then—"

"A new feller showed up."

It wasn't a question, but it did have a mote of suspicion about it. Like Sam didn't like the idea.

"And you know him."

That wasn't a question, either, but it made Rhett feel right prickly.

"What showed up was a wildcat with a silver bullet kissing his heart. Winifred pulled it out, and it turns out it's Digby Freeman, my foreman from the railroad. Nice feller." Rhett stared at Sam, hard. "But not my type, if you catch my drift. Dan and Winifred like him, although Dan doesn't like that Winifred does. You should come on out and meet him before you get too set against him."

Sam's head jerked back like he was surprised at himself. "Gosh, Rhett. I'm not set against him! I don't even know him! I know I can be jealous, but…I'll own that my reaction was right peculiar. Like some part of me just doesn't trust strangers anymore."

"The vampire part, you think?"

For all that he could see fine in the dark, Sam's hand fumbled for Rhett's and clutched it like he was drowning, cold as a waterlogged corpse.

"I…I don't know. I don't want it to be the vampire part, but I reckon it is. I don't want to change, but I keep finding myself changed. It's unsettling. I'm glad to be alive and strong, but there are these moments when I feel like…like someone else. God, I miss the sun, Rhett. If I'm changed, if I'm ornery or I take against a feller at first, it's not because I want to."

Rhett squeezed Sam's hand back, feeling the man's skin warm to his own. "A feller's got a right to change, now and again, I reckon. I know I reserve that right for myself. The idea is to change together. I'm not that fond of strangers these days, either. But Digby's no stranger, Sam, I swear. We lived in the same car with the same dozen men for weeks, and he never did anything that made me want to punch him in the mouth, much less kiss him on the mouth, and…" He chuckled. "That's pretty goddamn rare."

"So it is." With a businesslike sort of sigh, Sam went about straightening his clothes and patting down his hair and putting on his hat. As the darkness progressed, it was getting hard for Rhett to see what he was doing, but he knew Sam's motions, knew what the feller did every morning on the trail. And this was Sam's morning now, only instead of waking up next to Rhett, saddle by saddle beside the coals of the fire and kissed by sunrise, he'd woken up alone in the wagon.

Oh, lord.

If Rhett wanted to sleep by Sam's side now, he'd have to sleep during the day. And in the basement of the mission, with all its gory ghosts of dead monks ripped apart by giant lizards. A shiver went down Rhett's spine at the thought of cozying up down there in the cold.

"You okay, Rhett?"

Rhett shook himself like a dog throwing off water. "Goose walked over my grave, I reckon. I'm fine enough."

"Then let's go meet this new feller. And you got to get some sleep."

"No! I mean, later. I want to be with you. Got to eat first, in any case, maybe wash off the road dust." He gave Sam a hopeful grin. "I don't know if you recall, but Inés has a rather nice copper bathing tub, out back."

Sam made a throaty sort of rumble that made Rhett's knees go weak. "I do recall, yes."

Rhett fumbled for the door, but Sam opened it easily and jumped out, holding up a hand for Rhett. It wasn't even that dark outside, but the sun had definitely given up the ghost. Rhett grabbed Sam's hand, hopped down, and kissed Sam's sun-browned knuckles. When he looked up, Digby and Dan were gone, as were the various piles of chupacabra duds, which was convenient.

"What that smell?" Sam's head was up, his nostrils flaring and his eyes wide. "Blood?"

Rhett went on alert and searched the yard but didn't see anything untoward, nor did the twitch in his belly tell him anything other than the fact that a bath with Sam would be pretty nice. Then he noticed the lump out in the yard and nodded.

"Oh. That. We butchered the old black mare. She wasn't gonna make it long, and we needed meat."

"And you just left it out there?"

Rhett smiled at Sam's fussiness.

"Well, we did have an injured lion yowling in the barnyard. If you want to go back to butchering with me, I'll gladly help."

"I thought it was fresh," Sam said, disappointed. His head hung, all dejected-like. "I...I need blood. I hate to say it, I really do, but I haven't had anything since Emily, and that wasn't a real meal."

"Well you can have the rest of the horse, if you want it."

Sam reared back his head, scandalized. "I can't eat a dead horse! I need fresh blood."

"Well how the hell should I know that? I don't know the... the...vampire rules!"

Rhett realized that his voice had risen more than he'd wanted it to, and he was bickering like a chicken in the barnyard. Sam had realized it, too, and they both went over a bit embarrassed.

"What do you need, then? Is it just people? Can you drink from an animal? Does it hurt? Like, what if I held a horse for you, and you just sunk your teeth in for a bite? They got plenty of blood, right? Might have some extra in there? That new flea-bit stallion deserves it."

Sam looked everywhere but at Rhett before stomping determinedly to the horse carcass, carefully rolling up his sleeves, pulling out his Bowie knife, and getting to work. As soon as the first strip of wet meat plunked into the waiting pot, he started talking.

"Emily said human is best. Tastes the best, makes you strong, and they have the best reaction to the...the feeding. Which I reckon you've heard about?"

Rhett blushed and looked down. "A vampire whore once told me it feels pretty nice, to a feller, which is how they stay in business without actually whoring."

Sam nodded eagerly. "Yeah, and it made me feel a hell of a lot better, learning that. All those times I thought I'd...or the whores at the Leapin' Lizard had...but really, they just had a snack off me, and I wasn't the worse for wear. They were welcome to it. Anyway, I need blood every couple days or I'll get weak and frachetty. Horse and cow will do in a pinch, but cows are a lot nicer about it. You get a sleepy cow, and she just sits there, eyes down, chewing her cud, dreaming about cow stuff. Horses can be a bit persnickety, but I reckon I'd feel guilty, sucking on Blue like he was a pint of beer."

"What about monsters?"

"What about 'em?"

"I mean..." It was Rhett's turn to look away. "Can you feed on a monster, or do we taste...I don't know. Dirty? And does it feel nice? To a monster?"

Sam's unbloodied hand landed on Rhett's shoulder, and Rhett had no choice but to look into Sam's baby-blue eyes or know himself to be a coward.

"Rhett, you got to get over that. That thing where you think you're lesser. Monsters are people. They taste like people—well, most of 'em, I reckon. Those chupas tasted like week-old rattlesnake. But outside of taste, I'm starting to believe that the only people who think less of monsters are the folks who got power and don't want to share it. And I reckon the folks, like Jiddy back at the Las Moras Outpost, who'd rather lick the boots of the people in charge than own up to being what they are. You're not dirty. You're not lesser. And if I keep telling you that your whole damn life, maybe one day you'll start to believe me."

Rhett could feel his lips wobbling between a smile and a sob, and Sam's broad thumb swept down to scoop up a fat, betraying tear. Sticking his finger in his mouth, Sam chuckled.

"Almost like blood, but not quite. Too salty. Couldn't live off your tears, even if I wanted to."

Dashing the rest of the tears from his cheeks, Rhett muttered, "I ain't crying."

"Nothing wrong with it if you were. You're strong enough. You can cry a bit when it's needed."

"Crying's for girls."

Sam's hand grabbed Rhett's chin, newly forceful.

"Fool, I'm only going to say this once, so listen hard. There's nothing wrong with being a girl. Not saying you are one, just saying that you got a lot of pigheaded ideas, and I reckon you'd be a lot happier if you'd stop worrying so much about..." Sam's hands waggled in the air, one flashing horse blood. "I don't know. All this. Monsters and people and boys and girls and this and that. It's all just words. And I don't give a shit about words. I don't have to."

It was like Rhett had been slapped, all that stuff Sam had said. Ever since he'd left Pap and Mam's ranch, Rhett had wanted nothing more than to be a man and live a man's life. He'd always reckoned girls were terrible things and monsters were terrible things and not being white was a terrible thing, but Rhett was what he was, and he did what he did, and not a goddamn thing had been able to stop him, so far. So whatever he was? Well, it had to be okay.

If Sam thought it was okay, it was.

"Thanks, Sam," he said, soft as a cloud.

"You're welcome, Rhett. Now shut up and help me with this goddamn horse carcass."

They butchered the goddamn horse, and Rhett felt pretty good.

But what Sam had said itched him like a horsefly: He was

decidedly different, now that he was a vampire, inside and out. What other changes was he going to go through? How much of him was human, and how much of him was vampire? Who was he going to become?

And how were they gonna keep him fed?

CHAPTER 7

Carrying the pot of meat together, one on each side, Rhett and Sam headed for the mission's kitchen. Rhett felt an uncertain stirring in his gut that had nothing to do with monsters. So far, he'd always been the odd one out, the new feller. Now he had to deal with a new feller of his own. With just Dan and Digby around as fellow cowpokes, the idea of teaching a feller how to lasso a cow seemed pretty reasonable, even if there were no cows to be had. But now he was trying to consider what Sam might be thinking on top of that, whether Sam would mind him spending daylight time alone with Digby, and it got all confuddled. And then he got confuddled, because he wasn't much of a one to think about how someone else felt, first.

"I don't know if you want to eat this meat, Rhett," Sam said, nose wrinkling. "Smells off."

"It's barely a few hours old, and in November! I've et a lot worse meat than that. And it smells fine. As fine as raw meat can."

Sam deflated a bit. "Maybe it's my new nose. Alive smells good, already dead smells bad."

Thinking back to the railroad camp, it was Rhett's turn to wrinkle his nose. "Considering where I came from and where

I been, as long as there aren't living bugs in it and nobody's swabbed it out with a moldy mop, I reckon I'll be glad to eat."

The mission was lit with candles, and as they skirted past the chapel, Rhett could feel Inés buzzing with the angry hum of a nun who'd found the havoc he'd left behind, back when he thought he'd never see this place again. Trevisan's crows had attacked him in that chapel, or swarmed, or just set their sights on driving Rhett mad, and he'd retaliated by becoming a bird and killing as many of the foul, fake critters as possible. Which meant that when he'd walked away from the mission, he'd left a once holy room full of toppled relics and feathers, a magicked ball of wax splattered here or there with vulture shit for good measure. Hell, at least they hadn't been real birds, so there weren't any of their own body fluids or crunchy little bones anywhere. Still, Rhett was happy to hurry past to the kitchen, where they set the full pot down with a satisfying *clang*.

Winifred looked up, annoyed, from reading a book at the long dining table.

"Honestly, were you born in a barn?"

"In the dirt, more likely. You?" Rhett shot back.

Digby leaned his chair back and smirked. "It didn't come out much at the train yard, but it looks like there's a hell of a mouth on you, son."

Rhett's hands went to fists. "Don't call me son."

"He's always like this," Dan said, sounding like an exhausted parent.

Inés swept in, her usually immaculate black habit covered in feathers, bits of wax, and dust. Even through her veil, Rhett could feel her hard stare.

"You have been busy, Rhett."

He put his hands up and closed his eye in case she decided to lift her veil and be done with him. "Look, Inés, if you're asking about your chapel, that happened before we left for San Anton, and I do hope you'll believe me when I say they started it."

Inés made a low growl that turned into snorts and then great guffaws. Dan started chuckling and had no choice but to join her, and then Winifred and Sam followed suit. Digby, for all that he was new, couldn't help himself. Soon they were all laughing, mad as a bunch of goddamn hares.

Laughing at him.

Rhett turned red as a beet, half full of embarrassment and half full of rage. His hands back in fists, he struggled not to lash out, not to say something cruel to Winifred or punch Dan. He was more aware than ever that he was, in ways said and unsaid, the captain now. He had the badge. He called the shots. He was the one with the destiny, and they were, in effect, his Rangers. And good Captains didn't lash out. They took their licks. When he thought back to his own Captain and what he would do in this situation, he reckoned he would've just smiled and taken the high road. And so, fighting every fiber of his being, that's what he did.

"I was thinking about getting in a fight with some candles tomorrow," he said. "Maybe shout at a bush, if you've got a ready broom."

That just set them off howling even more uncontrollably, which made him grin.

It had actually worked.

He'd turned it back on 'em.

As their laughter died off and they set to wiping their eyes, Rhett felt like he'd done a good job and was just about finished. "What's for dinner?" he asked.

Inés tossed the feathers and wax into the yard and wiped off her hands. "Looks like you brought it. I have some bags of dried corn and beans hidden, but they won't be ready until tomorrow. Meat will have to do, tonight. We'll just need to get to work."

Rhett's jaw dropped open. "You ain't started cooking yet?"

Hands on her hips, the snakes under Inés's nun hat bristled and hissed. "I slept. And then I worked. You haven't slept. So go sleep, and take your rotten mood with you."

"But I got to—"

Dan put up a hand. "Rhett, you haven't slept in nearly two days. That's not healthy, even for the legendary Shadow."

"Don't you tell me to go to bed, Dan, I'll—"

"You're not going to win this one, fool."

Rhett just gawped, and Sam gently took his hand and pulled him away. "They're right, Rhett. You need sleep. We need you up to snuff. So come on. Let someone else worry for a while."

It felt all kinds of wrong, going to sleep when other folks were gonna be awake and working—and probably talking about him. Digby still didn't know his way around, and—

"Sam, we got to make you a bed down below," he said, allowing Sam to lead him down the hall. "It's more important than my sleep."

"No, it ain't."

And then they were alone, and Sam was sort of shoving, sort of hugging him down onto one of the cots in the old monk dormitory and he obliged by kicking off his boots. It wasn't a soft place by any means, but it was horizontal, and it wasn't moving or fighting or bleeding or needing him, so he sank down willingly enough. There was barely room for Sam to curl around him, but that just meant they were all pressed up close together, and that was home, and Rhett was just about to explain all the things that needed be done when he just drifted right off to sleep.

Unlike Sam during his new vampire sleep, Rhett still had dreams. Flashes of Trevisan and Cora and Meimei and Earl surfaced out of a fog that surrounded everything, that divided Rhett from Sam and the rest of his posse. He tossed and called out, and somewhere nearby a cool hand fell on his forehead and told him to *hush, fussy,* and he sank back down into quieter visions. He shivered, tucking his feet up, and then a blanket covered him, warm and smelling of horse, and he settled back down. And then things went deep and dark, and Rhett finally found rest.

When he woke, he wasn't alone, but it wasn't in the way he preferred. A single lantern lit the echoing room, showing him his fellow inhabitants. Dan slept a few cots over, on his back and still as a statue, and Digby was even farther away, a slab of a man on his side and muttering in his sleep. Sam was nowhere to be found, and the abject darkness suggested it was deep in the night. Somewhere, far off, Rhett could smell the sweet smoke of cooked meat, so he tossed off his blanket, slipped on his boots, took the lantern, and tiptoed to the kitchen. The blessed quiet was more than welcome—better than hearing the others laughing at his goddamn expense. The mission's ghosts were thankfully quiet, and in such scant light, he could barely see the old bloodstains seeping through the thick white of the walls.

In the kitchen, he found a big bowl overturned on the table with a rough drawing of an ugly bird with an eyepatch on it, done with a charred bit of stick.

"Very funny," he muttered, lifting away the bowl to find a plate of meat with some slimy greens.

He sat to eat, wary of the sound of wood scraping pewter,

how it cut through the blessed stillness of the night. A far-off hammering suggested that Sam was working in the basement, probably fitting out a bed to suit himself, so Rhett figured he could take a few moments alone to eat. He hadn't slept in a couple of days, sure, and he hadn't eaten in nearly as long, besides a few tough strips of old jerky. The ancient mare's meat was just as stringy and gristly as expected, but he'd eaten worse in his time and wasn't about to complain, although he surely did miss Conchita's tamales and something heartier to drink than the cold, mineral-tasting water from Inés's well. When he'd finished, he wiped his mouth off on his sleeve and took the lantern down the hallway to the open priest hole, the ladder sticking up out of it in a welcome and also terrifying sort of way.

"You down there, Sam?" he softly called, sticking his head down into the chill darkness.

"I am," Sam answered. "It's almost morning, though, so you'd best hurry."

As much as he hated to, Rhett left his lantern on the floor, stepped carefully onto the ladder, and clambered down. He noticed that the bouncier rungs had been replaced by new wood tightly bound with fresh rope. Once he realized the ladder wasn't nearly as dangerous as it had been before they left, he felt much better about letting it take his weight.

The cellar itself still was, unfortunately, something out of a nightmare. The clammy dirt ceiling seemed to press down, and the candles set into niches flickered uncertainly, casting ghastly shadows on the packed dirt walls that wore their bloodstains more proudly than the ones upstairs.

"Sam?"

"This way. Opposite the library."

When Inés had shown them the secret underground chamber

of hidden books about monsters and magic, Rhett hadn't realized there was another room down here. But in the opposite direction, he found another, smaller chamber lit with yet more yellow candles. It wasn't very large, and the scent suggested the monks had kept some sort of yeasty food down here, bags of grain or casks of beer or wine, maybe. Which would also explain the door built into the dirt, heavy iron hinges clinging to thick wooden jambs hammered into the earth. Much to Rhett's surprise, Sam had built himself a sort of bed on a wooden platform with a straw-stuffed tick spread over creaking ropes.

"How the hell'd you do that, Sam?"

Sam was currently lying on said bed looking happy as a cat that ate a canary, his elbows out and his bare feet crossed. "You been asleep for a long time, Rhett. I'm a fairly handy man." He crooked his finger at Rhett. "As you well know. Now c'mere and help me try it out."

Feeling self-conscious and small all of a sudden, Rhett stepped out of his boots and crawled onto the bed, which croaked under his weight.

"Is it gonna hold?" he asked.

"It's made to hold," Sam murmured, drawing Rhett up into the crook of his arm. "I grew up with seven kids in a bed this size. Weighed more than you and me, and wiggled more than us, too. Unless you'd like to try out just how much wiggling it can take?"

Rhett's first response was shyness, considering Dan and Digby and the rest were upstairs, but then he recalled that it was in the middle of the night, and they were all asleep, and what's more, there were ladders and hallways and doors between them. Nobody in their right mind would venture down into a basement as wretched as this one in the middle of the goddamn night unless they had a damn good reason. Which Rhett, strangely enough, did.

He lifted his face to Sam's as if offering himself up on a platter, and Sam tasted his lips, all tentative. "This is the first time we've been in a real bed together, ain't it?" he murmured.

"Well, there was that bed of hay," Rhett admitted.

Sam's fingers skimmed down Rhett's neck and plucked his first shirt button open.

"Hay don't count."

The next button came undone, and Rhett shivered, frozen and wanting.

Sam paused.

"Kiss me again, Sam," Rhett said, something like a plea.

But Sam's head fell back against the pillow. Rhett called his name again and gently nuzzled his neck, and then Rhett realized with a sinking heart that whether or not he wanted to be, Sam was asleep.

Rhett himself couldn't find such peace. With Sam unconscious, the room went from being a cozy little nest to a crypt, and the heavy dirt walls felt like they might fall at any time, and a creak outside suggested to Rhett's wildly beating heart that perhaps the giant Gila monsters had again found the breach behind the bookshelves and might storm in, razor teeth ready to kill, or at least maim.

"I love you, Sam, but I got...I got to go," Rhett muttered, planting a quick peck on Sam's cheek and backing out of the bed. He shook out his boots and plunked his feet into the cold, clammy leather and closed the great, creaking door and padded back to the ladder. Once he'd pulled himself up into the hallway overhead, somehow warmer and lighter despite the night's chill still holding off dawn, it was like a weight had lifted off his chest. Standing in the mission proper, the cellar sure enough looked like a hole into some cold, hateful hell. Rhett knelt and put his hands on the top rung of the ladder and shoved it down, making it clatter far below. He closed the trapdoor and pulled a rag rug over it.

This way, hopefully, nobody could get to Sam. For once, maybe, Sam would be safe.

It should've made Rhett feel secure.

It did not.

It was right peculiar, sitting around a breakfast table with everybody but Sam. Digby was cheerful, at least, and his conversation kept Rhett from thinking too hard about his own problems. For Digby, sleeping in a place where he was neither chained nor exposed to the elements was a right treat, and having fresh breakfast where he could smile and speak his mind was utterly glorious. He asked what felt to Rhett like a million goddamn questions—about Dan and Winifred, and Inés and the mission, and the Rangers, and just about everything a body might not know if he'd been kept a slave for several years. Rhett listened to the feller's own stories and learned a good bit about his history and grew annoyed at the prattling. For all that he liked joshing around a breakfast table, knowing too much about a feller's past made him downright uncomfortable. Probably because then that feller might ask him about his own past, and he'd get all squirrely and have to find a way to avoid the questions. He was enraged that he'd spent so much of his young life under Pap's rule when he now realized he could've run off years earlier. Pap probably hadn't even come looking for him. And of course he wanted to hide...well, most everything else about himself, too.

"So you and Sam, huh?" Digby said.

Rhett dropped his spoon and bristled. "Maybe. What about it?"

Digby put his hands up, his eyes innocent and wide for a feller out of diapers. "Nothing about it. Just something I noticed. Look, man, you don't spend a few years in a camp of men without changing your ideas of how men get along when there ain't no women. I got no problem with whatever you got going. Just trying to make conversation."

"Yes, me and Sam, then."

"Fair enough. And the...the..." He glanced sideways at Winifred.

"It ain't mine."

"Of course it ain't. Two women can't do that!"

Dan hissed in warning, and Rhett was on his feet, his fist cocked, before he realized it was happening.

"I like you, Digby, but do not mistake me," he said, low and unfriendly. "Not now and not ever. I ain't a woman."

Digby gave him a hell of a look but in no way appeared cowed. "Don't you even think about threatening to hit me. I lived with you. Close quarters, open trenches, for a couple of months. I know well enough what you got going on down there, for all you tried to hide it. And I don't much care. You pulled your weight and then some, and these folks trust you enough to lead 'em. I'm just trying to figure out how all these pieces fit together. But again, you're the boss. You say you're a man, I reckon that's how it is."

"Then are we done talking about personal matters, because I reckon work won't kill you, Digby."

"No, I reckon it won't."

"But jawin' like that might."

Digby shrugged and tipped his plate back to scrape the last of his breakfast into his maw. After he swallowed and daintily wiped off his lips with his bandanna, he grinned again, his former thunder forgotten. "You're the boss, boss. What we got on the docket today?"

Rhett didn't know what the hell a docket was, but he reckoned it had something to do with the list of shit Digby was going to have to accomplish to get back in his good graces after that crack about being a woman. So Rhett considered what needed doing.

"Well, somebody needs to go to the nearest town for supplies. And chickens. Breakfast ain't breakfast without eggs. And a cow, maybe, for milk and butter."

"I will do that," Inés said. "I am known, hereabouts. Whereas you…" She looked around the table, but Rhett knew damn well she was talking about him. "You look disreputable. Like you might cause trouble."

Dan pulled out his leather bag and slid several gold coins across the table. "Will this do?"

Inés slipped the coins into the sleeve of her habit and nodded. Rhett appreciated that instead of yapping any more, she just stood up and left.

"I need to help her unpack the wagon to make room," Winifred said, and she, too, left.

It was only the three fellers now, and Rhett waited to see if anybody else was gonna volunteer, as he had no rightly idea how to go about his goal of setting up a little ranch somewhere near the border. Had no idea, and hated to ask anybody else. Especially Dan. So of course Dan started yapping.

"Do you want to get rid of some deadweight, Rhett? Maybe sell off the clothes and boots we don't need, along with the saddles and tack?"

Rhett stroked his jaw, wishing he had the proper sort of stubble there to make it a raspy, manly sort of movement.

"Well, let's see. If we're setting up an outfit, we'll need more men. Do most fellers bring their own saddles and such?"

He looked to Digby, who just shrugged. "I've never been such a man," was all he said.

"With the Rangers, then, Dan?"

"Most men come on a horse with a saddle, tack, and guns. As you've seen, if they need something better, they take it as payment on the trail or use their pay to buy something new in town as we pass through. Cowpokes will bring their own kit, I think. But it's best to keep back the nicer saddles. Better to have them and not need them than need them and not have them, unless a man prefers bareback."

"Well, bareback don't allow for a Henry or saddlebags, so join the rest of us in the 1800s, grandpa," Rhett said, enjoying every goddamn word.

Dan snorted a laugh, and it felt like victory.

"So here's the thing I need to know," Rhett continued. "Our goal is to buy a little place near the border, but so far as I seen it, only white folks own land, and they don't much like selling it to fellers that look like us. Our only white feller ain't around during bank hours. So how do we get the land?"

"There are several scenarios to consider." Dan stroked his chin with a light rasp that bugged Rhett like a mosquito tickling his toes at midnight. "Considering none of us know how to build anything, I'm very much against starting from scratch, so forget lumber. That leaves taking and buying. We can do what we seem to always do, find a nest of monsters and rid the world of them and claim their property as our bounty. There will be those nests of chupacabras you're so anxious to eliminate, for all that it may be the death of us. Or perhaps we'll find something like the siren's little town, like Reveille. Or we can go over the border into Azteca, where white men don't rule, and make someone a deal. We don't have enough money to buy a place outright, but after we sell off what we need to and a few dozen horses, we might be close."

"Azteca," Rhett murmured. "Never thought of that. What's it like over there?"

Dan looked at Rhett like he was a damn fool. "Do you think the land knows there's a border, Rhett? Do you think the mountains are somehow different there? They may be called Durango and Azteca, but they are the same place under the same sky. Some parts are prairie, some parts are desert, but borders are just lines men draw in the sand to make themselves feel safe."

Outside, Rhett could hear the harness jingle as Inés and Winifred hooked Samson up; well, that was good sense, at least. Hook up the horse and bring the wagon closer to the mission to unload before setting off for whatever shitbird town Inés used for supplies. The silence inside drew out longer than Rhett liked. He was the captain, but he didn't know what to do, and that made him feel a fool. Plus, Dan had been the last person to say something wise and clever, and Rhett hated that, too.

"This how you-all decide what to do?" Digby asked. "Just... staring off into space?"

Dan wagged his head. "Rhett's Shadow sense usually guides us, and he's rarely this quiet. What is it, Rhett?"

Chewing his lip, Rhett stood up and turned this way and that.

"I'm not sure. Don't know how to explain it. Usually, I got a strong tug, something telling me which direction to go. I just match up that feeling to the available options and kick my horse in the right direction. But this time, I got several... little tugs. One out far to the west that I know is those goddamn chupacabras. One coming in from the northeast, feels like it's on the move. Hell, a couple things coming from that direction. And one due west, almost feels like..." He paused, felt tears prick his eyes, and had to force himself to swallow. "But it can't be that."

Dan leaned forward, avid. "You think there might be something at Las Moras, still?"

Rhett met his eyes and nodded. "Something. Don't know what. For all I know, sensitive as I'm getting, it could be a harpy having a snack. But all these little tugs—well, they don't tell me what to do next. I feel like I'm supposed to wait. Or go to Las Moras. Or wait, then go to Las Moras? Hellfire, this is not how it usually works."

"Damn, boy. Are you a dousing rod for trouble?" Digby asked, trying to understand.

"I do believe I am," Rhett said, pleased to be understood. "You still in?"

Digby laughed. "I'm a bit of a troublemaker myself, when I'm not chained up. So I might as well cause some trouble with you. Your friends here tell me you help folks, like you helped us back at the camp. That you free folks and fight for folks who can't fight for themselves and take down the monsters that would do ill to innocents. If that's true, then I'm still in."

Rhett rubbed his temples and thought about asking Winifred to trim down his unruly fuzz. But he was already exhausted and had a headache, and the sun was barely up. Not only that, but it would be twelve goddamn hours before he could see Sam again, and by then, he'd need to sleep. Maybe he'd start going to sleep after lunch, have a siesta like the sensible folks of Azteca did, and wake up again when Sam was around. But for now...

"Well, then. We'll do what we can do until we've got a

hankering to do something else. Let's go take care of the horses and sort some goods. Although how we're supposed to sell 'em without a white man holding the purse strings I'll never know." For Sam, he reflected, couldn't sell their stock during daylight hours, and most deals, he knew, had to happen under the telling eye of the sun.

"You'll be surprised when we get farther west," Dan said. "The faces get browner and friendlier."

"Then let's hurry the hell up and get going."

The morning passed quickly, at least. They began with the beasts. Not only did Rhett love moving among horses more than just about anything except moving under Sam, but he discovered that he enjoyed teaching—and that he was a good teacher. For all that Digby didn't know the first thing about breaking horses or moving cattle, he was curious and had an affinity for animals, and Rhett approved of the man's instincts. Turned out Digby had ridden, a little, but explanations about horse care had been less important than galloping off to war with the band that had adopted him when he was a child.

As Rhett and Dan considered the horseflesh milling about Inés's brokedown pen, Rhett explained how to judge a horse's confirmation and hooves and eye. He pointed to the various parts of a horse and told Digby what they were called, and he showed him how to lift up a hoof without getting stamped on or kicked. Dan began with his nose poked in too close, like he doubted Rhett could teach a donkey to bray, but as Rhett and Digby found their rhythm, Dan went to sort through clothes, boots, and saddles. Which felt pretty good to Rhett, as not only did he not like being stared at and examined, but he also took it as Dan's agreement that Rhett was a good judge of horseflesh and a proper enough teacher of people.

Digby took a liking to a thickly muscled buckskin, so Rhett

showed him how to halter the gelding and guide him out of the pen on a lead. It was right peculiar, describing to someone the words for how to do something Rhett felt like he'd known since before he could talk. Horses came as naturally to him as breathing, and he didn't even know how he knew the things he did. He just knew.

The work was going so well that they forgot to stop for lunch. Digby had picked out a saddle and was on horseback for the first time in years, and it was just too much fun to quit. A few hours later, Rhett realized that he needed to get to sleep if he had any hope of time with Sam, so he hollered for Dan and told him to teach Digby how to undo all the hard work he'd done tacking up.

For once, Dan was amused. "It's nice to see you happy, Rhett," he said, which just served to make Rhett grouchy again.

"I'm happy all the damn time," he growled. "I am a ray of goddamn sunshine."

Both Dan and Digby laughed at him as he skulked inside to eat some leftover breakfast and hit the hay in his cot.

He was so tired that he was asleep in no time, and then it was dark and Sam was whispering in his ear to wake up.

So it went for some time. Rhett split his time between darkness and light, working with Digby and Dan during the day and napping in the afternoon and mostly playing, if he was honest, with Sam at night. There wasn't much that could be done in the dark, if a feller wasn't on the trail and couldn't read. Most nights, first thing, Sam went off by himself to drink a few sleepy gulps from Inés's new cow while Rhett washed off the dust he caught during the day. They went for long rides just because they could, and Rhett came to know the curves and valleys of sleeping Durango intimately. The sound of coyotes calling, the rasp of a snake's dry hide, or the pop of a startled armadillo—these were the notes of the night's song he sang with Sam. He got to where he could see pretty good by moon or stars, could navigate without the sun.

They didn't talk all that much, he and Sam, aside from sweet whispers in Sam's little nest down below, where Rhett never felt quite comfortable but where they knew they could be more alone than anywhere else. Despite all their time together, Rhett couldn't help feeling like some part of Sam was far away and unreachable, and like maybe some part of himself was likewise hidden and would always be so. It was as if there had once been an open hallway, but now they were each trapped behind a closed door. But he didn't say anything of the sort. He learned, for once, to be quiet and take what was given, even if he wasn't sure it was what he wanted anymore.

Only during the day, really, did he have doubts.

Sunshine had always reminded him of Sam, and Sam had seemed most himself outside, laughing, blue sky and golden light caught in his hair and flickering in his eyes. But now Sam was a thing of moonlight, of stark black and furtive white. He didn't laugh as much as he once had.

Rhett didn't say anything about that, either.

Winifred started to swell up, although it happened so slowly that a feller couldn't really notice it, day by day. She left off her dresses and took to wearing a man's clothes, long shirts that gave her room to breathe and soft old doeskin leggings with a drawstring at the waist. She chatted to the new batch of chickens every morning, strewing corn for them and delighting in their chicks, and got tired in the afternoons. Often when Rhett would tuck into his cot, she'd already be asleep somewhere funny, curled up on a haystack or splayed over a rocking chair, the tips of her braids flapping in the wind. The cold had crept in, and Rhett realized she'd properly become part of his family when he found her huddled and snoring in a pew in the chapel and brought an old horse blanket to tuck around her so she wouldn't get cold.

Digby became a fine enough horseman pretty quick, although Rhett couldn't teach him a damn thing about cows using Inés's new placid white heifer. Many a morning they spent taking turns trying to lasso a stump, and although Digby didn't excel at that part of the work, it was like he and his buckskin, Hess, could read each other's minds. Digby's skill with a gun went from nothing to something, and they had to send Inés out to buy more bullets to rebuild their stores.

Because even when things felt settled, they really weren't.

All that time they spent living life at the mission, Rhett could feel those three points moving, ever closer, to where he waited. Northeast, due west, farther west into Azteca: They buzzed like flies in his mind. Finally, one day, it was just too goddamn much. He woke, sputtering in the cellar's darkness beside a sleeping Sam, and knew what had to happen.

"West," he said to the curious, sleepy faces at the breakfast table, dawn kissing the horizon. "We got to go west."

Dan, Digby, Winifred, and Inés looked up to stare him like they didn't know what to do with this information and would just like to finish their goddamn beans, thanks. At least he assumed Inés was likewise staring; he could hear the annoyed hissing of the snakes under her habit.

The tug had gone from a tickle to a yank, that quick. Overnight. All the calm Rhett had built up exploded like a bottle kissed by a bullet, and he was damn glad he and Sam had installed a lightproof box into the back of the wagon, because the only thing he knew was that they had to get on the road to Las Moras. Together. And soon.

"What's the hurry?" Digby asked, as he was the only one who didn't yet understand how things worked.

Rhett shook his head. "Doesn't matter. We just got to go."

"It takes him like this," Dan explained. "And we follow. Usually."

"Don't act like you know my ways," Rhett snapped.

Winifred smirked in that infuriating way she had. "He's pretty frachetty until we do, too."

Rhett focused on her, his eye narrowing. "What's this *we*? Girl, you're getting unwieldy, body and mind, and I can't lead you into danger. Even if I tried, your brother would skin me. Surely your mama coyote instincts have kicked in and told you to settle down and, I don't know, build yourself a nest. Or brick yourself into a cave to protect the rest of us from your sharp tongue."

Winifred's head jerked back like she'd been slapped. "This again? I thought we were past you telling me what to do."

"Maybe I'm thinking of your little one."

"Maybe as long as it's in my body, it's still my call."

Rhett looked to the girl's brother. "Dan, surely you're not gonna take her side this time?"

Dan's face was placid in that way he got when the Shadow called Rhett into danger, like he was watching a peculiar but expected part of nature unfold. "I won't say this again, so mark my words: My sister is her own keeper. I tried to keep her safe, and it didn't work. She's an adult, and she'll go where she will. If she chooses to go with you, it's your job to protect her. I suggest you hammer that into your hard head." The corner of his smile jerked up, just a little. "But if you want to take off this afternoon during her little catnap, I wouldn't argue."

In response, Winifred threw a tamale at him, and as it bounced off Dan's nose, Rhett couldn't help laughing. Winifred joined him, but Digby and Inés didn't.

"What about you, nun? You up for another adventure? Want to drive the wagon for us?"

Inés put down her spoon and turned to face him. As always, her face was hidden by her veil; it was impossible to guess her subtleties of expression. But Rhett knew enough about her now to know that she was giving the topic a good hard think, rolling the possibilities around in her head.

"The time will come when I go, but now is not that time," she finally said before continuing to nibble her breakfast, spooning beans under her veil.

"But if you don't go, then Sam can't go, because somebody's got to drive the wagon," Rhett protested.

"Then let Sam drive it. Or any one of you. I am not your servant."

Rhett hated the truth of it, but there it was. He needed to leave immediately, but now he'd have to wait until nightfall to ask Sam what he wanted to do.

"What's peculiar, Rhett, is that I don't feel the need to go, either."

This from Dan, and when Rhett turned to stare at the feller, he could tell his jaw was gaping, and he plunked it right shut.

"So Winifred wants to go, but Inés and Dan don't?"

"I didn't say I wanted to go," Winifred said. "Just that if I did, you couldn't stop me."

Much as he hated it, Rhett felt right dumbfounded. Every time, they'd followed him. Even when it hurt, even when it was unpleasant or downright dangerous. This was the first time Rhett had felt the Shadow's tug and watched his people, one by one, turn their backs on him.

"What the hell is happening?" he murmured.

"Perhaps this is a quest just for you, Rhett," Dan said. "Every other time you've gotten a wild hare, I've felt the need to move, to follow you, curled in my chest like a viper waiting to strike. It's itched me and prodded me to go, even when my better sense suggested it was a bad idea. But this time, strangely, I feel that perhaps you should go alone. We'll wait here for you. Take care of things as you see fit." He paused, looking over Rhett's shoulder through the door to the hallway that held the trapdoor to the basement. "And I'll tell Sam where you've gone, if the urge requires him to follow."

"I'll go," Digby said, very quietly. "I don't have strong feelings one way or the other, and I reckon it might be a good test of what I can do. Riding a horse around the mission ain't the same as going on the trail, right?"

"True enough," Rhett allowed, trying to hide his relief.

"Hey, you think it's gonna be dangerous? Like, does this Shadow of yours think it's gonna be a whole myriad of monsters—which means a hell of a lot, in case you didn't know—or something more like Trevisan?"

For all that Digby was smiling while he said it, Rhett could tell the man was hiding his biggest fear. Nobody, no matter how tough or strong or hard to kill, would want to subject himself to a feller like Trevisan twice. And as Rhett knew better than anybody, the world was full of Trevisans, even if they kept their true faces hidden most of the time.

Licking his lips, Rhett focused on the feeling in his middle. It was urgent, but it didn't feel...dangerous? Well, hell, everything in Durango was dangerous in one way or another. A man could die from leaving his beans out a day too long or stepping on a particularly angry scorpion.

"Whatever it is that's calling me...that thing ain't dangerous," Rhett said, not quite sure how to put a feeling he didn't truly understand into words that often failed him. "It ain't attacking. The way to it might be dangerous, but that's just how it is on the trail."

"And you're going to Las Moras," Dan repeated.

Rhett nodded. "Or what's left of it. I got to go fast." He slammed down his coffee and stood, boots clacking in the stillness. "And I got to go soon. So if you're coming along, Digby, best get packed. You got an hour." Before Digby had found a way to mention that he didn't know how to pack for such a journey, Rhett took pity on him and added, "Dan, will you help him? And Winifred, will you help me?"

The girl was caught by surprise, but Rhett often seemed

to catch her by surprise. She nodded and cocked her head, waiting.

"I need you to write a letter to Sam. If I tell you what I want to say, can you write it out?"

"I can do that, Rhett."

"Good. Rustle up whatever you need. I'll figure out what to say while I pack my gear."

With a nod, he was gone. He went to his bunk for a spare set of clothes, another binder cloth for his chest, and his rags—because his body seemed to always pick the worst possible time to remember that it had female parts and start bleeding like a stuck pig, for all that it had been decently reliable in his months at the mission. He grabbed up the old blanket he slept under and carried it out to the barn. When he whistled, Ragdoll looked at him like he was a fool and walked over—not like she was in a hurry, but like it was mostly her idea. Since it wasn't going to be the most punishing of trips, Rhett also caught up the little gray he'd picked out from the chupa horses, the one he called Squirrel. Squirrel was young and a little flighty but the pony knew well enough to follow Ragdoll's lead and would learn a lot from the trip.

As he saddled up and checked his saddlebags, Inés came out and tucked a tied cloth of food into one side, leaving an identical packet for Digby on top of a fence post.

"Be careful," she said, but Rhett could tell she thought it was pretty funny, telling the Shadow to be careful, which he never was.

With his two horses twitching their tails at the fence, Rhett went into the barn and loaded up on ammunition. A box of bullets for his pistols, a box of bullets for the Captain's old Henry, which looked mighty fine sticking up from Rhett's new saddle, also once the property of the Ranger leader. He slid his

Bowie knife out of his sheath and checked that it was honed, which it always was. And lastly, as he often did before a trip into the unknown, he pulled the leather bag on its string from around his neck and dumped the contents into his hand.

The teeth from the first vampire he'd ever killed, not knowing why he was being attacked in Pap's rotting barn. A tiny moccasin from the lair of the Cannibal Owl. The sand that had once been some of his friends. His first quarter, given to him by a kind cowpoke for breaking a bronc. All those treasures and many more, including a shiny button that had popped off one of Sam's shirts, as Rhett liked to think he took a bit of Sam with him everywhere he went.

As Digby came out to saddle Hess, Rhett wandered among the herd, checking teeth and hooves and coats, looking for wounds or signs of bullying among the silly beasts. His old, one-eyed mule, Blue, barreled up to him and rubbed his long nose on Rhett's shirt, leaving slobber stains. Rhett always looked closely, these days, to see how far the ancient, sway-backed nag might be from death. Blue had to be up in his thirties, and Pap hadn't taken good care of him because Pap didn't take good care of anything. But Blue didn't seem to mind; he was just glad to be alive, especially when Rhett was around.

"Look, I'm going away, but Dan'll take care of you, old man," Rhett said, rubbing the mule's bony forehead and scratching behind his ears. "Don't you go breaking a leg while I'm gone, you hear? Cuz Dan'll eat you. Dark-hearted, he is."

In response, Blue just butted Rhett in the shoulder and whuffled. He looked good, for his age, and Rhett was grateful that whatever power the Shadow had to call critters to him, his childhood friend had felt that call and been able to follow it.

"That one seems to like you more than most folks," Digby

noted as he cinched up his saddle as if he'd been doing it for years.

"Yeah, well, he's known me longer than most people, which is an argument to his own stupidity, I reckon. But I been feeding him a long time, sometimes from my own breakfast, so maybe that counts for something."

"He seems pretty old."

"He *is* pretty old."

"Say, is it true what you just said? That if a horse breaks a leg, you got to put him down?"

Rhett looked from Digby to Blue, his look thunderous. "First of all, don't ever think about putting down old Blue unless you wanna be put down next." Then he softened, because outside of its relation to Blue, it was a reasonable question before green fellers took to the trail. "Second, there is some truth to it. A horse with a broke leg can't carry you and it can't run away and it can't eat, and that means it's dead on its feet. So shooting it is a kindness. And using the meat, after that, is just making the best of what you got. Better you live off a good horse than leave him to rot for the vultures. That's why you always ride one horse and pony a second, if you can."

Digby nodded, slow, absorbing that, and put a hand on Blue's scarred old hide.

"I never knew how fragile these critters were," he said. "Break a leg, get put down. Eat the wrong thing, can't puke it up, get put down. Run too hard without getting cooled down right, fall over dead. A dozen peculiar maladies I never heard of, things a person could get fixed easy, and for a horse, it means you're dinner." He shook his head. "And still I begin to think they're the most majestic goddamn creatures the good Lord put on this here earth."

Rhett nodded approvingly. "No wonder I like you. You got a reasonable way of thinking. Mind if I check over your gear?"

Digby stepped back with a bow that suggested he wasn't sore about it, and Rhett checked his horse, saddle, bags, and kit. These days, Digby had taken to wearing a gun belt like every other man in Durango, and Dan had taught him how to keep his weapons clean. His hat had a proper sweaty rim, and he kept a kerch tied around his neck for the dust. He'd become more or less a proper cowpoke, at least as related to animals that weren't cows, but that wasn't his fault. Maybe they'd find some steers on the trail to drive along, just to give him some practice; heaven knew the damn things were everywhere, and most of 'em weren't wearing brands. Rhett would keep on the lookout.

"We ready?" Digby asked.

Rhett looked around the mission, wishing he could just pick up the whole damn thing like a fussy lady's hoopskirts and plunk it down near the border. Inés's place had just about everything they needed, although Rhett would've liked a bit more grazing and a nearby stream, as compared to the old well. It wasn't much of a home, and it wasn't his, but he didn't particularly want to leave it and head off toward some random itch that didn't have a known source. He could've been riding toward a monster, a man, a tornado—anything.

And ride toward it he would.

But first, he had to find Winifred.

He gave Digby a nod. "Soon."

When he moseyed into the kitchen, Winifred was already sitting at the table with some crinkly looking paper and a quill, practicing her letters.

"I'm used to finer things from Nueva Orleans," she said with a lopsided smile as he watched her struggle. "I wrote letters for the family and a few for me, and it seemed like they had endless amounts of crisp paper and smooth ink. This is a bit more rustic than what I'm used to."

"I reckon Sam won't care so much about that part. He's gonna be mad, anyway. Just make the words as good as you can."

She tipped her head, quill ready. "Well, that part's up to you, isn't it?"

Rhett cleared his throat and struggled to find words. It struck him that this was the first time anything he said had ever been written down where anybody could read it, where it would last forever. There was a kindness in the way most words came and went like smoke, leaving nothing behind. He often regretted things he'd said—and things he'd neglected to say—but this time, he had to get it right.

"Dear Sam," he began, speaking slowly so Winifred's scratching quill could keep up. "I got to go, and I hope you can understand why. The Shadow pulls me suddenly to Las Moras, but as nobody else feels pulled, I reckon it's a job for one. I do not have a bad feeling over it, so you should not worry. I will be quick and careful." He paused to let her catch up, wishing he could put the sort of sweet sentiments he whispered in the dark of night into the letter, but knowing he couldn't let Winifred see that tender part of himself that he'd denied her. "Whatever comes next I will need you by my side, so I urge you to make ready for a journey and a fight. Digby goes with me, so I am not alone, although I will keep the fire between us at night."

Rhett worried his lip with his teeth as he contemplated how to close the letter in a way that was true and manly, a way that said what he needed to say but kept things private. *Love* was out of the question, but *Fondly* seemed like something a feller might say to a sister he didn't hate too much. Winifred stopped writing and stared at him.

"Anything else?"

"Hush, you. I'm thinking on how to end it."

"That's easy, fool. Just say, 'Love, Rhett.' That's how folks end letters to the people they care for."

"Not men, you fool-headed woman." It came out gruff enough to be a growl.

"A man who believed in himself might. I'll just do it for you. *Love, Rhett.* There you go. You can mark it with your X, if you like."

Cussing her under his breath, Rhett took the feather she offered, held it awkwardly near the tip, and scratched a childish X, getting ink all over his hands in the process.

"I didn't say to write that," he added.

"And I didn't ask for permission. You love Sam, and Sam loves you, and everybody knows it, so stop acting like it's peculiar or some big secret."

Heat bloomed in Rhett's cheeks, but so did a sweet sort of joy. Everybody knew Sam loved him? He didn't even know that himself, sometimes.

"Well, then," was all he could say. "Many thanks for the letter. You'll see he gets it?"

Winifred smiled at him like he was a silly child, but not a horrible one. "Of course, Rhett. I know you're worried. But everything will be fine. Your gut tells you some things, and my gut tells me things, too."

But Rhett wasn't so sure. Every time the coyote girl seemed cocky, something terrible happened.

As much as he wanted to wait until sundown, Rhett's belly fought him like a carp on the line, calling him west. He and Digby left shortly after that, mounted on Hess and Squirrel with Ragdoll ponied off Rhett's saddle, nudging ahead as lead mares tended to do. Considering it was his first time on the trail, Digby didn't need the added confusion of ponying a horse, so Rhett could only hope they didn't find too much trouble. Dan, Winifred, and Inés waved from the yard in a way that made Rhett feel right peculiar, as if something final was occurring. When a feller left the Rangers or the Double TK Ranch, nobody stood around, waving at him. He wasn't getting on a goddamn train to cross the country. He sighed and waved back, annoyed that folks kept making things feel even stranger than they already did.

"So where's the trail?" Digby asked.

Rhett settled into the saddle, feeling his hips loosen up. "You're on it."

Looking around, Digby frowned. "I don't see any demarcation."

"Don't know what that is, but if you mean it should look like a trail, then you're confusing being on the trail with being on a road. The trail just means you're out in the world, headed somewhere. There ain't always a road, so to speak."

Digby frowned as he considered it. "That's right philosophical, Rhett. You consider yourself a philosophical man? Because there's something poetic about it. If you're going somewhere, forging a new trail, you're on the trail. It ain't a trail until you're on it. It didn't exist until you started, and you make it happen as you go along. Whichever way you go, that becomes the way."

Rhett groaned. "Oh, lord. You're starting to sound like Dan, and even worse, it almost makes sense. All I know is that I'm happiest on the trail, I think." He quickly amended that, though. "Happiest on the trail with Sam, I mean. Doesn't feel right, heading out before lunch and without him."

"You fellers go back, huh?" Digby asked, but he didn't wait for an answer, and Rhett didn't really want to give one, so he just let Digby talk. "I had me a wife, back up in Montana del Norte, pretty as a damn picture. Hell, I talk like it's in the past, but maybe she's alive still. Never went back. Figured I'd just get snatched up again. See, ol' Trevisan didn't just lure boys in with promises of payment in Calafia. He bought wagons full of chained men from rival bands, whether they were in the slaver's irons or the Ranger's. Good money in selling folks that can work, you know."

He looked to Rhett, gauging Rhett's reaction.

"Yeah, I know," Rhett said, looking away.

"Anyway, sometimes I think about going back home, seeing if she found another man to take up with or if she's pining for me." He chuckled, but it was forced and dark. "Not her band's way, pining for lost folks. So I figure it's respectful-like if I stay out here. Maybe I'll go home if I find me a gold nugget the size of a toad. Go home in my own wagon. That'd wake 'em up, huh? No point going back when I'm wearing a dead man's clothes and riding a horse I didn't pay for."

Rhett's head whipped around at that.

"Now on that point, I've got to disagree, Digby. Just because you didn't pay for something with coin don't mean it's worthless. A shirt is a shirt. After the first wear, once the sweat and dust soak in, nobody knows how new it is or where it came from. And a horse rides fine under a different rump. Hell, every horse I've ever ridden came from somebody else. What, you think you just come across a field of 'em growing, shiny and new and untouched, and pluck one up like it's a turnip? If you want something in this world, you got to take it fair and square."

"So you took my duds off them chupacabras fair and square?"

Rhett grinned. "Feller points his gun at me and shoots first, nothing's squarer than that."

It was agreeable, the way Digby listened to him without

scolding him and then settled back to chew on it a moment before speaking his thoughts. Made Rhett not hate talking so much. They rode along quite a while before Digby spoke again.

"That's some good sense, right there. That's some good sense."

Rhett nodded his appreciation of the compliment and nudged Squirrel in the direction that was tugging him. It was different, being on the trail with Digby. Calm and thoughtful, but not threatening like Dan got when he was quiet too long, like he was just thinking up new ways to ruin Rhett's day. Still, even though he was moving toward the Shadow's pull, Rhett felt another threat, far off, sitting on the horizon like thunder.

It was the chupacabras, he reckoned, way out west.

Waiting.

But he didn't know what for.

CHAPTER 9

A few days later, Rhett woke up with the sun and turned to where Sam usually lay. All he found was a bitty scorpion, which raised its tail as if to suggest it had been there first.

"All yours, friend," Rhett said, tugging on his boots and standing to stretch without being further threatened by a tiny feller with pincers.

Digby shifted under his blanket on the opposite side of the fire; it always took him just a little longer to rouse, probably because he'd not yet been awakened by the sort of attack Rhett had experienced so often on the trail. It had been a peaceful enough trip with plenty of chances for instruction that served to make Digby a right useful feller. They'd found a couple of scrawny little steers, sure enough, and Digby enjoyed driving the little fellers around. He called 'em Mack and Jack, and they were getting to think of him like their mama, which Rhett didn't much cotton to as related to cows. Still, Digby had a good seat on horseback now, and he'd even shot a fat turkey for supper. The man had already known how to make a fine fire and spit meat, which meant Rhett got to avoid his least favorite trail chores.

"We should hit Las Moras today," Rhett told him.

"How'd you know? I didn't see any signs."

Rhett snorted. "Who needs a sign when you got the Shadow? I can't read, but I know this area, and I know when what I'm looking for is nearby."

"Know what it is yet, this thing you seek?"

Digby rolled up to standing and splashed some water from his canteen over his face as he did every day. It befuddled Rhett, who liked a nice coating of dust.

"Don't know," he answered. It bothered him, not knowing, but he wouldn't let Digby see that. "Doesn't have...what do you call it, when something's real loud and fierce?"

"Ah." Digby grinned. He loved this game. Digby knew more big words than Dan did. "Intensity? Furor?"

"Sure. It don't have those. It's a real quiet thing, but important. Whenever fellers have been galloping up, guns drawn to cause harm, it's like...my heart knew it. It kicked in like a drum, and suddenly I knew I had to move. Whatever this is, it doesn't feel like that, but it's still pretty goddamn important." He looked west, considering. "Like it's waiting for me, but it won't wait forever."

Deep in the most secret and dark part of his heart, he thought maybe the Captain had somehow come back from the dead. Maybe a vampire had found him, and like Sam, he was different now but still the same. Or maybe...maybe...

Hell, Rhett couldn't think of any maybes. He could only hope.

Couldn't stop himself from hoping, in fact.

Even if he knew it was impossible and stupid, which is why he said nothing but just hurried to saddle his horse.

The closer they got to Las Moras and the more the buttes and arroyos looked familiar, the more antsy Rhett got. He was being reeled in, following the Shadow's suggestion—well, demand—and he still had not a single inkling of why. He'd looked for clues along the way, for signs that someone had passed this direction or for white smoke spiraling up into the winter sky, but Durango would not give up her secrets so easily.

"We're skipping lunch," he said. "Unless you want to stuff down some jerky. We're close. We just got to keep going a little longer."

"You're the boss, boss," Digby said, which Rhett appreciated. He understood that if a man who'd served under him had then been placed over him, he wouldn't have been half as friendly about it as Digby was currently being. This must be what a gentleman was, he reckoned.

"Well, so I am. Let's go, then!"

He'd spotted a tall orange butte that he recognized, and he couldn't hold off any longer, so he kicked Ragdoll into a gallop and laid low over her neck. Squirrel had no choice but to join up, and Digby's gelding caught on immediately. Soon all three horses were flat-out racing across the craggy skin of the prairie, kicking up stones and leaping over carved canyons. Rhett whipped off his hat and whooped, loving the feel of the cool winter air against his face, the sunbeams in his hair, like he was flying. For just a moment, he realized that he hadn't changed into the bird in weeks, and it was strange, so he shucked that thought off and kicked his mare harder. He could feel her snarl against the bit, but she pulled ahead of the other horses easy enough. Behind them, Mack and Jack struggled to keep up, their clunky bodies holding them down to the earth as they mooed in frustration.

As he reined up outside the valley, he couldn't help recalling the first time he'd seen the Las Moras Outpost of the Durango Rangers. Dan had brought Rhett here after he'd nearly died in the desert out west—and after he'd discovered his destiny as the Shadow. Sick, confused, lost—how little he'd known then. He hadn't learned he was a shapeshifter yet, had no idea that with the right prodding, he could become a lammergeier, as Trevisan had called it, maybe the biggest bird in Durango. He hadn't even known what a Ranger Outpost would be like. He'd just seen a long, low cabin bristling with unfriendly white fellers with guns. But they'd accepted him. Listened to him. Valued him. And one day, those same fellers had become Rhett's friends and fellow Rangers. And then, another day, most of 'em had turned on him because they couldn't stand to see a brown man made captain.

He'd shot most of 'em, that day.

And now, as he rode up that same path he'd trod before and skidded his mare to a stop, feeling her sides heave between his knees, it was all gone. There was no neat cabin, no cozy bunkhouse, no barn full of cockatrices and salamanders that needed feeding. Now there were just three burned-out husks, black and sharp against the orange ground. The tug in Rhett's belly was on high alert, and so was he, his gun pulled as he scanned the area for something dangerous that hadn't yet appeared.

"Hello?" he called, knowing it was a risk.

But anyone waiting to ambush him would've already shot, wouldn't they? Unless it was an animal sort of monster, but even then, it would've scented him long ago and come a-running.

No one answered his greeting. He pointed at Digby's gun belt and waited until the feller also had his weapon in hand. Rhett's ears were twitching, his eye scanning, his nose flaring for any sign of some foe. Nudging his mare forward, he hoped he wouldn't have to go all the way to the cabin's ruins. He'd left the Rangers burning on a pyre, as Rangers always burned their dead so they couldn't be turned into something worse than corpses, like Lobos. Rhett didn't want to see the bones he'd left behind that day, nor how the scavengers might've strewn them about like forgotten jacks.

"What is this place?" Digby asked.

"Our aim," Rhett said, knowing full well it wasn't enough.

Facing the main building, he added, "This used to be the Las Moras Outpost of the Durango Rangers. Me and Dan and Sam, we lived here. We wore our stars proudly."

"And then?"

"And then exactly what you see. It all went to shit."

"But why?"

Rhett chewed his lip. He could see them now, which meant Digby could, too: blackened bones, scattered on the hard ground. The critters had come for their due and left a mess of their own.

"That's a long story, but I assure you the wrong thing happened for the right reason."

"So why are we here?"

With a sigh, Rhett sat back in the saddle and considered. Why *were* they here? He still didn't know. The tug in his belly had quieted down like it was satisfied but not quite done with him. Was he just supposed to look at the havoc he'd wrought and feel like shit? Was there something here he needed to find to aid his next quest?

"I don't know, but I reckon we might as well make camp and wait it out."

The look Digby gave him suggested this seemed like a foolish idea, but Rhett didn't much care. Digby was a fine feller, but he didn't know much about how the Shadow worked yet. If it wanted Rhett here, it was for a reason. A necessary reason. Not necessarily a pleasant one.

"Go on. Gather some sticks for a fire. We'll settle over there, in the pen."

Because considering all the burned bits, the only part of the outpost that was still pretty were the fences, which Rhett had left untouched by fire. The grass had crept in, and the wood had held up, and he dismounted and led his horses and the two cattle into the pen and took the saddle off Ragdoll. The clever mare had her ears perked and was looking here and there, alert as hell, as if she knew something wasn't right. Or maybe she just remembered this place and liked it better full of fighting men and fine horses. In any case, although she lowered her head to graze, she did not relax, and neither did her rider.

As Digby hunted for anything that would still burn, Rhett went to the old well and started pulling up water to fill the trough, which had gone bone-dry the day they'd left. The first bucket got sucked right up by the ancient wood, but soon he had enough water for the three mounts and the steers to drink. He knew the feel of this particular bucket, as watering duty was always given to the lowest feller among the Rangers, and for a heartbreakingly short time, that had been Rhett. As the bucket handle dug into his fingers, he couldn't help recalling that that meant Sam had once held this bucket, done this same work, made this same walk from well to trough and seen the same splatters dry on his boot tips in the Durango sun.

A wash of heartsickness came over him, thinking about Sam. They hadn't spent this much time apart since Rhett's days in the train camp, and for all that the current situation was much more pleasant, it still didn't feel right. Sam would be asleep right now, but soon he'd be waking up, stretching and yawning in the bed he'd made, his pale chest shining in the darkness. Rhett was thinking about Sam, perhaps a bit too much, when he heard a crack over by the remains of the main cabin.

Ragdoll threw her head up, and Rhett followed suit, gun already drawn.

"Back me up," he murmured to Digby, real low, hoping that the feller's aim while under fire would be up to snuff.

From here, he couldn't see anything happening at the ruins, and the animals weren't acting like there was anything too dangerous about, but animals didn't know what the Shadow knew. Rhett crept, stealthy-like, between the white boards of the pen and approached the burned wreck, scanning the area with his eye and his gut to find the danger. Nothing presented itself, but danger could sometimes be sneaky and subtle.

"Who's there?" he barked.

When a coyote darted out of the rubble, he startled but didn't shoot. Digby, on the other hand, fired off a shot that didn't hit home. After throwing them a look of disgust, the dust-colored critter hightailed it into the hills.

"Normal coyote or Dan coyote, they're annoying little bastards," Rhett noted.

"That wasn't what we came here to see, right? And that wasn't a person? Because it didn't act like Dan, that's for sure."

Rhett shook his head; Digby hadn't seen Dan or Winifred in their coyote form yet, so of course he wouldn't know the difference. Most folks weren't sensitive enough to tell an animal from a monster, which is what had distinguished Dan and Rhett as Ranger Scouts. Apparently, Digby didn't share that sense.

"Don't reckon that's what the Shadow wanted, and it wasn't a person. Just a creature trying to get by. I normally don't begrudge such things, but I'd rather not watch my old friends get chewed on, so I don't mind the loss of your bullet."

He could tell Digby wanted to ask again about what had happened at Las Moras, but he figured Digby could take a look at his face and posture and know that he still wasn't gonna talk about it.

They made camp in the pen, and the winter-brown grass made a comfy enough mattress under Rhett's horse blanket. Digby shot a prairie chicken, and Rhett lured in some rabbits with a drop of blood, and they had more than enough meat for two and another little brown pelt for Winifred to add to her collection. Far as Rhett could figure, when her baby was born, Winifred was just gonna roll it up in all the skins she'd been collecting and drag it around on a sled. Fed but not yet sleepy, he and Digby sat across from each other, the fire ever between them.

"Tell me a story, Digby," Rhett asked, as he'd found that he actually liked to hear Digby talk. The feller was a born story-teller, and sometimes he told tall tales he'd heard along the way or wild legends from his new people up north, and sometimes he told real stories that had happened to him and folks he'd met, before the train camp. But he never, thankfully, talked of his time in that hellhole.

"What you want to hear about tonight?" Digby said, leaning back against his saddle with a grin, always pleased to be invited to yammer.

"Something real," Rhett decided. "Something that ain't sad."

Digby nodded, fist on his chin, thinking. "The not sad part's the hard part about reality."

"Don't I know it."

Finally, Digby settled in, staring into the fire. "Well, one time when I was a little boy, I was on an errand, running fast as I could so I wouldn't get whipped for shirking, and I accidentally ran headfirst into the Maman. She was the oldest lady on the plantation, and everybody knew she was a witch, even if all the older folk whispered that if she had any real power, she would've blasted every chain and lock on the island and made every whip turn to a viper in the overseer's hand.

122

"Now, I hadn't had cause to meet her before, because she kept to herself and mostly attended to the house mistress, who had every imagined disease you can invent. And of course she helped the girls who needed help getting rid of somethin', all quiet-like, and the men who took ill with the miasma or infected lashes, that sort of thing. But she didn't have cause to do anything with rascally little boys except in a threatening sort of way when we got too near her hut. And then I came around a corner too fast, hit her bony ol' knees, and knocked her flat on her back.

"I reckoned she'd curse me from the ground, and I'd grow me a tail. I was too young to change, you see, didn't even know what I was yet. A tail seemed a terrible thing to have. In that moment, I could've run away, and maybe she wouldn't have even known which of the whelps had knocked her over, but I couldn't bring myself to do it. I hopped up and hurried over and held out my hand and said, 'Apologies, Maman. I did not see you.'"

Digby paused to wipe imaginary sweat from his forehead; the night had gone deathly cold, but from Digby's past descriptions, Rhett could imagine the hot, wet stink of the plantation, the sugarcane shivering in a salty breeze as a little boy who'd never known anything but pain awaited more punishment.

"She let me help her up, and she was a tiny, bent old thing, and she stared at me so hard I reckoned she could see my giblets contract. She pointed at the medicine basket I'd made her drop, and I tell you what—I picked up her roots and plants and flowers quick as a damn bunny, tucked 'em all back in that basket neat as a boy can do. She took the basket and gave a firm sort of nod, like maybe she'd decided not to give me a tail that day, but just barely. And then she crooked a finger at me and said, '*Mon fils*, you gonna run headlong into trouble your whole life. But don't you never stop running.'"

He chuckled and shook his head. "And damn if she wasn't right."

Rhett drew his horse blanket up to his chin and stared at the stars. He wanted to know if you could see the same stars down in the islands where Digby had been born, but it seemed a little rude to ask.

"So what's your point?" he asked instead, because he often felt, with Digby, like the man wanted him to draw conclusions while never quite giving him enough information to do so, which made him feel a fool.

"My point is that you and I got that in common. We run at trouble, even knowing it's gonna hurt. We run out to meet it. Maybe that's why Dan doesn't understand you. He just waits for it. The world needs both kinds of men, I reckon, to make up for the fellers who run away whenever things get tough."

Settling back, elbows out and feet crossed, Rhett considered that. The sky was clear, the night cold but peaceful, and he missed his old buffalo robe like hell. And Sam. And even Dan, maybe, for all that Digby was right about his tendency to wait around being pretty annoying. There was something comforting about having everybody around the fire, where they belonged—and where he could keep an eye on 'em. He felt pretty far from home, just then, although he wouldn't say that out loud, ever. Not only because it made him sound like a whiner baby, but because Digby was obviously a hell of a lot farther from his own home, wherever that was.

"Digby, do you reckon—" he started, but he was interrupted by Ragdoll, who snorted and bugled. The sensible mare didn't do such things frequently, and Rhett crouched, gun in hand, to deal with whatever was coming. When he concentrated, he could feel it: that rumble in his tummy. Something coming near. The very something he was here to meet. But he didn't feel that urge to act, which was downright odd.

Ragdoll was at the fence, chest pressed up against the boards, with Hess and Squirrel worrying around her and the young steers cavorting like fools in their excitement. The mare stamped her feet and bugled again, and this time, another horse bugled back.

"Now, who could that be?" Digby said softly, appearing by Rhett's side, his gun drawn.

"You got the quiet of a cat, that's for sure," Rhett said in an appreciative sort of tone. "And I got no idea, but I reckon we're gonna find out."

"Do we hide or stand tall?"

Rhett drew a breath as he tasted the night air and threw out his senses for clues. His belly stirred, the Shadow anxious for whatever was coming, but he couldn't get a handle on what it was.

"We got a fire, three horses, and two fool steers giving away our position. We can't hide. So we go out and stand tall."

Unfolding from his crouch in the grass, Rhett shoved his pistol back in his belt, took the Henry off his saddle, and slipped between the fence boards. Whatever was coming was taking the usual road, and it wasn't going fast. It wasn't on attack. It was just moseying along. He could tell that much. But still, it pawed at him. Dangerous. But harmless. But evil. But innocent. Worry, but hope? The hairs rose along his arms and up the back of his neck.

Whatever it was, it was important. He put the Henry behind his neck and draped his wrists over it as the Captain had done upon meeting someone new. It was a position that suggested power, that said he was strong enough to be casual and leave his vulnerable belly open to harm for the split second it would take him to whip the gun around and blow a hole in whoever dared attack him. There was a manly laziness about the posture he appreciated.

"If I tell you to shoot, you shoot," he whispered to Digby.

"Aye-aye, Captain," Digby responded, and Rhett swole up a foot taller, felt like, to have the older man say such a thing.

Ragdoll and the other horse kept up their conversation, whinnying back and forth across the night, and Hess and Squirrel joined in while the steers caterwauled.

"Good thing we didn't need to hide," Rhett muttered.

"Do horses do this a lot?" Digby asked. "I've never heard such a thing before. Hollering to wake the damn dead."

Rhett's eye shot guiltily toward the blackened pyre. None of the Rangers would be waking up, he hoped.

Dark figures entered the valley, at least three on horseback, and Ragdoll pressed so hard against the fence that it creaked as she gave her loudest whinny yet, sounding excited and pleased. When the other horse whinnied back this time, Rhett had the oddest feeling that he'd heard exactly that horse before, and he racked his brain for folks he knew out in the world. Maybe it was some of the Las Moras scouts returning from Ranger duty elsewhere? He whipped his Henry off his neck and held it in both hands. That would be an awkward conversation that would end badly, and if such was the case, he might as well shoot first and save himself the trouble of watching another man's face wrinkle up into a scowl of disbelief and blame.

"Who's there?" he hollered, making his voice as deep and gruff as it could go.

He heard voices gabbling, low and indistinct, and then a lone voice called out, surprising the hell out of him.

"Is your brother, Revenge. You told me come, and I am here."

CHAPTER
10

Rhett dropped the Henry and ran, his heart just about to burst. If Revenge was here, and he wasn't alone, who were the others? Was his mother with them? Goddamn the night for being so dark! As he drew near with Digby hard on his heels, he picked out three horses and a couple of fellers on foot, making five people in all. Revenge slid off Puddin', and Rhett finally understood why Ragdoll had been so beside herself with joy. Rhett almost hugged his little paint horse first, but he figured his brother might take that the wrong way and stepped in, arms open, for a punishing embrace.

Revenge hadn't changed much, although he was dressed in white man duds, a plaid shirt and butternut britches and dusty brown boots. His hair hadn't changed, though, and neither had the stern set of his face, making him look years older than he was. The feller seemed always to be scowling, although his current scowl held a sort of triumph.

"Got good English, did you?" Rhett asked, trying to give the feller a compliment without being too obvious about it.

"English stupid language," Revenge said, shaking his head in disgust. "But I get enough."

Beyond him, Rhett saw his mother dismounting from a

sturdy brown pony, and he hurried over to help her. She chuckled and put a hand on his cheek.

"Don't need help," she said, her voice deep and warm. "But thanks."

When she'd rearranged her shawl, Rhett waited, hoping she'd want a hug. She opened her arms, and he just about knocked her over, squeezing her like he'd never been hugged before. He was breathless and elated all to hell, tickled pink that this was what the Shadow had brought him here to do. For so long, the tug in his gut had been hanging low like storm clouds, but it had really been a ray of sunshine, heading toward this moment, right where he needed to be. So why was his belly still grumbling like something dangerous was in the area?

Someone else hopped down off a big Medicine Hat paint, and when Rhett saw her, he knew she was the trouble he'd been waiting for, the reason the Shadow had sensed danger.

He knew what she was immediately, could smell the stink of it on her.

"You brought a goddamn Lobo?" he growled, pulling a pistol and fighting to keep his finger off the trigger.

The woman walked around her gelding as if Rhett were no threat. She was middle-aged and pretty and tough as old leather, her beaver hat pulled down and a stylized black tattoo gracing her chin.

"They told me you were a surly critter, and here you are," she said, her voice surprisingly high and musical and tinged with an old accent as faded as her calico shirt. "I'm Lizzie. You're Rhett. So that's out of the way, and you can stop staring at me like I'm gonna bite you."

Rhett turned back to Revenge and his mother, flanked now by Beans and Notch, who had followed on foot. When Rhett had left this foursome of folks several months ago, they'd had only a leather dwelling and the gift of Rhett's fat little paint horse. But now, they'd changed drastically. Beans and Notch looked tougher, stood taller. Revenge and Rhett's mama had enough speech to make themselves understood. And they'd somehow gotten their fool selves involved with a Lobo, which was about the same as shackling oneself to a rabid wolf.

"Did she eat that little coydog of yours, Revenge?" Rhett asked, his dander up.

"No!" Revenge barked.

"Buffalo trample," their mama said sadly.

Rhett felt bad for bringing it up as a joke, so he returned to the problem at hand.

"You-all know all Lobos are bad, right?"

Lizzie snorted. "And who told you that? Let me guess. A Durango Ranger." She spit on the ground at his feet, loosened her girth, and towed her horse toward the pen and the fire.

Rhett's head twitched back and forth. He wanted to catch up with his folks, but he also wanted to keep everybody safe, which meant he needed to kill the Lobo. And yet his folks felt safe enough around her, for certain. But if this Lizzie was dangerous, how were they alive instead of dead or Lobos themselves?

"Come on over by the fire so we can sort this out," he said, taking the reins from his mama and giving her brown mare a tug. The gentle critter followed easy enough, and his mama allowed it, and they all sort of trailed along behind him in silence until his brother broke in.

"Lizzie is friend," he said, voice harsh in admonishment. "Lobo not bad."

"All Lobo bad, fool. Everybody knows that."

"I do not know that."

"I do not know, too," his mama added in her gentle but stern way.

"Just come on," Rhett muttered, snatching up his dropped Henry and walking faster as he saw Lizzie entering the paddock and nearing Ragdoll. For all he knew, the Lobo might hurt his horse, and then he'd really lose his shit. But all she did was let her big gelding sniff at the other horses while she unsaddled him, a gesture that showed she understood horses and had respect for their ways. Once inside the pen, Rhett took care of his mama's mare, all the while keeping watch on the new folks. Poor Digby kinda skulked along behind him, unsure what was happening or what to do about it.

"We good, Rhett?" Digby asked.

"Hard to say, but I'm gonna find out."

Once all the horses were unsaddled and folks were taking their places around the fire, Rhett set to fretting that there wasn't more food to share. Nothing remained of the prairie hen but a carcass and a pile of feathers, and a rabbit could barely feed one hungry traveler. He was about to send Digby out hunting when his brother pulled a deer haunch out of his bag and set to cutting it into strips like a useful feller.

"Well then," Rhett said, settling into his place with his mama and brother by his side and the Lobo woman across the fire. "I'm right happy to see most of you, but I'm right doubtful about sleeping with a Lobo loose nearby. So why don't you tell me what you're doing here with my folks, Lobo woman."

Lizzie just snorted. "Why waste my breath? You won't trust me. Let them tell you."

Rhett looked to his brother and gave him a nod. "So what's happened since I left you-all, Revenge? Find any trouble?"

His brother took a deep breath, a firm set to his jaw attempting to make up for the fact that Revenge was younger even than Rhett. "You go, we stayed. Beans and Notch helped. Teach me speak to you. Mama, too. You say I find you when I speak, so I come."

"Well, yes, I reckoned all that. But what about the Lobo?"

"Lobo is a thing we don't know." His mother's face screwed up as she tried to find the words. "Did not know. Lizzie saw our fire, came warn us. Haskell was near." Her face went dark, and rage welled up in Rhett's chest. After he took care of the chupas, he told himself, he'd go after Haskell. For all the feller had done in the name of the Rangers, and for all those people he might yet hurt.

"I'll kill him, one day," he promised.

Lizzie gave him a sloppy grin. "Then you're not that bad, in my book."

He turned to her, focusing. "So you see a fire in the middle of nowhere and go over to tell the poor souls that the devil himself is nearby?"

Lizzie nodded and drank from her canteen. "Ayup. That's what I do. I can't take on Haskell's Rascals by my lone, don't want to get involved with the Ranger higher-ups, and can't get up a big enough posse to do real damage, not that I'd even want to. So I stay a few steps ahead of him and his men, let folks know when they're coming. For all their bluster and cruelty, his men are neither silent nor good at keeping secrets. Easy enough to know where he's headed next. All you've got to do is camp within a mile and keep your mouth shut."

Rhett chewed the inside of his cheek. "Fine. So you did a good deed. Why're you still with 'em instead of heading to your next campfire?"

He was watching Lizzie's face, just then, and he saw confusion and doubt flash there, clear as day.

"I don't really know. It felt like the right thing to do. I trust my gut. It's why I'm still alive."

"How'd you become a Lobo?"

Her eyes flashed fire. "How does anyone? Lobos found me and hurt me, and this is what I became."

But Rhett still wasn't convinced. "Okay, but why didn't they take you with 'em, then? As I understood it, Lobos collect the Lobos they make. Adding more teeth to the pack, so to say."

Lizzie barked a curse in another language and stood, rising tall against the fire. When she wrenched up her shirt, Rhett was fascinated and disgusted to see that a big ol' chunk of her side was gone from ribs to hip.

"They left after they took what they wanted and departed, and this is the shape of it. I am what was left over when they were done." She let her shirt drop and sat back down, pulling a flask from her saddlebag. "And the worst of their work didn't leave a scar."

"Did you chase 'em down? Get your revenge?"

Her look could've stripped paint off a fence. "What am I, one woman, to a pack of monsters? No, I have my petty revenges when I can and tell myself it's enough. That living past their cruelty is enough. And when it's not enough, there's the bottle."

On this particular topic, Rhett had quite a lot to say, and he couldn't help stabbing his finger in the air and barking, "Bullshit. One person can take down an entire pack of monsters. If you think of yourself as a force of nature instead of a…a…a victim. Petty ain't enough. You got to end 'em when you can."

It occurred to him, as he said the words, that he'd said *person* instead of *woman*. Because he got a feeling that whatever else Lizzie was, she was like him: beyond living up to other people's expectations. And, hell, maybe he was starting to think girls could do anything they goddamn wanted, anyway, especially when revenge was involved. But there were many kinds of revenge, he was learning. And the petty sort was not his personal choice. He preferred annihilation.

Lizzie settled back on her elbows and took another swig. "How pleasant for you, to have such powers and confidence.

To know your destiny. Some of us know we're just bugs, scraping along. So we try to make the bad men itch a little before we go."

"Lizzie is good," Revenge growled, looking up from where he was threading meat onto sticks, and Rhett thought he saw the twang of puppy love in his hotheaded little brother's eyes. Their mama nodded firmly. Even Beans and Notch bobbed their fool heads in agreement, not that Rhett gave much consideration to their thoughts.

"Maybe," Rhett said. "And maybe not." He sighed. "But I will admit you're nothing like the Lobos I met before. Who are all dead now, I might add. Just sand in the wind."

"Good," Lizzie growled. "Best place for 'em."

For a while there, it got quiet around the fire, and that's when Rhett remembered that he was the one in charge and needed to do something to set the tone. All the jobs had been done, and Revenge was putting meat on the fire. Ordering folks around was easy enough for him, but bringing two groups of strangers together around the fire for pleasant talk was beyond him.

"Uh, Digby, you know Notch and Beans, and you heard tell of Lizzie, but this is my brother Revenge and my mama...?"

He'd never addressed her by name, last time they'd met. He'd been too bowled over to meet her, the mother who'd lost him as a child, who'd slept as the Cannibal Owl whisked him away in its clacking fingers. It wasn't her fault, and he didn't blame her, but it did pain his heart, knowing what his life could've been if he hadn't been stolen. Winifred had told him his mama had changed her name from I Will Find Her to I Found Him, which sounded a hell of a lot more musical in her own language. Still, he needed something to call her, and it was the right time to find out.

"Finder," she said, and Rhett was about to tell her that wasn't no name, but then he reckoned a person could claim any name they goddamn wanted.

"Well it's right fine to meet you all," Digby said, tipping his hat and giving his broadest grin. "I'm Digby Freeman, and I'm from somewhere far away you ain't never heard of." He focused on Notch and Beans, who had been silent all this time, as they somehow always managed to be the lowest fellers on any totem pole. "Notch and Beans, as I live and breathe. But it sure is good to see you boys again! You-all know if anybody else from the ol' train camp got where they were going?"

"We don't know nothing," Notch said. "Found Rhett here, then he sent us along with his people."

Digby spun on Rhett, looking alarmed. "You left your mama with these two...fellers? Out in the middle of nowhere?"

Rhett bristled. "They're fine fellers, and you know it. And if not, she'd stick 'em with her knife, easy as pie." Finder held up her sharp little stick knife and smirked in support of his point. "There wasn't much choice. I was on my way to this outpost, right before it got burned down. The Shadow was driving me with spurs, and I couldn't take them into danger. I gave 'em my second favorite horse!"

His mama snorted and shook her head in amusement like he was quite the scalawag.

"Then why are they here now?"

Rhett looked around the campfire, meeting each person's eyes. "Because we all feel something stirring, don't we? It's whatever brought you to the mission, Digby. And what brought Lizzie to them, and them me, to the outpost. I told Revenge to come here to find me once his English got good enough, hopefully once the worst of the danger was over. But I'm starting to feel like the worst danger yet is on the horizon."

"I feel it," Lizzie said, her voice low. "Like thunder. Nothing substantial yet. But waiting."

Rhett nodded. "That's true enough."

"Fight is coming," Revenge said.

"And you'll stay the hell out of it! Both you and Mama!"

Revenge hopped up to his feet, his knife in hand.

"The fight is mine. You cannot steal it again!"

So Revenge was still mad that Rhett had taken down the Cannibal Owl, the destiny Revenge had been born to conquer. Not that Rhett had even known the feller existed, back when his destiny had sent him to hunt and destroy the child-stealing monster.

"Mama, you're okay with a little cub like him fighting? Because whatever we're up against, it'll claim casualties. People are gonna die." He touched the kerch over his gone eye. "Or lose things. Hell, I'm down an eye and a toe already and I feel pretty damn lucky by comparison." He glanced back at the burned skeleton of the ranch house. "Whatever's coming, some folks won't make it out alive."

His mother regarded him coolly. "My boys strong," she said, fist against her heart.

Rhett threw up his hands. "Some mother you are, sending her only two whelps out into some kind of war. Don't even know what's coming yet, but you're ready to see our backs."

His mother's lip quivered, and then she broke out laughing. Revenge and Lizzie joined her, and then everybody except Rhett was cackling. All Rhett could do was angrily poke at the fire with a stick.

"You-all ought to stop gabbing like crows and get some sleep. We got to head back to the mission tomorrow, where the rest of our people are." He glanced around the valley, feeling like perhaps he was surrounded by ghosts. "I don't like this place, not one bit."

As much as he'd once loved it here, he hated it now. He was beginning to see that his Rangers and his Captain weren't what the other Rangers of Durango were, and that a fine thing had been snuffed out. The Captain had told Rhett, there at the end, that he'd made some mistakes in his life and had tried to set them right. Rhett knew how that felt now. And he knew that for all he was set on doing the right thing, that didn't necessarily make him a good man. He'd be good, as good as he could—until Sam was threatened. Until anyone he loved was threatened.

All these folks around the fire were his now. He didn't know why fate kept sending folks to his doorstep, folks he knew or loved, but he understood that his job was to lead them. Not keep them safe. Not even shelter them. More like the Captain led his men. Danger was coming, and they'd be in the thick of it, yet they'd all been drawn to him for this reason, and they'd chosen to answer the call.

So he'd lead his people to the end, whatever it was. That's what the Shadow demanded.

They settled down, heads pillowed on saddlebags and horse blankets still damp with sweat. Instead of staring into Sam's blue eyes and matching the cowpoke's breathing until he was asleep, something he couldn't do ever again anywhere but underground in a goddamn crypt, Rhett stared at his mama by firelight. She was quiet and watchful and somehow hard, for all that she could be tender. She watched him, too. He hoped she was proud of him. And he wondered what it would be like, on the trail with her. Like Sam had once been, she was human, the only human among them all, and that made her precious.

And a liability.

It was like having a gaping wound wherever he went. Paining him, worrying him.

He'd half lost Sam. Now that he had his mama, he would do anything not to lose her, too.

For all his worries, Rhett slept just fine, and the Shadow slept, too. Lizzie took down some birds for breakfast, and everybody knew their way around a campfire, and they were soon on the road with Notch and Beans doubled up bareback on Squirrel. Rhett led the line, all his folks strung out behind him with Lizzie in back. He had a sort of animal sense that told him she was the most competent among the available crew, but that only served to make him more suspicious of her. Anybody could say they were good and harmless, but the truth of a person always came out, one way or another. And when it did come out, it was probably best if they weren't behind you, watching you, making their own dastardly plans.

The trip back to the mission was peaceful enough, and Rhett enjoyed the quiet days riding alongside his mother and brother, pleased to see they both shared his gift with horses. Digby did his part of shooting supper with Revenge and often rode along with Notch and Beans, although they didn't have much in common past the time they'd spent in the train car. Notch and Beans hadn't changed a whit, and they rode like they didn't have a firm bone in their bodies and might topple off their horse at any time. They still looked at Digby like they looked at Rhett: as a leader, someone higher up on life's ladder. The two fellers were followers, through and through, and Rhett reckoned that was just how it was. Not everybody could be the lead dog. Then again, he'd been a follower for years, up until the night he'd killed his first vampire and seen the way of the hidden world of monsters. And even after that, it had taken time, mesquite poisoning, and the careful teachings of men he mostly trusted to set him on the path to embracing his destiny.

The Shadow was mercifully silent, which meant that the tug Rhett felt, reeling him back to the mission, had to be Sam. Yes, Sam was different now. Hellfire, Rhett was different than he'd once been, too. But Rhett still craved Sam like a dying man craves water, and being away from Sam had only intensified his thirst. As the mission came into sight in late afternoon, he couldn't help nudging Ragdoll to a canter so he could see things settled and hurry down to the basement to be there when Sam woke up. The rest of the horses followed suit, and then old Blue the mule bugled his welcome, and suddenly everybody Rhett wanted to see was standing around in the yard, curious. Excepting Sam, of course. Rhett hopped down off his mare and stood there feeling silly.

"Well," Rhett said, one hand on Ragdoll's neck and feeling like a fool. "Here we are."

"So what called you to Las Moras wasn't…?" Dan asked.

Rhett shook his head. "Not a monster. Nothing bad. Just my folks here, making good on our agreement. Ain't that right, Revenge?"

"For once, you are right," Revenge said, making Dan break out into a rare grin.

Winifred had been watching the exchange, bemused, one hand on her lower back, as it had begun to ache her something fierce by nightfall after a day's ride or work, according to her constant complaints. Now she walked toward Rhett's mama, hands out.

"It's good to see you again, sister," she said, and Rhett's mama said, "Yes, it is good," and they hugged, and Rhett's heart ached that he couldn't be so comfortable in his ways, couldn't show his feelings as easily as these two women did, embracing each other and whispering and laughing together before heading off to the kitchen, hopefully to round up some grub.

As the women passed Inés, the nun said, "I think I'll join you," and followed them in, leaving Lizzie as the only woman outside the mission. Rhett reckoned that it was lonely being a wild woman out on the prairie, and that the women felt the same comfort in their kitchens as he felt taking his place around the fire at night, joshing and farting among fighting men. Lizzie, again, was a different sort of creature.

"Since Rhett is too rude to make introductions, I'm Dan." The feller strode to Lizzie, and she said, "Lizzie," and they shook hands like men did, and then as everybody else had met Dan, Rhett figured everything was done until Sam woke up and they had to do it all over again. Rhett didn't like the pageantry of it all; he reckoned folks could get to know one another in time, like he had in the train car. Then again, Rhett hadn't been raised in a crowd, just with two folks who hated him, so he figured he had a right to be skittish about such things.

"I reckon I'll see to the horses and our first two cattle," Digby said, taking Ragdoll's reins from Rhett to walk her along with Hess. Notch and Beans and Lizzie followed along, with Dan supervising. In a right peculiar turn of events, Rhett recognized that with so many competent folks around, he wasn't actually needed for chores. That meant he could do what he damn well pleased, which meant he hurried for the basement.

Since the ladder was down there, Rhett had to jump, but he knew well enough now that his monster body could take the impact. His feet went a little numb and his knees jangled as he landed on the packed dirt, but otherwise the only damage was to his mind. Just like every time he came down here, he could feel death soaking the walls, smell the dry, dusty musk of the giant lizards that had ended the mission's former occupants. But that didn't stop him. Except when he got to Sam's hidey-hole, he found the door was locked—from the inside.

No point in knocking. As he knew, Sam would be dead to the world until the moment some mysterious internal clock popped him awake like a rooster. So Rhett could either wait down here or go back upstairs and get fussed at by the women. It was bad enough with Winifred always on his back to keep his hair trimmed and Inés trying in vain to teach him not to slurp soup; now his mama was with them, and who knew what she would think about his rough ways?

"Hellfire," he muttered, moseying down the hall to the library.

A room full of books didn't mean much to a feller who didn't have his letters, and the volumes that had illustrations weren't very calming to the soul. Nothing but monsters and fellers in dresses with dumb haircuts getting chewed on by those monsters, although there was one really old book with a few inky cat paw prints on it that Inés had showed Rhett. He'd felt a kinship with that long-dead cat, a predator confined and taking its pleasure by mucking up the work of men who thought their shit didn't stink.

"Rhett? Is that you?"

Hearing Sam's voice made his heart go all pitter-pat-thunk. Sam's door unlocked and creaked open, and Rhett hurried back down the long, dark hall, hoping he didn't look and smell too horrible after several days on the trail.

"Sam, I—"

"There are new people here."

Sam stood in the doorway, golden brows drawn down over his once sunny blue eyes. When he talked, Rhett could just see the shiny white wink of his fangs. Rhett slowed and put his arms down to his sides, as Sam didn't look too interested in hugging, just then.

"Yep, there are. But you met most of 'em already, I reckon. It was my mama and Revenge, coming to meet me at Las Moras, like I told 'em to. They brought Notch and Beans. And there's another woman, Lizzie..."

"A Lobo."

Sam said it like a snarl, and Rhett recalled feeling about the same way a few days ago.

"Yeah, she's a Lobo. But since you're a vampire and you're not bad, I reckon you can cotton to the fact that she's a Lobo who's maybe not bad. My folks vouched for her, and we traveled with her for several days without a lick of trouble. She didn't change into a wolf at all, and she's a good shot for breakfast birds. Peculiar thing."

"I hate Lobos more than I used to, Rhett, and I used to hate Lobos a lot. Got a stench about 'em now."

Rhett sighed. "Well I'm not that fond of 'em myself, if you'll recall what I been through with Lobos." He gave Sam a significant look to remind the feller of the day Rhett had pretended to be a girl so the Lobos would think he was helpless and focus on hurting him instead of killing the Captain and a few dozen Durango Rangers they'd managed to ambush on the trail. The ruse had worked, but it had been too close a call for Rhett's comfort, and Sam had been against the idea from the beginning.

Sam's brow furrowed, showing he well remembered. "I do recall."

"Then give her a chance, just like everybody's gonna give you a chance." Feeling exasperated, he shrugged helplessly, hating himself for it. "Well, aren't you glad to see me? I missed you like hell, Sam. It's the truth. The trail's shit without you."

141

At that, Sam smiled, something close to the old Sam smile, which felt like the sun coming out from behind dark clouds.

"I did miss you, Rhett. I just worry. I wish I could be there to keep you safe. Before, when I slept, at least I could wake up if there were gunshots."

"Well, this time there weren't gunshots, so there was nothing to worry about. Easy little trip among friends."

Sam looked down at the floor and rubbed a hand through his hair, which was growing out in silky golden ringlets, making him look even more like an angel. "And Las Moras?"

Rhett looked down, too. "Still burned to ashes. Quiet. Nothing there."

"I guess I thought maybe—"

"Guess I did, too."

"I got your letter."

Without really meaning to, Rhett had shuffled close to Sam, and they crashed together in a mess of grief and need, all mouths and hands and panting like they'd run a mile. Sam walked Rhett backward into his bed, and Rhett sat down hard and tumbled into the covers, surprised as always to find that they were cold even after Sam had lain there all night.

When they were done with what they both needed, they lay there, Rhett's head nestled against Sam's chest, Sam's arm around him, and Sam humming some song Rhett had never heard before that sounded like it had come from a saloon piano. Rhett considered, for a moment, how odd it was that before, he had been the one cradling Sam's head. But he didn't mind where he was, not really. Part of being a good leader, he'd learned, was not trying to be in charge all the goddamn time. Still, he could feel Sam thrumming against him, as if it took a hell of a lot of care for the feller to hold still.

"Do you not want to be here, Sam?" he asked.

Sam planted a kiss on his forehead. "No, I do. I do. I just... I wake up with this energy. I need blood. Still haven't found a way to get it from a person. Inés's cow got kinda weak, and her milk thinned, so I had to drink from one of the horses the other night." He exhaled, and Rhett felt his shame in a huff of cool breath. "Not one we've named, just a fat one who seemed easy to catch. Didn't taste right. Like eating tripe when you're used to steak."

"I never had tripe nor steak," Rhett said.

"Like eating bugs, then."

Rhett had never eaten bugs, never been in that bad a shape as a human, but he didn't say so.

"Do you need to go to San Anton?" he asked, his voice unwillingly small in the dark.

"Maybe," Sam breathed. "Maybe."

"I'd rather you just drank from me."

"What? No! I told you no." Sam shuddered and edged away a little, and Rhett could've shrunk to the size of a bug himself, he felt so goddamn rejected.

"But why not? You need something, I got plenty of it. You can't kill me."

Sam shook his head, gently withdrew his arm, and stood, tugging his clothes back on and speaking hurriedly. "I can't explain it. Would you... would you milk your mama for your coffee? Would you cut off one of my toes if you were starving?"

Now Rhett stood to dress, feeling just as vexed. "Those are pretty goddamn different and you know it. At least try. Maybe just a little bit would hold you off. Emily said just a few pulls would do it." He exhaled and stood tall. "If I'm honest, which I always want to be with you, I'd rather you drank from me than some other man. It seems right personal. Taking... taking part of a person into yourself like that."

Sam turned away from him as he finished with his buttons. "It ain't personal. It's like..."

"You just said it was personal! You just said it was like milking my...goddammit, I can't say it. Either it is personal or it ain't. If I'm not good enough for you, just say so, but don't you dare go find another man and then come home to me with his stank all over you!"

Rhett gasped, surprised by his own outburst.

Sam snorted and went stiff.

"So that's how it is? You've used other people for your needs before—and I had to watch it happen. I reckon I'll do what I must. But I won't drink from you, and if you weren't so goddamn scared and pigheaded, you'd realize how much that means, coming from a hungry vampire. Guess I'll go welcome the new folks."

He walked past Rhett without so much as brushing his shoulder in the narrow space, and Rhett forced himself to stay there, suffering and cold, in the dark, until he'd heard Sam climb the ladder. As he climbed out himself, hearing the sounds of cooking supper and camaraderie in the kitchen, he felt more lonely than he had since he'd wandered the desert, alone except for Ragdoll. He'd never imagined hollering at Sam like that—and he'd never imagined Sam giving him the coldest of shoulders.

Steeling himself, he moseyed into the kitchen, trying to add an extra layer of mosey so the others wouldn't know he was worried to his very bones. About Sam, mostly, but also about everything else. Ever since leaving Pap's place, he'd been drawn somewhere. Now his gut told him to stay put and wait, and Rhett wasn't at all good at staying put.

It was easier to outrun a man's problems on horseback, and he reckoned this was one problem that couldn't be fought with fists or bullets.

"Evening," he said, entering the kitchen.

The women nodded at him from around the table, appearing far more comfortable than Rhett himself.

"Lovers' quarrel?" Winifred said with a sly smile.

"Oh, shut your hole," Rhett muttered, slinging himself onto the bench.

"Big heart makes big noise," his mama said, thumping her chest with a sympathetic smile. "You have a big heart."

Rhett snorted and shook his head. "You don't know me very well, Mama."

"I know Revenge. I know your father. I know."

"He is changed, Rhett," Inés said quietly. "The spider venom, and now this. You must give him time. Most people don't adapt as quickly as you can."

"How can I give him time if I can't even give him food?" Rhett muttered. "He won't let me...he won't...he won't take what I'd give him of my own free will."

Winifred shrugged and rubbed her belly with lazy fondness. "Giving and taking. No one said it was going to be easy."

"What was?"

"Love, you fool."

Rhett went over red. It was one thing for folks to guess, another thing for folks to privately know, and a very different thing to have it said aloud around folks he didn't know too well. Like his mama. Would she think him...wrong? But when he looked up at her, all skittish, she was smiling in a way that said she maybe knew how he felt, that it went beyond boys and girls and right and wrong.

"Need time, then talk." She raised her eyebrows. "And time when no words are needed, only bodies. That helps."

"Mama, please!" he yelped.

His mama and Winifred and Inés all laughed together,

cackling like tickled hens, so he got up and hurried out of the room and into the yard. It was that odd time when evening is over but it's not yet full dark, when the stars just start to peep one by one, and the coyotes try a little snippet of song, not quite sure if they're ready to tackle the whole thing. Over against Inés's fence, freshly mended, the men and Lizzie worked in the way men do when at their ease. Dan was helping Notch and Beans select easy mounts from the small herd, and Digby was working with his little steers, treating the horned beasts like giant puppies. Lizzie looked to the west, quiet and still, a cigarette burning between her lips, and Sam was among the herd, talking to his leggy geldings in that soft voice he used with animals and sometimes, sweetly, with Rhett. Rhett's heart ached with what a pretty scene it was, right before the truth whomped him back, reminding him that the moment wasn't actually that calm, and that it wasn't gonna last. Yes, for now, he was supposed to wait. But one day soon, he'd bolt up, heart beating like crazy, knowing it was time to go fight something else. He didn't know what and he didn't know when; he only knew it was gonna be a hell of a fight.

"I was thinking the little grullo might do for Notch," he said, walking up to the fence. "Kind eye, and he runs to fat, so he could use the movement."

"This one," Dan agreed, putting a hand on the pony, which nuzzled him and cocked a back foot.

"I don't know, Rhett. They all look scary to me," Notch said. "Can't we walk on our own feet? We're quick as horses. Just ask Lizzie."

Before Rhett could answer, Lizzie said, "You're quick at a walk, it's true. But whatever's coming's gonna be a hell of a lot faster. You're going to want to run, when it's on the horizon."

"But can't we just…"

Everyone looked at Beans, knowing full well what he meant. "Stay back and shirk the fight?" Rhett said, low and deadly. "Hang back while we take on whatever's coming?"

"We ain't fighters like you, Red-Eye!" Beans wailed. "They been trying to teach us how to shoot. Neither one of us is any good with a bow, and we just waste the shit out of bullets. Revenge can whup us both with one hand tied behind his back, and that ain't a joke."

Rhett stood there, thumbs in his pockets. "Then why the hell did you come here?"

Notch shrugged. "Where else would we go? We found folks to travel with, so we traveled with 'em. Ain't passed a town yet. I'd rather sweep up at a saloon. Some folks are—"

"Cowards?"

"Yes! Most of the goddamn world is, Rhett!" Sam barked. "Don't you get it? None of us can be what you are. We can't do what you can do. Even those of us who reckon fighting's the way to go are scared when we do it. You ain't a regular sort of feller, running headfirst into every tussle. You compare us to you, and we're gonna come up short, every time!"

"I didn't ask to be this!" Rhett hollered back, surprised to be on the end of a tail-chewing from a man who'd so recently turned his back. "I'm goddamn exhausted, but all I can do is keep going and figure maybe if I keep running into every fight first, I can keep y'all alive, cowards and fools included. You always been the best of us, Sam. Didn't you ever figure maybe I'm the one who ain't up to snuff? Didn't you ever consider that maybe I run headfirst into fights because I'd rather die if it meant you were safe? Don't you know I'd bleed out to feed you, if it would keep you by my side?"

Sam gawped like a fish and took a few steps closer. "I'm not the best. Not a glass teacup to be put on a high shelf and kept pretty, Rhett," he said, much softer and more like the old Sam. "I'm not an angel, and I never was. Probably closer to a devil now, I reckon. I hoped me being what I am now would help you see it—help you understand it. You keep putting me up on that shelf, looking up to me, I'm only gonna fall off one day. It's a lot to carry."

"I reckon I feel the same way. Nothing you could do would break me."

They moved closer with each word, and the others politely turned their backs and found other shit to do, talking to the horses or smoking cigarettes or wistfully describing a nice job in a saloon. Soon Sam's hand cupped the back of Rhett's head and pulled him close, their foreheads touching.

"How 'bout we both stay off shelves, then?" Rhett said.

"You stop asking me to drink your damn blood, and that'll do fine."

"It's just a sacrifice I'll have to make, I reckon."

Sam gave Rhett that old, sunny Sam smile.

"It's a deal then, angel," he said in a come-hithery sort of way that made Rhett's knees weak even as the word *angel* made him scowl.

They were just about to kiss when Rhett's belly did the wrong kind of flop and he drew his gun.

CHAPTER
11

W hat's wrong?" Sam said, but Rhett had to get some distance away and figure out what the Shadow was trying to tell him.

"I don't rightly know," he called over his shoulder as he jogged to the pens and monsters and around otherside of the the past mission.

Once he got into an open patch, he could feel it coming fast, for all that the night had fallen for good, and he couldn't see the horizon.

"Get your weapons!" he shouted, running back to where his people waited. "Get inside! They're coming!"

"Who?" Dan hollered back.

"I don't know, but it ain't good!"

His crew, at least, knew well enough by now not to question him too damn much. They ran for the mission, even Lizzie and the new folks, and once they were in the kitchen, Rhett followed and slammed the door and threw the bolt home. It was odd, how cheery and warm the kitchen was, all lit with golden candlelight and smelling of good supper, against the backdrop of death coming at a gallop from the starlit night outside.

"What is it?" Inés asked.

"I don't know and it don't matter but it wants to fight."

The nun nodded, while Rhett's mama drew a big-ass knife from somewhere on her person.

"What's the plan?" Winifred said, sensible as usual.

"And how much time do we have?" Dan added.

"And what the hell is going on?" Beans all but yodeled.

Rhett shook his head like a horse afflicted with summer flies. "Stop your yammering and let me think, dammit!"

Whatever it was, it was moving fast, and it was angry, but it wasn't that close yet. They had a little time—an hour, maybe. And in that time, Rhett had to get all his people, new and old, in position and ready to fight. In the dark, for all that it was only six in the evening. His first thought was for the tender folk—his mama, Winifred and her babe, Notch and Beans. The people who needed Rhett to keep them safe.

"Everybody who ain't fighting needs to go into the cellar and pull down the ladder. Once we cover up the trapdoor, nobody'll know it even exists." He looked at his mother. "That's you, too. And Winifred, for the love of all that's holy, I hope you'll take your whelp into consideration, or at least the fact that you ain't at your quickest these days."

Both women, of course, had objections.

"I fight," his mama said, holding up her big-ass knife—and her little stick knife, too. "I am fighter."

"She is fighter," Revenge affirmed solemnly, and Rhett was realizing his brother was the only feller he'd ever met who might have a bigger stick up his ass than Dan.

"You let our mama fight?" he asked, just about agoggle.

"Cannot stop her," Revenge said with a shrug. "Do not try. Waste time."

Rhett chuckled a little; he knew what it was to live with stubborn folks.

"And I won't go in the basement, but I will stay inside by

a window and do my shooting from behind a foot of adobe," Winifred said. "Just bring me a pile of guns and keep the bullets coming."

He wanted to growl, but Rhett just grumbled, "Well, if Buck comes a-knocking and asking after your health and safety, you just remember where I wanted you to stay: as far away from trouble as possible."

When he looked at Notch and Beans, he expected to see their knees and teeth knocking, but they both looked like they were trying to be upright sort of men, even if it went against their grain.

"And what about you two?"

Beans looked to Notch, by far the gutsier of the two. "Hell, Ned. If the women won't go in the cellar, I don't reckon we can. Maybe we can run around bringing bullets? Neither one of us can shoot for shit, but we can follow orders good enough."

Rhett nodded his approval. "That's a right brave thing to do, boys."

"I'll go up on the roof," Dan said. "With all my arrows and plenty of bullets. Try to pick some off before they get to you."

"I'll stay on the ground." Lizzie gave a feral grin. "When the wolf comes out, it tends to get messy."

"I reckon I'll do whatever you suggest, boss," Digby said in his usual, easy way. "Haven't been in a fight in a damn long time, and I reckon it'll be nice to stretch my legs a bit."

Rhett smiled and nodded. "All that sounds right sensible. What about you, Sam?"

Sam looked at Rhett like he was dumb as a possum. "Well, I'll stay with you, fool, as it should be. Ride out and meet whoever's coming. Give 'em a nice welcome. I can see better in the dark than anybody, I reckon."

That old familiar fear grabbed Rhett by the throat. For all

that Sam was no longer a soft, squishy, easily killed human, he still had one vital weakness. Unless...

He looked at the stack of pewter plates, waiting for dinner, and grinned.

"Inés, I know you care about all them books in the cellar, but do you maybe got a stack of books you don't care so much about?"

Funny how he could feel Inés glaring sharply, even when he'd never seen the eyes hidden under her veil.

"All books are precious, Rhett. Mine especially so."

"They as precious as a person's life?"

The nun sighed. "Just tell me what you want."

With his hand over his heart, Rhett said, "Remember how I sometimes wear that bitty bible in a pie plate over my chest? We all need to do that. If there's only one way you can die, and you can stop that from happening so easily, you need to do it. I thought about this when we went up against them chupas, but then nobody shot at us for a while, and I forgot. Everybody just needs a plate, a little book, and something to tie around 'em. Bit of cloth or a belt, it don't matter. And maybe give Winifred a washtub for her wee-un." He chuckled at his own joke, imagining Winifred wearing a copper tub tied over her bulge of a belly, but even she was nodding along with the cunning of his idea.

"That might be the most sensible thing you've ever said, Shadow." This from Dan, who rarely gave Rhett a compliment and never without some sort of insult in it.

"I will see what I can find," Inés said, standing and heading for the trapdoor to the cellar with a lamp in hand. "But we should snuff the candles and lanterns before they arrive. Or else they will see us better from outside than we will see them."

"Good point. And we will. You go get the books, and

everybody else go get whatever you need for battle and bring along something to strap the plate over you."

"And where are you going, Rhett?"

Rhett tipped his hat to Dan. "Well, nursemaid, I'm gonna take to the air and see if I can figure out what's coming at us."

"No need," Dan said, tipping his hat right back. "I suspect somebody has already had that notion."

Until that moment, Rhett hadn't noticed that his brother had quietly left the room. When he looked to his mother, Rhett found her smirking, half amused and half proud.

"Think alike," she said, tapping her temple. "Much same, my boys."

"Goddammit," Rhett muttered. "Goddamn your other boy. He don't take direction well."

Instead of saying anything, she pointed at him and raised her eyebrows.

"Yeah, I know. I know," he grumbled.

He stood and went outside, where he wasn't surprised to see his brother's cowpoke duds puddled in a shadow and a black form flapping away toward whatever was coming. He was mad, but it was a tired sort of mad. He didn't have the energy to strip down and chase his brother, maybe screech a bit and strike him out of the sky for being so dadgum rebellious. All these feelings he was having, all these fights he was running into—they were downright exhausting. Best thing he could do was get on with preparations, not double the task and possibly injure Revenge right when his skills were needed. Even if the boy was itchy as a flea, Rhett suspected he was a fine enough fighter. After all, they shared the same hot blood.

He walked back inside, where his mother was sorting through the pewter plates, holding each up to gauge its thickness—a clever thing to do.

"He a good fighter, my brother?" he asked.

Her smile was warm and proud. "Good fighter, yes. Good with bow, good with horse, good with knife. Learning gun." As Rhett nodded his approval, she added, "I teach him."

"You, too?"

The look she gave him was very familiar, the look he gave folks who assumed he was dumb as a possum.

"Brothers alike. Both take after me. And father. All good fighting. Many scars. But still alive."

"Then let's keep it that way." He stalked off, knowing that instead of getting his four weakest people into the safety of the cellar, he'd have the whole posse running around in a hail of bullets and arrows, possibly getting hurt. At least they'd cottoned to his idea of protecting their stupid hearts. Hearts, it turns out, were an awful lot of trouble, and that was before mysterious enemies were shooting at 'em.

With everybody else doing something useful, it looked like Rhett was the only one without a job. He gathered up his Henry, loaded all his guns, and strapped on his own pie plate and bible, slipping it under his binder and retying it tightly. He checked the edge of his knife and retied his eye kerch. He used the outhouse and filled his canteen and saddled up Ragdoll before realizing his mistake and going back in the pen to fetch BB instead. If he was going up against bad guys, it was true that Ragdoll had the biggest heart and seemed to know what he wanted before he told her what to do with heels and reins, but she was mortal, and a single shot almost anywhere could kill her—or get him spilled in the heat of battle. Now was the time to be grateful he'd brought along the Captain's gelded unicorn mount. Although he didn't have time to brush BB to a white sheen, he could tell the big beast was sensitive to the energy in the air and ready for a fight. Did BB hate waiting as much as Rhett did? Probably, judging by how the big feller danced around on his heavy, feathered hooves, snorting and looking north.

"Wish I had a pie plate wide enough for your big ol' heart," he told the massive steed, who stood at least eighteen hands and was hell to mount, even for a string bean of a cowpoke like Rhett and even when the beast was at his calmest.

BB nuzzled him in a friendly but polite sort of way. He was a good mount, but he didn't have Ragdoll's annoyed and stubborn insistence, and Rhett found that he liked a horse with thoughts of her own. The mare waited nearby, close enough to nudge him and give him a look that suggested she was only slightly insulted that he was paying his attentions to another mount. Rhett turned to rub her forehead and scratch behind her ears.

"My other womenfolk won't keep safe, but I hope you will, little fool," he murmured.

She snorted at him, sounding more like Winifred than anything else.

"Well, try." He shoved her neck toward the herd as he led BB out of the pen and tied him up by the barn to get him saddled.

Although Dan was getting settled up on the roof, Rhett was soon joined by Sam, Digby, and Lizzie, each finding their horse and getting ready for the fight. They were more silent than usual, as men often were when a threat was incoming. Thoughts roiled in Rhett's head. What was headed toward them? It wasn't from the west, so it likely wasn't the chupacabras. Was it a pack of Lobos, riding hell-bent for leather on their ponies and hungry for blood, liquor, and coin? Was it Herbert and Josephina from San Anton, dashing along in their wagon behind the sheriff, come to take Rhett away to hang for stealing their possessed child? Or was it something purely animal drawn to Rhett's Shadow self, the giant lizards again, or maybe the same sand wyrms that had taken the Captain's life?

"Who the hell knows," Rhett muttered, tightening his saddle and slipping on BB's big bridle.

But then a huge bird landed on the dusty ground and rippled over into a naked man that looked about like Rhett wished he did, and when he grinned smugly, Rhett reckoned the feller knew what was coming.

"Revenge, what'd you see?" he said, for all that he'd been looking forward to chewing his little brother out like the ass end of a rag doll for going off on his own, now he had to appreciate that Revenge had done something right useful, gathering all the information he could about the incoming threat. A leader like the Captain would've just assigned the boy the task in the first place, but Rhett apparently had a goddamn lot to learn.

"Many men," Revenge said, and he didn't say it like he was scared, but like he was in complete control. "On horseback. Chasing a monster."

Rhett tried to make sense of this. "So they ain't coming here, for us? For us, specifically?"

Revenge shrugged. "How would I know? But they come."

"How many men?"

Revenge held up all ten of his fingers, closed his hands to fists, and displayed the fingers again. "Maybe that many."

"Twenty men on horseback, coming here at a gallop. Hellfire."

Rhett had been talking to himself, but Revenge added, "And a monster."

"They armed?"

Revenge flapped his arms like he was a bird and said, "Don't know," and Rhett understood well enough; when he was a bird, he had trouble holding on to such slippery ideas as numbers and guns, too.

"I reckon that's good to know, then, and we'll go on getting ready just the same. Where do you want to be?"

Revenge scoffed, and Rhett wondered what the boy would look like if he wasn't frowning. "With you. On my horse. Out front."

Rhett realized with horror that Puddin' was now his brother's horse, and his brother was determined to ride the fat little paint gelding into battle. Although Rhett didn't like that a bit, he knew what it would mean to try to change things. If Revenge was half as possessive of his horse as Rhett was of Ragdoll, it would just start an unwinnable battle, right when they both needed to focus on the oncoming enemy instead of bickering over mustang ownership.

"I reckon you'll do fine. But you're gonna put on one of these." Rhett pulled down the neck of his shirt to show the plate strapped there with a bible underneath.

"I will not—"

"Protect your heart, dumbass. Protect your life. Our mama will skin me alive if you die."

A small smile from Revenge. "Yes, she will."

Rhett looked around, nodding to each person standing by their readied horse, a nod that spoke of trust and strength and determination. He realized Puddin' was still in the pen and hooked BB's reins over his saddle horn to fetch the pony as a sort of peace offering to his brother. As Revenge changed back into his clothes, Rhett realized for the first time that although he didn't generally have problems with nudity, it was a right peculiar thing, staring at his brother's bare brown buttocks as the feller turned his back to step into his pants.

Facing the mercifully clothed folks, he said, "Let's go on in, then. We got ten minutes, maybe, till we need to mount up. You fellers need your pie plates. You, too, Lizzie."

She shrugged and grinned. "I am fine, being a feller."

The rest of 'em walked toward the mission, but Rhett hung back to speak with Lizzie. Everybody else in this fight he knew or trusted or both. Most of his people had proved themselves in battle, or they were related to Rhett, which meant they were dangerous by nature. But Lizzie was the wild card.

"You look pretty happy about this fight, Lizzie."

Her grin grew a bit mad. "I am happy. The Lobo in me likes fighting. Likes blood. It's good, putting the wolf to use. Letting it run free. Like when a horse has been forced to walk too long, and you take off the halter, and they run so hard they leave a plume of dust."

"I reckon I know that feeling."

"I reckon I do, too." The word *reckon* brought out her accent, making her seem even more foreign, even more strange. And Rhett had to set her straight.

"Then let me tell you this, because all these other folks have rode with me and know my ways." He stopped and turned to face her, full-on, sure to meet her eyes with his own. "I will take a bullet for any of my men. I will ride out first, and I will use every bullet I have, and then I'll use my knife, and when I got nothing left, I'll go in on foot and use my fists. If you're on my side, I got your back. But if you betray me or hurt mine, I will rain hell down on you like fire, you hear me? You're either on my side or against me, and there ain't many people against me because I turned them all to ash or sand. What you saw at Las Moras? I did that. Me. By myself. Because those men turned on me. Do you understand?"

She cocked her head at him as if seeing him for the first time. "I think I do."

"Good. Then if you're still willing to fight with us, let's shake hands and prepare to turn whatever's coming into something fine and powdery."

She stuck out her hand, and he shook it. Her hand was rough and callused and dry, much like his own, and when he looked down, he saw that her nails were bitten to the quick and her pale skin was covered all over with silver scars, just like his. His bones ground together, and he squeezed back to punish her own bones, and then it was over.

"Let's do that, Shadow," Lizzie said, and she headed toward the mission with her long, awkward stride and disappeared through the open door.

"Let's do it indeed."

He took a moment to stand there, alone in the dark to which he'd grown so accustomed, hands on his hips and surveying the mission. The cobbled-together pen full of horses, all milling in excitement. The old barn with its sturdy posts and carefully mended adobe. The squat, dusty white walls of the place where monks had once lived and worshipped and worked and died, all for that cross up top, right over Inés's chapel. The mission wasn't Rhett's, by any stretch. He hadn't paid for the land, hadn't fought for it, hadn't staked a claim in the capital, hadn't taken it by force from a doer of terrible deeds. Hell, even Inés didn't actually own it, as she'd merely moved into an unwanted space left empty by a massacre that the monks' god hadn't cared enough to stop or clean up after. And yet, just now, Rhett felt a kinship with the place, a need to defend it from whatever was coming.

It wasn't his, and he wouldn't stay here, but until it was safe, he'd die for it.

He inclined his head, almost a bow.

"Well, then."

He continued on inside to find everyone sitting around the

table, just a-bristling with weapons. The lanterns and candles were so bright he had to squint.

"You lot look like a right dangerous crew," he said, and he meant it as the highest compliment.

"I reckon we are at that," Digby said with a grin.

"Everybody ready? Anybody got any questions?"

Notch raised his hand and opened his mouth, and Rhett slashed the air with his hand.

"Not you. You ain't fighting, so you just do what you're told. Revenge said we got around twenty fellers on horseback, coming at a gallop, chasing a monster. Don't know what sort. Don't know if it's good or bad. Don't know if the riders are good or bad. But I got a feeling there's gonna be a lot of bullets flying around, so keep your heart covered and kill what needs to die."

"But how will we know?" Digby asked. "What needs to die, that is."

Rhett gave him a dark grin. "You just watch what I'm shooting at and follow suit."

The table went silent, everybody looking from one to the other as if waiting for something to happen, and then it did happen. Rhett felt the insistent tug at his belly, the impulse that had been bugging him all along, suddenly twitch like a fish grabbing the bait.

"It's time," he said, lurching to his feet.

The others stood, too. He gave his mother a nod that he hoped said everything he needed to say. She nodded back, a knife in each fist and an utterly nonmaternal grin on her face, and he understood her well enough. He took off running, and footsteps pounded the dirt behind him, but he didn't have to look back. Digby, Sam, Revenge, and Lizzie followed. Their horses were all lined up with BB, and the beasts could feel it, too—the storm about to hit. Stamping and milling, ears pricked, nostrils flared wide. For all that the night was dry and cold, the sky as black as frozen skin, it still felt like thick clouds held lightning waiting to strike. When he looked back at the mission, he saw the candles and lanterns winking out, one by one.

Rhett untied BB's halter and mounted up, finding Sam behind him, the cowpoke's head a good bit shorter, thanks to the unicorn's towering height. Rhett was flooded with feelings—the sort a feller had before he might die. He wanted to kiss Sam, apologize for every cruel thing he'd ever said, with or without meaning to. He wanted to go down into Sam's hidey-hole and stay there together forever, because even a changed, angry, bloodthirsty, frachetty Sam was better than anything else in the world. But it was too late to say any of that, and his men needed to be hard, going into battle. They were in the saddle with nothing between them and possible death but a pokey little ridge and a measly little pie plate. Again, as always, fighting came first. The Shadow made sure it was so. There wasn't even time for a kiss, even if the dancing horses would've allowed it.

"Sam," Rhett said, hearing the strangled desperation in his own voice. "I—"

"I know, fool," Sam said, sweet and teasing. "I can see it in your eye. I'm as worried for you as you are for me. But we both got our protection." Sam pulled down his shirt, showing Rhett a tantalizing swatch of skin with golden, curly down and the rim of a pewter plate. "And we'll make up tonight, I promise."

Rhett swallowed hard and willed himself not to let a single goddamn traitor tear slip out.

"You better keep that promise, Sam."

And then, louder, so no one could mistake him.

"They're here."

CHAPTER 12

The first shape over the ridge wasn't a man on horseback, but a monster. Man-shaped, roughly. Brownish. Dangerously big and moving fast on long legs and yet…familiar. As Rhett kicked BB to a gallop and took off to meet the running critter, he recognized the shape in its hand, a battered black top hat.

"Don't hurt the monster!" he screamed as loud as he could, hoping the fellers galloping alongside could hear him, as well as the folks waiting inside the mission windows and Dan up on the roof. "He's a friend! Help him!"

Behind the running shape, two dozen men on horseback poured over the ridge, guns a-blazing, and Rhett fully understood what was happening.

"It's Haskell!" he shouted. "You want to kill something, kill him!"

He realized, as he rode, that he'd just sealed his own death warrant in threatening a duly appointed Major of the Durango Rangers, and that meant he was utterly done with the Rangers forever. It was a cheap price to pay if he got to end Eugene Haskell of the Lamartine Outpost, a bigoted asshole who'd conspired with one Bernard Trevisan and killed countless innocent monsters. The men who served under him were no better, and as far as Rhett was concerned, they deserved what they got.

Rhett was more than ready to give it to them.

Just then, Rhett was galloping past the monster, bullets flying overhead, and he barely had time to holler, "Head for the mission, Bill!" before he was right in the thick of things and the pacifistic sasquatch he'd met in Prospera's circus was the least of his worries.

Bullets flew at him, and he shot back, then they were head-on, and BB juddered as he barreled into the smaller horses.

"You cur!" one of the men shouted.

"Goddamn you!" hollered another, bleeding from the shoulder.

"That one's mine!"

Haskell was in the back of the pack, proving his cowardice as far as Rhett needed it proven. Seeing the other man slow his horse and take careful aim with a cruel grin, Rhett kicked BB all the harder, and the huge unicorn slammed into Haskell's horse, chest to chest, as a bullet pinged through Rhett's upper arm like a streak of hot grease. The smaller horse squealed and fell, taking Haskell with him. Rhett popped off two shots but didn't want to hurt the horse; it wasn't the horse's fault that his rider was an asshole. That moment of mercy was enough to give Haskell the chance to shoot his own flailing horse in the skull and pull him over, using the critter's belly to hide behind.

"That's low even for you," Rhett growled, taking every shot he could, now that the horse was beyond his help.

"There's a difference between animals and men, not that you'd know it," Haskell called, emptying his gun and hitting BB four or five times.

The unicorn bugled his fury and hopped around a bit, and Rhett realized that even if Haskell didn't know the secret to BB's longevity, he would eventually hit the big critter's vulnerable heart, at this range. Grabbing his Henry out of the saddle, Rhett slid off BB and slapped the gelding's big rump, sending him galloping back out of range.

It felt strange and stupid, being outnumbered and on foot against an enemy, but Rhett wasn't worried. His boys were harrying the Rascals, which meant it was just Rhett and the Lamartine leader. Haskell pinged off another shot, grazing Rhett's temple with a searing hot line that dripped blood down into his collar. He swiped at it with the side of his hand like it was no more worrisome than a flicker of bird shit.

Taking aim with the Henry, Rhett shot directly into the dead horse's neck, hoping the bullet would go straight through and hit Haskell. As the man didn't die or holler or do anything useful, Rhett had to concede that a dead horse was a thick thing, and he'd have to get closer to do real damage. As Haskell ducked down to reload his guns, Rhett looked back to the mission. Gunshots were popping every which way, along with the thwack of several bows and the thunk of their arrows hitting home, but most of Haskell's men were galloping around between the mission and Rhett's horsemen, taking their own potshots and howling foul curses.

Rhett aimed his Henry and waited for Haskell to pop up and take a shot.

The only way to kill a snake was to cut off the head. He'd worry about the rest of the so-called Rangers later.

Haskell had his gun reloaded, and his next bullet hit Rhett in the thigh, making him grunt.

"You're a shitty shot, Haskell," he muttered.

Step by step, he walked closer to the dead horse and the garbage person hiding behind it. Bullets zipped here and there—one even flicked off his pie plate with a ping of impact, but Rhett kept walking. He didn't bother with any more shots of his own. As soon as he got to the horse, there'd be no place else for Haskell to hide. No point in wasting his bullets.

"Howdy there, Eugene," he said, the Henry aimed right at the cowering bastard.

Fury and disgust lit the man's face. Haskell was in his fifties, white skin burned to a boiled pink with atrocious facial hair going to gray and mean little snake eyes. Once he knew he was cornered, and once it appeared Rhett wasn't ready to shoot him yet, he stood with a sneer, his gun aimed at Rhett's heart.

"That's Major Haskell to you, whelp. Or have you forgotten you took an oath?"

Bang.

Plunk.

Rhett grunted with the impact of pewter against his chest, and a bullet landed at his feet. He looked down at it and shot Haskell in the groin, making the feller double over, screaming.

"Never took an oath, and if I had, I reckon it's no longer applicable. And even if it was, even if I still cared to call myself a Ranger, it'd be Captain Whelp to you. You want another bullet?"

"I want you to die," Haskell growled, hands over his business as blood dripped in the dirt. "My men are gonna tear you to pieces for this."

Rhett squeezed the Henry's trigger, putting a bullet right into Haskell's chest, but not his heart. Haskell tried to cover all his wounds at once and failed, teeth gritted against the pain.

Good. Rhett wanted the man to suffer a bit, first, as all his victims had suffered.

"You killed most of my people, you know," Rhett said, all conversational-like. "Almost got my mama. I don't think I'll forgive that anytime soon."

"Good. Every dead Injun makes the world a better place. We're gonna make the Republic great again."

For that, Rhett shot him in the foot.

"Oh, I think getting rid of shitstains like you is what's gonna make the world a better place."

"Then do it, cur!"

Haskell exploded from his crouch, popping Rhett in the jaw with a wicked undercut and sending him sprawling backward in the dirt, his Henry out of reach and his gun belt half underneath him. Rhett's head bonked off the hard ground, temporarily stunning him. Everything went fuzzy and heavy, and then a knife skittered off his pie plate and lodged in the tender place under his arm, sinking in until it thudded against a rib.

"Why ain't you dead yet, Eugene?" he asked, pulling the knife out of his own chest and ramming it right back home in Haskell's thigh.

Haskell fell off Rhett and scrabbled to yank out the knife.

"You feel that?" Rhett said, real low and mean. "My blood's inside you now. You're not pure anymore. You're just a cur, like I am. You're weak, you're dying, and you're gonna do it with a piece of me inside you, pumping right through that sick piece of shit you call a heart."

Haskell howled his fury and slashed down. The knife arced for his head, and Rhett moved just enough to let the red-wet blade slash past his face and slam into the cold dirt. Haskell was losing a lot of blood now, and his face, although snarling, was starting to have that look fellers got when they realized they were dying and were real surprised about it.

"Bet you thought you'd live forever, didn't you?" Rhett taunted. "Bet you never thought anybody was smart enough or strong enough to tear you down. Well, guess what?" He stood, pulled Haskell's knife out of the ground, and with one vicious stab put it in the man's heart.

"There. Now you die like you wanted me to die: in pain, in the dirt, with no honor. Hell, I'll even sit you up so your dead eyes can watch me end your men. Who are too busy being assholes to even think about coming to save you. Guess you weren't much of a leader, huh?" He chuckled as he dragged Haskell over to his dead horse and leaned the feller up to sitting against his own saddle.

Haskell's mouth opened and closed like a fish, but no sound came out so Rhett kept talking.

"Which reminds me. That's two outposts of Rangers I've taken down. Never thought it would go this way. Thought I would ride with my Captain until the end of my days. That's how much I loved the man—a feeling your Rangers don't appear to share regarding you. But now I don't assume all Rangers are good folks. Anybody looks at me like I'm an animal instead of a man? I'll put him in the ground, where he can't do any more damage."

Knowing full well that an asshole like Haskell couldn't be trusted, Rhett took the feller's pistols and emptied the bullets into his own bag, tossing the weapons far away into the desert. The man's Henry, though—well, Dan or Digby might like a Henry of his own, for all that there were hundreds of hatch marks down the side that probably represented innocent lives.

"I'll leave you the knife, though." Rhett put the flat of his boot against the handle, pushed it a little farther into the man's chest. "Let you think about it a bit."

The moment the knife slid an inch deeper, Haskell's eyes went wide and then empty. His jaw hung open, his hands curled and coated in sandy blood. Rhett stared at the mess he'd created and felt right conflicted. For all that Haskell's death was deserved and necessary, it didn't feel good to confront a carcass all et up with holes and muck of his own making. Most of the critters Rhett killed puffed away in sand, but this one he had to look at, see what he'd done. He'd been cruel, and the aftertaste was bile.

"Good riddance, you piece of shit," he murmured, turning back to the mission to whistle for BB, who came galloping over, just as the Captain had taught him.

Rhett collected his own Henry and shoved it home in the saddle, reloaded his guns, and hopped up holding Haskell's Henry, which he figured would be a fitting way to ride into battle with the remaining Lamartine Rangers. Maybe killing some of Haskell's trained dogs would offset the many hatch marks carved into the steel. The fury of the fight still sang in his blood, and as he mounted up, BB reared and leaped into battle, running like hell toward the gunfire lighting up the night back at the mission.

With BB's great strides, it was only a five-minute gallop until he was close enough to see the battle firsthand, and only then did Rhett feel even the slightest twinge of worry. The way Haskell's men were milling around the mission, hunting for any way inside, reminded Rhett all too much of the way the Lobos had cornered the Captain and Rhett's former fellow Rangers. Dead bodies and a few screaming horses flopped on the dirt, the men peppered with arrows and the horses peppered with bullet holes and broken legs, but plenty of fellers were still in the saddle and causing a ruckus, and some horses calmly stood farther off, their saddles empty. Rhett saw one feller skittering up a drainpipe toward Dan and popped off a shot with Haskell's Henry, which he missed.

"Damn your gun," he muttered, correcting his aim. The

third shot took the man down, although the feller had time to pop off his own shots at Dan before he fell.

"You good, Dan?" Rhett called as a bullet shot straight through his arm and plopped out the other side. He paused to shoot the feller who'd shot him, and the man's horse, now riderless, turned a circle and fled.

"Out of arrows," Dan called. "Coming down. But there's a ruckus by the horse pen."

"Shit," Rhett muttered, turning BB on a dime and kicking him toward the pen and barn on the other side of the mission. As they barreled through the fight, Rhett felt many a bullet whiz past, and a few clipped him or stuck, but he'd grown accustomed to being shot and no longer let it bother him. The bullets would either go straight through or plop right back out. Some things couldn't be undone, but as long as he wasn't sand, most things could. He gave as well as he got and knocked at least two fellers off their horses. Hopefully the folks inside the mission could finish 'em off, if Rhett's bullets didn't do the trick.

Around the corner, Rhett found Revenge on his feet, wrestling with one of Haskell's fellers, a big brute of a man who had a goddamn ax in his hands. Revenge had a meaty slice in his leg that was healing up, but not nearly quick enough for Rhett's taste. He galloped up and shot the feller in the back with his Henry. As the man fell, Revenge plucked the ax from his hands and lopped off his head with a brutal, meaty thunk.

"My kill!" he shouted at Rhett. "No shoot!"

Rhett didn't have time to rub the aching space between his eyes and remind his little brother that death was very real and all around them and slightly more important than counting coup. Instead, he just tossed his brother Haskell's Henry, hollered, "With my apologies!," and rode toward the other side of the pen, where one of Haskell's Rangers was trying to pull down a loose board. As far as Rhett could figure, considering the ax-chopped boards lying around, they were trying to cause mayhem and do some damage, and a stampede of horses tended to do exactly that. He shot the feller neatly with his own Henry but didn't have time to replace the board.

A scream from the mission caught his attention, and he sighed and turned to race for the open door of the chapel. Four horses switched their tails irritably outside, and Rhett slid off BB and peeked in the door to find the fellers creeping around in the shadows. A greasy-looking Rascal was hefting one of Inés's gold crosses in his hand, and Rhett watched him snicker and tuck it in his bag. Rhett looked to the statue of Santa Muerte, and damn if she didn't look offended.

"You fellers shouldn't steal from gods," he said, and when the feller looked up, Rhett shot him.

The other three fellers drew their guns and popped 'em off, but Rhett was ready and had the thick wood door open as a shield. Wood splintered under a hail of bullets, and the second their pistols clicked on empty chambers, he flung the door closed and shot back, taking all three men down. When one of 'em went for another gun to shoot from the ground, Rhett emptied an entire pistol into him until he was nothing more than a gory rag doll.

"Just die easy, goddammit," he said. "I don't like doing this."

Every sense on high alert, the Shadow ducked behind a wooden pew before reloading his guns from the bullet bag hanging off his belt. He knew well enough what happened if his heart got hit, but he'd never known for sure what would happen if his brain got hit or, like the feller Revenge had just finished off, his head got flat-out lopped off. He didn't want to find out.

Reloaded and ready, he hurried to the door that led to the

hallway into the mission proper. It was still closed, so he put an ear to the wood. He heard gunshots aplenty, but nothing to indicate Haskell's fellers had gotten any farther into the actual mission. When he tried to open the door, he learned why: It was bolted.

"Aw, shit," he muttered, running back outside.

A bullet zipped past his ear, and he turned to shoot back, gun up. Winifred's eyes peeped over the windowsill, and he lowered his gun.

"Sorry, Rhett," she called.

"Oh, that's all right. I guess you earned a few shots—" he began, but then her eyes went crazy and her gun went back up, so he fell on his belly, arms over his head, as she popped off a full round of bullets.

The feller who'd been running for him toppled over like a cut tree, leaking out of six different wounds.

"Thanks," he said. "You got room for one more in there?"

Winifred grinned and waved him in. "Hurry up. I'll cover you. Skeeters are bad out there," she said.

She scanned the yard as he ran, put one hand on the high sill, and vaulted into the mission. From their posts at other windows, his mama and Inés looked up. Luckily, as Inés turned, she held her veil back down, because she'd apparently been dealing her own brand of death out that end, holding up a lantern so Haskell's fellers would have no choice but to see her deadly gorgon's eyes, should they look at the light.

"How many statues you made?" he asked her, standing and cracking his back.

"Four. Not handsome ones, sadly."

He snorted and reloaded his guns. He'd brought as many bullets as he could fit in his bullet pouch, but now he was almost out. Boxes and boxes waited on the mission table, though, so he crammed a fistful into his own pouch, just in case. Sums were not his strong suit, but there couldn't be that many fellers left.

"You-all see anybody still breathing out there?"

"Two on my side, but out of range," Inés said.

"Just one." This from his mama. She walked over, took the Henry from his hands, walked back to her window, put the big gun to her shoulder, and popped off a shot. "Now, none."

When she handed the gun back to Rhett, he felt a swell of pride. To think: He'd once thought women were useless. If he'd grown up with this fierce mama of his like he should've, the thought would've never crossed his mind.

Winifred stood with a groan. "And three over here. Looks like they're planning something."

Rhett joined her at the window. Far off, out in the prairie, lone rider joined the three fellers Winifred had counted. They were on their horses, far out of range, talking. Rhett didn't know if they'd found Haskell yet or if any of 'em had a plan other than to kill as many monsters as possible, but he didn't want to find out. He needed this over, and with no chance that Haskell's men could get out alive. Not only because then they might alert the Ranger headquarters of the problem, but also because any man who rode with Haskell had already decided which side of the line he was toeing with his life.

As Rhett was formulating his plan, the door opened. All three women spun, guns pointed, just as they had at Rhett's entrance. But it was just Dan, Lizzie, and Revenge. All three folks had taken their share of wounds, red splotches painting their duds and smeared across their faces—with Lizzie sporting an uncomfortable amount of gore around her grinning mouth. But nobody had suffered major damage, which made Rhett's heart relax for just a second.

"You-all seen Digby or Sam?" he asked.

Everyone shook their heads, and Rhett's heart kicked right back into beating like a war drum.

"Well, hell. Fellers, let's mount up and chase down those last few assholes before they get up to trouble."

He strode from the room, his posse behind him, knowing the women in the mission would keep watch. For all that they had come together in a right peculiar fashion, they were an effective crew, and each person had chosen a job that they could do and do well. He hadn't seen Beans or Notch in a long while, but that was just fine. Tenderfoot fellers and cowards were better out of the way than underfoot, causing trouble. As he'd learned with Earl, some folks just weren't cut out for fighting.

Folks like that? They needed to stay the hell out of Durango.

This time, Rhett didn't peek out the door. He flung it open and strutted out, feeling dangerous and ready to finish the job. It took a moment for his eye to readjust to the darkness, but he didn't need his sight to tell him Haskell's men had been slaughtered. Bodies littered the yard, some stuck full of arrows like porcupines and some riddled with bullet holes. A few fellers were moaning or trying to crawl away.

"Who wants to deal mercy?" he asked.

"Let me," Lizzie said, more of a growl than a request, and when he looked to her, her nose was starting to lengthen out into a golden-brown snout. He didn't want to see her go full Lobo, so he just nodded and kept walking.

He was headed for the horses to ride down Haskell's men, but he was hunting for Digby and Sam, too. They weren't anywhere obvious, and he couldn't make his shoulders relax; even as a human, he was all hunched up like the vulture. Would the Shadow know if Sam died? It seemed to know when he was in trouble, as if a thread of worry always connected them. But

Rhett didn't feel anything now except a sense of longing, and if either of the men were sand, he might never find what was left of 'em. Nothing to do but to keep walking.

The first thing he found out back was Digby, on his knees and crying. His little horse, Hess, lay on his side, his eyes rolling white and two bullet holes pouring sluggish blood from his gut.

"Didn't think I'd care so much, Red-Eye," Digby said, looking up and not bothering to wipe away his tears. Hell, the feller could look manly even as he sobbed.

Rhett knelt beside him, put a hand on the bigger man's shoulder. "You're supposed to care," he said. "People will let you down, but a good horse'll run for you until his heart stops."

"Can he get better?"

Rhett pointed to the puddle of slurry blood and shook his head sadly. "A horse can't live through a gut shot. Neither can a human. I'm sorry, Digby, but if you care for him at all, you'll put a bullet in his brain and help him stop hurting. Or if you like, you can hold him, and I'll do it for you. It...It's never easy, letting go of a friend."

Digby sighed and stroked the gelding's sweaty neck. "No, I'll do it. He's my horse."

Rhett stood and moved away, giving Digby room. The man stood with great dignity, used his kerch to mop off his face, and pulled out his gun, aiming it for Hess's head, unashamedly crying all the while.

"Put it against his skull, man. To be sure. To be quick."

Digby nodded. "If that's what it takes."

Digby knelt, hugged his pony's head, and whispered something into his tan ear. Poor Hess could barely move now, couldn't even thrash, but his eye rolled this way and that, showing that he was hurting and scared. Digby put his pistol against Hess's forehead and pulled the trigger, and the little horse jumped once and went mercifully slack.

"That's the hardest goddamn thing I ever did," Digby admitted, and Rhett clapped him on the back again.

"It won't be the last," he said softly. "That's life in Durango. You're gonna lose things. You just got to keep finding things worth losing."

Digby took a quiet moment before sniffling and straightening up. "Now what?"

"Now we find Sam and finish off Haskell's men. But if you'd care to collect their horses that ain't hurt and put 'em in the pen, that'd be a fine thing to do. You see one that takes your eye, you got first choice."

Digby sighed, a sorrowful sound. "Seems unkind to take up with a new horse, just like that."

Rhett's grin was wry. "You won't say that next time you got to ride somewhere. Now go on and get to work."

Digby headed for a lost-looking palomino, and Rhett walked away toward where BB waited, satisfied that Digby would do what needed to be done. Dan and Revenge joined him.

"You're getting good at this, Rhett," Dan observed.

"At killing Rangers? Yeah, I know."

"No," Dan corrected. "At leading men."

Rhett shrugged that away. "Hell, Dan. If there's one thing I know, it's how to kill and clean up the mess after, whether because it's needed or for mercy."

The way Dan considered that statement made Rhett realize how close he'd come to revealing what had happened to Earl, which was a secret he kept as his own form of mercy. The donkey shifter's suicide sat heavy on Rhett's heart, and Rhett didn't want everyone else to know the shame Earl had confessed in his final moments. Let them think Earl went out fighting bravely; that was the right thing to do. But Dan had always had an uncanny way of seeing straight to the worst parts of Rhett, and all along, the feller'd seemed to sense that something about Earl's death at the Las Moras Outpost didn't add up. It was a relief, turning his back on Dan and mounting up and sliding his Henry into its holster on the saddle, hunting the horizon for the dark clot of Haskell's men.

But when the others were ready to ride, Rhett still hadn't spotted the Rangers, and the Shadow's sense that usually guided him provided no clues.

"You boys see Haskell's last fellers anywhere? Or do you reckon they ran for it?"

Revenge shook his head, and Dan said, "If they were smart, they'd run. Does the Shadow not guide you to follow?"

"The Shadow ain't saying shit, and that's what concerns me. Let's head to where we saw 'em last, out by that bluff."

He kicked BB to an easy lope, and Dan and Revenge fanned out to his either side. A cloud covered the moon just then, and the prairie went black on black, ink shadows over indigo ground. He strained for anything the Shadow might give him, any direction or tug, but all he felt was a distinct lack of guidance.

Horses appeared over the horizon, and Rhett pulled his Henry and took aim, hearing the rasp of guns drawn on his either side.

"Don't shoot me, fool!"

It was Sam, and hearing his voice, Rhett lowered the gun and shouted, "Don't shoot!," just in case Dan and Revenge hadn't gotten the message. He slowed to a trot and then a walk as he recognized the form of Sam riding an unfamiliar horse, leading three more saddled ponies behind him.

"What the hell?" Rhett said as they stopped to face each other.

"I took care of the last of 'em," Sam said. "Fine horses, too. Ranger money buys a good saddle farther east, I reckon. Silver conchos and everything."

Rhett looked as closely as he could in the scant light, noting that Sam looked...better. Fuller, warmer, more alive. More human.

"Sam, what did you do?" he asked, and it came out more suspicious and cold than he'd meant it to.

Sam heard it, too, and bristled.

"I killed four of Haskell's Rascals, Rhett. Isn't that what I was supposed to do?"

The night went suddenly silent.

"Did you kill 'em with your teeth?"

"How the Sam Hill does it matter how they died? They're gone now. Those were the last of 'em. And I'm not hungry anymore. Seems pretty reasonable to me." When Rhett said nothing, Sam added, "You don't have to thank me, but you can sure as hell stop looking at me like I've betrayed you. This is what I am now, Rhett. And this is what I got to do if I want to stay alive. You wanted me alive, didn't you?"

"Yes," Rhett said, all ragged.

"Shadow, what is your problem?" Dan asked. "You more than anyone must understand that a creature can only be what it is. Sam has done nothing wrong."

"Yes," Revenge added. "Do not be stupid."

Rhett closed his eye. He needed space. He needed to understand all the feelings roiling inside him, pick them apart like tangled rope. He knew that Dan was right: He was being stupid.

Sam was a vampire now, and that was Rhett's doing, and a vampire had to drink blood. Drinking blood from villains killed in battle was right practical, exactly the sort of thing Rhett would've appreciated in pretty much any other feller in his posse. He certainly didn't begrudge Lizzie the bodies she was chewing on just now, letting her Lobo run rampant in a helpful sort of way. So why did it bother him so goddamn much? Why did Rhett hate the thought of Sam's mouth on a dying man's skin?

Why was it so goddamned hard to be in love with a vampire?

"God, I'm trying not to be stupid," he finally said, shaking his head ruefully. "I'm awful sorry, Sam. I think it's just my natural state."

"It's okay, Rhett," Sam said gently—more gently than Rhett deserved.

Dan chuckled. "I forget you're still just a kid, for all that you act like a man grown. What are you, sixteen, maybe? Hell, I was still making dumb decisions back then, and I wasn't even in relationships."

"Not me," Revenge said with great gravitas, reminding Rhett that his brother was even younger than he was. "I stay smart."

Sam tried to nudge his horse close, but it was a foreign horse and BB didn't immediately cotton to him. So they sat their mounts, separated by mere feet of space and yet also what felt like the whole goddamn world.

"You're not stupid, Rhett," Sam said. "I never thought you were. I just need you to try to understand who I am now. And maybe…maybe not just jump to anger when things get strange."

Rhett swallowed hard and took a strangled breath.

"Leave us alone, will you, boys?" he asked.

Dan and Revenge turned to canter away, and Rhett hopped

off BB. Sam slid off the new horse as well, and Rhett had his wits about him enough to grin a little at Sam's way of always picking the leggiest horse of a bunch, the one with the most unusual color pattern. This one was a blanket appaloosa, and Rhett could already tell Sam would claim the tall mare as spoils.

Realizing he had to make amends, Rhett decided to try something new: Tell the truth about something that shamed him. Even if it hurt like hell.

"Sam, I got a confession to make," Rhett said, his voice low so it wouldn't carry too far on the dark prairie.

"I'm listening."

"D'you remember the first time we met?"

"Well, sure. You rode up to the Ranger outpost with Dan. You were about half-dead, I reckon."

Rhett looked down, kicked a rock. "No, that wasn't it." His voice, to him, had never sounded so small and feminine, so he cleared his throat and tried again. "It was a long time ago. In Gloomy Bluebird."

"Gloomy Bluebird? You heard of that shit town?"

"It's where I grew up. And it's where I first saw you, working broncs at the Double TK."

Sam grinned. "That was a fine enough place. Monty and Poke and Boss Kimble. I don't recall meeting you, though." His knuckles brushed Rhett's. "I would've remembered."

"That's just, it, Sam. You didn't. Because I wasn't me. I was a little girl in a dirty dress and an old serape and pigtails, hanging on the fence. But I saw you. Even then, I felt like I knew you. Like I wanted to know you."

Sam shook his head like a dog getting rid of a fly. "I don't remember that at all. You joshing me?"

"Well, and why would you remember a little girl, staring at you? You were a man already, by their standards, working broncs. Point is, I reckon…well, Sam, I reckon you always been special to me. Reminded me of an angel, like the church folk used to sing about. Cloaked in sunlight, shining, better'n everybody else. And maybe…what I'm saying is that maybe it's hard to separate that angel from the real you, from who you are now."

Sam stopped and went stiff, and Rhett panicked and dropped BB's reins to grab for Sam's shoulders.

"But I want to, Sam! I want to, goddammit! I want all of who you are, and I'll burn every angel in heaven to get to you. I don't care about a little girl's dumbshit dreams. If I can decide to be who I want to be and forget the past, then I can by God give you the same courtesy. It's gonna be different from here on out, you hear me? No more golden angel. No more little girl with pigtails. No more shying away from blood. Just you and me, Sam. Just you and me."

Sam had been resisting him, fighting the grasp of Rhett's hands on his upper arms. He went tense all over, and Rhett could feel it in him, a power like floodwaters breaking out of a riverbed, and he steeled himself to run all night, on foot or on horseback, to chase Sam wherever the fool thought he could run to. But the tension broke, and Sam turned to him and exhaled, looking at the ground. And then he looked up and met Rhett's eye, and for the first time in their life so far together, Rhett saw Sam for exactly what he was and nothing more.

"I don't care about the past. I just love you," Sam said, ragged as all get-out.

"Me, too, Sam. Me, too."

"But you got to let me eat, Rhett. You can't look at me like I'm a devil. Because I might not be an angel, but I'm never gonna fall that far, vampire or no."

"You're right, Sam. I will."

"And you got to stop worrying about me so much."

Rhett spluttered a laugh. They were so close to being okay.

"Now that I can't promise. I love you too damn much to lie to you, so I tell you now that I'm always, always gonna worry."

"Well, then, I'll keep on worrying about you, too, fool."

Sam dropped his reins and reached for Rhett, cradling his face in hands that were warmer than they'd been since Sam had taken Trevisan's knife in the gut.

"Rhett," he murmured, all tenderness, "you got snakes living in your head. Let 'em go. They only make you miserable."

Rhett put his hands on Sam's and looked down at their kissing boot tips. "I'm trying to get untangled, Sam. Reckon I'm getting pretty close."

"Kiss already!" Revenge shouted from across the desert.

"Don't tell me what to do, you little shit!" Rhett shouted back, but then he lifted his face up to Sam's and kissed the hell out of him anyway.

The horses were stamping quite a bit by the time they were done, and Rhett felt mighty shy as they took their reins back up and moseyed toward the mission. It had to be getting close to dawn, Rhett reckoned, but Sam didn't seem to be in a hurry, and Rhett wasn't about to hasten his departure for the day. It had been another long-ass night, and Rhett was beyond exhausted, and he wondered if he'd ever sleep like a normal feller again.

"You coming to bed?" Sam asked, reading his mind and making him blush.

Rhett nodded. "Just got to check in with everybody first, make sure somebody keeps watch while we sleep in case more Rangers show up. And we got to see about Bill."

"Bill?"

"Sasquatch Bill," Rhett corrected. "The big hairy feller with the fine hat that Haskell and his men were chasing. I set him free from Prospera's chains before I killed the old witch. Big ol' feller wanted nothing more than to get north and disappear."

"So?"

"So we got to find out how he ended up here, on the opposite side of the damn country, chased by Rangers. Bill wouldn't hurt a fly."

"They probably just saw a monster on his lone and went for the kill."

"Maybe," Rhett said, swinging his reins as he walked. "But I doubt it."

CHAPTER
13

For all his curiosity about the sasquatch, Rhett still took his time with the chores outside. Bringing herds of unfamiliar horses together could be tricky, and it was a shame they only had one small, badly patched pen, which even now shuddered under the impact of lead mares and brassy stallions picking fights and testing each other. When they'd found a place out west to start their cattle company, he'd make sure they had the proper amount of fencing and a lot less balls. Hell, maybe they'd head back up to Las Moras and load all that lumber into the wagon. Not like anybody else was there to use it or would care to hunt down a fence thief.

Digby, at least, had gotten ahold of himself, and Dan had roped him and Revenge into helping him tow the dead bodies of Haskell's men into a big pile and divest them of their useful effects. They were Rangers, and they'd burn like Rangers. Looking at Haskell's Rascals, Rhett just wanted to see the blight of Haskell's taint gone off the world completely. Durango would be a better place without these fellers, that was for damn sure.

It was a shame how many horses had fallen in the fight, although Rhett was glad to see none of 'em were full of arrows;

probably Haskell's fool men panicking and shooting wide. There were five dead mounts, beside Hess, and Rhett's mouth twitched with frustration. These critters had had no quarrel, had just been doing their jobs, never knowing that the men they served were evil. And now they were lumps in the dust.

"Might as well butcher these fellers for winter, I reckon," he said, and Dan nodded his agreement and went to fetch Samson, the big draft horse, to help him drag the carcasses into the barn and string 'em up from the rafters, where wild things couldn't get at the ready meat.

Every job had willing hands doing work, and Rhett was heartened that they hadn't lost anybody. He knew already that the women inside were fine. But then he remembered...

"Notch and Beans?" he asked.

Every feller looked up and shrugged. Lizzie walked over, her face a mass of gore, and Rhett posed the same question.

"Too thin for my blood," she said with a laugh. Being a Lobo seemed to improve her temperament quite a bit.

Which didn't help. Maybe it was part of being a captain, but Rhett wanted all of his men accounted for and wouldn't be able to relax until he knew everyone's fate. Once inside the mission, he found at least one thing he was looking for: William the Sasquatch. The big feller sat on the floor, hat in his lap, looking lost and resigned and as exhausted as Rhett felt.

"Bill," Rhett said, tipping his own hat.

"Shadow," Bill said, flapping his topper. "I did wonder what drew me back here, and how curious that it is you, my good sir."

Rhett cut to the chase. "Why were they chasing you?"

Bill's huge, reddish-brown shoulders heaved like boulders. "They didn't say. So rude. They merely galloped into my camp and began shooting." He grimaced, showing huge canines. "With silver."

"I'll get the tweezer." Rhett turned to fetch Cora's old box from the shelf they now kept it on, then remembered to ask, "It ain't in a private-type area, is it?"

Bill's head wagged. "One in the upper arm, one in the lower leg. I have been running for nearly a day. If there's any food on hand, it would be much appreciated."

"Well, of course we'll feed you, fool. We got six—" He remembered Digby crying over Hess and corrected himself. "Five dead horses outside. Just carve yourself a leg, if Inés can't cook enough to fill you up." Rhett flapped a hand at Inés, who was dishing out supper by a pile of guns and bullet casings, and pulled down the doctor box. He recognized by now why he felt peevish: not only because Notch and Beans were still missing, but also because Bill had been drawn here, to him. And that's why this kind, dignified critter who just wanted to get off and live alone had been shot, and that's why he'd run for a day, and that's why he was now taking up a quarter of the dang kitchen surrounded by strangers.

First Digby had appeared.

Then Revenge and Finder and Lizzie, Notch and Beans.

Now Bill the Sasquatch.

Something was pulling these monsters toward Rhett, and Rhett didn't know what or why, and that made him as jumpy as a cat in a room full of rocking chairs. Except in his case, the rocking chairs were full of alchemists and chupacabras and Lobos, because regular ol' rocking chairs just weren't enough to goad Rhett Walker into action.

He still felt a wrenching pain in his chest when he opened Cora's box and had to think about her—and how unqualified he was to touch her most precious tools. But it had to be done, and Bill didn't need to suffer a moment longer while Rhett's foolish heart counted regrets. Winifred walked in while he was trying to part Bill's foot-long arm hair to hunt for the bullet, and the girl plucked the tweezers out of Rhett's hand.

"You're a brute," she explained, poking him in the back with the shiny tweezer. "And Bill is a gentle soul. He doesn't deserve to be prodded like a dang carcass. Go find something manly to do."

Frankly grateful, Rhett stood and clapped Bill on the back. "She probably just saved you from a world of pain, my friend. But before I get on to the next business, now that you're here, what do you plan on doing?"

Bill's face turned up, considering him with a mix of confusion and curiosity.

"I don't know. I just know that something drew me in this direction. I've always felt the pull of the north, tugging me home, but my footsteps led me here. Why do you think that might be?"

"Well, you'll recall my destiny?"

"A little. Human affairs are of no interest to me, really."

Rhett drew a deep breath and readied himself for ridicule. Might as well trot it out against a tough crowd and see how it went.

"I think we're gearing up for something. A war, maybe, or a big fight. There's something going on with the chupacabras over the border in Azteca, and I think they're planning something against us. Against me. All sorts of fellers are finding me now, all of 'em good fighters, or useful in this way or that. If I had to put money on it, I'd bet that in the coming days, we see more and more folks, maybe even strangers. Because whatever's coming, it's trouble, and it needs to be stopped."

Bill nodded, considering, his heavy brows drawn down over dark eyes full of feeling. "But I am not a fighter, and this is not my fight," he said softly, wincing as Winifred pulled a silver bullet out of his arm and holding a handkerchief over the freely bleeding wound that would quickly clot. "I'm a pacifist. A thinker. A quiet sort. I like the forest. Being alone."

"I know you do. I...I think plenty of us would like to sit this one out. But the same feeling that's bringing us together is gonna lead us forward. Together. I don't think we'll have a choice." He watched Bill's arm muscles ripple under his hair-like fur. "Besides, maybe you're not a fighter, but you look like you could win any damn case of fisticuffs around. You ever punched anybody?"

Bill drew back, affronted. "Of course not, my good sir."

Rhett grinned. "We'll give you a few days to recover from your run and bullet wounds and see what you can do."

"Perhaps I am capable, but what if I do not wish to fight?"

Winifred plucked the bullet out of Bill's leg and held it up to wink in the light. When he put out his flat hand, big enough to crush Rhett's entire skull, she dropped the smushed metal into his palm.

"When the fight comes to you, you learn what you truly want," she said, but gently. "Because then you learn what you're willing to fight for. Let's get you fed. Rhett, clean off the tweezer and get out of here before you scare folks away."

She tossed the blood- and hair-spattered tweezer at Rhett, who fumbled but ultimately kept hold of the slick metal and took it off to the trough, grumbling, "Just because you're full of baby don't mean you're full of knowing everything," fully aware of how ridiculous it sounded.

He washed and dried the tweezer, put it back in the case, and put the case back on its shelf, then went sniffing around for Beans and Notch. He found the fellers in Sam's hidey-hole, the door locked up tight. At first he was annoyed, and then he was furious. It was almost morning, and Sam needed that space.

He banged on the door with his fist, hearing the fellers whisper and snivel inside.

"You open up this door or so help me I will rip it down with an ax and drag you out through the jagged hole by your god-damn ears," he shouted.

"Well, who would open a door with someone saying that on the other side?" Notch asked.

Rhett quit his banging and considered the truth and cowardice of the statement. He had to try another tack.

"Since the fight is over—we won, if you're interested, and no thanks to you two—would you kindly consider getting out of the vampire's personal bunk before he gets back down here and discovers you two been rolling around in his blanket?"

The door burst open with Notch and Beans falling all over each other to get out of the narrow room.

"Vampire?" Beans yodeled, and Notch shook like a Chihuahua.

Rhett nodded, hands on his hips. "Yep. Who else you know requires a dark room in a dark cellar with a door that locks from the inside?"

Notch and Beans looked at each other like the world's greatest fools. "Why didn't we ask ourselves that very question?" Beans said.

"Doesn't matter. He'll be coming back soon, and I assure you, he can already smell you. And you're gonna be in close contact with him soon enough, once we get on the road. So you'd best get used to it."

He flapped his hands like he was shooing ducklings across a trail, and Notch and Beans herded each other up the hallway.

"You ain't upset with us?" Beans asked. "Running out during the fight?"

Rhett sighed the sigh of the woefully exhausted. "Not too

much. It was my own fault, thinking having an easy job would suddenly make you willing to handle a little bit of danger. You two told me to my face that you were cowards, and I should know by now that nothing in the world can change that. It's something bone deep. I can't change you, and you can't change me, so we got to find a way to get along. Now, you can leave this mission—and my posse—any moment you want, but you got to know that dangerous critters are all around us. If you leave, something bigger and meaner is bound to come along and make quick meat while you tremble. Or you can go along with us for a bit, and we'll put you to regular work when it's safe, and whenever there's trouble, you can do what you've always done and hide. Reckon I owe you for teaching my folks to talk good."

Notch and Beans looked at each other, and they had that look of an old married couple who've been together so long they don't have to use so many words anymore.

"That's right fair of you," Beans said.

"More than I'd expected," Notch allowed.

Rhett rubbed his temples, feeling bone weary and footsore. "Fine. Then get out of the cellar, fools, and don't get underfoot. Dinner—well, breakfast now, I reckon—will be ready shortly."

"What about you, Red-Eye?"

As soon as they were over to the ladder, Rhett dragged himself into Sam's bed and flopped into the mussed covers that smelled, wrongly, of someone else's fear.

"I'm gonna sleep until it's time to do something different."

And he did.

He was sleeping so hard he didn't even sense Sam returning, and when he woke up, Sam was already asleep. They'd missed each other completely, but judging by the protective way Sam's arms were wrapped around him and by the comfortable smile on the cowpoke's pinker-than-usual lips, Rhett reckoned it could be a lot worse. He crept upstairs and ate a late breakfast by himself at the long table, feeling profoundly alone.

By the time he was scraping his plate out into the chicken yard, newly anointed with chickens that had all somehow managed to live through the fight, Rhett reckoned he had lollygagged quite long enough. It was time to go, to move on to the next step of their plan and get situated farther west. He reckoned they'd start by pulling down the remaining boards from Las Moras, then find a place near the border and set up a new base of operations. There was no point in hanging around Inés's mission when they could meet the enemy head-on.

They had as much coin as they needed, Dan said, from selling off so many fine saddles and from looting their dead enemies, and Sam had rigged the wagon to suit himself with a lightproof box. Rhett's next puzzle was figuring out who to take with him on the scouting trip and who to leave behind. The mission was a useful place—water, space for the horses, easily defensible—and he wasn't ready to give it up completely yet. On the other hand, he didn't know what they would face after they'd scavenged Las Moras. Would they find a place quick or have to build one? Would they have trouble or mosey on in? Until he knew more, the horse herd had to be someplace safe and defensible, and that meant he had to split his posse in two, which he didn't like at all.

"Me and Sam have got to go, and that's just facts," he said, mostly to himself, as everybody but Sam ate lunch, cozied up around the table like they'd been together for years. "But we need fighting men here with the women, and we need folks that know horses to stay behind. We got a herd of four dozen out there, and they'll need seeing to. Goddammit, there just ain't enough of us to go around."

"And I must go," Dan said. "Because I know how to deal with white men, and because someone must keep you walking the line, Shadow."

Rhett rolled his eye. "Well, yeah, I figured that."

"But everyone else can stay. Between Digby and Revenge, they can run a mission with Lizzie and Bill's help, yes?"

"Yes," Digby and Revenge said at the same time, eyeing each other like butchers looking at the same hog.

"I will run my mission," Inés said, her voice carrying despite its softness. "As I have for many years. And the men may care for the horses, but do not forget: This place is mine." Her slender fingers fiddled with her veil, a good reminder of what truly lived under the nun's habit.

In the silence that followed this proclamation, Rhett's mama and Winifred stifled their chuckles, and Lizzie didn't even try. Beans and Notch had no further thoughts on the matter, and for all that Revenge probably had something to say, he was sitting right next to his mama, who carried a pretty big knife and was not above tearing him a new one if he got too mouthy. Digby, for all his skills, had always been a polite sort of feller, and Rhett knew he'd oblige Inés and help Revenge with the horses without acting too high-and-mighty about it. It was a fair enough deal. And they'd have Lizzie, too—Rhett was mostly sure she could be trusted now.

"Just one thing," Rhett said. He waited until the table went quiet again. "If you-all smell trouble, you don't take up your stations to defend this place. You head down into that cellar, pull down the ladder, and shut the hell up. We can get more horses and saddles, but..."

"We can't go replacing people," Digby said softly.

Rhett nodded his approval and looked around. The mission kept pretty neat, although he admitted to himself that he didn't know who did the work of keeping it running; he assumed the women did. He'd always been a messy sort and reckoned he made up for it in murdering ability.

"Then it's settled. We'll get ready and take off once Sam's awake. I suggest an afternoon nap, Dan. Won't want you falling asleep in the saddle."

Dan gave him the stink eye. "Oh, yes. It's definitely me who's trouble on the trail."

At that, Rhett grinned. "Well it's right gentlemanly of you to finally admit it."

Suddenly filled with energy now that the decision was made, Rhett hopped up and went to packing. They had plenty of clothes these days, so long as a feller didn't mind a few bullet holes or bloodstains. Rhett took the liberty of packing for Sam, selecting shirts in shades of blue that would bring out the feller's eyes. It was getting cold out, so he added rolls of socks and a couple of old knit scarves Inés had passed around, rough wool things in a plain, dark brown that Rhett now associated with dead monks. Outside, he oiled his saddle and Sam's, too, and packed their saddlebags with ammunition, making a mental note to teach somebody how to make bullets and cast silver while they were gone since the yard was full of free lead.

As the afternoon went long, the indigo shadows stretching across the pecking chickens, he pulled out Sam's blue roan and the appaloosa mare he'd favored from Haskell's spoils and brushed them to a shine alongside Ragdoll and BB. As for Squirrel...

He went inside to Digby and looked at the wall over the feller's head to make it less awkward for 'em both. "I'm right sorry about Hess, man. He was a good little pony. But if you've got a liking for Squirrel, well, I reckon you got first choice and she'll do you fine. I'll leave her behind, and you do as you see fit. Revenge has a good eye for horseflesh and could take a spill, if you see something else in the pen and don't want to be the first feller on a strange critter's back."

Digby put down the knife he was sharpening, the corner of his mouth lifting up. "You giving me your pony, Red-Eye?"

"Only fair."

"Well, that's appreciated. I'll mosey out tomorrow and see how she rides." He held out his hand, and Rhett shook it. Digby pulled him close, just a little, and the man's voice went over hard. "I know you carry worries on your back, but I promise you I'll step between your women and a bullet. I'll be wearing my pie plate and bible if I do, but I'll do it, and no mistake. You done good by me, for all I put you through hell in that train yard."

Rhett's eyes pricked, but he swallowed his sentiment right back down. "Shit, Digby. You kept me alive when I would've got myself killed. You didn't have a choice, and once you got here, I never expected anything less."

Digby stood, and they shook hands in that manly sort of way that said all sorts of things and ended with a nod of respect. By the time Winifred and Finder walked in, one holding a chicken carcass and the other a bag of feathers, the two men had returned to their places and looked like nothing had passed between them.

"And what do you want us to do while you're gone?" Winifred asked. "Make the beds and sing songs with the desert creatures?"

It was teasing enough, but if Rhett had been a horse, his ears would've flattened back. "I reckon you'll do the same thing you always do, which is whatever suits you. But if you know anything about making bullets and arrows, I'd be glad to see those stores built back up."

Winifred and Finder wore matching irritated scowls, and Rhett could tell Winifred spoke for them both. "Of course we know how to make arrows and bullets, idjit. You don't grow up on the ground in Durango and not know that. I can knap stone, too. And your mama's a hell of a shot. Honestly, Rhett, when will you stop underestimating us?"

"When he stops hating himself for being like you," Dan said, sauntering in with a grin, just ahead of Revenge, who had a new load of brush for the kitchen fire.

"At least Digby's on my side."

"Well, perhaps he doesn't know you as well as the rest of us."

It wasn't until that very moment that Rhett recognized his posse was joshing him again. Even though he felt attacked and surly about it, he reckoned it was part of his job to take it.

"Well, I'm sure you-all can disabuse him of that notion in a few days," he said with an easy grin. "Just make sure you tell him all about my various blunders while I'm on this scouting mission. He'll need all the dang facts."

Chuckles and grins met this statement, and Rhett felt settled, for once. Dan had nothing further smart to say, which was treat enough. Bill wandered in, looking lost, and Digby patted a chair, inviting the sasquatch to the table like it was a regular sort of thing, for all that the sturdy wooden stool creaked under his weight. And then Rhett heard the ladder scrape against the trapdoor and forgot everything else but Sam. By the time Rhett got there, Sam was already topside and bouncing in his boots.

"Something in the air," he said, pulling Rhett close for a tender kiss. "Time to go, ain't it?"

Rhett grinned. "You're awful good at reading my mind."

"Well, you got good ideas, most of the time."

They were soon outside, three fellers preparing their horses as the rest of the company watched. Notch and Beans kept fidgeting and scratching, like they were et up with guilt, and Rhett figured they deserved it. Digby and Revenge stood up front, both of 'em trying to look as competent and manly as possible. With Ragdoll saddled and BB packed up, Rhett suddenly realized what he'd forgotten—what they'd all forgotten: that Sam could no longer just ride around freely—and that they'd need a way to carry the lumber from Las Moras.

"Shit. The wagon. Samson."

He dropped his reins and rope and hurried into the pen to pull out the big draft horse and hitch him up to the wagon. Sam came over to help, for all that either of them could've done it alone.

"Who's gonna drive, Rhett?" he asked, because no Ranger in his right goddamn mind wanted to be the feller driving the ponderous wagon when he could be high-stepping on horseback.

Rhett considered, biting his lip. "Beans, come on!" he hollered. "You're driving."

He wasn't entirely sure Beans and Notch could separate from each other anymore; they were stuck together with fear like molasses. But apparently their fear of angering Rhett was stronger than the fear that cleaved them together, and soon Beans slunk over and clambered into the wagon seat.

"Do I got to, Rhett?" he asked.

Rhett shook his head and laughed. "Got to? Son, all you got to do is sit up here, nice and comfy, and let ol' Samson do the work."

He hurried back to Ragdoll and nearly mounted before his

heart tugged at him. He was in unfamiliar territory now, but he reckoned that meant he could do as he pleased, so he walked up to his mama and held out his arms in a half-hearted fashion that maybe wouldn't look too pathetic if she felt different. But she opened her arms with a warm smile and took him into a hug, and the scent of her was so familiar and good that it sparked something deep inside, triggering memories he didn't even know he had except in dreams, memories of paint ponies and firelight on deerskin and dancing and drums.

"You take care," he said.

"You, too," she said back.

He turned to his brother, who looked like he'd punch Rhett in the nose if he went in for a hug. "You take care of her," he said.

"Always do," Revenge shot back, arms crossed, prickly as a cactus.

Rhett cuffed the boy's shoulder. "I know that, fool," he said. To everybody else, he just nodded.

"All of y'all take care. And remember: If there's trouble, hide in the cellar. No use in fighting if you're going to lose."

"That's the least Rhett thing you've ever said," Dan acknowledged.

"Well, I wasn't talking to myself."

And then they were on the way. Rhett led on Ragdoll, ponying BB, who was placid enough for an eighteen-hand unicorn led along like a pup. Sam rode his blue roan, ponying his new horse from the chupa herd, the blanket appaloosa he called Kate. Dan took the rear behind the wagon on his forgettable chestnut, ponying another forgettable chestnut, choosing the lone path, as he so often did. They all followed the tug in Rhett's belly toward Las Moras.

It wasn't a strong tug, like last time. But then again, it wasn't a tug that suggested they could put off the trip. It was steady, even, but demanding.

Rhett suspected that there would be something waiting there besides unwanted lumber, but he had no idea what it might be. So he didn't mention it.

CHAPTER
14

They rode through the chilly night and settled down a bit before dawn. Rhett was bone weary, but then again, it felt like that was his natural state, these days. The pressure to keep working, to keep moving forward, was unrelenting. He'd said it was like thunder on the horizon, but it was also like the storm was chasing him, always just behind, threatening. A few more miles, a few more hours, and it felt like maybe he could get ahead and rest. But when he woke up from too little sleep plagued by ominous dreams, he began to see that he could never get far enough ahead to feel comfortable or safe.

Maybe that was destiny: a thing that never let up, a rider who never dropped the whip.

As they watered and hobbled the horses at an ice-crusted creek, Rhett realized another thing they'd forgotten: While Sam had built himself a lightproof box in the wagon for traveling the trail, Rhett was pretty certain it was a box built for one. Even if there was room for him in there, he'd be stuck inside, locked in until nightfall or taking the risk of exposing Sam to the elements and his possible death. He couldn't fall asleep touching Sam, much less holding him. The closest he could come was snuggling up to a wood box in the bed of a wagon that only made him relive some right uncomfortable decisions he'd made at a different part of his life. Did Sam know about the time Rhett had spent with Winifred in there, first fumbling and then…well…tumbling?

He shook his head. It didn't do to dwell; this was just one bitty part of life, not eternity. They'd get to Las Moras, tear down the fences and load up the wood, and move on to something more permanent. At least he was so dang tired he couldn't worry too much about what could go wrong, and at least the Shadow hadn't suddenly jerked him in some other direction. Like Sam, he'd probably be sleeping straight through the day, anyway.

"Lord, Red-Eye. My back feels like a broken chair," Beans moaned, hopping down from the wagon and leaning back with several pops of his bony spine.

"Yeah, well, those of us in the saddle feel that in our rumps and legs and arms, too, so I reckon you got off easy. Now let me teach you how to unhitch the horse, because from now on, it's your job."

Beans was a fumbly feller, but Samson was a stoic sort of horse, and they were soon ready to bed down for all that it was nearly dawn. Rhett didn't care about time of day anymore; he just needed sleep. They hadn't seen any game, so those who still ate food chewed on jerky and Inés's corn cakes, and Dan and Beans laid their bedrolls beneath the wagon, aiming for some shade during the day. So much for getting up to anything fun in Sam's final moments of wakefulness, with two bodies just below the boards. When he couldn't stop yawning and the sun was almost up, Rhett tipped his hat and followed Sam into the wagon.

"You doing okay for food, Sam?" he asked before significantly lowering his voice and leaning in right close. "You want me to ask Beans…?"

Sam pulled him in the rest of the way and set their foreheads together. "Naw. I ate my fill of Haskell's men yesterday. Should be good to go for a while. You can't tell it from the outside, but I'm all swole up like a dang tick on the inside. Reckon I'll sleep well." He looked down at the box and grimaced. "Although I'm right sorry there's no room for you in there."

Rhett looked at the box, too, and stopped himself from shuddering. "Oh, that's all right. I don't think I'd do so well in a box."

Sam chuckled, and Rhett felt it against his chest. "No, I don't suppose you would. Guess this is good night, then."

"Good night."

The kiss was tender and swift, and then Sam was climbing into the open box and pulling the lid down, throwing Rhett a last look of longing. A lock clicked, and Rhett felt the urge to pry it back open. It looked way too much like a coffin and made him distinctly uneasy. But he just tapped Shave and a Haircut on the box and felt a wash of comfort when Sam tapped back with Two Bits.

He slept on the wagon floor beside the box and couldn't decide if it was better or worse than the cold winter ground outside. He had his buffalo robe, at least—Sam claimed cold didn't bother him so much anymore, so Rhett had it all to himself. He could hear Beans shifting and farting all night—well, day—as the feller tended to do, but Dan was ever his still, stoic self. It wasn't Rhett's favorite way to pass a fit of sleep on the trail, and he missed the old camaraderie of the fire, but he reckoned it was more comfortable than Sam being dead, so he fumbled through it and just kept on going.

Nothing of note happened on the way up to Las Moras. It was slower going than Rhett would've liked, owing to the wagon, but it was a rare slice of time when the Shadow wasn't pushing and pulling him like two children playing tug-o-war. The nights were clear and cold, and the days were dry and bright. It could've been a lot worse.

As the buttes and mountains started to look achingly familiar, however, that old feeling started up in Rhett's gut. Not a tug so much as an alarm, like a bell ringing in Rhett's soul, hurrying him onward.

"Something's wrong," he muttered to Sam, who rode by his side.

Knowing that look, Sam straightened up and put a hand on his gun. "What?"

Rhett glared up ahead, scanning the night, searching his gut for some telling subtlety of feeling. Nothing seemed out of place. But to most folks, nothing usually was out of place.

"I don't know, but we got to hurry. Dan! Join up!"

Dan galloped his chestnut to meet them, just a few strides from where he'd been riding behind the wagon, alone with his thoughts and protecting their flank.

"What is it?"

"Damn, son. I don't know, but we got to go!" Rhett turned in the saddle. "Beans, you got a gun under your seat. Use it if you need to. We're riding up ahead."

"What is—"

"Shut up!"

And then he was kicking Ragdoll, and she ran like she'd been praying for an excuse. The familiar trail wasn't as worn clean as it used to be, but they both knew the steps. With Sam and Dan on either side, they flew through the night, every moment cranking Rhett's heart up a notch. There was nothing up ahead to betray what they were riding for—no smoke, no bullets, no scent of blood. But Rhett rode forward, anyway, pistol drawn and reins gathered in one hand, ready for anything.

What he found when the valley opened up on what had once been the Las Moras Outpost of the Durango Rangers was... nothing.

No people. No monsters. No smoke. No fire. No shiny new patch of sand.

He reined to a halt in the clearing and scanned every inch of land.

"What is it?" he asked, pathetically echoing the question other folks usually asked him.

"Hell if I know," Sam muttered.

"I don't sense anything," Dan added.

But Rhett's danger sense was tingling. He knew he was missing something. Something important. Something he'd ridden here to see. He hopped off Ragdoll and closed his eye. Whatever it was, it was that way. He walked, carefully, trying to feel with his gut more than his eye.

"You got something, Rhett?" Dan asked.

"Hush, fool. I'm trying."

He opened his eye, standing closer to what was left of the Outpost than he ever wanted to be, and realized it had been there all along.

Tied to one of the blackened porch posts of the burned-up cabin was a body—a body so dried out that it was more like a skeleton. Its clawed hands were bound with rope overhead, a long nail sticking it in place, and its feet were tied lower down. A black suit hung off it, fresh as if it'd been laundered that morning, for all that the body looked a thousand years old, like those mummies Rhett had heard about once in town.

"I know who that is," Rhett said, a peculiar chill settling over him. "It's that wendigo doctor. The one who came to help the Captain when he was wyrm-bit and dying. You-all remember him?"

"Doc Ashmore," Dan confirmed. "He wouldn't hurt a fly. Many a time I saw him getting pale and feisty when flesh wasn't available, but he wouldn't give in to it. Fought his nature every moment of his life."

"But who the hell would want to hurt him?" Sam asked. "He was right fair to everybody."

As soon as Rhett had identified the body, the Shadow calmed down, as if he'd solved a damn puzzle. The area didn't feel dangerous, and he wasn't worried about any monsters lurking nearby, although he didn't know if he would sense humans who weren't intent on causing harm. The valley felt as empty as the moon and just as cold, wind whispering through the brush and careening around the rocks and whistling through the charred remains of what had once been a damn good life.

He stepped closer to the corpse and did his best not to flinch as he opened the doc's shirt to inspect his chest.

"Here's what I don't get. If you don't stab a monster in the heart, I always heard a feller could go on living. Some things grow back, although silver can mess a critter up." He touched his gone eye without meaning to, the hole always aching. "But the doc is dead as a doornail, and there's his chest with his heart still in it. Or at least he ain't sand. So what happened?"

Dan stepped close, taking the doc's wrists in each hand and yanking him down off the nail. There was no blood, no spray; just the creak of a dead tree in winter. It was as if what was left of the doc didn't weigh more than a tumbleweed, and Dan tugged his feet free and laid him down on the ground.

"Wish we had a lantern," Dan said. "For all that my eyesight has gotten accustomed to the night, I'd like a better look at our old friend."

Sam sighed and looked away; Rhett had noticed he was always uncomfortable when time of day came up. "Yeah, well, you'll get your daylight soon enough. I can see fine, and I can smell, too, and I tell you now his heart's still in there, shriveled up as a black walnut. More importantly, there's not a drop of blood in 'im. He's totally empty. Dry as a bone."

Dan being Dan, he turned the body over and checked for a hole in the back, some sort of open window into the doctor's heartmeat, but he found only leathery skin under the tidy black jacket. "Of course you're right," he said to soften the insult. He stood and put his hands on his hips. "There are other ways to kill a monster, Rhett," he said, quiet as if someone still might overhear what should be kept secret, for all that it was early morning in the darkest part of night in the middle of nowhere. "Cut off a head—that won't grow back. Hell, slice a body into too many pieces and throw them too far away, and they won't be able to crawl back together. All the things I know about killing a monster without taking the heart involve the grisly use of knives or teeth, or the Lobo way of eating out all the parts a creature needs most and leaving a hollow carcass. But this. This...draining. Sam, could a vampire do this?"

Sam cocked his head and sucked his teeth, and Rhett saw his fangs flash in the low light. "Reckon I don't know all that much about what I am yet, but it would take more than one vampire, I know that much. We don't like to finish out a body—the blood gets slow and slurry, tastes like death. Even the other night, with four fellers...well, you know how a beer gets foam? You could say I just sucked off the foam. It's enough to kill, but I wouldn't say I even took a tenth of what any of 'em had inside. Not that I have room for that much blood." He knelt by the body, put cold white hands on its face. "There would be teeth marks. More than one set. On the neck." His face colored—Rhett could see it, that's how bright he went. "Or on the groin, Emily said. There's a...a big vein down there. If you're already down there." He cleared his throat and looked away. "But I don't see tooth marks up top, if that's what you're asking."

Rhett walked around the body, frowning. The sun would've been mighty helpful, just then, but he wasn't about to tell Sam that, and he didn't want to gallop back to the slowly trundling wagon for a lantern, either. Something about what was left of the doc—he wasn't ready to leave it. Something was bothering him. And who knew if the body would float away like dandelion fluff or be stolen by an enterprising coyote or suddenly decide to shift into sand, taking any clues about its unnatural death with it.

"Somebody did this," he said. "This...well, shit. Obviously it wasn't natural. Nobody decides to tie up their hands and feet and nail themselves to a goddamn post." He spit in the dirt, far away from the doc. "But there's a purpose to it. We were supposed to see it. No." He kicked a stone, listened to it roll away, the only sound for miles. "*I* was supposed to see it."

And Sam and Dan knew him well, so nobody said, "But why?" Because of course that was the question on everybody's mind.

The body suddenly shifted, and Rhett jumped. The dark and the prairie's wind, well, it could do things to a feller.

But then the body did something that it should not have been able to do because it had been drained down to jerky, light as a wasp nest.

It spoke.

In a voice that was a sorry shade of the doctor Rhett had met, it said two words.

"El...Rey..."

CHAPTER 15

All three men drew their guns on principle, even though the doc was clearly not a threat.

"How the hell did he talk?" Sam yelped.

Dan stuck his gun back home and knelt, putting a hand on the doc's chest. Not the body, not the carcass, Rhett realized. The man. The doc was still in there, somehow.

"Doc, can this be undone?" Dan asked.

The doc said nothing, just let a moan escape like the sound of a leather hinge giving up.

"Doc, do you want us to end it?"

Another moan, air whistling through a cave.

And then a sound that almost sounded like "Yeah."

Dan whipped out his knife, but Rhett stopped him with a hand and got low to look into what was left of the doc's face. The feller couldn't have opened his eyes, even if he'd wanted to—they were all sunk away in their sockets, dry and twisted as old leather. But Rhett figured a feller knew when somebody was in his face, so he got there.

"What the hell is El Rey? You got anything else to tell us?"

The sound the doc made after that didn't need syllables to read as sarcastic.

"He can't tell us anything, Rhett. We've got to do the merciful thing," Dan explained, his knife hovering over the doc's chest.

"But he's in there! He knows what we're up against! He knows why this was done! Can't we...fill him up? Give him water? Or whatever a wendigo needs?"

Dan gave him the *Rhett, you're dumb as a possum* look. "A wendigo needs human flesh. A lot of it."

Rhett looked back over his shoulder to the place where Beans would soon drive up in the wagon. He didn't much want to feed a corpse chunks of meat and water, but he sure as hell did want answers.

"Well, what if—"

But Dan said something in his own language then slammed his knife home in the shriveled chest. The doc's body turned to the saddest little puddle of sand Rhett had ever seen, his clothes drifting down into a mournful pile.

"Goddammit, Dan!" he growled.

Dan sheathed his knife and stood.

"Goddamn you, Shadow. That man needed mercy more than you need an interrogation. Remember who you are."

Rhett's hands went into fists, and he kicked the pile of clothes. "I'm the feller who knows something terrible is coming and who can't stop worrying that everybody he loves is gonna die in the fight! I'm the feller who needs answers more than I need to go on being good!"

Dan shook his head like he was ashamed. "If you love us, Rhett, you've got to walk the line. You might be the Shadow, but if you make innocent people suffer to pursue your own ends, then maybe the Shadow isn't what we need after all."

"I never been here to be what you need, you high-and-mighty bastard. I'm here to do what needs doing, even when it's ugly work. And it would've been goddamn useful to see that body in the daylight and figure out how all the goddamn blood came out so we know how to keep ours on the inside. Goddamn." Rhett pinched a bit of the doc's sand and slipped it into the pouch around his neck, one more weight to carry.

"The king," Dan said softly.

"What'd you say?"

"El Rey. It's Aztecan for *the king*."

"King of what?"

Dan held up his hands. "I assume we're going to find out whether we want to or not."

"That ain't helpful."

Rhett whipped his hat off and rubbed his hair as he paced. His need to be here, in the ruins of his old Outpost, had frittered away on the wind with the doc's sand, and he was full of piss and vinegar and ready to be gone again.

But he couldn't go, could he?

"You like his remains so much, you search him for clues," he said to Dan, finally hearing the jingle of the wagon's approach.

"What are you gonna do, Rhett?" Sam asked, glancing toward the east as if checking for a sudden assault by the morning sun.

Rhett realized he was still holding his gun, rammed it home, and stalked to the wagon like he was hell-bent on killing something.

"I'm gonna get a crowbar and start taking down that fence," he said. "I need to tear something apart, and I reckon I can do that in a useful way instead of in my usual way."

Beans pulled Samson to a halt unnecessarily as Rhett took the gentle gelding's bridle in hand.

"Everything good, Red-Eye?"

Rhett snorted his amusement at that question. Hell, when

in his life had everything been good for a single moment? Even Rhett's most cherished interludes had been stolen, surrounded by a sea of troubles.

"Hell no, it ain't. Now, hold that horse while I get the tools."

Beans knew him well enough to say no more, and as Rhett stalked back toward the outpost's board fence, a crowbar in one hand and an old red tool kit in the other, he hollered, "Follow me. With the horse and wagon, though. Not on foot."

Because just as Beans knew him now, Rhett knew Beans was the sort of feller to get down and trot after Rhett while leaving the wagon behind, which was not helpful. He heard the jingle of traces in his wake and reckoned even Beans could follow a man through darkness and stop a horse by a fence.

As he marched, Sam passed him, touring his horse back toward the wagon.

"Is it time?" Rhett asked him.

Sam gave a sad sigh. "Just about. I told Dan to make sure you get your rest, too. Can't have you pulling boards all day and being surly all night."

Normally, Rhett would've stopped to pat Sam's leg or pull him down for a peck on the cheek, but Rhett was beyond such comforts at the moment and merely waved, saying, "Sleep sweet, Sam. See you tomorrow night, when I'll try to be less of a bastard." All the rage and confusion inside him—he didn't want to poison Sam with it. The feller had no choice but to sleep for twelve hours; he shouldn't have to do it carrying Rhett's dread like an extra saddlebag.

Soon, the sun was coming up and Rhett was tearing down a fence while his friends slept. When the crisp morning breeze stirred up the sand, Rhett looked up at the pink-painted clouds.

"Whatever happened to you, doc, I hope it don't happen again," he said, to nobody and nothing in particular.

The only response was a prickle down the back of his neck.

He spun slowly in a circle, scanning the horizon in every direction, crowbar in his blistered, bleeding hand, but the Shadow sensed nothing.

Rhett knew better.

It took two nights, more or less, to pull down all the boards from the outpost's horse pens, yank out all the nails, and stack the wood in the wagon. Rhett, Dan, and Sam took turns sleeping and working on the fences while Beans got sent to hunt for bits of bullet metal in the ruins. Rhett spent most of his time demolishing the fence, which felt damn fine. It was hard, destructive, angry work, and it suited him. By the time they had filled the wagon with warped boards and buckets of used nails hammered straight again on the barn's half-melted anvil, he was more than ready to bid farewell to the Las Moras Outpost forever. He'd said his good-byes long ago, and even if it kept pulling him back, he was about to start resisting if it kept it up.

They napped through the afternoon, and when Sam woke, Rhett was feeling right spry and ready for the trail, for all that he ached in every bone and his hands were a mess of blisters that hadn't healed before they'd broken again. He kept waiting for the Shadow to give him some indication of what to do next, but it continued feeling less like a tug and more like an all-over buzz.

"Where to?" he asked Dan as they swung up into the saddle.

Dan's grin was a bit too wry for his taste. "Why, I thought that was up to you."

"We both know it's never up to me, you sassy bastard. But right now, I ain't receiving any messages from the Shadow. I'll follow you to any border town you think might sell us some land or a hut. Except Gloomy Bluebird."

"Who the hell would want to live there?" Dan asked with feigned innocence, and Rhett just snorted.

"I know where the doc lived," Sam said, real quiet. He'd been squinting at the tail end of the sunset like it might reach out and slap him, and now he looked right troubled. Rhett was starting to hope they'd come upon some no-good humans soon, as he could tell Sam was getting hungry, and he could also tell that Beans would shit a brick if Sam tried to drink from him.

"Why the hell would we want to go to the doc's place?" Rhett asked, but not in a cruel way.

"I mean, I want to know what happened to him. Don't you? Might be something dangerous. Besides, he was a nice enough feller. Captain sent me out to fetch him once with Virgil, told me I needed to know the way. He lived in a little farmhouse with a barn just big enough for his horse. It's west, right over the border, out by itself a bit but just an hour's ride from a little town called Rona. It's a wild place where folks go to hide out from Durango and Azteca law, lots of gunfights, so the doc did okay with . . . with what he needed." Sam swallowed hard and licked his lips, and it wasn't in the way that made Rhett feel all loose in the nethers. It was in the way of a thirsty man thinking about a sloppy shot of whiskey.

"What about that town called Darling?" Dan reminded him.

But Rhett didn't even have to think twice or consult the Shadow. What Sam had suggested? It just felt right.

"Forget Darling. I'm with Sam—let's go to the doc's place. Both so we can maybe find out what happened, and because that farmhouse might make a good base."

Beans gaped at him. "You wanna go steal his house, Rhett? Just like that?"

Rhett would've flushed with shame even a few months ago to hear anyone talk about him like that, but the time for piddling around with the feelings of folks who didn't matter was past.

"It ain't stealing if he's dead, fool. I take it the wendigo didn't have any family about?" He looked to Sam, who shrugged. "No? Fine, then. It ain't stealing. Something's coming, boys. I told you—it's waiting over the horizon, like thunder, and it's building up power just like a storm. We got to get settled someplace and get ready to defend it." He held up a finger to silence Beans, who had girded his slender loins to protest. "Now, if we go and he's got a little wendigo wife or whatever, we'll tip our hats and leave after giving her the bad news and our condolences. But if we find an empty house and we can use it to save folks that are gonna need saving, I reckon that the doc would be glad to know we were there. Don't you?"

Beans shook his head. "It just don't seem right, moving in like that."

Rhett looked to Dan, who snorted to suggest he was staying the hell out of it. Sam had a hard look about his mouth but gave Rhett a nod of understanding.

"I didn't say it was right, Beans. I said it was what needed to be done. So that's what we're doing. That's how we do everything. And while we're building shit, you can go into that town and stay there, if you don't like the way we operate. Find a saloon to sweep." He turned BB to the west and gave the unicorn a nudge to get him moving. "So everybody gets something they want and something they don't. Seems fair enough, don't it?"

After a moment, Sam steered his mount to ride next to Rhett, and Beans hopped up on the box and whickered to Samson to get the big draft moving, and Dan fell in behind the wagon, to which the rest of the ponies were tied. It would be slower going now that the wagon was full of wood, but it would be worth it. Wood wasn't easy to come by, this far west, and wherever they ended up, there would be horses that would need to be penned and protected. Rhett knew that much.

They rode silent in the dark for a while, but Rhett was no good at being quiet when he was full of worry.

"Sam, do you still dream?" he asked, almost out of nowhere.

"When I'm asleep, you mean?"

"Well, yeah."

Sam cocked his head, considering. "Not like I used to. It used to be weird stuff, like my socks turned into snakes but I stuck my feet in 'em anyway and wore my boots like that, with snake teeth in my knees like garters. But now it's more... colors and feelings, I guess. Mostly red. Lots of black. Peaceful. Although it's right peculiar not waking up to go piss."

Rhett smiled to himself. Sam had always awakened at least once a night to sleepwalk over to whatever seemed the most like a bush.

"I don't toss and turn, neither. Just lay there like a corpse, I reckon." Sam looked over at Rhett, a bit worried. "Am I?" he asked. "Like a corpse?"

"Of course not," Rhett hastened to say. "You breathe, and your mouth turns up in a little smile sometimes. But you do stick to one pose, mostly, instead of squirming as you used to."

"Well maybe I get comfortable and you're the one who's fussy."

"That's me. Fussy Rhett, they call me."

They laughed, and things were easy again, but then Sam looked over at him, sharp.

"Wait, Rhett. Why'd you ask me about dreaming?"

"Oh." Rhett looked down at his Henry, considering. "I used

to have dreams. About things that were gonna happen, sometimes. When we were chasing the Cannibal Owl or Trevisan or when Buck was nearby. But I feel like I'm not dreaming the way I used to. It's like I'm always lost, wandering around in fog. Or smoke. Or sand."

"Maybe it's because you mess up your sleep something awful to be with me."

Rhett snorted. "Of all the fool things to feel bad about. I get enough sleep, and I do enough work, and it's nobody's goddamn business when I choose to do either." He grinned at Sam. "Or when I do other things." Which was as close as he could come to telling Sam that his hated courses were over and after a good wash in a cool stream, he'd be available for said things, if they could sneak off for a moment alone.

Sam grinned back, wolfish. "Well, maybe it would be nice having a farmhouse and a bed after all." Then he turned grim again, and Rhett felt like the moment was gone too soon. "But we got to think of the doc first. It ain't right, what happened to him. And Dan didn't find anything in his clothes?"

Rhett shook his head. "We couldn't find anything. I keep thinking I should've stopped Dan from knifing the poor critter. We could've found marks to tell us what got him, probably, if we'd only waited until daylight."

"Naw. I'm with Dan. Mercy comes first."

"But sometimes withholding that mercy can save more lives. Whatever hurt the doc…well, it's gonna hurt somebody again. You don't do that to a man once and live a good life, go back to being harmless."

Sam rubbed his eyes with the back of his sleeve. "We all got to pick where we land in that field of gray, I reckon. I'm always gonna choose mercy."

"And I might not always get the chance."

They rode on for some time in silence.

When it began to rain, that, too, felt like a mercy.

And when Rhett next slept, he wandered, lost, in the mist.

In between the rain and Sam's condition, it took them two days to get to the doc's place, although Sam said it could be done in less than a day if a feller was unencumbered and had a fast horse. Rhett just didn't want Sam to feel bad, so he suggested the problem was that Beans was farting so much that it made Samson ornery, which gave everyone something to laugh about. As much as Rhett didn't like to ride up to a new place in the dark, Sam was the only person who knew where it was, hidden as the doc had kept it from outsiders. Not only that, but if Rhett was going into a new place that might hold possible dangers, he'd rather have Sam on his side than the sunshine.

Sam led them past high rocks, winding into a canyon, pueblos and rock formations rising all around them. The pitch-black holes and strange paintings struck Rhett as right eerie and peculiar, but he wasn't gonna say shit about how other folks had once lived. It was empty now, Sam said. The doc had explained to him once, while riding through, that a plague had wiped them out—a plague brought by white fellers, spread by blankets. And once the people had all died, the white fellers hadn't even wanted the homes. They just wanted the people gone, and gone they were. By the time Doc Ashmore showed up, everything was empty, and he'd dragged out all the blankets he could find and burned the lot. The night wind felt stark as a pointed finger poking Rhett in the chest. These ghosts were as uneasy as he was.

They pulled their horses to a halt, the wagon creaking dangerously behind Samson. It was a narrow trail, but so far, Beans and the big-boned but agile gelding had managed it. Dan rode up from behind the wagon, and Sam said, "Doc Ashmore's place is around the corner. Can't miss it. He had a horse and a hollering donkey and some chickens just for looks, but that was it, as far as I know." He paused, and the night creatures made no comment. "Rhett, I hate to say it, but I don't hear his donkey."

Rhett shifted in his saddle, feeling his sentiments rise in an unpleasant sort of way. If the doc's donkey was anything like Rhett's ancient mule, Blue, he would've been hollering his fool head off. Which meant that the donkey was either gone or dead. And that only upped Rhett's dander more, as he couldn't think about a dead donkey without thinking about Earl. And once he started thinking about Earl, the Irish shifter's death rattled through his head like a goddamn player piano, filling him with regret and self-loathing and the other sort of emotional shit that made it harder to fight.

"Let's go, then," Rhett said, preferring to run headfirst into trouble over dealing with the part of Earl's ghost that lingered in his heart.

He kicked BB to a trot, navigating the rocks easily with Sam and Dan on his tail. He could see, just ahead, where the pueblos opened up into a green-speckled valley, and he pulled his gun, expecting trouble. The Shadow didn't sense anything unusual, but Rhett was starting to doubt what the Shadow could currently contribute; whatever they were facing seemed somehow beyond its powers. He could feel the monster natures of Dan and Sam and Beans and BB, tugging at his belly with a small, familiar wobble, but everything else in the world felt like fireflies in fog, a little buzz that couldn't be hunted nor tracked. And Rhett didn't like that.

The pueblos became stark rock walls, and the doc's lonely farmhouse came into view. It was two stories tall and thin as a toothpick, seemed like, rising up from the red dirt with a squat little barn off to the side. It looked like failure made flesh, like some man had paid for his dreams and brought them here to plant them, and they had risen up scrawny and already crumbling. Rhett didn't want to set a goddamn foot in the place, and he began to understand why Sam hadn't been that taken with the idea.

"Looks pretty dead to me," Rhett said, immediately regretting his choice of words.

"No donkey, no horse." Sam frowned. "Maybe he was out riding when it happened? The donkey went along with him, see, carrying his doctor box and things. He always knew if he was tending Rangers, he'd be gone a few days." His tone suggested he knew it was a stupid sort of hope.

"Fuck it," Rhett said, pulling his gun and kicking the big unicorn to his rumbling canter.

The closer Rhett got to the doc's old house, the more he knew he wanted nothing to do with it. He didn't want to live there, much less go to the trouble of defending such a shitty, thin little building. Every whistle of wind would squeeze through those cracks. A shadow of snow would dust the floor. The summers would be like sitting inside a walnut's skin, hard and dry. It was a crust of a place, one that would provide neither protection nor pleasure. No one, he reckoned, had ever been happy here.

But as he drew near, he felt that ripple over his skin telling him something wasn't right. Like the Shadow couldn't quite identify the problem but damn well knew there was one. The hairs all up his arms and the back of his neck went on point, and his stomach just about jumped out of his mouth, but there was nothing to fight, nothing to kill, nothing that called to him. And that only made him long to fight all the harder. He felt small and stupid and helpless. So helpless.

"Where the hell is it?" he bellowed.

"Rhett," Sam called, his voice sad.

"Where? You point me at something that needs killing, and I'll kill it. I'll kill it dead!"

"Rhett, look up."

Rhett yanked hard on the reins, and BB just about sat in his haste to obey. The gelding danced under Rhett's tight hands as Rhett backed him up and let his eyes crawl over the front of the wind-washed gray house as it rose up against the blanket of stars. There were no details, only layers upon layers of shadow.

Windows without glass. An open door. The second story. A crumbling roof.

A weathervane up top.

And tied to it, a small shape.

Shriveled. Bloodless.

Just like the doc, but smaller.

And Rhett knew exactly who it was.

CHAPTER 16

Oh goddammit. Oh goddamn. Who would do this?" Rhett leaped off his horse and ran in the front door of the doc's house, uncaring of any danger that might be waiting therein. "We got to get her down!"

He had his knife drawn as he muddled through the simple, narrow building. The stairs were easy to find, and as he pounded up them, he could feel their brittle give. The doc had been a slight man, and Rhett himself was not large, but his desperation and fury gave him weight. Up top, there was only a narrow hall and one bedroom, and in the center of it, an open window, ragged curtains gently billowing in and out as if the house were breathing. Rhett stuck his head out, seeing only the horses switching their tails below. Footsteps told him his friends were following him, although they were taking their time, being safe.

"How do we get up there?" he asked as Dan came into view. For all that Dan was a vexful bastard, he did have a certain crisp way of thinking that came in handy when Rhett felt the most out of control, as he did now. When he got like this, his instinct was to hit, barge, run, kill. Stepping back to think, though? That was the hard part.

"An attic," Dan said. "See? The ceiling is flat, but the roof is slanted."

"Found it!" Sam called from the hall, and Rhett ran to him.

Sam had pulled down a little door in the ceiling, which was low and oppressive, and a gust of chill air whistled down.

"Boost me up."

Sam bent over, hands cupped together, and without another word, Rhett sheathed his knife, took a jogging step, and let Sam's hands catapult him upward. His belly landed on the edge, and he dragged himself onto the floor up above, the boards not pleased by their new burden. He couldn't stand—could barely crouch, but for once he was grateful for the wretched house's many faults. The roof felt as poorly constructed as everything else, and after he'd felt every which way and howled his desperation, unable to find any sort of hatch to the outside while stumbling and clawing in the dark, he found a crack that showed the twinkle of stars and began to tear at the wood, prying up a loose board, and then another, his hands bloody and torn, until he'd made a hole just big enough for his narrow shoulders.

Heights had once frightened him, but not now. When a body was mostly unkillable and felt at home in the sky, there were worse things to fear than untidy falls over hard-packed earth. He scrambled out onto the roof, digging his fingers into the cracks between rough shingles, until he clung to the base of the iron weathervane and had no choice but to confront what hung there like an empty sail.

No.

Not what.

Who.

"Meimei," he whispered.

The last time he'd seen the little girl, she'd been leaving on horseback with her older sister, hugging Cora's waist from her perch on a pony's rump. He hadn't really known this girl, but he'd given months of his life—and one of his pinky toes—to hunt and destroy the alchemist who'd taken her hostage. She'd been human, which meant that unlike the wendigo doctor, there was no way she could be alive now. And thank goodness. Because whatever had happened to the doctor had also befallen this child. She was a dry husk, nothing left but papery skin wrapped in cloth.

"Goddammit."

He didn't want to touch her—it felt like sacrilege. But he had to get her down. It was horrible, the thought of her up here, flying like some evil asshole's flag. And where was her sister? Before he reached for his knife, Rhett scanned the area around the farmhouse but neither saw nor felt any indication that Cora was nearby.

He swiftly sawed through the ropes holding Meimei to the weathervane, and she was so fragile that he had to go slow for fear of snapping off some part of what was left of her. She was so slight now, more delicate even than in life, and her little cloth shoes rasped against the roof like a skeleton's finger bones clawing at a door.

Rhett had seen and done a lot of horrific things in his life, but this one? Beat the hell out of them all. By the time he was done, he was a mess of tears and snot, and he took the little girl's body in both hands and went to the hole in the roof.

"Dan?"

"I'm here." Rhett knew he would be. That was the thing about Dan. Irksome as he was, when something terrible needed doing, Dan would never shirk it. He would wait in the shadows, patient and silent, and do it.

"Take her down. Be careful."

"I will."

Rhett passed the tiny body through the crack in the roof, as careful as if he'd been handling dynamite, and Dan took it, tender as if he were holding an infant. Rhett quickly scanned the roof for clues but knew he would find nothing. Whoever was doing this was likewise careful, and if they wanted something found, it would be. He crawled down into the attic, chilled to the bone and plastered with snot, and felt a million years older when he'd dropped back onto the floor below.

Sam joined them, and the three men stood there in the dark a moment, holding the dead child between them, unsure what to do.

"We need to bury her. I...I don't know if I can bring myself to do it." Rhett's voice quavered. "She's so small, Sam. So small."

A tear slid down Dan's cheek, the first one Rhett had seen. "We have to burn her. Or she might turn into something else. We still don't know what...what's been done. Or why."

"She's dead." Sam's voice was as small and firm as Rhett had ever heard it. "Nothing here is alive. Nothing. Nothing could be brought back."

Rhett thought back—to Trevisan, to the Lobos.

"Never say never." Dan's voice, speaking for Rhett's mind, brooked no refusal.

When Sam's head bowed in agreement, Rhett groaned and said, "Fine. We burn her. But tomorrow. We got to see this body in the sunlight. Got to see what marks were left on it. There's got to be something here. Something we're missing." He didn't say so, but he didn't want to rifle the small body in the dark. He wanted to touch her as little as possible, with as much respect as possible. Not like he was plundering an enemy for treasure.

222

He took the burden from Dan and carried Meimei to the iron bedstead. The blankets were tucked in tighter than an armadillo's asshole, and Rhett couldn't handle another fight, so he just laid the tiny body atop the coverlet. They stood around the bed, and the room felt so cold, and Rhett didn't know if he'd rather tear down the world with his bare hands or crawl into the wagon and sleep forever. He felt utterly empty—of life, of energy, of hope. So he wiped the mess off his face with his bandanna and sniffled and took his hat off.

There were a million things he wanted to say, but he wasn't a man of words, so all that came out was, "This ain't right."

"A child's death never is."

"I know that, Dan, you ass. But everything about this is wrong. It was done for a purpose. But she was innocent. And why the hell tie her to the roof? And where's Cora?"

Dan sighed and didn't bother to wipe off his own tears. "Sometimes you have to grow accustomed to not knowing."

"I don't have to do anything of the sort."

"C'mere, Rhett." Sam's voice was soft, his arms open, and Rhett threw himself against the cowpoke's chest, burying his face in Sam's flannel shirt. Sam rubbed his back and murmured sweet things to him like he was a baby horse with a lost mama, and Rhett went right back to crying, his fists tangled in Sam's shirt and his hat forgotten, on the floor. Dan disappeared, and Rhett didn't care. Just then, all he needed was Sam.

"Why's it feel like everything I touch dies?" he whispered into Sam's chest.

"Hush, fool. Everything dies. That's how life works."

"But it feels like...like...death is just flat-out drawn to me. Like a stream drawing thirsty horses."

Sam chuckled, a fond rumble against Rhett's cheek. "You just see it that way because you're the center of your own goddamn world. You think I ain't lost people? I lost plenty of people. You just got to keep going. Find reasons to keep going. Find people who make you want to keep going, even when you think you can't."

Rhett pulled away, swiped his sleeve across his face. Out the window, he saw Dan unsaddling the horses and leading them to a small pen. Far off, the wagon was trundling up, Samson's head down and weary.

"Maybe I should run away. Become one of those...those people who live off alone?"

"A hermit?"

"Maybe. I just keep thinking that maybe if I stopped letting the Shadow yank my chain, if I just sat my ass down and refused to chase things, maybe death would stop following me around."

Rhett was facing away, and Sam put a hand on his shoulder but seemed to understand that Rhett couldn't stand more than a kind touch, just then. "Death doesn't follow anybody around. It's just always there. Everywhere. All around. Doesn't matter where you run. It'll find you. Like Haskell's men. You didn't ask for that."

"I did in my own heart," Rhett admitted, a mere whisper. "I wanted to kill 'em. Every one."

"Well, you got your wish, I reckon."

Rhett fought the urge to say, "So did you," and mercifully, for once, won. Instead, what came out was, "I'm tired, Sam. I'm just so goddamned tired."

"It's getting sunup soon. You need sleep. Come with me. Let me comfort you."

It sounded goddamn ridiculous, hearing it said out loud, but it was also a hell of an invitation and one Rhett would not turn down. If there was any place to lose himself, Sam was better than some old hermit hidey-hole out in the desert.

"As long as Beans hasn't stunk up the wagon," Rhett said, trying to remember how to smile.

Sam took his hand and led him out of the room, and Rhett gave himself the gift of not looking at Meimei's body, stiff and light and tiny and brittle and still, on the bed.

Rhett slept in a bit, meaning he didn't wake up until afternoon, and he felt like shit about that. If he was a good person, thoughts of Meimei would've woken him up, spurring him to figure out why she'd died and to punish the monster responsible. But he'd slept hard, deep and undreaming, and he found he couldn't be sorry. Dan didn't give him any shit over it, at least, and Beans was still asleep under the wagon himself. Rhett checked that Sam's box was locked up tight before shoving his feet back into his boots and hopping down onto the dry red earth. The sun felt strange now, and he had to shield his eyes against the unwanted brightness and chilling cold. Being in open space was a blessing after the terrible mess of the wagon, which was packed to the gills with boards and nails and had left very little room for maneuvering the night before. They'd ended up tangled in the open box. He'd slept curled beside it.

He didn't see Dan outside at first, but he reckoned the Shadow would at least have the sense to let him know the feller was in danger. Rhett walked around the house and barn, hollering at the top of his lungs, and was just about to shuck his clothes and turn into the bird to get a better look from the sky when Dan came moseying up from the old pueblos, barefoot and dusty but smiling.

"What the hell are you so happy about?" Rhett asked.

"Trust you to be offended that I'm smiling," Dan said, shaking his head. "Thing is, this is a good area for what you want to do—and don't you dare interrupt me, or I'll slap you." Rhett closed his mouth. "I know the house isn't right. Everything about it feels terrible, even more so after we found Meimei. But what we've got here is a space nobody wants. We have plenty of wood for fences, and I went scouting this morning. These pueblos are perfect. Lots of room. Dry places for storage. Dark places for Sam. It's defensible. And no one comes here. It's close to the border, just a day from the nearest town. It's perfect."

Rhett frowned, because Rhett mostly frowned.

"So you want to give up the house and move into the rocks?" Dan grinned.

"Yes, that's exactly what I think we should do. We can bring another load in the wagon, furniture and cooking utensils— but this place was built to hold dozens of people, maybe hundreds. There are already ovens and bed niches and carefully crafted outhouses. And anyone coming here looking for you will ride up to that house like a fool." He shook his head in disgust. "White men don't even see the rocks as homes, you know. Just…animal dens. So let's do the smart thing and take advantage of that."

"Wait. Why should I care what white men think?"

"Did you hit your head while you were asleep? The Rangers are white, and whether or not you remember it, they're eventually going to come after you. You've taken out two outposts single-handedly, and one day, the boss men will find out. They may not be able to tell you're a monster, but they know you're a threat. And they will hunt you down."

It was Rhett's turn to snort. "They don't know a goddamn thing about me."

"Don't be stupid." Dan pulled his old Ranger badge out of somewhere and held it up to the light, and of course it was just as shiny and well kept as it had been when he'd worn it proudly.

"Captain made you a Ranger. That means he had to inform the main office, put you on payroll and deduct your bullets, all that. Then he made you a Scout, which means there are papers somewhere giving you permission to range around under his command. And I guarantee that when you visited Haskell, he wrote that up for his superiors. Fellers you don't like the look of show up at your outpost, asking pointed questions and saying they're Rangers, you report that. So your name will be floating around back east, and believe me, Rhett: One day, someone will connect it to the deeds you've done." He held up a hand. "All of which I agree had to happen. But it's not going to look so simple from the outside, so we'd best prepare for war."

Rhett rubbed his face, wishing like hell he had stubble. "I just want to be left alone."

Dan put his badge away and started walking toward the farmhouse. "Yeah, well, you should've thought about that before you started killing shit and calling it your destiny."

Rhett jogged to catch up. "Wait. Where the hell are you going?"

Dan gave him that look. "To see to Meimei, fool. Best get it done while you're still fresh. Grisly work doesn't keep."

Rhett didn't have anything useful to grumble at that truth, so he caught up, and together they walked up to the sinister-looking farmhouse. They stood in front of the door for a shade too long, neither one wanting to step inside and hear again the lonely splintering creak of old wood. But it had to be done, and Rhett didn't want another preacherly reminder from Dan, so he heaved out a sigh and pushed the door open.

It looked different during the day but still wasn't a place he'd choose to spend time. It was as spare a space as he'd ever seen. Even Mam and Pap, poor as they'd been, had scattered their sad shack with a collection of junk ranging from old buffalo skulls to half-fixed saddles and piles of ragged horse blankets that had frozen in place with sweat. The doc's place was empty and clean, all gray boards and a few neat stacks of ugly things—shirts, blankets, papers going yellow. He had a small table and one stern chair, a rag rug underneath showing even wear that suggested he turned it at regular intervals. Nothing hung on the walls. The only clutter Rhett could see was in the other room, which held a desk covered in books, pens, and half-dried-out jars of ink. It was surrounded by shelves of more heavy books and a wall of doctor-type tools, all gleamingly clean.

"He was a weird feller," Rhett noted.

"Doctors always are."

There was a door out of the office, but it just led outside and didn't have anything special about it. The doors had no locks, and the windows had only plain white sheets as curtains and shutters for when the weather got especially bad. The floor had been swept clean, and although Rhett wondered if maybe the murderer had done that to cover his tracks, he felt like it was pretty in character for the doc to have floors so tidy a feller could eat off 'em. Not that the doctor ate in that sort of way.

The stairs were waiting, though, and Rhett was sick of postponing his lunch out of disgust and fear.

"Well, here we go," he said, tromping up.

Just like last night, the steps bowed and groaned, and the hallway upstairs now seemed stuffy and smaller, just a box with a window. They'd shut the bedroom door, and Rhett's fingers tingled as he reached for the cold porcelain knob. He didn't want to see this, but he had to. No matter what he did, his life seemed rife with shit he didn't want to do but had no choice about. Whether it was forced drudgery for Pap and Mam or enjoying the supposed freedom of a cowpoke or the Shadow, it was just another long list of tasks.

And the only way to get to the next task was to open the damn door and get on with it.

So he did.

And there, on the other side, was Meimei.

She was unchanged from last night, but seeing her in the light of day brought the tears back full force, making Rhett's heart ache for Sam's comfort. In the dark, there were only shadows, but in the light, every detail was laid uncomfortably, luridly bare. The little girl was around six, small for her age thanks to years spent locked in a cage in Bernard Trevisan's personal train car. Her short black hair, silky as a bird's wing, was attached to a head that now looked more like a shriveled-up apple. The girl's golden skin was dry as paper, her mouth open like she was wailing. Her hands were up like she'd been fending someone off—and failing. And Rhett didn't want to get any closer, but goddammit, he had to.

"Hellfire, I hate this. C'mon, Dan."

He stepped up to the bed with Dan by his side.

"You see anything?"

Dan sighed and gently moved the girl's collar down. She was wearing an old dress, much faded and patched, like the little girls wore in town, and it hurt Rhett's heart to think of her and Cora in a shop in San Anton, selecting this secondhand dress from what someone else had discarded so they could throw Herbert and Josephina off their trail.

"Why'd you start with the neck?" Rhett asked.

Dan looked at him sharply. "Because that's where vampires and Lobos bite. I figured I'd look there before I began undressing her."

"Don't you dare—!"

Dan faced him, frowning. "You think I want to undress a dead child, you idjit? Of course I don't want to. But if we want

229

to find what killed her, we have to find the marks. And I don't see any on her face or hands. Do you?"

"No."

"Then let's start with what we can see before we look for things too terrible to contemplate."

As gentle as Rhett had ever seen him, Dan inspected the girl's hands, rolled her sleeves up her arms as far as they could go, and regarded the bare calves above her shoes. They found nothing that would point to a cause of death, and Dan turned to Rhett looking serious as hell. "We have to do this, Shadow. Start at the feet or the throat?"

Rhett shuddered. "The throat."

Dan nodded in agreement and gently turned the girl onto her side to unbutton her dress down the back. Rhett had done and seen a lot of terrible things, but nothing as horrible and wrong as this, and he comforted himself by whispering under his breath that he would find whoever or whatever had done it and make them suffer.

"Here."

Rhett looked up from red-tinted visions of carnage to find Dan pointing at the base of the child's neck, hidden by her dress, where a slender cut showed in her skin. It was puckered but small and clean, considering how dry her skin was, and it would've been easy to miss in the darkness—on Meimei or on the doc.

"Someone bled her from here. It's a neat cut. Not teeth. No bloodstains, no scab, nothing ragged. Almost like they used a . . . an instrument or a machine."

"A machine?"

"Hellfire, Rhett. Do I look like I know? I've seen about every bite a creature can inflict on human flesh, and this is something entirely new. Almost like a doctor did it. But a cut like that from a knife couldn't do...this to a body."

Rhett leaned in close and hated that Dan was right.

"You don't think—"

"No. I don't think the wendigo did it. It's not like he'd find a child, bleed her out, and tie her to his own weathervane before riding to Las Moras and killing himself in the same manner. But it doesn't make much sense, I'll give you that."

Rhett had expected to feel some sort of relief, finding the child's death wound. Finding teeth marks he could match to a beast, or acid saliva, or a bullet. But all he had were more questions and heaps more anger than he had ever thought possible.

"There's got to be something here." With less gentleness, he felt along the sides of the child's chest and down her waist. She'd been tiny when alive, but now she was more like a corn husk doll, and he had to hold down his gullet, which he'd never been good at. Finally, his fingertips found a lump. He reached into a pocket sewn into the side of the girl's dress and withdrew something.

He knew what it was before he'd held it up to the light.

He had thought he couldn't get angrier, but now he had.

It was a bag.

Just a small leather bag.

When he opened it, he found silvery sand and a hank of silky black hair.

CHAPTER 17

Just like that, he knew.

Cora was dead.

Beautiful, fierce, fiery, sweet Cora was gone.

Whatever had killed Meimei had killed her sister, too.

Her sister, the dragon.

Which meant that their murderer was not only monstrous but also very, very powerful.

"God, I hope he got Cora before Meimei," Rhett said, his voice a ragged thread.

Dan rubbed his eyes. "There's no good order this could happen in."

"No. But it was Cora's worst fear, losing her sister."

"I imagine it was Meimei's worst fear, too."

"You shut the hell up, Dan! With your being clever. These girls are dead. Our girls. I loved Cora!" He glanced guiltily to the window, wondering if sleeping vampires could hear things. "Not for long, and not like Sam, but some kind of love. I cared for the girl. Held her in my arms and laughed with her. Comforted her. You never saw that part of us, but...we had something there. A little spark. It died. Hell, I probably killed it. But I still cared." He was crying again, tears soaking down his chin and throat and into his binder. "For all our quarrels, I always cared."

"We know one thing now for sure, then," Dan said, rage simmering in his quiet, thoughtful voice. "This isn't a coincidence. This isn't random monsters being drawn to you. Whatever is happening? It's all connected." He cocked his head. "I'd ask you if you have any enemies, but we both know you have more than most. The question is: Which enemy is still alive, and which one has the need and the resources to do something like this?"

"The more important question is why can't I feel it? Why is the Shadow letting me down?"

Rhett needed something to do, so he pulled the little leather bag from its loop around his neck and stuffed the hank of hair inside, along with a pinch of sand.

"The Shadow can't let you down, Rhett." Dan met his eye. "It's a force. It can't be fickle or fall asleep. So whoever is doing this must be purposefully working in ways that the Shadow can't detect."

That made a hell of a lot of sense, as much as Rhett hated to admit it. He started pacing, nodding. "Yeah. Yeah. It's been right peculiar lately. Not working at all the way it normally does. I thought maybe it was changing, maybe I was changing. But maybe it's just that the enemy is..."

"Evolving?"

"Being an asshole. You don't think Trevisan—"

"Is alive? No. You ended him for certain. He can't be El Rey."

"Then who is he? The king. King of getting on my goddamn nerves. And he's a damn sight smarter than I'd hoped. So now I got El Rey after me, and I got the chupacabras after me..." Rhett trailed off and shook his head. "Hellfire, Dan. I bet El Rey is the one stirring up the damn chupas out west in the first place!"

"I was wondering when you'd come to that conclusion," Dan said in his preachiest sort of way.

Rhett was about to dog cuss the man, but he was a leader now, and he had to get a grip on himself. He stopped to gaze down at Meimei and find his focus. Each time he looked, really looked at what was left of the child, it was like getting punched in the heart. A realization dawned on him, horrific as it unfolded.

"Oh, sweet goddamn. Dan, we left 'em there. All our people. We just left 'em at the damn mission!"

"Yes, and?"

"Alone! Without me!" He finally stopped pacing and stared Dan down. "Shit. I got to go. Now. You burn the child. Say your prayers, do whatever will make her rest easy. Unload the wood and leave Beans here with a gun. Then you and Sam drive this wagon back to San Anton as fast as Samson will go."

"Rhett, slow down. I don't understand. You're going back alone?"

But Rhett was already at the door. "I got to, Dan. If El Rey and the chupas get to 'em first, they're all dead. Drained, like this. I can't let that happen. Tell Sam I'm sorry to leave without him. No. First, tell him that I love him. Then tell him I'm sorry. Then tell him to hurry."

Rhett was already out the door, boots thumping down the creaking stairs. Outside, he paused just a moment to fling Cora's sand into the wind. "You'd want to be here near Meimei, I know," he whispered. "I hope you found that cantankerous grandpa of yours, wherever you are. I hope you feel free." He paused, looked down, saw teardrops splash onto the cracked orange earth and get soaked right up. "I'm sorry I failed you so many times."

And then he was saddling BB, knowing the big bastard

would run until his damn heart quit pumping. He wouldn't risk Ragdoll if he could help it—hell, he'd already risked everybody else. When the mare nuzzled his arm from the pen, he roughly patted her nose. "Sorry, girl. I need a monster for this job, and that unicorn's a hell of a monster. You're too good for the likes of me." She snorted as if in agreement but bumped his shoulder with her nose, and he reckoned that was as close as he'd get to forgiveness. As he swung up into the saddle, Dan hollered his name, and Rhett looked up to find him standing in the front door, holding a small shape wrapped in the doc's coverlet.

"What?" he asked, BB dancing underneath him, feeling the thrum of needing to run.

"Be careful," Dan said.

"I always—no. You're right. I never am, am I? But that's what's kept me alive. I'd rather be fast than careful, just now. You be careful. Take care of Sam."

Dan's stare was level and dangerous. "And you take care of my sister."

Rhett shook his head and kicked his mount, shouting, "I did that a while back, and you got right annoyed with me, if I remember correctly." And then he was galloping like a bat out of hell, smiling grimly. But he was kind enough to holler, "You know I will, fool!" right before he was out of shouting range.

It was a straight shot east, and the days and nights blurred together. BB had the heart and wind of a monster, and he could gallop for hours if the terrain allowed it. Pressed for time as they were, Rhett didn't go wide around the rises or hunt for better river crossings. He kicked the unicorn up hills, sometimes having to walk behind, pulling himself up using the gelding's long, white tail. They forged rivers in the pouring rain and slept under lightning-black trees, and when Rhett reckoned he didn't have time to hunt scarce and flighty game in the desert, he turned into the bird and found something good and dead to fill his belly. It was a brief joy, riding the thermals, free of a man's thoughts. But he couldn't let himself stray too far from human. He needed his anger, needed his worry to drive him, and the bird took him too far away from his feelings, from what forced him to keep going. He'd almost lost himself there once, and he wouldn't do so again. Not now, when his people needed him most.

When he nodded off in his exhaustion and thought he couldn't sit in the saddle another moment, he'd think about Meimei and Cora and the doc, and he'd imagine his mama with that shriveled, paper-thin skin, or Revenge turned into a pile of bloody sand, and he'd kick his wearied mount and they'd struggle up the next hill. His belly tugged him toward the mission, but he felt delicate as a cat on a fence, waiting for any sense of an emergency, for that feeling he got when the danger was so close as to make it unavoidable. That feeling didn't come, but that didn't slow him down. Whoever El Rey was, whatever the bastard was doing with the chupas, however he was maneuvering things, Rhett hadn't felt Cora and Meimei in trouble, and that meant that he couldn't count on the Shadow anymore.

He could only count on Rhett.

Once Ned, once Nat, once Nettie.

No matter what name he'd been given or taken for his own, the core of him remained the same: He would scrabble to stay on his feet, no matter what. For the longest time, he'd just had to keep himself alive, sometimes against what felt like impossible odds. But now he had all these people who depended on him. He'd tried to think of them only as his posse, as the folks who helped him fight for what was right—or who just so happened to show up in his life needing to be saved. But he could no longer avoid the realization that he had a family now, and whether they wanted it or not, whether *he* wanted it or not, his job was to keep them safe or die trying.

He lost track of time completely as he rode, a bandanna over his nose and mouth to keep out the dust, but he snapped out of the funk the moment he recognized the area around Inés's mission. It was going on lunch, judging by the sun, and when he whooped and kicked BB, it was half with worry and half with a thought for eating real food he hadn't pecked out of a blackened carcass. The Shadow told him nothing but that there were some monsters ahead, none of them intent on his own harm, but he didn't take that as seriously anymore. It still felt like a slight buzzing everywhere, like bees in smoke, and he wondered if El Rey, or some underling or necromancer, had cursed him or poisoned him or done something to mute his powers.

"Goddamn silly," he murmured to himself as he cantered up to the mission's front door and slid off the ragged, sweat- and dust-crusted unicorn onto numb feet and shaking legs. He didn't even bother to hitch BB up, just hooked his reins over the saddle horn and let the big feller go and trusted him to find his way around the mission to the water trough.

"Who's about?" he hollered, both guns drawn, expecting a fight.

Hellfire. Or what if El Rey had already got here? Silence had never been so sinister.

The mission's yard was still and quiet, the ground still twinkling with the remnants of last night's hard rain turned to ice, not yet burned off by the winter sun. Rhett waited to hear a welcoming bugle from Blue the mule around back, but he heard…nothing.

So he shot into the air, once.

And waited.

Still no bugle. Still no footsteps.

And then an arrow thwacked into his shoulder.

He spun for the window the arrow had come out of, guns pointed.

"Don't shoot at the mission, you asshole!" Winifred yelled.

"At least I shot at the sky, you bitch!" he yelled right back. "Are we under attack or not?"

"Only by you, fool!"

"Well, I'm the only one with a hole in my hide!"

"Then take off your bandanna and put up your damn guns before that changes, you jumpy idjit!"

"Goddamn your eyes, then, Coyote Girl!"

He shoved his guns back into his holster and yanked out the arrow, which at least hadn't been launched with full force. Noting the feather pattern, he snorted and cracked it over his knee before tossing it on the ground.

"Some welcome, Mama!"

The front door opened, and Winifred stood there, quiver over her shoulder, belly bulging out. "Some grand return, shooting a gun! And you're wearing a strange poncho and a villain's mask. Of course we panicked. Sorry about the arrow, though."

"I ain't even wearing my pie plate, and the poncho was for the rain! I was so worried about you-all that I dropped everything and galloped back here, and what thanks do I get? An arrow in the dang arm."

His mama and Revenge appeared in the door, as well as Digby and Lizzie and Inés and Notch. Rhett was overcome with relief to see them all alive and unharmed but still, honestly, pretty pissed off about getting shot. Arrows apparently stung more than bullets. And it reminded him of how foolish he'd been not to wear his pie plate before riding into what could've been any sort of trap set by El Rey or the chupacabras or any one of his many enemies.

Winifred closed the distance and rubbed his arm and chucked him under the chin. "You want a piece of penny candy? That looks like it hurts a wittle bit."

"I hate you," Rhett muttered, but there was no venom in it. His exhaustion was hitting him like a steam train, the fury of the final gallop draining out of his system. "You-all ain't had any trouble at all? Any strange folks showing up?"

"Funny you should ask," Inés answered. "Because strange folk have definitely begun to show up."

Winifred said something in her own language, speaking through the door, and five fellers came out. Rhett vaguely remembered them from a few months back—Little Eagle and his men, a group of fellers who'd attacked Rhett's posse to steal a large herd of horses before Rhett had offered them half the herd just to go the hell away. Fine fellers, once they'd received some horseflesh to feed their band and settled down around the fire to share some meat.

Rhett nodded. "Y'all are welcome, I reckon. What brought you here?"

As he expected, Little Eagle and his second, Slippery Snake, shared a look and shrugged. "We don't know. But here we are."

"How are your people? Those horses help out?"

Slippery Snake looked away, his face hard.

"Haskell," Little Eagle said. "We lost so many. We heard he was nearby and came hunting him. But now we hear it was you who ended him."

Rhett nodded, tears in his eyes. "And that's the truth. But I am sorry if I stole your revenge."

"He does that a lot," Rhett's brother said, and Rhett didn't know if it was a joke or not.

"As long as he's gone," Little Eagle said. "That's all that matters. We hear you're waiting for a fight."

Rhett nodded and walked up to the doorway, where everybody was watching. They stepped back to let him inside, and he followed his nose to the kitchen and fell onto the nearest half-eaten-through plate without bothering to ask whose it had once been. After days of trail food and then vulture food, the beans were heaven, and the tender meat—well, he nearly et himself sick using only his fingers.

Bill the Sasquatch walked in holding a teacup, raised a hairy eyebrow, and asked, "Hungry?"

"Starving," Rhett replied. "You gettin' on?"

Bill nodded. "It grows crowded here, and the barn is squalid."

Rhett just nodded along like he knew what that meant.

Now that everyone else had followed him into the kitchen and sat down, Rhett pushed back from the table and let out an enormous belch that tasted more than he preferred of a scavenger's breakfast.

"Well, I got good news and bad news on that front. Everybody here?"

He looked around the room. Bill, Inés, Winifred, his mama, his brother, Digby, Lizzie, Notch, Little Eagle, Slippery Snake, and three more Javelina fellers he didn't know but who looked like they'd been through a few fights and come out the other side okay.

"We're here," Winifred said, giving him the look of deep suspicion and reproach she shared with her brother Dan.

"The bad news is that we got to pack up and head out quicker than I'd hoped. Whatever's coming—it's already playing with us. We got to Las Moras and found the Rangers' wendigo doctor—an old friend, I guess—nearly dead. Weird, mysterious sort of work it was, too. Feller was drained to nothing but

240

didn't have the means to die, and Dan did the merciful thing and put him out of his misery. So we went to the doc's house and found…" He'd been doing his best impersonation of the sort of feller who was always in charge, who always knew what to say and said everything like it was just a harmless romp in the past. But when he got to the part about what they'd found at the doc's house, his throat closed up and his eyes pricked and he felt all that food he'd shoveled down start to edge up his gorge.

"What?" Winifred said, kinder this time, a hand on his arm.

"Meimei," he croaked. "Same treatment. Sucked dry, dry as paper. Didn't weigh as much as a folded shirt, seemed like. But she was human, so she was just…dead."

"And what about Cora?" Winifred was on full alert now, and Rhett realized he'd forgotten that, like him, Winifred had a prior relationship with Cora, one that might've been more sisterly or it might've been more personal than that. Probably both.

"Gone," he whispered. "Found a bag of sand in the child's pocket. Had this in it." He pulled the leather bag from around his neck and tenderly fished out the hank of hair.

Winifred's fingers danced over the inky black. "Maybe it's not hers."

Rhett shook his head. "That's the dumbest thing you ever said to me, and you know it."

Winifred tried to say something, but her voice caught, and all that came out was a sort of surprised gasp of a sob. Rhett understood, but he didn't know what he could say that would make her feel any better, that would take any of the goddamn sting of it away, so he carefully divided the lock of hair into two slender hanks, put one back in his bag, and slid the other toward Winifred, letting his fingers brush hers, ever so quickly.

"Thanks," she muttered, slipping the last of Cora into her own little bag of memories.

Rhett cleared his throat. "So maybe you can all see why we got to stay together and move west. That was the bad news. The good news is that we found a place. A good place. A defensible place. The doc's old farmhouse is—well, it ain't a building I'd want to bed down in. But there's a whole city of pueblos, carved out of rock, and Dan says it's got more than enough room for all of us and anybody else that shows up to fight or hide. It'll be a damn sight more comfortable than the mission's getting, unless you-all like sleeping in the same bunkroom." He glanced at Bill. "I reckon you snore something fierce."

The great shoulders gave a heaving shrug.

"Dan and Sam are on the way with the wagon, but I reckon it'll take 'em another day at least, maybe two. So gather up what you need. Bundle it however you see fit, and roll up a mattress from your bunk. Find the ponies you like. And get ready to move."

"Just like that?" Inés asked.

Rhett gave the tiny nun his full attention, even though all he saw was the white sheet of her veil. "Just like that," he agreed. "And if you decide you need to stay here, that's your business. But I can't protect you if you do. Nobody can. The best chance you've got to stay alive—and maybe do some good—is to stick with this posse and go to a safer place."

"How is this place not safe?" the nun pressed, her voice sharp and snippy and her arms up in frustration.

Rhett looked all around, wishing he was a man of words instead of a man of fists and blades and bullets. Most of the things he felt he didn't know how to say, and the things he did say always seemed like they came out wrong.

"This place is fine. We seen how defensible it is, as long as nobody knows about the giant lizard burrow that opens into the cellar. But what if they do? We're leaving. If you stay here alone, when will you sleep? How are you gonna watch every window and door and secret hidey-hole, all day and night? Will you just live a regular ol' life, knowing something's after me and might come here to find me, and . . . well, it's beginning to look like they're killing everybody I ever met? Cora thought leaving me was the safe thing, and now look what happened to her."

Inés muttered a string of Aztecan under her breath that sounded less than godly. "This place . . . churches are protected! By the gods!"

"Yeah, well, tell that to the monks whose blood painted those walls."

Rhett's exhaustion hit him full force. Explaining the obvious to someone who didn't want to accept it was downright destructive to a man's constitution.

"And now that you all know you're in mortal peril, I'm gonna go find me an empty bunk and sleep for a while. Would somebody see to my unicorn? He's probably found his way to the trough. And make sure my old mule Blue is doing okay. I didn't hear him when I came in."

Rhett's chair scraped back as he stood. He felt dog tired in every bone. But the silence around the table . . . well, it was unnerving.

"You're right," Digby said. "It's downright peculiar, not hearing that ol' bastard hollering his hellos. And he'd holler his hellos at a cactus."

A sick drop hit Rhett's stomach.

"Goddammit," he muttered, turning away from the lumpy and narrow but still horizontal beds and heading for the back door.

The rest of the crew was behind him, his panic rising with every step. He threw open the back door to find horses in all sorts of places they shouldn't be. The pen was just smashed to pieces, and several of the horses—familiar ones—were all clustered together where it had been. But old Blue the mule was nowhere to be seen.

"Did you-all have a stampede you're not telling me about?" he asked, drawing his gun.

"They were fine this morning." Digby's voice was a rasp of fear. "I swear. I emptied out the trough and brought fresh water. Even gave ol' Blue his oats. Everything was fine, Rhett, I swear on my life."

Rhett hopped down onto the dirt, took a few steps, and then was running to where the horses clustered, looking up in confusion.

"Move it, assholes," he hollered, fighting his way to the center of the herd.

There, splayed on the ground, was Blue the one-eyed mule, his belly torn open and empty.

CHAPTER
18

A howl clawed out of Rhett's throat as his hands shoved the flanks of the still-living horses aside. He fell to his knees by Blue's head, the old mule's gone eye pointing skyward. He put a hand on the critter's side and found it still warm. This, this... horror...had happened recently.

"He's still nearby!" Rhett shouted. "Y'all find him!"

"Does the Shadow feel anything?" Winifred asked, her hand on his shoulder.

He shook her off. "No, the goddamn Shadow doesn't goddamn feel anything. If I'd felt something, I would've been out here shooting mule killers full of holes." He looked around frantically. "Nobody heard anything? Saw anything? Heard wild animals about?" He searched for Lizzie and found her, baring his teeth. "Did you get hungry, Lobo?"

The look on her face was too honest and disgusted to be anything but horror. "No! Heavens no! I would not kill a mule! Lobos don't crave animal flesh. And look here." She pointed to the edges of the wound. "These are the marks of a knife, not teeth. A lobo's bite is a jagged, torn thing. But this is clean."

He hated to admit she was right, but she was. It was a clean cut, like somebody had just decided to cut a window in an old mule's stomach for fun. Except...

"But where's all...all his...oh, hellfire. His insides?"

He had to stop and mop off his face. After days in the desert on the run, after all he'd been through, he was surprised he had enough juice left for tears at all. But for old Blue...he would've cried blood.

Back on Pap and Mam's farm, horses and cows had come and gone. Pap won 'em in a game of poker or stole 'em off somebody drunker than him, and it was up to the slave girl, Nettie, to fix what ailed the critters, body and mind, so they could be sold. She'd gentled colts and schooled bastard stallions and fattened up scrawny critters on the cheapest of mash, but old Blue had been the ugliest thing to holler in their sorry old twig pen. Which must've been why he got to stay, and for years he was the only friendly face in a world full of hate. One-eyed, ugly, patchy, bony, swaybacked. Nobody wanted him. Nothing about that mule had ever been beautiful except maybe his kindness...but to Nettie and now Rhett, everything about him had been beautiful. And someone had snuffed out that beauty. Snuffed out everything.

Rhett realized, with dawning horror and rage, that he would never again hear that welcoming bugle that meant he was home.

"There's got to be some clue!" he shouted. He thought about digging around in the empty belly of the mule but couldn't bring himself to do it. So he stood and looked at the ground, but all he found were hoof prints and the familiar lines of his own boots. "Spread out. Look for boot prints. Look for drops of blood fallen off the knife. There's got to be some goddamn sign of what happened here."

His friends looked at him, then at one another, but nobody moved.

Rhett pulled his gun.

"Move, goddammit!"

They fanned out, looking scared and sorry, and that was how he felt, too. Both for what had happened and for any appearance of threatening his friends. His job was to lead these people, not wave guns at them so they'd turn away and not see his tears. He studied the ground, went from horse to horse looking for anything peculiar, but there was nothing to be found. The Shadow felt nothing. Rhett felt everything.

"Come on back," he hollered. "There's just . . . nothing."

They crept back toward him like kicked dogs, and he pulled up his kerch and rubbed his gone eye. Hell, even that reminded him of Blue. They'd been fellows, ever since the Cannibal Owl's minion had shot Rhett in the eye with silver. He went back to what was left of Blue, noting how sad and hollowed out the poor ol' critter was. Truth be told, Rhett had known Blue wouldn't last but a few more winters, even if he was real lucky. But nobody deserved to go out like this—nobody except evil monsters. Blue's gone eye was pointing straight up, an ugly valley of worn skin pulled over the mule's skull. Curious, Rhett lifted the heavy head to look at Blue's remaining eye, and what he found there chilled his heart.

The eye was gone, and set in its orbit was a shiny new quarter.

For several long moments, Rhett squatted there, the coin cold and wet in the palm of his hand.

He knew what it meant.

And it didn't make sense.

It was impossible, in fact.

And it wasn't good.

"What you got there?" Digby asked. "Find something?"

"I did."

"What is it?"

"The worst goddamn thing I can conceive of."

Digby scratched his head. "A quarter? I can conceive of worse things, if I'm honest."

Winifred and Inés joined him now, the others who knew him less well keeping their distance, probably in case he pulled his gun again like a fool. He sighed like his heart was breaking, which it was, and pulled out the leather bag around his neck for the second time that day. He dug around inside it and fetched an identical quarter, albeit one not wet with eyeball gunk and mule blood.

"This is the first quarter I ever earned," Rhett said. "At the Double TK Ranch in Gloomy Bluebird." He didn't even care about keeping his secrets anymore, because clearly, someone else was using his past against him, and he wouldn't give up any more of his power by hiding. "A feller named Monty gave it to me for breaking a horse. He was a top hand. Taught me everything I know."

"What happened to him?" Winifred asked, in that way she had that suggested she already knew and was probably pretty close to the damnable truth.

"We got attacked by a chupacabra," Rhett said, voice ragged. "On our lone while the rest of the ranch was headed out to rustle some of Juan de Blanco's cattle. This young feller turned, and he came after us, and Monty... well, he died in the attack."

"He got bitten?"

Rhett gave Inés a hard look. "No. I was aiming for the chupa, and the shot ripped through him and hit Monty in the head. There. So now you know. I'm a monster. I do bad things. I killed Monty. Closest thing I had to a father, and I killed him."

Winifred shook her head like none of that mattered. "It was an accident, Rhett. Let it go. But he didn't become a chupa, is what you're saying? Because when a chupa bites you…"

Rhett slashed a hand between them. "No. He died. Deader than dead. In my arms as I apologized a hundred times. So whoever left this quarter must know about that. They're trying to scare me. Trying to rile me up." He pulled his kerch back down over his gone eye. "And hell if it ain't working."

He set off walking for the kitchen, but when he got to the door, he stopped.

"Digby, Lizzie, Little Eagle. If you-all wouldn't mind, would you set to rebuilding that fence and rustling up the horses? And then get your shit ready to go, because we got to hurry. As soon as that wagon gets here, we load it and we're off."

No one spoke, but everyone nodded and moved off to tend their business. Digby set to oversee the fence while Little Eagle's men gathered the horses, who were at least done being startled and back to being agitated and saddened by their dead fellow. Inés and Winifred followed Rhett, and he could almost feel them in his wake, having one of those silent conversations women had when they figured they knew better.

"So who could it be that knows about your past and wants to rile you?" Winifred asked.

Rhett breathed out through his nose as he started moving weapons and bags of bullets onto the kitchen table from the various places he'd stashed them.

"Chuck was the feller who turned into a chupa and attacked us. Before he…when he was human, he was snotty and thought his shit didn't stink, so about the same as any green-horn. We got on, though. I would say he was a friend. I thought I killed him, but now that I think about it…" He trailed off as realization dawned.

"Shit. I didn't hit his heart. Didn't turn him to sand. I didn't know, back then. Got a bullet through his throat and figured he was a goner. I had to run before the other fellers from the ranch found us. Found me. But knowing what I know now, I reckon...I reckon that little chupa shit is still alive."

Inés nodded. "So that is one suspect. Do you think this Chuck is clever and angry enough to do this? Could he be El Rey?"

Rhett fought the urge to spit on the floor, knowing how much the nun hated that. "I guess Sandy Claus could be El Rey, for all we know. Chuck wasn't a cunning feller, but I could see why he'd maybe hold a grudge. Inés, do your books say anything about killing chupacabras? Maybe stuff they're scared of?"

Inés stood. "The library always knows. I will go see what I can find."

Winifred stayed, and Rhett could feel her sympathy, and it made him downright itchy. He hated to be the subject of anyone's pity, even if he was still wearing the tear tracks from the death of his oldest friend.

"Dan will know more," she said reassuringly. "And Sam. The Rangers said—"

"Yeah, and the Rangers said vampires and Lobos were all evil, so what the hell do they know? Sam and Lizzie ain't what the Rangers said they'd be. So, excusing the Captain, I don't give a shit about Rangers anymore." He looked her up and down. "Are you ready to go? Gonna drive the wagon and be reasonable?"

The girl snorted and stood, one hand always on her belly. "I have a perfectly good horse, Rhett. And two perfectly good hands that can still shoot perfectly good guns."

"All that racket can't be good for your perfectly good spawn."

She shook her head at him as she sashayed out of the room. "Oh, she won't be perfectly good. And don't worry. Action keeps her lively."

Left alone in the kitchen, he rolled the quarter back and forth on the scarred wood table. Was it possible El Rey was Chuck, infused with evil chupacabra powers and pestering Rhett for leaving him in the desert with a torn throat? Or maybe someone who just knew about those days, who'd talked to Chuck or Poke or maybe even Boss Kimble and heard about the apparently senseless killing? Maybe there really were Wanted posters around the area, condemning a feller named Nat for murdering Monty, and somebody had taken it a bit too serious? Rhett knew well enough that there were plenty of cowpokes at the Double TK who hadn't taken kindly to seeing a mixed-breed boy added on to the crew and praised for his fine hand with a bronco right there at dinner. But what El Rey was doing, assuming all these murders were being committed by him or on his behalf—it went deeper than merely nettling a feller. It was personal.

"I just don't know, goddammit," he said to the quarters. "I just don't know." He wiped the gunk off the new quarter and stuck 'em both back in his bag. Later on, he'd add a little braid from Blue's tail. His bag, he couldn't help noticing, was getting pretty goddamn full of mementos.

And then he dragged himself downstairs into Sam's old hidey-hole and buried his face in the bare, crackling mattress, desperate for a whiff of the absent Sam and the simple feeling of safety.

He didn't find either.

When he woke again, Sam was beside him, doing the vampire's imitation of death. There was a brief feeling of relief, knowing that Sam and Dan had made it back, but it couldn't outweigh all the goddamn tragedy. Rhett had no idea what time it was, whether he'd slept for five hours or five days. He'd lost his pocket watch long ago—the one he'd earned on his first Ranger mission, after killing the siren of Reveille—and although he didn't miss the Rangers, he missed knowing what time it was. He planted a kiss on Sam's cheek, pulled on his boots, and headed for the ladder, hearing all sorts of busy footsteps overhead.

Up top, he found it to be lunchtime, and everybody was doing their part to get ready to eat. Inés and Rhett's mama were dishing up the food, Winifred was sending all the men back outside to wash up because they looked like they'd rolled in manure, and Dan was sitting at the table, poring over one of Inés's big old books.

"Welcome back, Dan."

"Chupacabras," Dan said, all preacher-like, without looking up. "You sure do know how to pick your enemies, Shadow. Even the Rangers hate chupacabras. Wiry, tough to kill, with a mad edge that most other monsters don't have. Something about living in nests together makes them willing to die in a pile instead of focusing on saving their own skins. And they'll eat any meat, which makes them less picky than vampires or Lobos." He looked up to meet Rhett's eye. "And we lost your horse on the trail."

"Goddammit, what?"

Rhett was barely awake, and he was already furious again. "You only had six damn horses to contend with! All you had to do was pony her off the wagon! Ragdoll is a sensible mare. A lead mare. She wouldn't just wander off!"

"You think I don't know that? That's why I brought it up first."

Rhett slammed his ass into a chair and pulled his short hair through his fingers. "Because they told you what happened to Blue, and now you reckon El Rey's got plans for Ragdoll. Goddamn. Goddammit. Goddamn!" He stood and threw the chair across the room, which wasn't very far. It crashed into the wall, but it was a well-built piece of furniture and a thick-built wall, so nothing happened except Rhett made a ruckus that made his mama look up from rolling tamales by a window and give him the stink eye.

"I didn't feel anything, Rhett. Sam didn't smell anything. No monsters, no wobble. She was just…gone."

He looked up at Digby, who was whittling on the bench, trying to act like he wasn't there, or at least like nobody should throw a chair at him or chew him out.

"Digby, are all the other horses here?"

Digby looked up and nodded slowly. "So far as I know. All the ones we done named are here, and the rest of 'em seem the same. Poor critters keep going to the spot where the mule was and sniffing the ground like they can't believe he's gone. Reckon I know how that feels." He cleared his throat and dashed at his eyes. "We drug him off and buried him for you, in case you're worried. Next to Hess. Put rocks overtop to keep the coyotes out. Seemed like the right thing to do. Saved you a bit of his tail." Digby slid a little hank of wiry black hair across the table, tied off with a bit of twine.

Rhett walked over to Digby and put a firm hand on the feller's shoulder. "I won't forget that kindness, Digby. Thank you." He tucked the hair away in his bag, feeling like the damn thing weighed a million pounds, it was so full of death.

As more folks came in from outside, Rhett got all skittish and headed in the opposite direction, hollering, "Save me some supper, you indolents."

Soon he stood alone in the overcast afternoon and stared out at the mission yard, hands on hips, feeling like a patchwork quilt falling apart at the seams. Every time he took care of one thing, something else began to rip away. Kill Trevisan, almost lose Sam—and lose part of Sam. Find his mama and brother, lose Cora and Meimei. Find a new base, lose Blue. Be reunited with Sam, know that Ragdoll was gone, out of his reach. The day seemed to reflect his feelings, half weak sun and half dark, threatening clouds. Rhett could smell the rain coming, could almost feel the earth around him opening up to it like a hungry mouth that ached for kissing. But the ground always knew there would be more rain, and Rhett had no idea if his life would ever have room for more than a solitary second of mercy and rest before something even worse came along.

In that moment, his heart could've broken, to think about the sadness of having a destiny.

Folks thought they wanted one, thought they were heroes meant for greatness. But being a hero with a destiny was shit, and the only way out was death.

"Goddammit," he growled at the clouds.

With a huff of annoyance, he went to the barn for his saddle, finding everything half in disarray and half neatly packed for a voyage. He soon had BB ready to go, his Henry in the holster, and his face set in what felt like a tooth-grinding scowl.

"Where going?" Revenge asked, appearing out of nowhere in that quiet way he had.

"To find my mare," Rhett growled.

"I come."

Rhett was too angry to find words to argue, and he reckoned it was never a bad thing to have help when you were looking for something, so he just nodded and swung into the saddle. There was electricity in the air, and he was about to urge his mount forward when he felt Revenge's hand on his boot.

"What the sweet hell?"

Revenge shook his head like Rhett was a fool and pointed to the sky. "Fly, idjit" was all he said.

And as much as he hated to admit it, Rhett knew his brother was right. Why go out on horseback in the big world when you could take to the air?

"Fine" was all he said.

He was soon out of the saddle and stripping down, daring his brother to say a goddamn thing about what was under his clothes. The boy looked away, feigning disinterest, as he, too, undressed, and then Rhett took a running leap and was pumping his wings into the sky. It was a grand relief, letting human thoughts and feelings drop away. When he became the bird, he could hold on to one thought, generally, and just now, that thought was of a rangy little dust-brown appaloosa mare with a bottlebrush tail. The bird soaring just a little below him squawked and peeled away, headed west, and the bird that was Rhett trained his sharp eye on the ground.

In bird form, he felt the storm building, could feel the air currents twitching in his flight feathers. He had time; he knew that, too. Lightning was coming, but it wasn't here yet. Down below, he scanned the ground for anything out of the ordinary and found nothing. Even with the ugly edges of San Anton on the cusp of his vision, the land showed nothing more than the usual creatures hiding out before the storm. He ranged north a bit, up into the hills, where it got greener. Somewhere in the bird's mind, Rhett focused on the horse...and on what it might mean if a human sort of shape was sighted. That's as far as the thought went, though; the bird had his limits.

And then he saw something.

Several somethings.

Horses.

And when there were horses, there were often men.

The bird spiraled down, king of the currents, to get a closer look.

The horses were traveling in a loose herd, and the bird understood immediately that there were no riders. These horses were wild. But one of them was familiar, and it was enough to tug him down to the ground, where he touched down, lolloped, and stumbled to human feet. He'd landed far away enough to avoid detection, but he could still watch the horses from behind a rock formation.

Naked and more curious than anything else, Rhett watched his mare enter a courtship dance with a big mustang stallion. She'd never shown any interest in any of the stallions they'd kept in the herd, and as lead mare, she'd never allowed any of the horses to mount her, but his ugly little Ragdoll was playing her part with a sturdy, sensible looking paint of fine conformation. Rhett thought to stop her, but then he remembered that she was a wild thing doing what wild things did, and stopping her would be outside of their friendship. It would be a hell of an inconvenience, having her bred and unrideable for a while, but he also liked the thought of his nippy little mare trotting around the pen with a fine and spotty colt behind her, kicking up his heels.

He'd expected to find her gutted and dead or ponied behind a passel of chupacabras, and instead, he found his mare in a private moment of hope, and he couldn't stop himself from smiling. Even when everything was pretty much terrible, there was still something to look forward to on the other side, even if it was just seeing which color this wild mustang stud's baby would be.

The horses did what horses do, several times, and Rhett almost intervened when the stallion bit Ragdoll, hard, on the neck. But if the mare was fine with it, what the hell business was it of Rhett's? After the third mounting, Ragdoll spun around, gave the stallion a hell of a look, and took off at a gallop, her path headed directly back toward the mission.

"I guess she got what she needed," Rhett muttered.

He changed back to the bird, took to the sky, and lazily followed the galloping horse back home. He never did find any sign of what had happened to Blue, nor did he see any people or monsters running away from the mission. When he landed at dusk, naked and weary, Sam was waiting for him on the shadow side of the barn.

CHAPTER
19

I was worried," Sam called before Rhett had even picked up his britches.

Rhett blushed despite knowing Sam had seen everything he had. "My horse was missing. I had to find her."

Sam gave him a moment while he got dressed, but as soon as Rhett's shirt was mostly buttoned, long arms wrapped around him. "I let her back in the pen for you. I'm glad she's okay," Sam whispered in his ear, sending shivers up and down his spine. "I heard about Blue. This is..."

"Not my week," Rhett finished for him, clutching Sam just as tight as Sam was clutching him, like they were drowning. "But at least you're here now, and Ragdoll didn't get hollowed out or bled, and we can get the hell on with things."

When Sam didn't speak for a few minutes, Rhett felt the cruel clutch of panic again. "Or has something else happened? I wasn't gone that long, goddammit! Is it Revenge? Did he not come back?" He finished buttoning his shirt with shaky hands, and Sam caught his fingers and held them tight.

"Revenge is back. Ragdoll's in the pen. Nothing else happened. Everything is fine. Gosh, Rhett. I've never seen you so jumpy." He gently redid all Rhett's cattywampus buttons, and

Rhett stood there and quivered, feeling a little embarrassed but mostly just glad.

" 'Course I'm jumpy. I lost two friends in a couple of days, and we got to admit that whatever El Rey and the damn chupas are doing, the Shadow doesn't know how to fight it."

Sam snorted and cupped his face. "Oh, when the time comes, I'm confident the Shadow will know how to fight it. El Rey might be wily, and his chupacabras might be rowdy, but none of 'em can beat you when it comes down to a fight."

"Lord, I hope you're right."

Together, they went back around the barn, where everything was business. Rhett's posse had learned to operate in darkness. The wagon was backed up and hung with lanterns, and Dan was barking orders at people, careful to make sure that the wagon was packed tight as a turtle's butt around Sam's box. For a moment, Rhett regretted that they'd abandoned Cora's old wagon from the train yard so easily, but then he noticed a smaller wagon being kitted out and realized that of course Inés had one, too. The woman had made supply runs into town before they'd shown up, hadn't she? Everybody was busy carrying things here and there, and Rhett saw Cora's doctoring box stacked up with another tool kit. Digby started pulling out the riding horses with help from Slippery Snake. Everything was under control. He felt like taking charge, but dang if there was anything else that needed doing. So Sam followed him as he followed his nose to the kitchen, where he found a plate covered with a bowl waiting by an empty coffee mug, with a pot perking in the oven's coals.

"You doing all right, Sam?" he asked as he settled down amid the chaos to down the last fine meal he was likely to have for some time. He nodded at the food, in case Sam didn't catch his meaning.

Sam shrugged with the guilty look of a good dog who'd stolen meat from the table. "All right enough. I stopped by the town outside the doc's farm—Rona? Wild little place, almost all outlaws and fugitives. Found a feller beating a dog in a back alley and let him know I didn't think that was the way to go. When I was done, he didn't seem to notice. Got all dreamy and was petting the dog instead. So I reckon I'm good for a few days." His blue eyes went all pleading. "It wasn't...I mean... it was just food, Rhett, I swear. He was ugly as sin and smelled like the inside of a trapper's drawers."

Rhett sighed and brushed Sam's knuckles with a quick finger. "I know. I got to get used to it, and I know that. You did what you had to do. Just keep picking ugly fellers who deserve it, will you? I'm a vain man."

The grin he got in response smacked of Sam's old sunbeam self, and Rhett went back to sucking down Inés's tamales and fatback with gusto.

They were soon on the trail, a long line of horses in the pitch-black night. Rhett and Sam led off on their mounts, and damn if Ragdoll didn't feel like she was proud of herself—prancing, the little vixen, even if nobody could see it. Then came Winifred on Kachina riding beside Rhett's mama, then Revenge and the fellers of Little Eagle's band. Next were the two wagons, driven by Notch and Inés with Sasquatch Bill striding alongside, then their herd of nearly fifty horses now. Dan rode behind the herd as usual, but Digby had gotten attached to the stock and rode with 'em, his two wild steers keeping pace like large and dedicated hounds. Lizzie, strange critter that she was, rode very last on her Medicine Hat horse, several lengths behind Dan. It seemed a peculiar place, but she didn't quite fit in with anybody, and Rhett reckoned that if something terrible came from behind in the dark of night, he'd be glad enough to have a Lobo between it and the horses. And him.

As they rode, following Rhett's gut back to the doc's place, he was on full alert. The night air was thick and cold, the stars and moon entirely blotted out by low, heavy clouds that seemed like they might choose at any second to dump buckets of freezing rain. The sensation of thunder waiting on the edge of the world now felt more like eyes always on him, buzzing like flies. Whatever El Rey's game was, it was clear to Rhett that the asshole had somehow found a way around the Shadow's defenses. He could snatch people and critters and do terrible things, and Rhett's belly didn't even give the smallest flip. It just kept on buzzing, making him feel like he was surrounded, like something was coming but not quite arrived. And it was exhausting. Everything was exhausting. Rhett felt about like old Blue had looked just before he'd died.

Dan rode up every now and then, as he always did, to check in with Rhett and Sam, and for once, Rhett wanted to know the man's thoughts.

"Dan, you told me that your folks used to talk about the Shadow. Is that right?"

Dan's look was flat. "Yes. Before they were massacred. You know that."

"Did they know how it works? The...the...belly-flipping thing?"

Dan's lips twitched as he considered the question but didn't smile. "No. Even you don't know how it works. The legends I was told only said that the Shadow would rise to fight evil. It felt like hope in the darkness. When a mother found an empty cradle or Lobos howled in the hills, we whispered that one day the Shadow would come and make things right."

Rhett swallowed down a ball of shame that felt about like vulture bile. He hadn't made much right, and he knew it. "So how does this El Rey feller know how to best me?"

"He doesn't, fool. He just knows enough to trick you."

"And how the hell would he know that? Only the folks nearest me know how it works. And none of you-all would go telling some random asshole about my weaknesses. And no monster could get close enough to ask."

Now he got the dumb-as-a-possum look he'd been bracing himself for. "El Rey likes killing things, Rhett, which means he probably likes torturing them. He most likely asked Cora and the doc for information on you, and with the right leverage, they gave it. If someone threatened Meimei, you know full well Cora would tell them anything they wanted to know, even if it could be used to hurt you. Caring for someone like that is a weakness."

"And we don't know everyone El Rey has found," Sam broke in. "Only the ones he wanted you to find. Or the ones we found so far."

That was a punch in the gut that Rhett hadn't considered— and a damn dark thought from sweet ol' Sam. Who else knew him and might be tied to a post somewhere, drained of blood and dry as a tumbleweed, just waiting to be discovered?

Hell, there weren't that many people left he cared about in the world, and they were right here with him.

"We got to keep an eye out," Rhett said, voice low. "Who knows if he's waiting to pick folks off? Nobody goes off for a piss alone. Nobody chases a loose horse. If we hear gunfire, we circle up instead of scattering. We got to tell everybody, and soon."

"Let me."

Rhett was surprised to hear Dan volunteer for such an activity.

"Why you?"

"Because my heart's not in it like yours is. It's floating in your eyes like a worm wiggling for fish. You care about everybody here, even the ones you don't like, and seeing you worried will only make the others jumpier. They need to see you strong."

Rubbing a hand over his face, Rhett had no choice but to agree. "Fine, then. Tell 'em what you like. Just make sure we don't lose nobody. Not even a horse. Already lost too many damn beasts this week."

Dan nodded and rode back to tell the rest of the folk, spread out as they were, and Sam rode closer to Rhett, his boot knocking against Rhett's in a companionable sort of way.

"Don't take it so hard, Rhett."

"Take what hard?"

"The fact that everybody knows you got a big ol' heart and care too damn much."

Rhett's teeth ground, his shoulders hunched, and it made complete sense that the dense clouds would choose exactly that moment to start spitting rain. He yanked his hat down and stared straight ahead between Ragdoll's ears, but there wasn't much to see, just darkness that seemed pretty goddamn endless. He'd heard it said once that if you weren't the lead dog, the scenery never changed, but that sounded like the kind of bullshit folks came up with when they'd spent too long staring at ugly wallpaper, trapped in big houses and tiny lives. And when they'd never led an entire crew to their probable death through a goddamn rainstorm in the middle of winter.

"What I'm taking hard is that I keep losing the only folks I can stand in the world and I don't have an enemy to punch in the teeth for it," Rhett muttered, but loud enough to be heard over the rain.

"It ain't easy," Sam agreed, because even as a vampire, Sam was agreeable.

"Sam, tell me a story. About what'll happen after we kill El Rey and his chupas."

Sam sighed and sat back a little in his saddle, staring up at the sky like it was full of sunshine and rainbows instead of clouds and indigo nothing. The rain streaked down his face, but it didn't seem to bother him at all. He wasn't even shivering.

"Well, I reckon we won't lose anybody this time, since we got a hell of a crew and we have our pie plates." He tapped his chest and produced a light clank. "We'll have them pueblos all set up, big enough to house anybody that shows up needing a little space. These folks that find you—we can start a little community there, share what we got, and live peaceably away from the Rangers. We've got a fine herd of horses, and we'll start gathering up some cattle. I know a bit about good breeding, and I reckon I can build up a fine herd, keep some nice bulls for meat and cows for milk and butter. We can start a garden, get some fresh greens. Hell, maybe some strawberries, come summer. I used to love 'em, but now—well. It's fine, though, tending growing things. Winifred can have her pup in the dirt or in that farmhouse, and we can take to the trail again any time we want to do some rustling. Our own little town. What would we call it?"

Rhett let himself get lost in the picture Sam painted. It was always nice weather in that place, the pueblos clean and smoke puffing up cheerfully through the rock. The horses were fat and sassy and the cows produced plenty of milk and meat. Ragdoll's colt was a fine stallion, like his father, the kind of horse that a picky mare would travel a hundred miles to find. Rhett would raise that colt gentle as a puppy, and that shining coat of spots would never be marred by whip nor spur.

"We'd call it Walker, I reckon, after the Captain."

"I could see that. We'd find a blacksmith, have him make

up a brand with a big ol' curly *W* on it. Mark all our cattle, fair and square. And if ol' Juan de Blanco came for 'em in the night, we'd chase him off, guns a-blasting."

Lightning struck up ahead, and the horses danced and balked, breaking the vision as everyone fought to stay in the saddle.

"That was a right pretty story, Sam," Rhett allowed. "I'd wish on every star in the sky to see it come to pass."

"It's funny." The wind snatched Sam's voice, making it seem far away. "When I picture it, it's daylight. Blue skies and sun. But I'll never see that again, will I? I ain't saying I'm ungrateful," he hurried to add, "or that I'd rather see no skies because I was dead in the ground or a pile of sand. Just that it's funny how a feller can imagine something impossible, and when you're dreaming it, you forget that part. That it's not possible."

"I reckon everybody wants what they can't have, Sam," Rhett said. "But what really matters is what you do when you realize you're never gonna get it."

"What are you saying, Rhett?"

The panic of lightning had passed, and their horses went on, companionably walking side by side, but Rhett and Sam were entirely focused on each other. Rhett was saying a million things, but he didn't want to break it down, because that wasn't something he was good at. If he could've rounded up the possibilities and shot 'em like ducks in a barrel, that would've been easier.

"I guess I'm saying you take what you can get, for as long as you can have it, and if you can't see the sun, you goddamn learn to love the moon."

Sam's smile lit up, and Rhett knew he understood. Sam always understood.

He was starting to get a little goofy-eyed, staring into Sam's sweet face like that, noting that even in the dark, rain pouring, soaked to the skin, Sam was perfect. But then his belly twitched.

"What the hell?" he muttered, breaking the connection and focusing his attention on their surroundings.

They weren't far from the mission and hadn't even crossed the first river yet, but something had changed. Those buzzing flies in the mist of the Shadow's world—well, one of 'em had turned into a hornet. It didn't feel like something attacking, didn't feel like the chupacabras had felt, coming up over that ridge. But it felt...

"What's the word for when something's out there, wishing you harm? But it ain't coming for your skin just yet?"

Sam raised an eyebrow. "Hell, Rhett. If it wishes you harm, I just reckon it's evil. And dumb."

"Malevolent," Winifred hollered over the patter of the rain, and Rhett cursed the girl for having a coyote's sharp hearing and teeth to match. He hated that she might've overheard their earlier interlude, but there wasn't a damn thing he could do about it.

"That's what it feels like," he muttered. "Something waiting for us. Up ahead."

"You and me could gallop up together," Sam offered. "Guns out and pie plates on. Clear the path for everybody else."

Rhett shook his head. "Won't help. Whatever it is, it's just gonna keep waiting. And this ain't good weather to gallop up. Guns might not even fire. Goddamn squall."

With each step, Rhett felt like he might crack a tooth, he was grinding his jaw so hard. His body was cold and tense, and it soon took up an ache that made him shiver. Soaked to the bone, half-blind by the dark of the night, and responsible for fifteen lives, a herd of horses, and three dumber-than-usual cows, Rhett felt like he was pinned down, forced into uselessness. Was this how the Captain had felt, always caring for others, as if they were bluebird eggs cupped in a callused hand? Rhett preferred being free, and in another life, he could see himself turning into the bird and flapping away to find a tree with a nice, empty hole in it and think about delicious dead things. Figuring all his gunpowder would be soaked, he pulled out his Bowie knife, checking the hone of the blade and finding it respectable.

"I'm gonna trot back and talk to the other fellers," he told Sam. "You keep leading us in this same direction."

Sam nodded in the competent, manly way that made Rhett feel giddy, although he took pains to hide it. "You got it, boss."

"Don't call me boss, fool."

Sam's grin was teasing with just a hint of fang. "Then what do I call you?"

Rhett thought about it a moment before answering, "Partner," and trotting off before Sam could say anything else on the topic.

When he reached Winifred and his mama, he turned his mare to walk with them.

"You need more big words?" Winifred asked. "I have a plethora."

"Maybe you could find a doctor for that, then," he responded. "What I need is folks with bows and arrows at the ready, or maybe that little rock sling of yours."

Both women straightened up, their smiles disappearing.

"Do you expect trouble?" Winifred asked, and Rhett's mama murmured, "He *is* trouble."

"Not me." Rhett barely managed not to call his mama a fool. "But something's coming. No, not coming. Lying in wait. It's that word you said that starts with *mal*. I reckon the guns are too soaked to be any good, so I figured I'd tell everybody to get ready with their other weapons, just in case."

"Just in case what?"

Rhett rolled his eye at Winifred, although it was too dark to see it well. "In case what usually happens to us happens, and we end up in a dumb fight. The most important thing is that folks stick together. We can't let whoever or whatever it is pick us off or separate us. El Rey and his chupacabra fellers would love to get their damn hands on you. So if there's an ambush, you-all head for the wagon." He held up a hand. "I'm not saying you got to get in it and throw your skirts over your bonnets, shrieking like you saw a mouse in the flour. Just that everybody, man or woman, needs to stay close so we can keep this bastard from getting what he wants."

Rhett's mama drew her knife and gave him a solid sort of look.

"Together," she said.

"Together," he responded. Then he looked to Winifred. "Even the annoying folks."

He rode on, giving the same speech to Digby and Revenge, to Dan and Little Eagle and his men, and lastly, to Lizzie. She didn't seem troubled by the rain, but she didn't seem troubled by much anything. Rhett found her to be a very strange creature, and after his little speech, she just nodded like he'd been remarking on the weather.

"You don't got no questions?" he asked.

She shook her head, sending water flying. "Everything you said makes sense. I don't argue with sense. My best weapon is merely to stop being human. It's a relief."

That caught his attention. "So you're saying you like being a Lobo?"

Her smile was rueful, showing crooked teeth. "When I am a Lobo, I like being a Lobo. I don't worry about people or weather or money or food or the next watering hole. I wholly become the wolf. And there is always food."

"You mean humans."

"There are always humans."

"And you don't feel bad about that?"

She sighed and gazed out into the darkness. "Everyone hurts people. At least when I do it, it's fast and beneficial. I try to stay near those who could use the punishment. Why do you think I am here, in Durango, instead of somewhere civilized? I come from Europa. These people are not my people. I can never go back to them. To my people."

"That's a dastardly damn worldview. Killing folks just because they ain't yours."

She regarded him coolly. "Well, if it will make you feel better, I promise not to kill the folks that are yours, either. You must think of me as a weapon, Rhett. A weapon that works in all weather, day or night, hot or cold. Point me at the enemy and get out of the way. Many men would kill for a tame Lobo."

"Woman, I don't for a second think of you as tame. I ain't that foolish."

Finally, Lizzie laughed. "Then Dan is correct. You are smarter than I had assumed."

If he was honest with himself, Lizzie was getting downright creepy, her grin just a little off, so he tipped his hat in thanks, dumping a gallon of water, and trotted back up to the front of the line, where he ever so slightly adjusted their path. It was funny, how he'd never really had to navigate on his own—he just let the Shadow lead him. Other folks used the stars, the sun, maps, landmarks. Rhett had no idea how Dan got where he was going, and he didn't really care. As for himself, he just went in whatever direction his Shadow sense suggested, and it had always led him right.

Or had it?

He wasn't, after all, where he truly wanted to be.

Not yet.

He had to get through El Rey first.

"Everybody good, Rhett?" Sam asked.

"I don't know about good, but they're ready for whatever's coming." He frowned. "Or they think they are, which is about as much as we can expect."

"But you can't get a sense of it? If it's one feller or a posse? Or a monster?"

Rhett closed his eyes as his hips rolled with Ragdoll's walk, focusing on his belly.

"It's close. It's not moving. It's...hell, Sam. I can't explain it. It's bad, but it ain't coming for us."

"The siren of Reveille wasn't coming for us, either," Sam reminded him. "Just sitting there, a-waiting like a spider in a web."

Not knowing was about driving Rhett mad, but it didn't feel like the siren, either, and he didn't want to argue with Sam or answer any more questions about something that just made him feel angry and confused.

"I don't rightly what it is," was all he said. "But it's damn close."

The sound of rushing water overlay the rain, and Rhett saw the signs of their first river crossing up ahead, thick clusters of stocky trees and brush. The ground, so hard and thirsty, grew just the tiniest bit soft. Rhett didn't relish wading into the ink-black river, had always hated the sensation of a horse swimming the deep part in the middle, being swept just a little downstream as muddy water soaked up his ass crack. He reckoned the horses didn't like it, either, and floating the wagon was always a pain and a worry. At least this river wasn't the widest or the deepest.

"Hellfire," he muttered, kicking Ragdoll into the running water and preparing himself for the worst, which didn't come. The water barely went up to her knees, and the wagons wouldn't even have to float. It was a fine thing that the crossing happened before the rain had really turned into a gullywasher, and an even finer thing that whatever he'd been dreading wasn't a water thing lying in wait. Sam splashed out of the river behind him, and Rhett was about to turn and watch the rest of his folks cross, ready to leap in and save anybody who looked troubled, for all that he couldn't swim. He couldn't drown, either, supposedly, so it wasn't such a threat.

But then he felt a sick tug on his belly, and he urged his horse to press a little farther into the copse beyond the river. He pulled his knife and squinted through the rain, ready for anything.

Or so he thought.

What he found was another body. This one human and not quite dead.

It was someone he'd hoped to never see again.

CHAPTER
20

It was Pap.

The man's body was nailed to the biggest tree around, which wasn't all that big. He wasn't fully drained, like the others had been, but Rhett could tell the feller had taken some damage. Pap was in his fifties, as far as Rhett knew, white as sour milk unless he was drunk or turning red as a beet while hollering at his slave girl for burning the eggs. Just now, Pap was naked as a jaybird, and that was just another reason Rhett didn't want to look at him, his sad old man's belly plopping over his shriveled parts like his body was embarrassed of itself.

"Help!" Pap cried, catching sight of him. It was a wheedly sound cutting through the rain. "Please!"

Please was a word Pap had never used with Nettie Lonesome, and for just one moment, Rhett let that soak in: The white feller who had used him as a slave was now begging him for help. But the moment didn't last long, because even if Rhett hated Pap, Rhett couldn't leave him here and keep walking.

He got off his horse, handed Sam the reins, and took a step forward.

"What is this, Rhett?" Sam asked.

But Rhett just held up a hand. This moment? Was between him and Pap.

"Who did this to you?" he asked the caterwauling fool.

Pap's eyes ran a familiar, crafty tally as he took in the cowpoke approaching him. Rhett could imagine the thoughts puffing past: a colored boy, but his clothes were fine, his saddle had silver conchos, and he was armed to the teeth on a fit horse, plus he was the only salvation to be had in the empty nothing of Durango.

"Oh, please, sir. Please help me down. I need a doctor. I feel faint. You got to see that I need help!" Pap whined.

Rhett spit on the ground.

"Oh, I can see it. Now, again, tell me: Who did this to you?"

Pap wriggled and moaned and wept, and Sam dismounted and sidled up close. "Rhett, you got to do the merciful thing. Let him answer once he's been cut down. The poor man is suffering."

Rhett turned to Sam, gave him a meaningful look, and said in a voice he'd never used before with Sam, a hard and implacable voice, "Me and this man got a history, and he can have his mercy when I have my answers."

Sam looked like—well, like Rhett had struck him right across the face, but he backed off.

All this time, Pap watched them, but as soon as Rhett had turned back to him, he started blubbering again. "Oh, please, sir, your friend is right, I been used so bad. Lord, it hurts! Take me down, please!"

Rhett shook his head once and stepped close—close enough to touch, if Pap's hands hadn't been nailed to the tree overhead, just like the doc's had been.

"Do you know who I am?" he asked.

Pap looked him up and down again, still crafty but now also distrusting and suspicious. Which was understandable, as anyone Pap might recognize would also know what a piece of shit Pap was.

"No, sir, I don't believe I do, but you strike me as a gentleman." He made his bloodshot eyes all wobbly as a soft-boiled egg, and Rhett fought the urge to spit again.

"Well, how about this. You tell me who did this to you, and I'll take you down and tell you who I am."

Pap swallowed hard, and Rhett couldn't believe he could look shifty while half-dead and nailed to a tree, but the bastard managed it.

"I don't know," he said, following it up more quickly with "and that's the truth! They wore masks. A bunch of fellers, with one in charge and barking orders. It was all in Aztecan. I don't know what they said. One of the fellers cut open my neck and put something in there, something like a worm, and they took a big jar of my blood, and oh sir, please take me down. I'm dizzy and sick, and I need a sawbones so bad, and I got to get home to my poor beloved wife!"

"What were the masks like?"

That stopped Pap's stream of mouth diarrhea. "What?"

"The masks. What did they look like?"

Pap's head wagged. "It was the middle of the night. They were wearing maybe dark sheets? Some of 'em looked like skeletons. Dragged me off the porch rocker some time after midnight, tied me up, and tossed me over a horse. Left my poor wife all alone as she slept. The Rangers need to know! And the sheriff! Sir, please! Just…you got to get me down. I'm dying, sure enough."

"Rhett, take him down," Sam said, and this was a new voice for him, too. Commanding and not to be argued with.

Rhett narrowed his eyes. "I'll do it in my own time. But you got to believe me: Whatever he suffers just now, he deserves it and more."

But he couldn't stand the way Sam was looking at him, and the rest of the company was starting to gather around curiously after crossing the river, so Rhett stepped forward and inspected the nails holding Pap to the tree.

"Somebody get me a claw hammer from the tool kit in the wagon." He looked at Pap's hateful face. "Unless you want me to just yank you off the nails?"

"No! Please! Mercy! I beg you!" Pap started snuffling all over himself, and Rhett smelled urine, a sharp stench he knew well from a life lived at this man's beck and call.

It was Digby who finally brought the hammer, and Rhett was glad the women stayed back, away from this new danger. He didn't feel any other malevolent things nearby, though— just Pap. That's what he was meant to see. Pap had been left here for him, a new kind of torture.

"You want me to hold him, Rhett?" Digby asked.

"He don't deserve it, but if that'll help you sleep at night, you go ahead."

Rhett pried out the nail in Pap's hands first, and Digby barely had time to catch the naked feller and lower him to the ground. Wailing and blubbering, the old man writhed in the mud, trying to find some way to be that wasn't a world of hurt with his feet still pierced. After taking his sweet time, Rhett also pulled out the foot nail, and Pap finally splayed out on his back. Staring down at his former so-called father from overhead, looming over his first enemy, blood-slick hammer in hand, Rhett knew full well that if it had been only him and Pap here, alone, in the desert, in the dark, that the hammer would've come crashing down again and again, mashing what

Pap considered a brain into a bloody pulp. But they weren't alone. There were people here. Rhett's people. And even if they tried to understand the depths of his bitterness, they would certainly not accept that kind of justice.

"What'd they do with the blood they took?" Rhett asked.

"Jesus wept, Rhett. Have some compassion." Sam threw him the look one gives a tantrumming child and knelt, offering his canteen to Pap and helping the old man drink with shaking hands.

"Do you—would you have any whiskey?" Pap asked. "To fortify the blood. Medicinal-like. It's been a hell of a few nights, I tell you what."

"Fucking pathetic," Rhett muttered.

"He's had a shock," Sam countered. "I seen you take a shot when you're suffering. Why would you deny him that? What the hell has this man done to you?"

Rhett tossed the hammer away so he'd stop holding it like a weapon.

"Let me just fill you all in at once, then, but don't you dare give this piece of shit a single drop of liquor. This is Pap. A long time ago, he found a little brown baby out in the middle of nowhere, and instead of looking for her family, he took her in and raised her nothing like a daughter." Rhett's mama hissed, and Revenge said something low and deadly like a promise. But Rhett wasn't done.

"He named her Nettie Lonesome, and he taught her with whips and slaps and boots to the ribs how to do all his work. She cooked, cleaned, begged around town for him. Mended his fences. Broke the nags he won at cards so he could sell 'em. Dodged the empty bottles of rotgut he threw at her as he called her every bad thing you can think of. Tried to touch her when she was a-bathing, a couple times, when he figured she was old enough to use in a new way, but she took precautions after that. And then Nettie ran away and became Rhett Walker, and Rhett Walker doesn't dole out mercy." He stopped to spit in the man's tear-streaked face. "Not to his kind of monster."

Finder stepped in and spit, too, and Revenge held up his knife in a way that suggested that if Rhett took the first stab, he'd be glad to finish things off. Then they both walked off into the darkness.

Pap pretended they didn't exist as he wiped the spit off his face like it was just rain and squinted, and the look in his eyes was a straight-up lie. "Nettie, girl? My beloved Nettie? Is that you? Why, I have prayed every day for your safe return to our loving embrace. Me and Mam missed you so much—"

Rhett drew his knife and crouched, silencing the man with a blade pressed to red lips.

"Don't put my name in that lying mouth," he said, low and deadly. "Or I'll close it for you."

The night went quiet, nothing but the soft patter of rain and the feel of Rhett's blood thrumming in his temples. Was there anything he'd ever wanted in life as much as he wanted to kill this man and know that he was officially and forever gone?

Yes.

Yes, goddammit.

Rhett wanted Sam to stop looking at him like that, like Rhett was the villain.

"Give him some food," Rhett said. "Not jerky. Something softer. The asshole has bad teeth, what few teeth he has left. And anybody found giving him liquor will answer to me. Can you walk?"

Pap looked up at him, his face a mess of guilt and worry and hatred. It was pleasant, at least, to be the feller on his feet instead of the one on his ass and hurting.

"They took half my blood, girl. Of course I can't walk."

Rhett backhanded him. He couldn't help it.

"I'm no girl, and you'll want to watch your goddamn tongue." He paced for a moment. "Feed him. I got to . . . I got to think, goddammit! Where's Dan?"

He headed back toward the river and found Dan with Little Eagle and his men, all of them working on getting the horse herd and steers across the river. Some of the critters were acting like they'd never seen water before, shying and bucking like fools. All the men could do was rope them, one by one, and lead them to where their friends hollered for them on the other shore. Rhett splashed across and tossed his rope over a mare's neck, glad for some reasonable work to throw himself into, bodily.

"Dan, I got to talk to you!" he shouted into the storm, which was wilder out from under the trees.

"What did I do now?"

"Nothing. I got a . . . a problem. The thing we were headed toward—the bad thing. Turns out it's the asshole who raised me. Half-drained, nailed up, still alive, and still an asshole. I want to kill him, but Sam just sees a sad old man who's half-dead and needs a doctor."

Dan snorted as he released a horse on the other side of the river. "And you just see the asshole."

"I just see what's always been there. He ain't changed."

"But you have, Rhett. You have changed."

"Hell yes, I have. And the new me don't take kindly to being lied to and called a girl. The new me has folks to save and work to do, and I can't do that if I'm having to look at his sorry face every day. Why the hell would El Rey do this?"

Rhett released the little mare and turned back, his toes

almost in the water. Dan grabbed him by the shoulders, claiming his full attention. For once, Rhett allowed it.

"El Rey is doing this to mess with you. Look how it tears you apart. You're angry, bitter, sad, cruel, fighting with the person you love best—he did this to you on purpose. If you follow your instincts and hurt this man, your people will learn to distrust you, will begin to see you as the monster. But if you do the right thing and help this creature who has hurt you, you are the only one who suffers." Dan snorted and shook his head in a sad chuckle. "Well, and your mama and brother, with you. This El Rey is a genius, Rhett. He knows how to get to you. He could send dozens, hundreds of armed men on horseback after you, but nothing would cause you as much pain as one sad old man nailed to a tree."

Rhett chewed his lip. "What you say may be true enough, but it don't tell me what to do."

Dan grunted and waded into the river to fetch another dumb horse. "You know what you have to do. You always know. You just wanted somebody else to tell you not to do the bad, easy thing."

It wasn't a long distance back to where the others waited, but to Rhett, it felt like he was walking across the entire dang Republic, dragging his conscience behind him like a sack of lead. He found Sam and Digby helping Pap sit up, wrapped in a horse blanket, as Winifred and Inés fussed over the old man's nail wounds. Because for all that Pap was a monster, he wasn't the sort who healed quickly. He was the sort who festered, whose body's own natural instincts were rejection and putrefaction. Sam had the canteen in hand, chatting, but while Rhett watched, Digby stood and stormed away.

"All right, Digby?" Rhett asked.

"I begin to see what's got you set against him," Digby muttered. "Feller doesn't think too highly of my ancestry. Didn't want me to touch him, like he figures black skin is catching. Can't even read, can he?"

"No, he cannot."

"I can read." Digby spit. "But some folks just enjoy being ignorant, don't they? Wallowing in shit, telling you they smell like roses."

Rhett nodded. "Well, get ready to keep shoveling it. We got to get him to a town. I won't carry him farther than that. But we can't leave him out here."

Digby looked around the little valley. "That's a shame. It'd be a right nice place, otherwise. Reckon I'll stay with the horses."

Rhett resisted the instinct to apologize for Pap, as if the old asshole was his responsibility, his fault. Digby tipped his hat and headed on, and Rhett girded his loins against the coming unpleasantry. His gorge rose as he got close and heard Pap talking to Sam like they were equals and on the same side, which they weren't in any way.

"Sam here tells me you got plenty of horses and goods," Pap said, doing his best to give Rhett a smile and mostly failing. "That you're rich."

Rhett gave Sam a cool look. "I'm not rich, no. My friends and I have plans, but they're none of your goddamn business."

Pap's lips curled into that cruel, disbelieving grin of his, the one that said Nettie had burned the eggs on purpose or failed by not begging enough money or cornmeal off folks in town and was somehow hiding riches under her ragged dress. "Well as your father who's kept you and fed you all these years, I'd say you owe me."

Pap was still on the ground, and Rhett was still standing

over him, and Rhett slowly drew one of his pistols and pointed it right at Pap's forehead.

"Forgive me if I don't see things your way. I don't owe you a goddamn thing, but if you keep insisting, I know exactly where to put a silver bullet, and you can keep the change."

That was the wrong thing to say to this particular sort of man, as Pap's eyes lit up. "You got silver? Where?"

Rhett cussed himself, eyes closed, before shoving his gun back in his holster.

"Enough resting," he hollered, loud enough for everyone to hear over the rain. "Let's get back on the trail and make good time while the night is quiet. Eat something, if you must, and get ready to keep on."

It was pleasing, how no one talked back regarding this pronouncement, but instead how they fussed with packs and pulled out jerky and went to refill canteens at the river.

"Where do you want him?" Sam asked, inclining his head toward Pap.

"In a hole in the ground," Rhett snapped.

Sam's brow furrowed down like a confused puppy. "I'm trying to help you, Rhett. Trying to help you take care of this burden. Why won't you let me?"

Rhett sighed and tried to unclench his fists. "He'll need to ride on the wagon box, I reckon. He's lost too much blood to sit a horse, and he's got a terrible seat, anyway. Horses just hate him. What a surprise."

"Why, Nettie, how can you tell such tales? Who was it that taught you how to ride?"

Rhett crouched and looked the old man right in the eye. "My mama, before I got stolen away. Now, if you know what's good for you and don't want to taste my knuckles against your teeth, don't speak to me again."

He stood and walked off to stand among the trees, glad that Pap didn't try any of his weasely nonsense after that. Sam spoke to him in a murmur, knowing Rhett was beyond hearing any kindness given to the man. Out of the corner of his eye, Rhett saw Sam help Pap stand and then guide the old man to the wagon, where he half lifted him up into the wagon box.

"Gonna smell like skunk in there now," Rhett muttered.

He focused on the horse herd and checking Ragdoll's damp girth before swinging up in the saddle and counting out his people. It was something he'd started doing, every so often, to soothe himself. When everyone was in their place, doing the right thing, he felt much better about the world. If only he hadn't had Pap to contend with—and the ongoing threat of El Rey—he would've been relatively content.

Back on the trail, Sam rode by his side, up front, silent. Rhett hated it—the feeling that Sam didn't approve of something about him, especially something that went back so old and so deep. Rhett could change a shirt or cut his hair to suit Sam, but he couldn't go in and cut out the festering wound Pap had left in his soul, nor the bitterness that seeped out of it. That wound would never heal, most like.

But didn't most folks have some sort of wound like that, the chancre they'd grown around, a thing that had shaped them? Lord knew Dan had a chip on his shoulder about the white men and what they'd done to his people, and Winifred had all sorts of chips about all sorts of things. But what did Sam have? What bruise did he carry with him? As far as Rhett knew, outside of the usual tragedies of lost friends and the loneliness of being different, Sam had never suffered the way he had. Maybe that was what made Sam seem so sunny: He hadn't been shaped by tragedy.

"You think me unkind," Rhett finally said, unable to mosey along in silence any longer.

"Only to him," Sam admitted.

"He used me as a slave."

"I ain't arguing that."

"Then what, Sam? You think that's something a person can forgive? Twelve years of cruelty? Of being starved and beaten and hated? You think I can look at him for one second without hating us both?"

Sam looked about like he'd been slapped. "Why would you hate yourself, Rhett?"

"Because I let it happen!" It came out all ragged, and Rhett felt about like he had been running for miles. "Because I took it. Everything he said to me, I soaked it up like thirsty earth. He's why I hate myself, Sam. Why I think I'm no good. I try not to let it in, but it's always there, stuck down in the bedrock of me like a railroad spike. He told me I was stupid, too brown, ugly, useless, scrawny, slow, and because nobody told me different, I believed it. And now I hate myself for letting him teach me how to hate myself, and it's all a big, ugly circle, and I just wish he was dead so I could figure out how to live on the other side of it."

Grateful that the darkness hid his tears, Rhett still turned away. Having Pap nearby brought his feelings up near the surface, and he resented the hell out of it. But Sam had a right to know—the good and the bad.

"I can't live like that," he muttered, once he had control of his voice again. "I try to be good, but I ain't that good, and I don't think I'd want to be."

"He's just a sad old man. We'll be rid of him soon. He's not worth killing."

283

"That don't mean he's got a right to inflict himself on my life. I'm not gonna kill him, Sam, but I'm not gonna give him my buffalo robe and favorite horse, neither. We're dropping him off at the next nearest town, and that's the end of it."

A few steps more, and Rhett felt a seeping sickness in his chest. Was this how it would all end, with Sam? After everything they'd been through, would it come down to Sam's big heart and an old, hateful white man who only showed his true face to powerless folks? Because Rhett reckoned he could take a lot of abuse, but he wouldn't take that. A man had to draw a line in the sand, and that was Rhett's line.

"Well, Rhett, I guess...I guess that's fair."

"No, you don't."

"I was raised to help folks. And then the Rangers taught me that my job was to help folks. And I reckon that even if we leave him in town, he'll need money and a horse."

"He'll just buy whiskey and gamble the horse away, Sam. A cow don't change its spots."

"But if we can help—"

"We're helping. Didn't kill him. Didn't leave him there. Every feller's got to make his own way. When I left Pap's place—when I ran away—I had nothing. It was good for me. Maybe it'll be good for him, too."

"I reckon you're right, then."

The horses walked on, and Rhett took care to keep his back straight, his chin up. Inside, he felt like he was all hunched up, sorrowful as an old turtle, but he wouldn't let that show. Not where Pap might see.

"So where are we headed? Because I reckon we're a bit off course."

At that, Rhett glanced over at Sam, offered a small smile. "Wherever the Shadow leads. It's telling me to go this way, which is still mostly west toward the doc's house, which is the way I wanted to go, anyway." He closed his eyes for a moment and listened to what the Shadow offered. "Everything's still as buzzy as a thundercloud, coming in slow and black, but there's something...something building. This way."

"Before we get to the doc's place?"

Rhett shook his head. "I don't rightly."

"Do you think we'll hit a town soon?"

Rhett's smile disappeared. "Hope so."

Sam sighed, and a sorrowful sound it was. "There's just so much we don't know."

"But there's plenty we do know." Rhett scooched his horse over, knocked his boot against Sam's. "We got everything we need right here. We just got to get through one more adventure."

"One more adventure. You keep saying that."

"What else could I say?"

"You could say it and mean it, Rhett. One more, and then you stop fighting and settle down."

Rhett looked to the west, toward the doc's house, toward the tug in his belly.

"One more fight, then, Sam. After that, we'll settle down. Raiding the reasonable chupas out west like regular ol' cowpokes."

Another sigh. "I hope so, Rhett. For a young man and a monster, I'm tired to my very bones."

"Me, too, Sam. Lord, me, too."

They rode on, and it was right peaceful. The rain fell off, and the clouds revealed a nice bit of starlight, for all that they were freezing cold and squelched in their saddles. Rhett ate some jerky and drank his water and almost managed to forget that Pap was riding along with them, asleep on the wagon box, as far away from Notch as he could get. As dawn approached and Sam yawned, Rhett grimly realized that a sleeping, vulnerable Sam was going to be just a few feet away from the lurking evil that was Pap, and he was supremely glad that Sam had installed locks inside his sleeping box. He had half a mind to sit on the dang thing himself all day, guns drawn, just in case Pap had any ideas about hurting Sam.

But then he realized: Pap didn't know Sam was a vampire. Or that Rhett was a shapeshifter. Until a human had killed a monster, they didn't even know monsters existed. To Pap, Sam was just another bright young white feller who might be separated from his coins if he felt friendly enough or didn't have a good poker face. Rhett exhaled, grateful for one small mercy.

He didn't have long to relax, though. The bottom dropped out of his belly just before dawn, and he felt the next great leap of fear and dread that told him something horrible was waiting somewhere up ahead. Without meaning to, he gasped.

"What is it, Rhett?"

Sam had purple bags under his bright blue eyes and looked pale as a ghost, and Rhett didn't want to trouble him too much.

"Nothing, Sam. You go on to bed." He nudged his horse over and leaned in for a quick peck on Sam's cheek. The smile felt counterfeit on his lips, but he did his best.

Sam's sleepy smile sent Rhett's heart all aflutter, despite the worry. "I reckon I don't have much of a choice." Kicking his horse up ahead, Sam signaled Notch to stop the wagon, tied up his pony to the side, and hopped in the back. Pap being Pap, he slept through the whole thing.

Once they were moving again, Rhett followed that old familiar tug in his belly. Not like something was coming; again, more like something was waiting. It was close now. Cussing to himself, he sent Digby up front to lead the group.

"I got to scout a bit up ahead," he said. "You keep on going this direction, due west."

"But what about you, boss?" Digby asked. "Shouldn't you stay with us, send your brother out instead?"

"No," Rhett barked, a little too sharply. Then, softer, "He's got good eyes and ears, but he doesn't have what the Shadow has. Either I'll come back, or you'll come find me when you get there. I'm going the same way you are, just faster."

"Is there something wrong?"

Rhett considered the question and offered the truth. "I don't know yet, but I'm bound to find out."

He kicked his mare to a gallop and took off across the cold red earth. Something was calling him forward, and he didn't want to go, but he had to. It wouldn't wait. There was urgency to it, a tug that wouldn't be denied. Deep down, he knew: El Rey had left him another present.

It wasn't long before he found what he was looking for. Up on a ridge, silhouetted against the dark sky and kissed by the rising sun's pink glow, was a mound of earth. And out of that mound burst a rough-made cross, just two sticks roped loosely together. Up closer, Rhett found something even more troubling: the tube-like shaft of a willow catkin, poking up from the pile of dirt. When he put his finger to the tip, he felt warm, wet breath.

Without waiting for his friends to arrive, he started digging with his bare hands.

CHAPTER
21

The mounded soil was easy enough to move, for all that the rain had flattened it down. The grave was recently dug, Rhett reckoned. Hours old at most. Fat stones tumbled away as he shoveled aside loose pebbles and sand. His fingertips soon went ragged, but he knew well enough how quickly they would heal.

"If you're gonna leave me fresh graves, you might as well leave a shovel behind," Rhett grumbled to himself, trying to slow the frantic beating of his heart. He couldn't help running through the list in his head of people he had left in the world who weren't dead or sand, but he couldn't come up with anybody El Rey might know about who Rhett wanted alive. He was losing folks, sure enough, one by one.

Finally he'd gotten most of the mound scraped off, and then he was burrowing into the ground like a rabbit, clawing the sandy red earth away. About that time, Digby showed up, walking quiet as a cat and standing overhead for a few moments before quietly murmuring, "Let me get you a shovel."

He went to touch the catkin, but Rhett hissed, "Leave it. Somebody's down there."

"Down in . . . the grave?"

Rhett shot him a look. "Where the hell else, Digby?"

Shaking his head, Digby walked off, muttering, "This is the strangest damn crew I've ever met, and that is saying quite a lot."

When he returned, Digby had a shovel, and Rhett snatched it from him.

"I was gonna help. Figured you could use a few moments of rest."

"Whoever's down there was put there for me, so I reckon I'll be the one to find 'em," Rhett snapped. It was well past time for him to go to sleep, he knew, and he was being needlessly rude. He blew out a breath. "I'm much obliged, Digby, and my apologies for being short. You want to be useful, how 'bout you help the other folks set up a camp here. It's a reasonable enough spot, and I reckon we're beat."

Digby looked around doubtfully. "As you say, boss."

"Well, shit, Digby, if you don't like it, you can go on and pick somewhere else, and when I'm done building sandcastles, I'll come find you."

Digby paused a moment, thinking, as Rhett began to shovel dirt out of the hole at a much more respectable rate than he'd done with only his bare hands.

"I reckon we'll move up a little to the next creek, then. It ain't far. You just holler if you need..." Digby looked down into the open grave. "Anything."

Alone again, Rhett really put his back into the work, always being careful of that little catkin tube that was providing some-body with the air that was the only thing standing between them and death alone in the dark. He couldn't help thinking about the first real grave he'd ever dug, when he'd shot the witch Prospera, thinking she was a monster who'd recognize a stern warning, and had instead killed the frail old woman. Digging graves wasn't a big part of killing monsters or being a

Ranger, but the fact remained that graves had a way of making a feller contemplate life, and Rhett in that moment could only think of his life as a series of deaths, those he'd caused by accident or very much on purpose.

And he wanted nothing more to do with death.

Finally, his shovel scraped on wood, and he stepped back and looked around to see who might be nearby. The answer was: nobody. Digby had taken the whole crew ahead, as he'd said he would, and although Rhett could hear the horses whinnying and the two little steers lowing somewhere not too far off, he couldn't see anybody. Fair enough. He'd rather find out who was in the grave by his lonesome.

It took a bit of time, getting all the dirt off the pine box while keeping that catkin in place. It wasn't a deep grave, but it was deep enough, and Rhett wished to hell he knew who'd gone to the trouble of digging it and why. He reckoned it was done on behalf of El Rey, but he also figured the feller wasn't doing his own dirty work. If El Rey had been nearby, close enough to leave Pap behind, Rhett surely would've felt it—the Shadow would've felt it. That had to be what the clever bastard was doing—sending his lessers to do his dirty work so the Shadow wouldn't go on alert to the danger nearby. El Rey himself was staying annoyingly out of reach. Out of range.

Finally, Rhett had most of the coffin box free of dirt and stuck the shovel's blade in to pry off the top. It was nailed on good and tight, but he didn't have the time or care to go fetch the claw hammer from the wagon. Whoever was in the coffin had been in there for a while, and who knew how bad off they might be? The catkin was fed through a small hole in the top boards, but Rhett couldn't see anything within besides darkness.

"You okay?" he hollered.

The only answer was a soft and ragged thumping and something like a muffled *Mmph!*

It took a lot of wiggling and ramming, but he finally got some of the nails pried up, and he grabbed the top of the coffin with two hands and yanked with all his strength. Nails squealed and wood splintered as the top board went flying, taking the catkin tube with it, and what Rhett saw inside didn't make him feel a lick better.

Whoever it was, they were all wound up in a shroud. And he'd taken away their breathing tube.

"I'm getting you out, you hear me?" he hollered. "You just hold on!"

With gentle, bleeding hands, he reached in to grab the wrapped figure. The moment he touched it, it began to buck and wriggle as if trying to get away. Well, hell, if somebody had wound him up and put him in a coffin with nothing but a bitty breathing tube, he'd be a bit jumpy, too. The tube had been inserted between bits of the white fabric, so Rhett laid the person on the ground and went for the face wrappings, trying to make sure whoever it was could breathe.

The first thing he saw were chapped pink lips, and they said, "Oh, thank the Lord."

And then he knew who it was and had to stop himself from tossing the figure back into the box and shoveling dirt right back on top. The shovel felt sharp and hard in his hands; one good thwack, and those pink lips wouldn't need the catkin tube to breathe anymore.

"I was too late," he could hear himself saying to Digby and Dan. "Been buried too long."

But when he considered what it would mean to lie to Sam's face, and whether he was even capable of doing it...well, he just took the shovel and walked toward camp, leaving the bundle there to caterwaul. It wasn't the longest of walks, and Rhett's head was still hot and his eyes pricking with tears when he got there. He tied Ragdoll up next to Sam's blue roan at the wagon and went over to the fire.

"Well, who was it?" Digby asked, and Rhett had to grit his teeth to hold in his cruel remarks.

He tossed the shovel down and pointed at Pap, who was warming his ruined hands over the flames, wearing clean clothes and wrapped in a nicer horse blanket and holding a canteen like he was some kind of precious invalid.

"Ask him. It's his goddamn wife."

Pap's face went through confusion to hope with a quick slide of slyness in between. "It's my Millie? My sweet girl? But I thought she was safe back home. I thought—"

Rhett stopped where he was and pointed his gun at the old man. "Save your goddamn lies. If you want her, you'd best go help her out of her shroud. Her mouth's out, so she can breathe, and I reckon she can lie as well as you."

"You just left her there?" Pap asked, the old anger flashing in his eyes.

"She ain't mine to worry over."

"Shame on you. That woman raised you!"

The gun pressed against Pap's cheek, the cold sun reflected in the barrel. "That's not the word for what you two did, and I'll thank you to stop trying to play on my friends or my heart with your lies. It won't work. I got a long memory for trouble." He turned to Digby. "Anybody kill anything worth eating? I swear I could eat a horse."

Digby's disgusted glare suggested he'd had enough of Pap's company himself. "Yeah. Little Eagle's boys had some good hunting. They're off butchering everything just now. Although I reckon there's still some things as could still use butchering."

At least Digby was on his side, then. Well, and the feller had been in manacles of his own before, hadn't he? Born into servitude, escaped, and then snatched right back up and delivered to Trevisan. Rhett glanced around and noticed that his mama and Winifred had their own fire, some way off, and he didn't blame them a bit for keeping their distance.

Since they were settling in for the day, he went over to Ragdoll to unsaddle her and hobble her for grazing. He took care of Sam's horse, too, and the routine actions brought him the tiniest sliver of peace. Looking up at the high sun and the puffs of his own white breath against the deep blue sky, he was grateful, at least, that it was winter. Sleeping under the summer sun would've left them sweating buckets, and the creeks would've been dry, making it harder on the horses. They were all soaked, but the horses didn't mind that. At least Sam was safe where he was. It wasn't easy to maneuver through the wagon's load of goods, but Rhett snaked a hand in under the canvas and patted Sam's box.

"Wish you were here," he whispered. "I could use a kind word, just now."

There was no answer, of course. He wandered over to where Little Eagle, Slippery Snake, and Revenge were cleaning game while their compatriots cut meat into strips to dry or tossed fatty bits into the stew pot they used while traveling.

"Good hunting?" Rhett asked.

Revenge looked up and grunted. "Always good hunt. Why you don't hunt?"

"I was digging up assholes in coffins," Rhett explained.

Confusion colored his brother's face. "How can dig asshole?" he asked.

Little Eagle chuckled and rolled his eyes at the boy. "No, that asshole dug up a coffin," he said, pointing at Rhett and miming the use of a shovel.

At that, Revenge looked comically startled. "Who dead?"

"I don't have time for this," Rhett grumbled as Little Eagle's men laughed.

He next visited Winifred and Finder, who were sifting through their foraging baskets by the fire, picking out herbs and green things to go in the stew.

"You two doing all right?" he asked, preparing himself for more trouble.

"We're fine," Winifred said, slicing a potato into the pot. "Did I hear you were digging up a grave?"

"Little gift from El Rey." He inspected the blisters already healing on his palms. "It's Mam. The lady who raised me, if you can call it that. Pap's woman. I didn't unwrap her all the way, but I reckon it's the same old story. Half-drained of blood and itching to piss me off."

"What is he doing?" Winifred asked. "This El Rey. It makes no sense."

"I know that."

"He keeps leaving things for you."

"I know that, too."

"The doc and Cora and Meimei dead, and Pap and Mam alive…"

"Don't you see, woman?" he hollered. "He's poking the damn bear. Stoking my fire. Doing whatever he can to get under my skin. The bastard's playing with me!"

Winifred sucked her teeth. "Almost like chess but with very real pawns."

"It ain't chess. I don't got pieces of my own to play."

Neither of them added that that was because most of Rhett's pawns were already dead somehow, nor that every time someone had attempted to teach Rhett how to play chess, he'd gotten pissed off and flipped the board. They were facing El Rey, but they didn't have the Rangers, didn't have the dragon, didn't have the doctor. For all the folks who'd been pulled toward Rhett out in the middle of the prairie, none of them were particularly powerful. Not deadweight, certainly... but not dragons.

"It ain't fair," he muttered.

"Nothing is." This from his mama, who would know.

"So what do I do?" he asked, almost pleading and past caring.

His mama looked him right in the eye, her backbone as straight as an arrow. "Keep fighting until you die," she said.

"Aw, hell. That ain't very chipper. I was hoping for something... hopeful."

"Look around." Winifred shrugged. "This is all the hope we have. You, and us. That's been enough before now. Figure out how to make it enough still."

But it wasn't enough for Rhett anymore. He was tired, body and soul. And the farther west they went, the closer they were to El Rey's territory, the less he felt like he was going to be enough to stop the monster.

"Oh, goddammit," he muttered.

"Come," his mother said, and although he normally would've grumbled an excuse and wandered away to do something manly, he was just tired enough and beat enough to fall to sitting by her side. She pulled him down to her lap, and oddly, he let her, and she knocked off his bedraggled hat and ran strong fingers over his dusty hair in a way that ran shivers up his spine.

The song she sang then was the one he remembered from when he was little, before Pap and Mam, the one that had taught him how to change. The one that said he was perfect, just as he was: a comforting thought. As his eyelid blinked shut, she stroked his cheek.

"Don't worry," she murmured as he fought against sleep. "Bad people can't hurt you. I am here, this time."

And although Rhett knew he could kill Pap and Mam with any weapon in the world, his mother's words comforted him more than his own lethality. She would protect him with her life, fragile and human as she was. Rhett Hennessy, born Fierce Rabbit, fell asleep in his mother's arms, and for a brief but beautiful moment, found some peace.

When he woke up, he was alone and cold under a horse blanket, the smaller fire gone out and the afternoon settling into dusk. Somebody must've helped Pap fetch Mam, as the wiry old bitch was sitting there by the bigger fire, parched but grim, her bracketed mouth already frowning and her tongue as sharp as a hatchet.

"There's that little chickenshit that left me lying in a shroud," she said. "Good for nothing. Always said you were good for nothing."

Rhett just took his place by the fire and accepted a plate of food, eating quickly as he waited for Sam to wake up and ignoring Pap and Mam completely. As the first stars poked out, he hurried to the private side of the wagon so Sam wouldn't have to hear the poison being spewed directly at him.

"What's going on, Rhett?" Sam asked, rubbing his eyes as he hopped down to the ground.

"El Rey sent along Pap's woman, Mam. Found her bundled up in a coffin. I reckon he's trying to nettle me."

"And it's working?"

Rhett couldn't help it; he grabbed Sam's neck and pulled the feller in close, setting their foreheads together. "Hell yes, it's working. First he took folks I cared about and killed 'em, and now he's sending back folks I hate but can't kill. He's taunting me. Dogging me. He's got me pent up like a rat in a cage. Will you come away with me for a while?"

Sam wrapped his arms around Rhett and pulled him close, their lips almost touching. "Away to where?"

"Anywhere. Say we're going hunting or scouting. I just need...I just need..."

Low and rumbly, Sam supplied the word. "Release?"

"Lord, yes," Rhett said, all shaky with need.

They disappeared for less than an hour and returned with a rattlesnake for the next meal. Sam had always been good at catching the damn things. As for Rhett, he felt like he'd slipped into cool water, like for just a little while there, nothing could touch him. Reconnecting with Sam was like that; a primal need that stilled his heart and reminded him things were worth fighting for. Sam gave him the courage to go back to the campfire and get folks ready to continue on the journey. As far as Rhett could tell, they should reach the doc's place by morning, which meant at least that they'd sleep out of the harsh glare of the winter sun and harsher whistling wind. And that he could plop Pap and Mam in the wagon and send Dan off to deliver them to Rona. Hell, he'd have them blindfolded first so they couldn't find their way back; Pap couldn't navigate his own boot. It was a hellish cruelty that they weren't currently near a town where the assholes could be disposed of.

They were soon fed and back on the trail, Rhett and Sam riding far ahead of the wagon and herd. It was a cloudy night, nary a star to be seen, and the air bit like an old blind dog on its last legs. As he began to recognize nearby landmarks, Rhett's spirits lifted a bit. Finally, they were close to their goal. He could see beyond El Rey now. They were gonna beat the bastard, whatever and whoever he was, and then he and Sam could have their tidy little ranch they'd talked about in whispered moments, naked and soft, in the darkness. They even had plenty of fellers around to help out, if Rhett's folks and Digby and Little Eagle and Lizzie all wanted to stick around. Although he'd originally wanted to build a new Ranger outpost, Rhett reckoned this future suited him even better, as now he'd have no boss back east to tell him what to do. Every time he looked at Pap, he remembered the chafe of following orders and was glad to be done with it.

"Wanna run?" he asked Sam, feeling more energetic than he had in days.

"Hell yes," Sam answered with a grin. "Always."

Rhett was riding BB just then, and although the big unicorn gelding wasn't as canny at understanding Rhett's feelings as Ragdoll was, he knew well enough when he was being asked for a gallop. Rhett savored the bunch of haunches and the way BB always stretched his neck out like he was racing for his life. Beside him, Sam's leggy appaloosa snorted and accepted the challenge. It was like flying, peeling across the desert at night, nothing but hoofbeats on hard earth and puffs of breath. He'd once been too cautious to run a horse at night, but now the night felt like home. Warm sides breathing between Rhett's knees, dirty white mane clutched in frozen fingers, he lay low over BB's neck and felt that lift, so like flying without taking the bird's form. Sam whooped beside him, and it was an even race as they tore through the valley and had to slow a bit to wind around the boulders and buttes.

They were trotting through a rocky patch when the first flicker of worry pinged Rhett's stomach. Something was very wrong—something up ahead. He wanted to kick BB to a gallop, but there was no way the unicorn could get Rhett to the doc's place any faster than he was already moving, not without ramming a rock wall or tripping over a stone in the dry arroyo.

"Shit," Rhett muttered.

Sam looked over, his grin gone. "What now?"

The way he asked it—like he'd been expecting trouble and was disappointed Rhett had let it interfere with their precious time alone—stung Rhett's heart a little.

"I don't know," he muttered. "I never do."

"Monsters?"

Rhett sighed heavily. "I wish it were that easy."

Because he couldn't feel minds set against him, racing toward him, waiting for him. He couldn't sense anything but wrongness, that constant buzzing on the edge of his mind that meant bad things were coming. He was starting to realize it meant that bad things were here, and not the sort of bad things he'd ever be able to catch and kill. El Rey was slippery as a mudskipper, and for all that Rhett knew El Rey had masterminded whatever waited at the doc's place, he knew the big boss himself wasn't part of it, nor even near. Rhett could feel him, just a little, a faraway heartbeat in Azteca, sick and dark as the pus in an old wound.

They came around the last curve, and Rhett didn't have to wonder what was wrong anymore.

The doc's house was on fire.

And someone inside was screaming.

CHAPTER
22

You hear that?" Sam asked, but Rhett just kicked his horse, hard, and aimed for the flaming building. He passed the stack of wood boards they'd collected from Las Moras to build their pens, also on fire, and skidded to a halt, swinging out of the saddle in one spare movement.

He didn't have much experience with fires and had only been in one once, back when the Captain had set fire to the siren's town, Reveille. That wood had been new and snapped with sap, but the doc's house was old and dry and going up even faster. The screams inside sounded like a woman, and Rhett wished to hell he'd counted heads in his own company recently to make sure all his womenfolk were accounted for. Not knowing who or what El Rey was, he didn't know how the feller managed to snatch folks, but he had to assume the bastard was good at it, and fast when he wanted to be.

"I'm going in," he said, tossing his buffalo rug and hat on the ground and handing Sam his reins.

"What do you want me to do?" Sam had an arm over his eyes, his fangs out as he turned away from the flames. Rhett wondered if they burned him, as the sun would, but didn't have time to worry about that.

"Stay put, Sam, and don't get hurt. That's all I'd ask."

And then Rhett was running for the front door, an open black hole surrounded by leaping orange flames. The voice inside was screaming itself ragged, beyond words and pleas, just a throat scraped raw by terror.

The heat was a slap in the face, an immediate pressure hungry for tinder. Rhett pulled his bandanna down over his nose and mouth and shielded his good eye with his arm, trying to figure out where the screams were coming from. For all the fights he'd fought without a second thought, this fire was something new. It commanded from all sides, licked and drove and hungered, and he soon lost track of where the door was. He was surrounded by walls of flame, his lungs on fire and his lips bubbling dry and his eye about to squash from the push of heat.

"Who's there?" he called, a dirty rasp of breath, but he could barely hear the sound himself.

His brain kicked in, suggesting that an asshole like El Rey would stash whoever they were trying to torture upstairs so Rhett's job would be that much harder while also putting him in danger, so Rhett ran for the rotting stairs and pounded his way upward, feeling the wood creak and crack and break in his wake, the boards falling into the hellfire below. Upstairs on the landing, the screaming was louder, and the flames were just a little bit less pressing. Rhett dropped to his knees and took a deep breath, as it seemed the smoke clustered higher up.

He realized, as he crouched there, sucking in deep breaths of almost-clean air, that whoever was screaming was definitely a woman.

Could it be that El Rey had kept Cora alive, maybe just cut off a hank of her hair and left it behind with the bag of sand in Meimei's pocket to make him hurt? Rhett's heart kicked up a notch, and he crawled toward the bedroom, knowing that's where she'd be. Sure enough, he saw ropes tied around the bedposts and booted feet bucking in vain. The screams kicked into overdrive, and he hurried along the side of the bed, finding yet more ropes binding wrists, a blanket hiding the screamer and shielding her from the worst of the smoke.

"Hold on," he rasped. "I got you."

Whipping out his Bowie knife, he sawed through the ropes, arms first and then feet. He didn't remove the blanket, knowing that whoever it was would be better off breathing in less smoke and not seeing what was happening around the room. Gathering up the covered form, Rhett felt the body shift against him in alarm, then relax. The screams stopped.

"Please help me," a voice said, too ragged to identify.

"I'm trying," he responded.

He went for the stairs, but the flames were licking straight up, the wood boards broken or gone. Which he'd known, hadn't he? But he'd had to try. There was only one other choice, so he went to the bedroom window, shoving a boot through to smash the thick bottle glass. As soon as the night air swept in, the fire whooped and hollered and flicked at his back, and he cursed himself for not knowing that would happen. He didn't have much of a choice now. The room was being enveloped in fire, and there wasn't anything else for it.

"Catch her, Sam!" he called, and he carefully dropped the blanketed form out the window, trusting that Sam and the folks waiting below would do their best to soften her fall. As soon as she was out of his arms, he leaped out the window, wishing like hell he'd had time to shed his clothes and fly. But no. The bird couldn't help him now. He hit the frozen ground, hard, on a boot and then his shoulder, feeling the snap of a bone and rolling several times before fetching up on his back.

"Goddammit," he rasped, pulling the bandanna off his nose and mouth so he could suck in the cold, fresh air.

Overhead, the fire burned with a raging, primal sort of satisfaction. Flames whooshed out the open window, and something down below exploded, sending sparks into the sky. It would've been pretty, had it not destroyed a good many of Rhett's dreams. Maybe not the house, so much, but the wood they'd labored to bring from Las Moras, which would've made the pens to hold their horses and cattle. All his plans, going up in smoke.

"Goddammit all to hell," he said again, sighing sadly.

His hearing had gone all cattywampus in the fire, but now it came back, the fire's crackling like merry music behind the rustle of voices.

"Are you okay?"

"What happened?"

"Did you see who did it?"

"Here. Drink some water."

As he held stone still and waited for the dull ache in his leg to subside, his monster bones knitting up fresh and clean, he tried to quiet his breathing. He needed to hear the voice of the person he'd saved, needed to know that there was some chance Cora was still alive and just another pawn in El Rey's game. And yet some part of him didn't want to look, didn't want to hear, didn't want to know that he was as dumb as the little white children in town who thought Sandy Claus would bring them oranges and penny candy if they were good. From her earliest days, Nettie Lonesome had known that Sandy Claus was a lie, and that even if he was real, he wouldn't have treats for the likes of her. And yet that child who he'd once been had lain awake every Christmas, waiting to hear the clickety clack of reindeer feet on the falling-down roof.

He'd never heard a damn thing. Well, except the clink of Pap's bottle.

"More water," the voice said, and it was so familiar, just tickling the edge of his memories.

Rhett rolled up to sitting and looked over.

His heart sank.

It wasn't Cora.

It was the last goddamn female he could've ever wanted to see, after Mam.

"Well, Miss Regina," he muttered. "What's a lady like you doing in a burning house like this?"

"You," that lady spat, glaring at him from a face black with smoke. "Again."

"And you. I should've known."

"As should I. Tragedy just trails in your wake."

"And you keep getting yourself almost burned up."

Her eyebrows were about singed, but they knitted down in fury. "It's never my idea!"

He tried to stand and failed. "Let me guess. El Rey kidnapped you and tied you up in that bed and set the house on fire. A present, just for me."

Dan held out his canteen, and Regina took it like a queen and drank with grace, her eyes never leaving Rhett's. Her other arm was cradled to her chest, probably broken, thanks to the frailty of human bodies. "Since the day you found me in Reveille, not a good thing has happened," she began in that annoyingly dramatic way she had. "I lost my child and husband to the Cannibal Owl, fell into this hellish world of outlaws, played lady's maid to a...a German! And then your Captain"—she spat the word, and Rhett's dislike went up a notch—"left me in another nothing town on the edge of nowhere. Barely gave me enough money to buy a meal. Couldn't find work. So I sold the only thing I had. Men passed me from hand to hand. I finally found a place, a little farm on the edge of nowhere with a man I didn't hate too much, and now here I am. Stolen from my bed in the night, just like my sweet child, my Marjorie."

She had a haunted, strange look about her, and she told her story like she was reciting bible verses to a sympathetic audience, and Rhett reckoned that she wasn't right in the head. And how could she be, after all she'd been through? When he'd first found her in the siren's town of Reveille, she'd been locked up in jail, heavy with a child to be given to the Cannibal Owl. Since then, she was right: Nothing good had happened to her. But Rhett wasn't about to take responsibility for that.

"Check her for a knife, Sam," Rhett said, hand on his own weapon to make sure it was still there. "She's got a way of trying to stab me when she ought to be thanking me."

"Thank you? For what now?" the woman spluttered. She was somehow more gaunt than the last time Rhett had found her, recently widowed and working as housegirl for a dwarf woman in Burlesville. She'd followed him into the night, tried to stab him, and then dogged his steps until he and Earl had returned to the Las Moras Outpost. The last Rhett had seen of the woman, she'd been sitting on the Captain's wagon box with the Rangers' cook, Conchita, giving him much the same look she was giving him now, a glare that suggested she'd like nothing more than to see him roasting over a spit.

"I just saved you from dying in a burning house, you harpy!" he snapped.

"And broke my arm to boot! Did it ever occur to you that I wanted to die?" she snapped right back. "You keep saving me and demanding thanks, but I'd thank you to walk out of my life forever and let me choose my own exit. I'd rather burn than see your face ever again!"

"That's not what you were screaming when you was tied to that bed!"

"I would've shut my mouth if I thought you were the only person who could hear me!"

Healed or not, Rhett was done sitting on the cold, hard ground, listening to his sins. He stood, holding himself carefully on his good leg, and lurched back toward his horse to collect his hat and buffalo robe.

"I'll be leaving you then," he said. "For the last time."

The burning house lit up the night, the pile of flaming boards in front of it turning Rhett's stomach. Hat in place and buffalo skin weighing down his shoulders, he angled away from it all and limped toward the pueblos. Those, at least, were something El Rey couldn't burn. Maybe the feller had filled them with venomous snakes and cow shit. Because it looked like El Rey knew every step of Rhett's journey and was determined to make it unbearable. Even here, the one place that might've felt like hope. But of course El Rey would use that against him, too. Rhett was dogged by his invisible goddamn enemy.

As he shuffled through the crowd, he kept his eyes on that pueblo up ahead, determined to look no one in the eye. Winifred, Finder, Revenge, Lizzie, Digby, Little Eagle, Slippery Snake. Even Bill the Sasquatch, hat in hand and looking sorrowful. Rhett moved through the clot of folks like he was walking through fog, and once he was on the other side, he said, "Find a pueblo that suits you and set up shop. I'd suggest getting high enough that you need a ladder. Rock don't burn. Sleep with weapons in hand. We'll talk in the morning." He snorted. "Or whenever we wake up." After a few more shuffling steps, he added, "And don't believe a goddamn thing that fool woman says of me. She's addlepated."

He dragged himself toward a random pueblo, hoping it would have an especially dark room in back that would keep Sam safe during the day. But Sam stayed with Regina instead of following Rhett, so Rhett just hobbled to the wall of rock and clambered up the primitive ladder awkward as hell and collapsed on the floor and felt sorry for himself. That was just like Sam—a gentleman, even when the lady in question didn't deserve a lick of his time and would probably cuss his face for smiling.

It was another low blow from El Rey, bringing Regina back into Rhett's life. The woman seemed to speak of the worst of his failures. He'd taken too long to kill the siren of Reveille, who'd killed Regina's husband. And then he'd taken too long to find the Cannibal Owl, and it had swooped in to steal Regina's day-old girlchild right from the cradle. And then he'd showed up right after Regina tried and failed to hang herself. And then he'd neglected to die when she'd stabbed him to get her revenge. If regret had taken human form, it would've looked and sounded a lot like the skinny fishwife still shrieking about Rhett's many faults over by the burning house that had nearly consumed her.

"If you want to die so much, just walk right back in that door," Rhett muttered, his knees going weak as he rocked between the walls of the pueblo, hunting for a place to lie down. "Every day, I see that door and choose not to go in it. Earl went in it, that cowardly little shit, and I carry him with me. And I carry you, too. None of it's ever your fault, is it, Regina? Always got to find a stronger soul to shoulder your burden. Well, I'm done carrying shit for other people. You carry it yourself, or you choose the easy road and walk back into that burning house. But you make the choice. Not me."

Something soft snuck in under his cheek, and his eye

blinked open. He'd fallen asleep, somehow, splayed across the hard stone.

"What were you saying?" Sam whispered, pulling Rhett closer and tucking the buffalo robe over them both.

"Oh, Sam. I was…I was saying…a man's got to choose."

"Choose what?"

Everything was confusing and dark, caught between dreams and waking life, and Rhett's lungs felt like they'd been scraped raw with a rusty knife. He couldn't quite remember what he'd been thinking, for all that it had felt like a promise.

"I don't get to choose," he tried again.

"I know you don't, Rhett. I know."

"He keeps taking away the wrong things. Killing what I love, reminding me what I hate. Mixing it all up. We got to kill him, Sam. We got to kill El Rey."

"I know it. You will."

And then it struck Rhett like lightning, and he bolted up onto his elbow. "Goddammit, Sam. That's it. He knows what makes me weak."

"Whazzat?"

The sweet thump Rhett heard suggested Sam's head had fallen back, and Rhett could tell that sunrise had claimed him. Rhett frantically felt for Sam's body, wishing for a lantern or any way to see anything in the pitch-black of the cave. The pueblo seemed solid enough but now he wanted to know for himself that it was safe, that they were alone, that there was no back door into their refuge.

Because Rhett had finally understood his enemy.

El Rey knew him, truly and personally knew him, and he knew what made the Shadow weak.

And that meant that Sam was in the most danger of all.

Exhausted as he was, Rhett was fully awake from that moment. With an enemy like El Rey, there was no safety. Hell, he hadn't even set someone to keep watch, so who knew what kind of dangers were skulking around outside? If El Rey knew how to get around the Shadow, maybe he needed to get a damn hound dog like the one his brother had once had—and lost in a buffalo stampede. His enemy was setting his aggressions in motion all sideways, not sending his folks against Rhett directly, as that would set up the Shadow's hackles. Instead, it was a raid here, a Pap there, a fire—little actions with big rewards when it came to getting Rhett's dander up and making his brain stop working and his gun arm kick in. He wasn't thinking straight, and that meant he was always a step behind.

Best he could figure, El Rey wanted him dead, but he wanted him to suffer, first.

It was like a cat playing with a mouse . . . and Rhett was more accustomed to being the dog.

Rhett left Sam under the buffalo robe and felt his way into the outer rooms of the pueblo, so carefully carved from the stone. His eye felt like it was full of sand and his mouth tasted like charred meat, and he blinked against the bright daylight, seeing spots. His saddlebags and Henry were out here, bless Sam's sweet self, along with a skinned rattlesnake hanging from the ceiling. So thoughtful of Sam to leave breakfast.

It was a peculiar afternoon outside, to be sure. The doc's house was a smoldering ruin, jagged black sticks poking up from a burned spot, gently smoking. The boards from Las Moras resembled an all-too-familiar pyre, white smoke spiraling into the chill blue sky. The wagons sat there, forgotten, full of all their worldly goods, and Rhett smacked his head when he considered how vulnerable his people were. They needed to get those goods distributed and squirreled away into various pueblos as soon as possible, before El Rey could destroy what little capital they had left. Another fire, and they were sitting ducks. Beans had slept through thing, snug in a pueblo.

The horse herd was spread around, the riding mounts hobbled and the cattle roaming a bit off, cropping the spare grass. Rhett found Ragdoll and BB and Samson among them, glad that they were safe. Even his old horse, Puddin', the paint he'd given to his brother, was a welcome sight. He'd never get used to that falling feeling he got when he looked at a herd and didn't see Blue or hear the creature's ear-splitting bugle. His hands went to fists as he considered all that El Rey had taken from him.

Instead of spending the time to set up a campfire, he stirred the ashes of the Las Moras fence wood and staked up the rattlesnake to roast. He fetched the kettle from the wagon and scooped up water from the doc's well to boil, checking it first to make sure El Rey hadn't thrown a dead skunk down to poison them, as it seemed just the sort of thing the bastard would do to make life harder. But the water was sweet and the coffee woke him up a good bit, helped clear the thick, smoky fug from his mind. They had a lot of work to do today, and Rhett needed to be ready for it.

He tried to give folks time to wake up on their own, but the contrary turkeys just kept on sleeping, so when he'd finally had enough of waiting, he brought out his pie tin and a wooden spoon and walked around banging the hell out of it.

"Wake up, fools!" he hollered. "El Rey's coming."

"Now?" Winifred asked, poking her head out of a pueblo, her hair rumpled and her eyes scrunched shut against the sun.

"Well, he didn't give me a timetable, but I reckon he ain't one to wait. Now get up and get to work. We can rest once the fight is over."

"Wake me up when he gets here," she grumbled, disappearing back into her pueblo. "I got a bullet with his name on it."

Most of the other folks, being fighters or nomads by nature and not being deeply gravid, answered Rhett's call. They clambered down ragged old ladders and went about their usual camp business. Inés went to make breakfast in the hot coals of the fire, and Little Eagle and his fellers produced a string of prairie birds, already skinned and dressed, to add to Sam's snake. As the sleepy camp woke up, Rhett doled out jobs, distributing guns and bags of ammunition among the pueblos and requesting aid regarding building up defenses. At least they only had one side to worry about—the back of the pueblo was thick rock and four stories high, and even El Rey couldn't vex them from that direction. He did set Revenge to hunting down all the extra ladders he could find, as that would keep El Rey and his men, or chupacabras, or whoever he bossed around, from getting into the pueblos proper.

Soon they were all busy as beavers, and Rhett felt relief mixed in with his worry. They were here. They were together. They were off the trail. Their only goal now was to kill El Rey and survive, and that was the kind of goal that Rhett liked best. And when Sam showed up at sunset, he smiled for the first time in what felt like days. Things were finally looking up.

CHAPTER 23

"When do you think he'll attack?" Sam asked when he emerged just after dusk and saw the preparations being made around the camp. He'd joined Rhett over by the horses, where they both felt most at home.

Good smells were coming from the campfire, and folks were preparing to settle in for supper. Far as Rhett could tell, everyone's clocks should've been turning back to normal, without the demands of the trail and Sam's schedule driving them. But for now, it was dark, and they were awake and lively. He personally missed waking at dawn and bedding down regular at night. Part of him felt bad about that, like he should crave the darkness and Sam, but the rest of him knew that the winter nights were mighty long and that the sun brought warmth and relief, especially after a hard day's work like they'd all put in today. Revenge had been dogging Rhett's footsteps all along, but Rhett didn't want him out of his sight, so he didn't snap at the boy.

"I don't rightly know when he'll strike next," Rhett told Sam. "I just assume he's got some dastardly plan already in place."

"We will fight," Revenge said with a manly nod. But Rhett just wanted a private moment with Sam.

"Go back to our mama and keep her safe," he said peevishly. "Quit following me around like a dang puppy. We'll fight, sure enough, but not just now."

Revenge muttered at him in his own language and slunk over to the fire, where it sounded like he gave his mama an earful about Rhett's many faults.

"All I wanted was to find 'em," Rhett said to the twinkling stars. "My family. But now I'll be damned if I didn't wish they were far away and had never met me. They'd be safer."

"Things don't always go the way you expect. I know I'm glad to be here with you now."

Rhett grinned at Sam. "I'm glad, too."

It was going to be a cold night. Rhett had packed on an old coat he'd found in the wagon and wrapped a warm flannel around his neck, the pie plate and bible back over his heart. The enemy, after all, knew Rhett was here. He'd encouraged everybody else to wear the same sort of protection, but that was all he could do. Much like Regina, from here on out, they could make their own choices regarding the thin line between life and death.

"So what can I do? What do you need?" Sam asked, and the simplicity and tenderness of the question just about made Rhett's throat close up. Folks had been doing what he told 'em to, whether stoically or grudgingly, but nobody had asked a damn thing about Rhett's own needs.

"We just got to figure out how to defend this place. Since El Rey knows where we are but we don't know where he is, I reckon he'll either pester us to death or come up on us all stealthy-like. So we got to be ready for him. You could scout a bit, if you think it'd help."

"Dan was always the better scout," Sam admitted. "Feller can sense a monster almost as well as you can. I'm more of a . . .

well, a second-in-command, you know? Real good at following orders."

Rhett considered him in the scant light, noting that Sam looked waxy and pale, his eyes feverish. "I reckon you'd do us all a favor if you got some blood in you. Ask Notch or Beans. Or, hell, go on and suck on Pap and Mam. They won't taste good, but they're made of meat."

Sam pulled a face. "Ugh. No. I reckon they'd taste like sour milk and gone beer. But I could take 'em off to Rona for you. Be back hours before daylight, and that's one less thing to worry about."

It only took a moment's consideration to realize that getting Sam away from the pueblos would be the best way to keep the feller safe—especially since Sam had his vampire senses and would be ready for any sort of attack. "That's a damn fine idea. And Regina, too. Leave her with a doctor and some gold, and leave the other two—hell, they'll end up at a saloon anyway, so pick the cheapest one you can find and drop 'em like a hot potato. Give 'em enough coin to ease my conscience." He clapped Sam on the shoulder. "And get some blood while you're there."

Sam looked up, all hopeful. "You don't mind?"

"I need you strong and ready to fight, Sam. I need that more than anything. I can get through whatever's coming if I got you by my side." Rhett fought not to wince; it was almost not a lie. Thanks to their recent revelations, he couldn't tell Sam that what he wanted most was to get through El Rey with Sam so far away that the bastard would never find him.

Sam's grin all but sparkled—the boy loved being useful. And pleasing Rhett. "Best get moving, then. Daylight don't wait."

"No, it don't."

Rhett didn't even look around to see who was watching

before he pulled Sam in for a desperate kiss that was like air to a drowning man. Sam's cold lips warmed to his, his bristles scraping Rhett's cheeks and heating him down to his numb toes. This was a good plan: Sam would get blood and get away from the target on Rhett's back, Rhett would get rid of the three hated humans currently in his care, all of whom made his innards jump like a frog in a hot skillet, blunting his senses for the real dangers. And if El Rey's minions went after Sam, Rhett knew they'd get their asses kicked. Most folks who tangled up close with a vampire didn't live.

As Sam headed over to the herd to pick out some easy ponies for his charges, Rhett got far away so Pap, Mam, and Regina couldn't stripe his hide with their foul tongues. He found Dan, Digby, and Lizzie at the narrow neck of the trail to the pueblos. Dan and Digby were setting spikes of wood into the dirt, aimed away at just the right height to harry incoming horses, and Lizzie was carefully cutting prickly pears and cactuses, rolling them over to build a sort of barricade.

"So they won't be able to surprise us from this direction," Rhett said, grinning. "That's smart work."

"You're welcome," Dan said, grunting as he fitted another spike into the ground. Judging by the burnt edges, it had been a wood board that hadn't fully burned, and somebody had taken the trouble to snap off one end in a jagged spear.

"Looks like you-all got everything taken care of down this way," Rhett said, hands on hips and, for once, satisfied.

"Perhaps," Lizzie said, standing up to wipe sweat off her brow. "But I'm unsettled. Someone has been here. A chupaca-bra. I can smell him. But the smell is off. Very strange."

Rhett shrugged. "I reckon El Rey had to send a feller to set the fires, and that wasn't even a full day ago. How long's your snoot able to smell folks that are gone?"

Lizzie's mouth twitched, her see-through eyebrows drawn down. "Hard to say. But this was more recent than that. After we arrived, I think."

That got Rhett's dander up. "While we were sleeping?"

She nodded once. "Just so."

"Well, maybe you can take a moment off cactus duty and sniff around. Make sure he's not still hiding out nearby. See if he came from this direction or from around the doc's house."

"Too many scents." Her nose wrinkled up, starting to blacken over like a Lobo's nose. "Hard to follow. But I will try."

Lizzie stalked off, and Rhett gave Dan and Digby his full attention. "Listen up, fellers. We got a ragtag crew here, and I reckon most of 'em are good men, but outside of Sam, I trust you two the most. I trust you to do what's right, and I trust you to do what I ask, when I ask it. So whatever's coming, I'm counting on you. To help me, and to make the other folks see." They both got that hard-eyed stare fellers get when they're committing to die for the right cause, and Rhett gave it back with interest. "Dan, I want you to know my first command is that we get your sister and my mama somewhere safe. They're gonna wanna fight, because they're fighters. But between you and me, I reckon this is the time to ignore that and do our duty by protecting them. You agree?"

Dan nodded. "You know I do."

"Now, some of them pueblos go right deep into the rock, and some have hidey-holes that go up and down between 'em. We haven't had time to explore everything, I know, but I figure that might work—have the vulnerable folks hide in back, behind some old junk. Or, if you think it's best, we can truss 'em up like chickens and carry 'em off to town. Inés, too. But my mama's the last human we got under our watch, and El Rey is looking to wound me where it hurts most, so I got to outfox him."

"Then don't hide her away." Dan's face was heading into preacher territory, grim and clever in that way that nettled Rhett. "If El Rey is watching, she's the first one he'll go for. My sister, for all that I want her safe, has the protection of the god. And that cat shaman curse, which suggests they'll have to kill her more than once for it to stick. I also know there's no way she'd consent to being packed off like a carpetbag. It might be best to put them in one of the highest pueblos and have them pull up the ladder behind. They're both good with arrows. And guns. And knives."

"So let them fight, but put them high up on a shelf?" Rhett tapped his lip, considering. "Yeah, you've the right of it. If I hide 'em away, I'll just worry. Better to keep them in plain sight but untouchable."

For just a moment, he thought of Sam, alone on the prairie with three fools and the light of a crescent moon, and his heart stuttered. Had he done the wrong thing? The Shadow wasn't worried. Sam was a creature of the night now, and a damned competent Ranger on top of that, and it wasn't a long ride.

"Then I'll leave you to tell the ladies our plan," Rhett said, strolling away.

Dan cussed at him under his breath, but Digby jogged to catch up.

"I don't like this," he said, voice low. "Something's hitting me wrong. If El Rey knows we're here, why ain't he attacking now, while we're all scattered and got our guards down?"

Irritation made Rhett grind his teeth. "How the hell should I know, Digby? I ain't the man's bosom friend. Maybe he's gathering his crew, or maybe he don't see too good in the dark. Maybe he wants to let me stew in my own juices, not knowing what's gonna happen. All I know is that he's coming, and soon. I can feel it in my gut."

Damn, could he ever. Those dark clouds that had pressed on him for weeks felt so heavy and near that his brain ached in his skull. It felt like the hours before a tornado he'd lived through as a child in Gloomy Bluebird, as the sky went yellowish green like an old bruise and the wind went so still that tumbleweeds ceased to tumble. The world held its breath, waiting for violence, and the people trapped under those black clouds could do nothing but huddle together in the dark, praying that catastrophe would strike even one house over.

This time, there were no such hopes. El Rey would strike, and he wouldn't miss.

The hardest part was knowing, bone deep, that El Rey understood him, while Rhett knew almost nothing of his foe. Even if it was Chuck, he didn't know Chuck that well. He didn't know why El Rey was out to get him. He had to assume, as his feelings coalesced, that his chupacabra problem and his El Rey problem were one and the same. The gathered clouds had come together, and they were on the move.

But why? Most chupas just played checkers with horses and cattle across the border, raiding into Durango and returning to their lairs with plenty of meat and coin. The only thing they liked better than riding fancy horses was eating less fancy horses. But El Rey seemed to want more, and it involved getting Rhett out of the way. But why Rhett? Was it personal because he was who he was, or was it just a powerful enemy working to get rid of the biggest threat to his plans, the mythical Shadow? Was it cat and mouse, or an unusually cruel cat going after a very specific mouse?

"I reckon I'd feel better if we checked all our weapons and ammunition," Digby said. "Would it be all right if I made a round of the pueblos? We got to make sure loaded guns are waiting at every window and door, don't you agree?"

Rhett's lips twitched. "If it'll make you feel better, Digby, you go right on ahead."

With all his prime fellers given their duties, Rhett wandered over to the fire, where he claimed the dregs of the coffee and a stick of rattlesnake. Inés had that calm way about her as she rolled up tamales, and it was a right pleasant moment, sitting there, eating and drinking, without anybody asking him for anything. But finally, as always happened, he couldn't keep his goddamn mouth shut.

"You been praying?" he asked the nun.

She shrugged. "Praying makes people feel better. The gods do as they will."

"You regret coming here with us?"

That earned a rich laugh. "Regret is a stupid word, Rhett. Every choice we make closes a different door. Like many people here, I feel drawn to you, to your cause. I'm here for a reason. Perhaps that reason is to lift my veil and kill as many enemies as possible. Perhaps it is otherwise. But I'm here, and here I'll stay, and if I survive the attack, I'll make another choice."

He chewed, considering. "You make good tamales, at least."

"Yes, well, one should always go to war with a full stomach."

His head whipped around, one eyebrow up. "You believe that?"

She laughed again. "No. Your Captain once told me that the bowels tend to loosen before battle, so I won't be eating too much, just now."

He snorted and shook his head. "Woman, you defy all."

"Defiance is itself a sort of prayer."

Tossing his stick into the fire and wiping the snake grease off his lips, he stood and moseyed to the horses, where he discussed defending the herd with Little Eagle. As Rhett had correctly surmised upon meeting the feller, Little Eagle was a fine hand with horseflesh and shared Rhett's belief that the horses would be better off away from El Rey's fight. Two of Little Eagle's men would take them, in two separate herds, just a little way away from the pueblos.

"You sure you can trust 'em?" Rhett asked, eyeing Otter Paws and Forked Stick, neither of whom he knew too well.

"With my life," Little Eagle said, looking pretty damn offended. "My son and my nephew!"

"Well you should've said so, you old tomcat," Rhett joshed, cuffing Little Eagle on the arm. "You don't look old enough to have a grown son!"

"I'm not old enough to lose a grown son. So they will go. Slippery Snake and Walks Fast will stay here and fight." The two fellers in question nodded along, and Rhett realized that these fellers were all who were left of Little Eagle's people, so far as he knew.

"You lost your folks, mostly, I know, so I got to ask." Rhett chewed his lip for a second, trying not to cause offense, which he most always did. "Why are you-all willing to fight? You could just take a few horses and mosey off somewhere else where there's less trouble. I wouldn't try to stop you."

Little Eagle snorted and cuffed Rhett right back on the arm, hard enough to bruise. "We tried running away from every fight, and that didn't work. Got to face the buffalo head-on for the surest shot."

"A final stand, you reckon? And then you think Durango will be clean of bad guys?"

Little Eagle gave Rhett a sad, pitying sort of look. "Durango is just one name. This place has many names. No edges. Its spirit can't be killed. There will always be evil things here, and there will always be another fight. But this time, we will win, even if it costs us."

"Damn," Rhett murmured as he strolled away. "Keep talking like that, you'll have me believing it, too."

Looking around the camp, he reckoned he'd spoken to everyone who needed talking to. Dan would handle Finder and Winifred, which was a pleasant relief. But now Rhett had one more feller to talk to, and it wasn't going to be all wise words and the hard cuff of a fighting man's friendly hand.

He had to find his brother and tell him to get the hell away. To fly.

Not for long. Just for the fight.

For even if Revenge saw himself as a grown man and a good fighter, Rhett still saw the little brother he'd just met and the only family his mama would have left, if El Rey won the day. And as the older brother, it was Rhett's job to keep the rabid little pup safe. A bird riding the thermals would survive.

He didn't find Revenge back with the horses, nor with the folks building the barricade. He wasn't near the fire, and Rhett hadn't caught a glimpse of him among the pueblos with his mama. Hadn't seen the boy since he'd snapped at him, back when he was talking to Sam. He looked over by the wagon, by the smoldering ruins of the house, and a sick sense of worry kicked up in his belly.

Where the hell was that boy?

Rhett was just about to start shouting when he was interrupted by Digby doing some shouting of his own.

"Rhett! Get over here, now!"

Rhett came at a run, hunting for Digby in the pueblos and finding the man leaning out a window, holding up a bag of bullets.

"You find my brother?"

Digby's face screwed up in annoyance. "What? No. We got a problem, though."

"Well, what is it?"

Digby turned the bag upside down out the pueblo window. A bunch of sand and rocks tumbled to the ground.

"Our ammunition is gone, Rhett. All of it."

CHAPTER 24

They went from room to room, bag to bag and box to box, and it was true. All the bullets they'd so carefully packed and placed had been replaced with sand, dirt, and rocks, weighted such that if you weren't paying much attention and you picked 'em up, you wouldn't notice.

"Oh, goddamn," Rhett muttered. "This means all we've got..."

"Is in our guns," Dan finished for him.

Rhett's stomach roiled like he'd eaten a live gopher. Even with a wagon full of ammunition, he hadn't felt that good about the coming fight. Chupacabras were monsters, and monsters were hard to kill. And chupas were known for their trick riding, hiding behind their horses and shooting under their bellies as they galloped past. At least when they checked the guns they did have, their ammo was still safe in the chambers.

"Lizzie smelled 'im," Rhett murmured, sifting a bag of rocks through his fingers. "He must've snuck in while we were sleeping. Clever son of a bitch. I reckon they didn't think we'd notice until we were in the thick of the fight." He looked to Digby. "You're a good feller, you know that?"

Digby looked down. "If I was good, I would've noticed a hell of a lot earlier."

Rhett waved a hand. "What's done is done. We ain't never fought something like this. At least we know now. We got to make shots count. We got to wear our pie plates. And we got to make as many arrows as we can. Dan, you and Winifred can do that, right?"

Dan looked around the valley and frowned. "Not much of the right kind of stone here, but we can try. Does your mother know how to make arrowheads?"

"Hell if I know. Ask her yourself. And find out where my brother is."

Winifred walked up just then, and Rhett tossed her a rock, which she caught. "At least you got plenty of ammo for your sling," he said.

She tossed it back, harder, smacking him in the head. "Which I hear I'll be using from the penthouse."

He rubbed the burning knot on his head, grateful that bruises no longer lasted. "If you won't think of yourself, think of the child. At least I'm not trying to stop you from fighting this time. Just trying to give you a bigger choice of targets."

"Idjit."

"Fishwife."

She shoved his shoulder and went to the fire for more food. His mama walked up next carrying a lantern, and she looked like she had a bone to pick.

"Where is brother?" she said, prissier than Dan.

"Why, I thought you would know!" he shot back. "I haven't seen him in hours."

He reckoned his face went through the same contortions as hers did, just then. Surprise, anger, and worry. Because the boy was gone, they were both mad about it, and now they were coming to the same conclusion.

"That little shit went scouting," Rhett said.

"He looks for El Rey—as the bird."

"I know that. That's what I said. Goddammit!"

Rhett kicked the pile of rocks he'd just dropped. "And I don't have time to turn and go looking for him. It's getting on daylight. Sam'll be back soon. And we got to...I don't know. Make weapons. Or traps. Hellfire!"

He stared at the night sky, which might've been beautiful in another life, one where the king of the goddamn chupacabras wasn't personally gunning for Rhett. In that life, his brother hadn't shucked his clothes and taken to the air, and Sam wasn't running late from his trip to Rona, and everybody wasn't looking at Rhett like he could somehow fix it all.

"Found his clothes!" Digby shouted, running up with the boy's ill-fit cowpoke duds and boots. "Around the back side of the pueblo. Reckon he didn't want anyone to know he was gone."

"He wanted to be a goddamn hero," Rhett murmured.

"Like his brother," his mother added, a wry twist to her lips.

"Goddamn fool."

For several long moments, Rhett didn't know what to do. His brother was gone, all the horses were out of range, and it was close enough to daylight that if he took to the sky, he'd miss seeing Sam and knowing that all had gone well on his trip to town. Luckily, just then, he heard horses calling and ran to where Sam ponied three mounts, coming in from Rona.

"Sam! Thank goodness. Everything hereabouts is going to shit. How was town?"

Sam swung down, grinning, and put an arm around Rhett. His cheeks were pink, his eyes were dancing, and there was a welcome warmth in his hands.

"Town was fine enough," Sam said. "I'm fat and sassy, and everybody's where you wanted 'em. Pap and Mam dog cussed me the whole way there, but as soon as I gave 'em a bottle of rot-gut whiskey and a pile of coins, they settled down at a table and shut up. I left Miss Regina with a doctor, and I swear he was making eyes at her. Gangly young feller, had just taken over for the old sawbones, who'd died of a social disease. So maybe she'll make a good end, after all." He yawned, jaw cracking. "But I'm just about set for bed now. What all went wrong, did you say?"

Rhett buried his forehead in Sam's neck, breathing him in, appreciating the rare warmth in the man's skin. "Nothing. Doesn't seem to matter now. Well, they stole all our bullets and my dumbshit brother is missing, and I'm pretty sure El Rey is the king of the chupacabras that want me dead, and I'm just about asleep on my feet, but other than that..."

"Well El Rey ain't here now, so walk me to bed and tell me all about it, will you?" Sam tugged Rhett's hand toward their pueblo, and Rhett got that little swoop in his belly that suggested they might do more than talk. Inés was right about a feller's bowels acting up before a fight, but maybe she didn't know that a feller had certain cravings even before that, when he was just thinking about facing down death and needed to lose a bit of himself, and Rhett would gladly see those cravings met.

Walking backward, Rhett tipped his hat to the grim crew watching his every move. "I'll be back in three shakes of a lamb's tail, and we'll figure it all out," he promised.

Even as he said it, he felt like a selfish little shit. But maybe his brother would come back soon, and then there wouldn't be that much to worry about anyway, would there? He'd always come back before.

Slippery Snake moseyed up to untie the ponied horses, and Sam passed his reins to Digby, but his horse didn't take it well. The dancing appaloosa skittered back, throwing her head and screaming as she reared, and Rhett instantly went to attention.

His belly flipped the wrong way, hard, and he fell to his knees, upchucking rattlesnake.

"What is it, Rhett? What's wrong?"

Rhett stood, shaking, and said, "El Rey and his boys. They're here."

CHAPTER
25

He turned to Sam, one hand on his gun. "Sam, we got to—"

But Sam was walking backward toward the pueblos like he couldn't stop himself, his blue eyes et up with fear.

"I can't, Rhett! I got to get in the dark. The sun's coming up. It's almost here. I got to . . . I got . . . Hellfire!"

Sam ran to Rhett like he was running through molasses, kissed him hard on the mouth, and ran for the pueblo, hollering "I'm sorry!" over his shoulder.

Rhett looked to his crew, what was left of it. His face hardened up, and he took a deep breath.

"I reckon you all know what to do," he said. "It's all we got left. We fight."

Nobody moved, so Rhett took the upset appaloosa's reins from Digby, whipped off the critter's bridle, and smacked her hard on the rump, sending her and the other three ponies in a mad gallop past the doc's destroyed house.

"Find your place to take a stand," Rhett said. "You know what to do. Waiting was the hard part, and the hard part's over. Now we just got to live to see tomorrow."

Dan was the first to take off, then everyone else ran in a different direction. For all that they hadn't had as much time to prepare as Rhett had hoped, and for all that they were past exhausted, and for all that they had far fewer bullets, they were a tough and ready crew. Rhett scurried up a ladder into his designated pueblo and fit his Henry to his shoulder, squinting to see what was coming.

The plume of dirt cutting through dawn was too big to be missed, even if the Shadow's tug hadn't made it clear that the fight Rhett had been dreading for weeks was finally here. They'd known something terrible was coming, and now here it was, bearing down like a twister. From far off, they looked like men, mostly, but as they came into view, they were wearing hoods of black fabric, some with skulls and bones drawn in stark white paint. They were dressed up like cowpokes under that, and it was impossible to tell what they were.

They clung to their horses like geckos screeching their war cries. As they came in close, many of them tossed off their masks, revealing exactly what Rhett had expected: chupacabras. Gray faces with round snake eyes, slit noses, and lipless mouths peeled back over rows and rows of teeth. Judging by their hair, plenty of 'em were Aztecan, as the Captain had said most chupas were, or had once been. But Rhett saw whites and blacks among them, and Injuns, too. Hell, even women. The figure riding up front was bent over a huge white steed, a unicorn, but he had his hat pulled down and still wore his black mask, painted with a grinning skull. That had to be El Rey. Before Rhett could focus on who El Rey might be and aim for the bastard's heart, a bullet pinged off the pueblo wall just below him, and he had to duck down.

"Pie plates!" he hollered at his people. "Take care and aim sly!"

When he popped back up, El Rey was past him, his men pounding behind him, past the unfinished barrier. Waiting a moment, Rhett took aim and shot a horse in the middle of the following herd, hating himself for the dirty move. If he could damage several chupas and hurt their mounts in one swoop, he'd get more done than if he picked one feller off with a shot to the heart. His aim was true, and the horse went down in the center of the pack, screaming as it knocked over its fellows like bowling pins. Chupas went flying, and one went out in a puff of sand as he got trampled by the herd.

More sand puffs followed as arrows and bullets rained down from the pueblos—although it was more like a drizzle. Rhett had expected to have the upper hand in this fight, enough bullets to take down a thousand chupas, but it looked like they'd barely have enough among 'em to dole out one to an enemy's heart. They were vastly outnumbered; there had to be at least sixty chupacabras, armed to the teeth—probably with Rhett's bullets.

He glanced behind him to the makeshift door that hid Sam's cave. For all that he wanted to jump down to the ground and start taking out chupas in a more personal way, he was the only thing standing between an unconscious Sam and a knife in the heart.

"Goddammit," he murmured, taking aim and squeezing the trigger. The shot went wide and hit the chupa in the shoulder. Just as Rhett would've done, the little bastard just laughed and kept riding.

The herd passed by, following El Rey to wherever he was going, and Rhett aimed his shotgun but ultimately recognized that hitting a heart was a lot easier from the front than the back, and he couldn't waste a single bullet for the sake of anger or argument. The herd circled back around to face the pueblos, coming to a halt just out of range, and a man's voice rang out.

"Come on now, Shadow. Don't you wanna fight me?"

The voice was familiar yet utterly different, cloying and cruel and muffled by the black hood. El Rey's face was hidden, his hands gloved, his unicorn dancing under him.

"If I fight you and win, will you go back to whatever hell you came from?" Rhett hollered back, hoping to buy some time. Because he wanted nothing more than to get his hands around El Rey's throat and squeeze, but he wasn't about to leave Sam unprotected. And if he ventured to call out for one of his own men to stand guard, the chupas would know he had something worth guarding.

El Rey laughed, and the chupacabras arrayed around him snickered and hissed.

"You can't beat me," El Rey said. "But how about this? I'll let you watch me kill everybody you love, and then I'll help you become something new."

A ladder shoved up through the hole in the floor of Rhett's pueblo, and he aimed his pistol before recognizing Dan, who pointed at Sam's door and gave Rhett the sort of nod that a feller can count on.

"Become what, a particularly ugly pile of sand?" Rhett yelled, trying to buy some more time.

He checked his pie plate and the Captain's bitty bible and adjusted his eye kerch and yet again checked the bullets in his revolvers and his Henry, as if the bullets might disappear if he didn't keep them properly counted.

"Better than that. I'll make you what I am. And then you can help me drive the humans out of Durango. It's ours by right."

That was not what Rhett had expected, so he looked over the wall to see what El Rey was about. A deadly sort of calm had come over the Shadow, along with a new curiosity about his foe. The Cannibal Owl had been dangerous but dumb,

and Trevisan had been smart but arrogant. El Rey was...
something different altogether.

"By 'ours' do you mean you and the chupacabras? Because I
reckon y'all are too ugly to been in charge of anything useful."

El Rey barked a laugh and fired a shot off toward Winifred, who'd been taking careful aim out of her pueblo. She fell
straight back, and Rhett's heart kicked up a notch, hoping that
wherever she was hit, it wasn't permanent.

"Not just the chupas. The monsters. Think about it. Chupas,
vampires, Lobos, shifters. We're stronger. Faster. Harder to kill.
The superior species. And yet we let them kill our bands, push
us farther and farther into the desert, into Azteca. Durango
is rightfully ours." He inclined his head, then tipped up his
hat to show Rhett the skull painted where his face should've
been. "And I do thank you for your hard work. Taking out two
Ranger outposts in one year is a hell of a way to help the cause."

Rhett flushed with shame.

"I didn't do it for you," Rhett yelled.

"You might as well have," El Rey replied, like they were having a pleasant chat over cards. "The end result was the same. I
wanted 'em gone and you took 'em out. I reckon I owe you one.
So look here."

Rhett peeked over the wall and saw El Rey yank a rope trail-
ing off his saddle. Whatever was on the end of that rope, Rhett
knew it wasn't good, and that it definitely wasn't going to go
toward paying a debt. Tug by tug, he was mesmerized, watching El Rey's gloved hands reel it in.

When he saw what it was, thrashing in the air as El Rey
pulled it up, it took everything he had not to jump down there,
knife in fist.

It was his brother.

Revenge.

Revenge in bird form, spitted on two arrows.

Rhett hadn't seen his brother as the lammergeier in a while, not through human eyes, and the boy had shed his immature plumage to look exactly like Rhett had been told he did. A vulture's vulture, with a peach-orange ruff and a big, ugly head. The bird's beak was open, panting, and it was clear that the boy couldn't change back to human, skewered as he was between the arrows. His eye met Rhett's, and it was like being struck by lightning. Rhett could barely breathe, his entire body going rigid with fear and rage. But he couldn't let his foe see that.

"You brought me an ugly chicken?" Rhett said, trying not to sound like El Rey held a chunk of his heart in his murdering hands.

"I know full well he's your brother, idjit. I've had men watching you for months. The funny thing about your little Shadow powers is that if a person ain't hell-bent on hurting you, you don't know which way to go. Your friend Cora told me all about that. You're like a guard dog with a bad nose. Hell, I had one of my boys standing over you while you were sleeping. Told him I was interested in you, wanted to recruit you. Told him not to harm a hair on your head. You never even knew."

El Rey held one of the arrows and gave Revenge a shake, and the bird gave a pathetic screech and held very still. That arrow—one of 'em or both—had to be right close to the boy's heart.

"Well, you got me beat, El Rey. You're a hell of a cunning feller. Now are you gonna give me that bird or just jerk him around?"

Rhett hated himself the most, in that moment, for being a bad liar. The fear and yearning in his voice made it high as a girl's, and the chupas hissed their laughs to hear him brought so low.

For his part, El Rey tossed the bird on the ground, arrows and all. Revenge tried to flutter, but his wings didn't seem to work—must've had his flight muscles pinned. He hit the ground hard and squealed like a baby, then lay there, still as death except for his blinking red eye, aimed straight up.

"Come on down and take him, Rhett."

El Rey looked up at Rhett as his mount pounded an impatient hoof. Rhett still couldn't see much of the feller's face; he fancied he caught a flash of eyes through the mask, but he couldn't guess as to their color. He glanced at Dan, who gave him the sort of look that suggested nobody would get through Sam's door until Dan was sand, and Rhett gave him the sort of look that thanked him in a manly and final sort of way. They nodded to each other and Rhett gently leaned his Henry against the wall and went for the ladder with only his gun belt hanging loose on his hips: two guns and a knife.

Climbing up, he had felt safe and clever, but as he climbed down, he felt every bend and creak of the wood in the ladder, every aching bone and singed hair, every exhausted muscle, every yard of air between him and the ground. He felt human and fragile and dumb and dog-tired, in that moment, thinking back to reckon which night a chupacabra might've stood over him, knife in hand, smiling a snake's grin. For all that he'd always gone into fights with a wild madness, flinging himself at danger, it was a new thing to crawl down to it, heart in his throat, ready to fall on his knees in the dirt and beg for his brother's life, if that was what was required.

This was one enemy he couldn't just fight with his hands and his weapons. This time, he was gonna have to use his brain. And Rhett did not consider himself a smart man.

There were two more ladders between him and the ground, and when his boots hit the sandstone on the middle floor, it did not feel a bit sturdy. He wobbled, and his hands had gone all bloodless, and the Shadow was tugging him hard toward El Rey, like it was trying to make up for lost time in pointing out where the danger waited. He passed by his mother, and she wordlessly put a hand on his shoulder, and he stopped and put a hand over her hand and felt as if his heart would break. The bottom story of the pueblo was empty by design, just a porch, and as soon as he was there, his mama pulled the ladder up behind him and gave him a look that told him to come back with his brother or don't come back at all.

As he stood and straightened, every foul move by El Rey flashed through his head. Every person taken, every fire, every bullet, every bugle of an old mule, lost forever. All of it had come to this moment, and combined, it made him feel like a goddamn fool and weak as a kitten. But that was exactly what El Rey wanted, wasn't it? To take away Rhett's control.

And if there was one thing Rhett hated, it was a feller thinking he had the upper hand.

He put his shoulders back and his chin up and added a good bit of swagger to his walk, thumbs tucked casually in his gun belt. Step by step, he approached El Rey and his passel of chupas, all looking down at him from on horseback, all watching him avidly with their lizard eyes and a hungry look about their mouths, or else a grim black hood. Maybe a vampire or Lobo could get turned and still be okay, but Rhett knew now that chupacabras were just assholes, and that was a fact. He stopped when his boot tips were just about touching Revenge and nudged the bird that was his brother, but gently.

"Can I have him now?" he asked.

El Rey laughed and looked up to where Rhett's mama stood, arms crossed, watching. "Well—"

Quick as a viper, Rhett sliced the rope with his Bowie knife, snatched one of the arrows stuck through Revenge, and used it to lob his brother with all his might into the upper stories of the pueblos. He didn't turn to watch and see what happened, just stood there and calmly slid his Bowie knife home in its sheath. Judging by the gasp from the chupa crowd and by El Rey's answering growl, his brother was safe.

"You said I could take him if I came down," he said, innocent as pie.

"You goddamn whelp—" El Rey began, but Rhett was done being called names. He whipped out his pistol, put it to the unicorn's chest, and pulled the trigger. The big critter dissolved in sand, and El Rey fell hard, still in the saddle and awkward as hell. A few chupas popped off shots as their horses revolted, and Rhett felt the burn of a bullet in his shoulder, but everything he had was focused on El Rey, because when he'd fallen, his hat had gone askew, and Rhett could see his eyes, and Rhett knew him, goddammit.

He knew him.

CHAPTER
26

Well, I thought for sure you were dead," Rhett said, gun pointed at the feller's heart. "Monty."

Snorting a laugh, Monty took off his hat and pulled off his black hood and smoothed down his white mustache, his blue eyes never leaving Rhett's. His skin was a little grayish and rough-looking, and his lips seemed too thin and his teeth too pointy, but he looked more human than his men, which struck Rhett as odd.

"Took you long enough to find me out. Nat," he said, his voice taunting.

"Well, you're uglier than I remember."

Every chupa in the pack had a gun pointed at Rhett, and at that, they cocked 'em. Some of the fellers closed in the circle behind him, and Rhett was fairly certain that for all his own ability to live through just about anything, maybe fifty fellers with a hundred guns would eventually find a way around his pie plate.

"Don't kill him, boys," Monty said. "Save him for me."

Monty stood, and Rhett let him, for all that he wanted to fill the feller full of lead. But there was something peculiar about Monty he didn't quite understand, and the way the feller was grinning now suggested that Rhett's usual tactics were understood, expected, and primed to fail.

"You don't look much like a chupa, for their king," Rhett noted. "For being El Rey."

Monty smirked, an expression Rhett had never seen on the man before. "Well, I'm only half chupa. See, when you shot me and left me for dead—beside a still-breathing chupacabra, I might add, and thanks for that—I was pretty sure I was a goner. And then, when I started to wake up, I was fairly certain I was gonna be one of these snake-faced wretches, much like your old friend Chuck. Come on out and say hello, boy."

One of the chupas pushed through the herd on his black gelding, and Rhett recognized what was left of the boy he'd joshed with on the Double TK Ranch. Chuck looked about like he had the morning he turned, which is to say like a farm boy turned murder lizard, but he shared the cruel glint in Monty's eye and had a hell of a lot more teeth.

"Well, hey there, Nettie, you girl," Chuck said, all mocking, as he stroked a finger past the white knot of scar tissue on his throat from Rhett's bullet, so long ago. It took everything Rhett had not to shoot him and let the cards fall as they may.

"See, Chuck couldn't quite turn me, but that chupa blood has a way of keeping a feller going, even if he seems mostly dead. So they brought me this drink they make. One of their old brujahs came up with it. They call it Devil's Brew, and it takes quite a lot of blood, as your friends Cora and Meimei and Pap and Mam and Regina and that rangy ol' wendigo doc and even that pathetic old mule can tell you. And a few other old friends of yours that I left scattered around, but that you never found." He stopped and chuckled. "Well, they could tell you if they were here and breathing. But some are dead and some you sent off like naughty children, ain't that so? You got quite a way of getting troublesome folk out of your purview. Still, I need blood on the regular, along with the brujah's blend, so they provided their contribution." He whipped a flask from the pocket of his coat and took a swig, a poisonous brown drop sliding from the corner of his mouth down his throat, leaving a sick, slug-like trail.

"So what the hell are you, then?" Rhett asked. "Besides an asshole."

Monty licked his lips, his tongue disturbingly long. "Something new. Half monster, half human. Twice as mean. Twice as hard to kill. I reckon you might say I'm mostly dead, and what's left over just wants to watch the world burn. And see you in particular bleed out like a stuck pig."

The child in Rhett who'd once idolized Monty couldn't help asking, "But why?"

Monty whipped out his pistol and fired quick shots around the pueblo, so fast that Rhett knew his mama and Digby had taken bullets. He heard their grunts of pain and surprise but didn't see sand or hear a scream, though, so maybe the feller was just trying to hold everybody at bay a while longer. Rhett held up his hands with a quieting motion and met Dan's eye, hoping the others would take heed and not do anything stupid.

"Why. Why? Because you killed the man you knew, and I'm what's left." Monty walked toward Rhett, his spurs ringing in the quiet, and they watched each other, unblinking. "When I woke up, surrounded by chupacabras and dried out and gasping in Azteca, this is what I was, so this is what I'm doing. All I can think about is destroying you. Hurting you. And then using what's left to get rid of all these goddamn humans. You been hunting your own kind, girl, and that's not the way to be." He smiled, and his eyes twinkled. "You trust your old pal Monty, right?"

Rhett cocked his head and looked into the blue eyes of the man he'd once loved like a father.

"I want to," he said, considering.

And then he bashed his forehead into Monty's nose. As the feller reeled back, Rhett yanked out his gun, stepped back, and shot Monty right in the chest.

"But I can't."

CHAPTER 27

All hell broke loose, but Rhett couldn't stop staring at Monty. Shot at close range by a revolver to the heart, Monty should've been nothing but a pile of ugly sand. Instead, he had a gaping wound full of slurry blood and an amused smile. He hadn't even fallen over.

"Don't listen so good, do you? I ain't that kind of monster."

Moving faster than he had any right to, Monty punched Rhett in the face, and Rhett reeled back, feeling a tooth loosen in his jaw. He kept hold of his gun, at least, and popped off another shot at Monty's thigh, hoping to slow the bastard down. All around them, the chupacabras tried to rein in their panicking horses and keep circled so Rhett couldn't escape.

And then Monty hollered, "Screw it. Kill 'em all, boys!," and it was like lightning had struck the chupa pack. They took off in every direction, some on horses and some on foot. A few were clever enough to gallop over to a pueblo, stand up in the saddle, dig their clawlike fingertips into the sandstone, and shimmy upward like the lizards they so resembled. Rhett was watching the insanity all around, hunting for Dan guarding Sam, when Monty's knife plunged into his side, just under his ribs.

"You weren't listening, Nettie Lonesome."

"The name's Rhett Walker, you son of a bitch, and I don't value anything you have to say."

He pulled out the knife with a fresh spurt of blood that made Monty breathe in appreciatively and lick his lips.

"You don't have much of a choice but to listen. You got maybe a dozen people, and I got five times that. You got maybe a hundred bullets, and I got all the ones you left unguarded in your little wagon. You got a heart aching for my knife, and I got a body that'll keep going no matter what. So if I wanna talk, you're by God going to listen. You used to enjoy my instruction."

With Monty's knife in one hand, Rhett took a swipe at his belly while popping off another shot, this one glancing off the feller's shoulder. Monty just laughed, the bullet nothing but a bitty hole and the knife slicing through air. Somewhere among the pueblos, a cry of pain was met with a gust of sand, and Rhett had to force himself not to look up and see if it was one of his people. More and more such sounds hit him as he faced off with his once mentor, circling each other like mad dogs in the street.

"I see you, watching that door up top. Your special friend is asleep in there, ain't he? A vampire. You'll remember I had cause to know Samuel Hennessy myself. I taught the boy plenty." Monty's eyebrow raised knowingly. "Plenty."

That got Rhett's blood up in a way nothing else had. He'd known Sam had been with other people, and also that Sam had considered Monty a mentor, but there was no way they could've . . . done that. The thought of Sam with the much older man made Rhett's stomach turn, and the look on Monty's face suggested that that was exactly what he wanted Rhett to feel.

It's all lies, Rhett told himself. *Just another way to get my dander up. He wants me stupid, wants me to make a mistake.*

But El Rey wasn't done hitting Rhett's soft spots. "Seems to me Sam wouldn't want to be a vampire. A monster. Sweet boy like that. I do wonder that he doesn't look at you and shudder. Not only at what you are, but at what you hide. Tell me, what did he say, the first time he pulled down your britches and knew you couldn't give him what he craved?"

Rhett couldn't stop himself; he roared his rage and tackled Monty to the ground, the knife skittering away as they landed. Monty was laughing as Rhett elbowed and kicked him, hunting for some vulnerable place to wound. But there were already wounds, and they were just oozing closed. Not like Rhett's skin did, quiet and neat, but like swamp water sucking up the ground, seeping and slurping and re-forming. A horse galloped by, jumping over them just in time, hooves nearly taking out Rhett's fingers. But all he cared about was hurting Monty. Ending Monty.

And it wasn't working. If a bullet to the heart wouldn't work, what the hell would?

A sound overhead caught his attention—a war cry. He glanced up and saw a shape falling from the pueblo to land a breath away. His brother, Revenge, naked and furious, bleeding from his wounds and wielding a stone ax.

"No, fool! He's mine! Get the hell away—" Rhett yelled.

The words died in his throat as Monty flung his knife, easy as you please, right into the boy's chest. Revenge didn't have time to do anything. He puffed into sand. And was gone.

CHAPTER
28

Monty's knife hit the ground in a shower of sand that blew into Rhett's eyes, merging with the tears that had already sprung up. But Rhett was taking up Revenge's ax, a crude thing of stone and sinew, and he took a swipe at Monty's throat. He nicked it but didn't quite slash it open, as Monty rolled back and onto his heels.

"That's what I admire about you, Nat," he said, like they were having a josh over breakfast. "You don't stop when the folks you love die. Don't even say a few words over 'em or shed a few tears. Just turn your back and keep on going."

"That's the only reason I'm alive," Rhett growled.

Monty put a hand to the slurry blood oozing out of his neck. "That won't matter for long. I can change that." Louder, he shouted, "Boys! Bring 'em down to me. Alive, if they still are."

As Monty stood, Rhett pulled both his revolvers out and emptied them into his once friend. He went for every soft spot he could—groin, belly, chest, neck, even one in Monty's cheek. But Monty didn't fight back or try to stop it. Just let the bullets find him. They didn't seem to hurt him or even slow him down, and Rhett soon tossed down his guns and took up his own Bowie knife.

"You done, whelp?" Monty asked, looking amused and almost bored.

"Not likely," Rhett spat.

He'd stopped paying attention to the chupacabras swarming over the pueblos, but now he had to watch as several fellers dragged down his people. Winifred and Finder and Digby, still in human form, as if the feller still thought guns and bullets could turn the tide when a lion's wrath would've done more damage. Lizzie had a wolf's head, a silver bullet eating through her furry golden cheek as she howled, but the chupas had her in silver irons and dragged her forward with the rest. Dan wasn't there, nor were Little Eagle or Slippery Snake or Walks Fast or Inés. And Sam, if Sam was still alive, was way up high in the dark, unconscious and vulnerable. Rhett struggled to stop himself from looking up there to see if his worst nightmare was coming true.

"Look what you've done to your mama," Monty said. He snatched Finder's chin in his dirty fingers and held her head still, giving Rhett little chance to focus on anything else. The proud woman's face was streaked with tears, a bullet hole oozing blood in her upper arm and her eyes sparking with rebellion and fury. She had never looked more human than in that moment, and Rhett had never felt more helpless.

"You did this to me," Finder hissed at Monty. "Not him."

Monty chuckled. "Well, ma'am, begging your pardon, but I do believe that's an interesting philosophical debate for another time. But the point is that I'm here because of your son. If he'd killed poor Chuck or taken me with him, I'm sure you'd have a nice enough life with your two boys in the doc's old house. Our mistakes make us who we are, and I am just one of your child's many mistakes."

"You leave her alone," Rhett said, real low. He raised his

knife hand, but a bullet pinged off his fingers, forcing him to drop the knife. As his hand jerked, spilling blood, a rope got tossed over his head and shoulders, pinning both his arms to his sides.

"Settle down," Monty reminded him in that old, patient tone. "This ain't your show. It's mine. And I'm gonna show you something special. Something you've never seen before."

"And what's that?"

Monty smiled a smile that held no kindness. "Resurrection." Lifting his revolver, he shot Rhett's mama in the forehead.

"No!" Rhett screamed, and he writhed and fought and spit, but the rope was tight, and he knew well enough when a human had no hope. Sam's gut wound had given him less than a day to live, and his mama was already on the ground, her mouth open and silent.

Loss crashed down, the world shattered. It was as if the most precious, fragile part of Rhett's heart had fallen with her, and he could barely remember who he was through the sobs racking his frame.

"Chuck?" Monty said. "Go on."

The chupacabra that had once been a sweet if braggy young cowpoke curled over Rhett's mama and gave Rhett a lizard grin before sinking his rows of teeth into her flesh, right over the bleeding bullet wound in her arm. Rhett shuddered and fought and cried as he saw Chuck's foul tongue caress his mama's dying flesh, licking up the blood.

"Just wait," Monty warned, giving Rhett a wink, as if he had any goddamn choice. Chuck lifted away and stood, moaning in a sick sort of way and licking bits of flesh off his cheeks.

The only thing worse than watching his mama die was watching her open her eyes, already going dry and wide, their warm brown edging into a poisonous mustard yellow. Her lips darkened and went gray and pulled back over teeth gone sharp and jagged. A crushed bullet popped out of the hole in her forehead and rolled harmlessly to the ground. She shook her head and sat up, every movement perverted from the graceful older woman to what was now a chupacabra wearing her long, dark hair like a wig. Her shoulders hunched up, her hands clawed over, and when she stood and looked at Rhett, her eyes were as empty of humanity as Monty's.

"Let us eat him," she said, licking her lips, and it felt to Rhett like every good thing in the world was gone.

"That's not even my best magic trick," Monty said, and Rhett realized that the feller had put his knife to Rhett's throat. He just about didn't care anymore. If Monty had set out to cause him pain, the feller had won his stupid game. The hot bite of metal against his jugular couldn't hurt him more than losing his brother and his mama in the same goddamn hour.

"I give up," he said, going limp in the ropes. "You win. You wanted me to suffer, and I reckon I can't suffer more than this. So just kill me or take what you want, and get on with it. You can have Durango. I don't want to be here anymore."

Monty's smile then was just about the most evil thing Rhett had ever seen, and that was saying something.

"Good answer. I do like winning. But I'm not done, so let's see what else I can do." Monty took his knife away from Rhett's throat and held it up, blood shining on the blade. "Shall we see what that Injun whore is carrying? You wanna place your bet if it's a boy or another useless little girl?"

Rhett looked to Winifred in alarm, which meant he was watching her face when it went from fear and surprise to determination. She let out a bloodcurdling cry and shifted to coyote form, shrinking out of the ropes that held her and darting right for Monty's leg. Apparently, for all his spying on folks, and for

346

all she'd stayed human while she was pregnant, Monty hadn't known that Winifred could transform at all. His look of surprise was a beautiful thing.

As the chupas behind him argued about what to do, Rhett, too, transformed, chucking his clothes and the binding ropes and flopping out as a right ugly bird. Monty was trying to stab the coyote that was going after his nethers, and Rhett pulled that string in his gut and became a man again, snatching his brother's ax off the ground and elbowing Monty in the face as the feller focused on Winifred. The chupas all started firing their guns willy-nilly, and a few arrows rained down from the highest pueblos, and Rhett had a moment to realize that he'd lost his goddamn pie plate when he'd shed his clothes and his binder, leaving his heart exposed, along with the rest of his skin. It didn't matter. He had to kill Monty.

A yelp suggested Winifred had taken a bad bullet, but that didn't stop her from harrying Monty, brave and vicious as hell, and Rhett took two more bullets as he maneuvered behind the man who'd taught him how to gentle a horse, the man who'd first understood and accepted that the little girl who watched the cowpokes from the white-painted boards didn't want to be a girl at all. Monty had called him Nat, given him the gift of letting him begin his life as a man, and he had to accept that that version of Monty was gone. This bleeding, angry, hateful thing focused on killing a woman and her baby was nothing but a monster.

Sliding around behind Monty, Rhett grabbed the feller's white hair, pulled back his head, and slit his throat from ear to ear with Revenge's ax.

Rhett had never felt a blade scrape against the tough tube of a man's throat before, and it jarred him to the bone. The whole time, Monty was laughing that sick laugh of his, the blood gurgling out.

"Why won't you die?" Rhett muttered, and he yanked that hank of old man hair all the harder.

Whatever he'd done to Monty's throat kept the feller from mouthing off, but a knife swiped in, skittering over Rhett's bare ribs in a burning arc, and Chuck hissed, "Because he can't, dumbass."

Rhett dropped Monty and squared off with the younger chupa now, seeing nothing of the old Chuck in the monster's slitted eyes. "Dumbass yourself. Everything can die. You just got to figure out how."

They took turns lunging at each other as the battle raged on, and Rhett mostly forgot he was naked until Chuck's Bowie knife sliced open one of his tits, which he conveniently forgot most of the time.

"Goddamn your eyes, Chuck!" he howled, dancing back and sparing a glance at his chest to find it jaggedly flayed open like Sunday bacon.

Chuck laughed a cruel laugh. "You even fight like a girl."

Before Rhett could find the right words to answer to that, an arrow thwacked into Chuck's eye, and the feller stumbled back and fell on his ass, scrabbling at his face and hissing.

"Thanks, Dan, but this one is mine." Without glancing overhead, Rhett stabbed Chuck right in the heart with his Bowie knife and watched him turn to sand. Regret twisted in his gut; there were so few people left who'd ever been kind to him.

"So long, shithead," he said.

He pulled Chuck's revolvers out of his holster and stood to see where the fight had gone.

Digby and Lizzie were harrying the chupacabras in their shifter forms, an enormous lion and a dirty gold wolf ripping out throats and spitting out chunks of acid-edged flesh. Winifred wasn't nearby, and at first Rhett was certain she'd taken a hit and turned to sand despite any protection from the god or the cat shaman who'd cursed—or, hell, blessed—her. But then he saw her, naked and round in human form, skittering up a ladder. He followed her progress to find Dan up high, battling three chupacabras and taking plenty of licks for his trouble.

"Goddammit," Rhett muttered.

There were maybe a dozen chupas on the ground and fighting still, but Rhett could leave them for Digby and Lizzie. He shot the ones who came after him with Chuck's guns until he was out of bullets, then picked up the guns in the next holster he found in a puddle of sand and clothes and kept shooting. He'd taken plenty of bullets by the time he got to the ladder and struggled to climb with blood-slicked hands. Looking down at himself wasn't an option. He hated his body at the best of times, and just now it was bare to the world and full of holes, some regular bullets and some silver popping out at intervals, and his chest was a mess of garbled flesh.

None of that mattered. He had to save Dan if he wanted any hope of saving Sam.

Up and up he climbed, and folks shot at him from the ground, but he saved his bullets and just climbed faster. Three ladders and he stopped, not quite at the top rungs, aiming for one of the chupas fussing with Dan. The fellers were slick with blood and acid and writhed like snakes, but he managed to grab one by the boot and yank him down through the hole. While the feller tried to regain his feet on the floor below, Rhett got him in the heart, and that left just two chupas between Dan and Rhett, which wasn't too bad a game.

Dragging himself out of the ladder hole on his belly, he winced to feel his chest closing up all wrong; must've been a silver knife. It looked like a raw ham poorly butchered, and it hurt like hell, and he gritted his teeth and stood to put a gun to the back of a chupa's head. When he pulled the trigger, the chupa's face exploded all over Dan. But instead of it being a good thing, Dan started shrieking his fool head off and dancing around, and Rhett realized that the acid in the chupa's blood and spit was all over Dan's face and eyes.

"Goddammit!" he hollered.

As the flailing chupa caught hold of Dan and dripped more acid blood all over him, the other chupa saw his opening and went for Sam's door. It was wedged into the wall pretty tight, but the feller pried it off like the top of a tin of peaches and dove into the darkness beyond.

"Sorry, Dan," Rhett muttered, chasing the chupacabra into the hole and feeling the acid burn his bare feet as he stepped through a puddle of what was left of the exploded chupacabra's face.

After the bright sunshine outside, Sam's hidey-hole was a pitch-black eternity with no way to aim a gun. Rhett closed his eye and let the Shadow guide him. He could feel the chupa, likewise blind but following his goddamn snake nose to the black hump of Sam's sleeping body, could feel the feller's sick excitement at catching his prey unaware.

"Hey, asshole," Rhett said.

But the chupa didn't turn around or attack.

Rhett heard him move, slithering, and launched himself in that direction.

The chupa sidestepped him, and the room filled with the blinding burst of gunfire.

But not aimed at Rhett.

At Sam.

CHAPTER
30

N o!"

Rhett flung himself at the chupacabra, taking the critter
down hard on the stone floor. A rib popped as they landed,
but it served only to fuel Rhett's rage. The chupa writhed in
his grip, moving like an angry snake, all muscle and spit, sharp
fingernails digging into Rhett's soft spots and teeth scraping
along Rhett's shoulder hungrily. Rhett elbowed him in the face
and hunted for a likewise soft spot to put his gun. It wasn't the
heart, but it would do, and he pulled the trigger and felt the
chupa jump at the close impact. It kept clawing him, though,
struggling against him, and Rhett shot him again. Then he
heard it. A familiar voice.

"That you, Nat?"

He stilled, knowing it instantly.

"Hellfire, Poke. Not you, too?"

The dusty chuckle tugged at his heartstrings. The older feller
had been kind, back at the Double TK Ranch. "You know me.
I go where Monty goes. Some of us weren't meant for—"

A knife landed in Rhett's leg, and he cussed himself for letting old-timey feelings make him soft.

"Fuck you, Poke, you chupacabra bastard!"

He wrestled the chupa with renewed rage, but it didn't escape him that in all their rolling around, they didn't knock into Sam. He felt Sam's blankets and straw tick under his bare, scraped knees, but not the cold, still body that should've been there.

Poke managed to stab him again, and Rhett felt up the body entangled with his until his fingers found nipping teeth. He struggled with the gun, getting it up against the feller's biting chin, and pulled the trigger. Acid blood and chunks of bone splashed all over him, but at least Poke couldn't see or smell or talk with that sweet old familiar voice anymore. As Poke's clutching fingers sought his face, Rhett felt down the feller's ruined chin, down his neck, all the way to his chest. He put the gun's barrel there, pulled the trigger, and collapsed in a puff of sand and an old man's tobacco-smoke smelling clothes.

The cave was quiet. Rhett's skin burned. Poke was gone. But when he felt around the straw tick and the blanket, hunting for Sam, desperate and crying and hurting, all he found was yet more sand.

CHAPTER 31

Stumbling naked into daylight, Rhett was blinded. He cupped a hand over his good eye and strained to hear the sounds of the ongoing fight. There was Lizzie's growl, and somewhere else, a cat's shriek of fury.

"Dan?" he called. "You out here?"

"Barely," Dan said, and the dryness of his voice made Rhett grin. If Dan was still feeling salty, he wasn't quite dead yet. But that grin disappeared.

"Dan, it's Sam. He's gone. I can't—"

"Shut up, fool. There are more chupacabras that need killing."

"But he ain't—"

"I told you to shut up and do your damn job!"

Another chupa skittered up the ladder, and Dan struggled to boot him in the face and mostly failed. Rhett could see now, and what he saw of Dan's eyes—it wasn't good.

"You blind, Dan?" he asked, more gentle than usual.

"Mostly, asshole. Now kill him."

Scrabbling for a gun on the ground, Rhett obliged. It took three shots before the chupa puffed into sand.

"How many more are there, Rhett?"

"But…hell. Do you think it'll fix itself? Your eyes? Or is it like silver?" He unconsciously touched the tight pink scar tissue over his own destroyed eye.

Dan's voice went hard and angry. "How many goddamn chupacabras?"

Rhett pulled himself up to peek over the wall.

"Just six that I can see."

"Then start shooting. Or go down there with a knife. Just kill them."

"Hell, Dan. I know that. But you got to tell me if Sam's alive."

"For once in your sweet goddamn life would you shut up about Sam and think of someone else? You're the Shadow! People need you! You've already lost enough! So go finish off the chupas!" Dan slammed a fist into the sandstone and didn't even seem to feel it. He was fetched up against the wall, full of bullet holes and knife wounds, his eyes turned up to the sky and gone white like an old man's.

"He's all I got left!" Rhett screamed. "My mama, my brother—"

Dan clumsily caught his shoulders, his hands slick with blood. "Do your fucking job, Rhett."

Overcome with loss, naked and weary, Rhett felt the full shame of his selfishness crash down.

"I guess I will, Dan."

Rhett gathered up fresh bullets from the holsters of the dead chupas and reloaded before climbing down the ladder. He moved slow and sad now, like he was caught in quicksand. He didn't care that he was naked and completely exposed, that he was mauled, that he had no protection for his heart.

Sam was his heart. Had been his heart. And it looked like Sam was gone.

Just like his mama and Revenge.

He moved through the battlefield like a ghost. Bullets slammed into him but didn't bother him more than mosquitoes on a summer night. He put down three chupas until all that were left were the two fellers tussling with Digby and Lizzie and a single figure still on the ground. As he got closer, knife in hand, he realized it was Monty. Monty, whose throat was slit, but who flat-out refused to die. The feller's chest was still moving up and down, bubbling blood out of the open hole in his neck with every breath as the wound slowly, so slowly, closed up.

"Slit your damn throat and you still won't leave me be," Rhett said, tired beyond his bones and half-empty of blood himself.

"I...still...won..." Monty hissed. Rhett bent over to hear him better. "Killed...everybody...you love. You might...as well...be dead."

Rhett sighed and plucked up some twigs and bits of dry grass, dropping them on Monty's shirt.

"You might be right at that. You always did know best. But the thing about coming from nothing is that you know what to do when you're back there again. If surviving's all I got left, then hell, I'll survive. I seen worse. You can't kill what's good inside me, even if you lost everything that was good inside you."

Moving like Mam the morning after a bender, Rhett went through the motions he'd once performed himself, then delegated to Earl. Gathering tinder, twisting a stick between his abraded palms. When the first tiny spark caught, he blew on it, gentle and slow, coaxing it to life. He fed it little bits of grass and fluff until it sputtered into a flame, and then he placed that flame on the pile of tinder on Monty's shirt and watched the fabric catch. As it ate into the plaid, he stood to look down into the first face he reckoned he'd ever loved.

"Another old man I cared for taught me that you got to burn your dead so they don't come back to haunt you. I've shot you in the heart and slit your throat, so I reckon this has got to be the only gift I have left to give the man you used to be."

The flames licked and burned and caught, blooming out of Monty's chest. When his hands rose to bat at it, Rhett sighed and picked up the rope that had once held his brother, and with it he tied Monty's wrists together, dragging them over his head and holding them there as the flames consumed him. Monty began to twist and writhe, his mouth open in a silent scream, but nothing came out except a hissing noise that sounded less like a chupacabra and more like a little snake trying to save himself from becoming supper.

"You wanted to watch the world burn? Well, now I just want to watch you burn and let the world go on about its business."

He stood there, watching, until Monty was nothing but a blackened husk amid the flames, surrounded by patches of soft, fresh sand.

And then he fetched a shovel from the wagon and bashed that husk to ashes and spread the ashes all around.

He would not kill Monty a third time.

CHAPTER 32

Rhett?"

Rhett opened his gummy eye to find a flannel shirt carefully draped over his naked body and Digby standing nearby. It was getting on to evening, the day gone cold and the sky edging into the purple of a fresh bruise. He'd woken up feeling worse, he reckoned, but not by much. Despite the wounds, many of which contained itchy goddamn silver bullets that needed to be removed, he just felt numb.

"What?"

"It's just that you been sleeping all day. Me and Lizzie, we tried to make things nicer, but we thought you might want to come away from . . . from the ashes. Find you a nicer place to sleep, come nightfall."

Rhett sat up, rubbing his eye and gasping as the wound on his bosom reopened.

"Fucking silver," he murmured. "We got to get us a new saw-bones. Just don't tell 'em we already lost two."

"He is delirious," Lizzie said, a little farther off. "It takes people like that, sometimes."

"What does?" Digby asked.

"War."

Grunting, Rhett stood on wobbling legs, clutching the shirt to his front. "I need some clothes. My spare clothes. And boots. Not these goddamn chupacabra duds. Up in the top pueblo, and I do apologize for the trouble."

A brief chuckle from Dan echoed overhead. "If Rhett's apologizing, you know he feels like shit." Before Rhett could retort, his clothes fluttered down to land in the dirt, followed by the two hard thumps of a pair of boots.

He didn't even pause before sliding into his pants and buttoning up his shirt. For once, he didn't bother with a binder. With his chest mangled, it would only pain him.

"You're a sight."

Rhett looked up, grinning, to hear Winifred's voice from another pueblo.

"Well, hell. I wasn't looking to take you to a fancy dress ball," he shot back, which was as close as he'd come to telling her he was goddamn happy she was still alive. "Not that you'd fit in a fancy dress now, anyway."

"Yes, Rhett. The baby's fine, even with my shifting. Thanks for asking." The ladder creaked as she climbed down and walked over. She had dark purple bags under her eyes and a few new scars, and she still limped from her troublesome foot, but he'd been expecting a lot worse.

"How's your brother?" he asked, real low.

"Pissed off!" Dan's voice came from the upper pueblo. "And my sense of hearing is even better now, so don't you dare try to mother hen me."

"Well, ain't you gonna come down here?" Rhett asked. "Join..." He looked around, finding only three people. "Hell, what's left of our crew?"

Dan's sigh was loud, even from that distance. "If I must."

It took the feller some time to navigate, but since he didn't fall down or walk into anything, Rhett figured he still had some of his vision. He couldn't help staring as Dan moseyed up, and Dan snapped, "I can still see shapes and shadows. I can still ride a horse."

"At least you'll never try to teach me how to shoot a bow again."

Dan's teeth ground in that old familiar way. "You pick the dumbest shit to be happy about."

It all rushed back in that moment: Sam was gone.

They'd beat El Rey and his chupacabras, but Sam was gone.

And his mama, and Revenge, and all the rest. Hell, even Inés, probably.

"There's...There's...oh, hell, Dan. Don't talk to me about happy. Not now."

Without meaning to, he fell to his knees, face in his hands, his many wounds forgotten. "Not without Sam."

The next sound he heard sent his fingers for a gun that wasn't there.

"Who the fuck is laughing right now?" he asked, low and deadly.

"Always with the melodrama."

That wry voice gave him the tiniest bit of hope. "Inés? But I thought..."

He looked up and saw her standing at a different pueblo, one he hadn't explored before. The nun looked calm and unruffled, her habit as neat as a pin as she stood in a forest of chupacabra statues, all the same gray stone as the ones that had decorated the chapel of her mission in San Anton. It was so easy to forget the tiny nun was a gorgon, and that her fighting style involved merely lifting up her veil and letting the enemy look into her eyes.

"You think a lot of things, Rhett. That doesn't make them true."

Her lightness, her humor...it rankled him. "What the hell were you doing when we needed you on the ground?"

"Silly boy," she said. "I was here. For good reason I was fighting a different kind of battle."

"What the hell does that mean?"

She held up a gloved hand, gesturing to the open door in the wall behind her. "I was guarding something important."

And then damn if Samuel Hennessy didn't walk right out of it.

Chapter 33

Wounds or no, exhaustion or no, Rhett had never moved as fast as he did just then, scurrying up the ladders like a goddamn squirrel, his heart beating like a drum.

"Sam? What the—how were—are you? How are you alive?"

He dragged himself up beside Inés, and even through her veil, he could feel her smug amusement. For once, it didn't bother him.

"I guarded him," she said simply.

"After we moved him," Dan added. "Under a thick blanket."

Rhett dodged a row of chupacabra statues and barreled into Sam's arms. All his pain was forgotten as he buried his nose in Sam's neck and left tears there in exchange.

"I thought I'd lost you," he murmured.

"I went to sleep fearing the same thing." Sam's voice was ragged with feeling, his own tears coursing down Rhett's face. "I guess we won?"

"We lost...we lost a lot of people, Sam. It wasn't a pretty fight. But you're here. You're here now, and that's enough."

"Speaking only for myself, I'm glad several of us are still here," Inés said. "But I'll leave you two to discuss it." Sweeping her long skirts back, she climbed down the ladder with the grace of a duchess on a grand staircase, and Rhett turned all his attention to Sam.

"No more fighting," he said.

Sam chuckled, a sweet sound indeed.

"I don't believe it for a second, but I appreciate the thought."

CHAPTER
34

The good thing about fighting monsters was that the cleanup wasn't a problem. A little extra sand just blew away on the desert wind, and even Monty's ashes were easily swept away by Inés's broom. Rhett gathered up a pinch of the sand where his mama and brother had died and added it to his little bag. He kept Revenge's ax and Finder's quiver, too, for all that looking at them pained his heart. They never did find Beans or Notch, and there was no way to know if the fellers had died valiantly or run away rather than face the chupacabras.

They gathered up guns and holsters and clothes and boots to save for later and collected what coins and bullets they could from Monty's men. It took time to round up the horses, but as soon as Little Eagle's men brought back the rest of the herd, along with an antelope they'd shot for dinner, every abandoned mount in the county bugled a request to join their crew.

Rhett moved among them, patting Ragdoll and Puddin' and Squirrel and BB and yanking saddles down off the new horses so they wouldn't have to suffer sore backs or bellies. Digby's two steers came lolloping up, mooing like the world's worst watchdogs, and Digby fell to scratching them under their chins and behind their ears like the world's worst cattleman while

Squirrel nipped his shoulder for her due attention. Sasquatch Bill climbed down off the top of the pueblo, where he'd been waiting with a pile of rocks and a couple of boulders, watching the other side for chupa reinforcements, as close as the pacifist could come to pulling his weight. Outside of the folks they'd lost, it was a pretty fine night of relief.

The moon was full and the stars were out, and Winifred picked bullets out of Rhett with that old, hated tweezer as Inés held a lantern aloft.

"You women just love jabbing me," Rhett groused as bits of bloody silver hit his pie plate.

"We do." Winifred rolled a crumpled bullet between her fingers. "That's why we cleave to you."

That made him squirm. "So will you leave, now that you don't feel that...that tug anymore? Because if I can't feel it, which I don't, I reckon you don't, either."

Because ever since Monty had died, that ominous, dark feeling had just floated away. Rhett felt, as much as he could, free. And it didn't feel as fine as he'd hoped it would. He'd gotten used to having folks around, and for all that he told himself Sam was enough, he was sick of patching holes in his heart when his chosen folks were lost. He wanted them to stay.

"Oh, I think I'll stick around awhile," Winifred said. "This baby needs a solid roof over her head, and Kachina is carrying a foal, and my brother says this is sacred ground. Not many places left where you can just pick your home and not be chased off the land by white men. But they'll never want this place. It's too wild and haunted."

"And that don't worry you?"

Winifred dropped another silver bullet in the pan and poked Rhett in the kidneys, making him giggle in a horrible fashion.

"Fool. I myself am wild and haunted. I'll fit right in."

Time got lazy, after that. Rhett told Sam his stories, and Dan and Digby and Lizzie and Inés and Winifred all had to correct him and tell their own, more correct versions. Sam couldn't believe his old friend Monty had gone bad and done so much damage, and when Rhett told him that Poke had been the one who came closest to killing him while he slept, he'd been downright shocked.

"They were fine fellers!" Sam argued.

"Until they weren't."

"That's true of anyone," Dan added. "Even the kindest dog can turn."

"Well, sure. If it gets rabies." Rhett jabbed his stick in the fire. "It wasn't Poke's fault, what happened. And I ain't saying it's mine," he hastened to inform Sam, as it was a point they'd argued over quite a bit. "I was young and I didn't know any better, back with Monty and Chuck. But Monty was something different, and he went looking for those good ol' boys we knew. And he turned 'em. And that's that."

"You're worried about it, aren't you?" Dan's white eyes seemed to see right through him. "The Devil's Brew he talked about. The brujah drink."

Rhett shrugged, feeling every wound, especially the one in his chest. "Worried, yes. But worried enough to go out looking for trouble? Hell no."

That seemed to appease Sam for the moment, but Rhett could tell the talks weren't over.

The next day, sick of watching him squirm as the silver-inflicted wound refused to heal, Inés doped Rhett with laudanum and removed his hurt bosom, cutting under the silver's damage and sealing the skin with a hot knife's blade. He felt downright lopsided when he woke up, but he thanked her nonetheless. After a few days, he asked her to take off the other one, and at first she wouldn't. Then, seeing how much happier he was, she took that one off, too. He didn't need the binder anymore. And for all that his chest was a mess of scars, he felt more like himself than he ever had, and Sam never had any complaint.

Bill the Sasquatch took his leave, doffing his hat and heading up north. Little Eagle's son, Otter Paws, spent more and more time with Winifred until he'd up and moved into her pueblo. For all that Dan's vision had gone bad, he still knew horses and could knap stone, and he did get a bit less preachy. The feller turned into a coyote more often and took off during the night, claiming that in his other form, at least his nose and ears could tell him everything he needed to know. Digby took to collecting and raising cattle, and the herd grew by leaps and bounds. Somehow, the ruse to make a cattle outfit had produced a mighty fine cattle outfit. Lizzie disappeared for a few nights each month and came back in better humor, but otherwise didn't act much like a Lobo. Inés moved her books into her pueblo, one by one, until the wagon was empty.

Ragdoll did indeed have a handsome colt, a buckskin paint with a wild blue eye. Rhett named him Pie and raised him up so sweet that even as a stallion, he'd let Winifred's daughter, Frederica, play at his feet without stamping a hoof or whipping his tail. Slowly but with thought, Rhett and Sam built up a mighty fine herd, and if Ragdoll disappeared every now and then, he knew she'd come back carrying the finest foal in Durango. Sam disappeared every now and then, too, but he came back warm and pink and happy, so Rhett learned to live with slight discontent if it meant the feller he loved was taken care of.

Ever so slowly, as he healed, Rhett realized that nobody felt like leaving at all. His people didn't abandon him. They were building their own little town of monsters.

His life, he realized, had somehow become worth more than a sweet goddamn.

— Epilogue —

Rhett and Sam had a place they liked to sit on a pretty night and watch the stars. Maybe the white folks in Rona favored rocking chairs on a porch, but Sam and Rhett liked to ride their horses out into the desert and climb an old trail to the top of a flat butte. Up there, the stars seemed near enough to touch, twinkling like Rhett supposed diamonds would, if he'd ever had the chance to see them.

They lay there one spring night, on their backs, Rhett's head pillowed on Sam's chest and their fingers loosely intertwined. Sam had fed recently in Rona, and Rhett savored the warmth of his skin. For monsters, they were getting a bit long in the tooth, but Rhett didn't mind the streaks of white in Sam's golden hair and beard. He could only ever remember how close he'd come to losing him, not once but twice.

"It's right peaceful," Sam said, as he often did now that things were.

"Except for Frederica. I don't care if she's half god, she's got no business trick riding like that."

"And Ebenezer's hell-bent to follow in her footsteps. And he's not half god at all, even if Otter Paws fancies himself as such. If that boy were human, I reckon we'd have picked his brains up off the ground years ago and presented them to Winifred on a pie plate. Climbing all over the damn pueblo like lizards, both of 'em."

Rhett couldn't help chuckling. "Hellfire, Sam. You sound like an old woman."

"We both do."

"I reckon it's better than the alternative."

Sam's thumb rubbed over Rhett's scarred fingers.

"D'you ever feel it anymore, Rhett?"

Rhett let out a sigh. "The Shadow, I reckon you mean."

"I do. I just . . . I can't believe that after all that time it kicked your ass around Durango, it just went quiet. Just like that."

Rhett sat up and looked down into Sam's blue eyes. In all these years, he hadn't forgotten what they looked like in the light of the sun. For decades, he'd seen nothing but the moon reflected there. And he reckoned it was time to tell the truth.

"I still feel it, Sam. I've always felt it."

Sam sat up, too, worry making ridges across his forehead. "Always?"

Rhett had to look away for this part. "Yeah. I told you-all it was gone, but it never left. I felt it tug me this way and that. Felt monsters pass by within a bullet's distance. Knew when a Lobo set foot in Rona, knew when it killed. I've always known."

"Then why—"

"Because I promised you, Sam. I told you I'd give it up, and I did. The Shadow claimed a hell of a lot of good folks, folks I loved. I wasn't going to come that close again. So I just ignored it. I reckon plenty of men have something inside 'em like that, some monster that whispers to 'em all night. Pap's whiskey bottle probably had a similar voice. Men who whore or play cards know that whisper. Hell, even anger's got a whisper like that, always urging a feller to go a step too far. And I realized after

El Rey, after Monty, that...I didn't have to listen. Didn't have to obey. At first, I thought it would be the hardest thing I'd ever done. But then I realized." He reached out to stroke Sam's cheek. "It was the easiest decision I've ever made."

But Sam was shaking his head, like he didn't understand, which was exactly why Rhett hadn't told him. "But that's your destiny. Folks need you."

Rhett nodded. "They do. And they're right here. I did my time. I fought great monsters. I helped folks. But there's nothing wrong with choosing your own path. And Sam, I chose you."

Sam leaned in for a kiss, and Rhett just about stopped breathing, it was so sweet.

"I got to tell you, Sam," Rhett said, watching the stars swirl overhead. "This is a fine enough destiny for me."

ACKNOWLEDGMENTS

Hat tips and gratitude go out to the Orbit team past and present for keeping Rhett in the saddle: Nivia Evans, Lindsey Hall, Devi Pillai, Lauren Panepinto, Lisa Marie Pompilio, Tim Paul, Ellen Wright, Sarah Guan, and every cheerleader, sales staff member, and copy editor along the way.

And many, many back-slapping hugs to the readers who stayed with Rhett and me to the end. Happy trails until we meet again!

extras

orbit

www.orbitbooks.net

about the author

Lila Bowen is a pseudonym for Delilah S. Dawson. Find her online at whimsydark.com.

Find out more about Lila Bowen and other Orbit authors by registering for the free monthly newsletter at www.orbitbooks.net.

CHAPTER I

The sky was fading to ultramarine in the east over the Victoria Embankment when a battered Mini pulled in to the curb, not far from Blackfriars Bridge. Here and there in the maples lining the riverside walk, the morning's first sparrows had begun to sing.

A woman got out of the car and shut the door, swore, put down her bags, and shut the door again with more applied force; some fellow motorist had bashed into the panel at some time in the past and bent it sufficiently to make this a production every damn time. The Mini really needed to be replaced, but even with her inherited Harley Street consulting rooms Greta Helsing was not exactly drowning in cash.

She glowered at the car and then at the world in general, glancing around to make sure no one was watching her from the shadows. Satisfied, she picked up her black working bag and the shapeless oversize monster that was her current handbag and went to ring the doorbell. It was time to replace the handbag, too. The leather on this one was holding up but the lining was beginning to go, and Greta had limited patience regarding the retrieval of items from the mysterious dimension behind the lining itself.

The house to which she had been summoned was one of a

row of magnificent old buildings separating Temple Gardens from the Embankment, mostly taken over by lawyers and publishing firms these days. It was a testament to this particular homeowner's rather special powers of persuasion that nobody had succeeded in buying the house out from under him and turning it into offices for overpriced attorneys, she thought, and then had to smile at the idea of anybody dislodging Edmund Ruthven from the lair he'd inhabited these two hundred years or more. He was as much a fixture of London as Lord Nelson on his pillar, albeit less encrusted with birdlime.

"Greta," said the fixture, opening the door. "Thanks for coming out on a Sunday. I know it's late."

She was just about as tall as he was, five foot five and a bit, which made it easy to look right into his eyes and be struck every single time by the fact that they were very large, so pale a grey they looked silver-white except for the dark ring at the edge of the iris, and fringed with heavy soot-black lashes of the sort you saw in advertisements for mascara. He looked tired, she thought. Tired, and older than the fortyish he usually appeared. The extreme pallor was normal, vivid against the pure slicked-back black of his hair, but the worried line between his eyebrows was not.

"It's not Sunday night, it's Monday morning," she said. "No worries, Ruthven. Tell me everything; I know you didn't go into lots of detail on the phone."

"Of course." He offered to take her coat. "I'll make you some coffee."

The entryway of the Embankment house was floored in black-and-white-checkered marble, and a large bronze ibis stood on a little side table where the mail and car keys and shopping lists were to be found. The mirror behind this reflected Greta dimly and greenly, like a woman underwater; she peered into it, making a face at herself, and tucked back her hair. It was pale Scandinavian blonde and cut like Liszt's in an off-the-shoulder bob, fine enough to slither free of whatever she used to pull it back; today it was in the process of escaping from a thoroughly childish headband. She kept meaning to have it all chopped off and be done with it but never seemed to find the time.

Greta Helsing was thirty-four, unmarried, and had taken over her late father's specialized medical practice after a brief stint as an internist at King's College Hospital. For the past five years she had run a bare-bones clinic out of Wilfert Helsing's old rooms in Harley Street, treating a patient base that to the majority of the population did not, technically, when you got right down to it, exist. It was a family thing.

There had never been much doubt which subspecialty of medicine she would pursue, once she began her training: treating the differently alive was not only more interesting than catering to the ordinary human population, it was in many ways a great deal more rewarding. She took a lot of satisfaction in being able to provide help to particularly underserved clients.

Greta's patients could largely be classified under the heading of *monstrous*—in its descriptive, rather than pejorative, sense: vampires, were-creatures, mummies, banshees, ghouls, bogeymen, the occasional arthritic barrow-wight. She herself was solidly and entirely human, with no noticeable eldritch qualities or powers whatsoever, not even a flicker of metaphysical sensitivity. Some of her patients found it difficult to trust a human physician at first, but Greta had built up an extremely good reputation over the five years she had been practicing supernatural medicine, largely by word of mouth: *Go to Helsing, she's reliable.*

And *discreet*. That was the first and fundamental tenet, after all. Keeping her patients safe meant keeping them secret, and

Greta was good with secrets. She made sure the magical wards around her doorway in Harley Street were kept up properly, protecting anyone who approached from prying eyes.

Ruthven appeared in the kitchen doorway, outlined by light spilling warm over the black-and-white marble. "Greta?" he said, and she straightened up, realizing she'd been staring into the mirror without really seeing it for several minutes now. It really *was* late. Fatigue lapped heavily at the pilings of her mind.

"Sorry," she said, coming to join him, and a little of that heaviness lifted as they passed through into the familiar warmth and brightness of the kitchen. It was all blue tile and blond wood, the cheerful rose-gold of polished copper pots and pans balancing the sleek chill of stainless steel, and right now it was also full of the scent of really *good* coffee. Ruthven's espresso machine was a La Cimbali, and it was serious business.

He handed her a large pottery mug. She recognized it as one of the set he generally used for blood, and had to smile a little, looking down at the contents—and then abruptly had to clamp down on a wave of thoroughly inconvenient emotion. There was no reason that Ruthven doing goddamn *latte art* for her at half-past four in the morning should make her want to cry.

He was *good* at it, too, which was a little infuriating; then again she supposed that with as much free time on his hands as he had on his, and as much disposable income, she might find herself learning and polishing new skills simply to stave off the encroaching spectre of boredom. Ruthven didn't go in for your standard-variety vampire angst, which was refreshing, but Greta knew very well he had bouts of something not unlike depression—especially in the winter—and he needed things to *do*.

She, however, *had* things to do, Greta reminded herself, taking a sip of the latte and closing her eyes for a moment. This was coffee that actually tasted as good as, if not better than, it smelled. *Focus,* she thought. This was not a social call. The lack of urgency in Ruthven's manner led her to believe that the situation was not immediately dire, but she was nonetheless here to do her job.

Greta licked coffee foam from her upper lip. "So," she said. "Tell me what happened."

"I was—" Ruthven sighed, leaning against the counter with his arms folded. "To be honest I was sitting around twiddling my thumbs and writing nasty letters to the *Times* about how much I loathe these execrable skyscrapers somebody keeps allowing vandals to build all over the city. I'd got to a particularly cutting phrase about the one that sets people's cars on fire, when somebody knocked on the door."

The passive-aggressive-letter stage tended to indicate that his levels of ennui were reaching critical intensity. Greta just nodded, watching him.

"I don't know if you've ever read an ancient penny-dreadful called *Varney the Vampyre, or The Feast of Blood,*" he went on.

"Ages ago," she said. She'd read practically all the horror classics, well-known and otherwise, for research purposes rather than to enjoy their literary merit. Most of them were to some extent entertainingly wrong about the individuals they claimed to depict. "It was quite a lot funnier than your unofficial biography, but I'm not sure it was *meant* to be."

Ruthven made a face. John Polidori's *The Vampyre* was, he insisted, mostly libel—the very mention of the book was sufficient to bring on indignant protestations that he and the Lord Ruthven featured in the narrative shared little more than a name. "At least the authors got the spelling right, unlike bloody Polidori," he said.

"I think probably *Feast of Blood* is about as historically accurate as *The Vampyre*, which is to say *not very*, but it does have the taxonomy right. Varney, unlike me, *is* a vampyre with a *y*."

"A lunar sensitive? I haven't actually met one before," she said, clinical interest surfacing through the fatigue. The vampires she knew were all classic draculines, like Ruthven himself and the handful of others in London. Lunar sensitives were rarer than the draculine vampires for a couple of reasons, chief among which was the fact that they were violently—and inconveniently—allergic to the blood of anyone but virgins. They did have the handy characteristic of being resurrected by moonlight every time they got themselves killed, which presumably came as some small comfort in the process of succumbing to violent throes of gastric distress brought on by dietary indiscretion.

"Well," Ruthven said, "now's your chance. He showed up on my doorstep, completely unannounced, looking like thirty kinds of warmed-over hell, and collapsed in the hallway. He is at the moment sleeping on the drawing room sofa, and I want you to look at him for me. I don't *think* there's any real danger, but he's been hurt—some maniacs apparently attacked him with a knife—and I'd feel better if you had a look."

Ruthven had lit a fire, despite the relative mildness of the evening, and the creature lying on the sofa was covered with two blankets. Greta glanced from him to Ruthven, who shrugged a little, that line of worry between his eyebrows very visible.

According to him, Sir Francis Varney, title and all, had come out of his faint quite quickly and perked up after some first aid and the administration of a nice hot mug of suitable and brandy-laced blood. Ruthven kept a selection of the stuff in his expensive fridge and freezer, stocked by Greta via fairly illegal supply chain management—she knew someone who knew someone who worked in a blood bank and was not above rescuing rejected units from the biohazard incinerator.

Sir Francis had drunk the whole of the mug's contents with every evidence of satisfaction and promptly gone to sleep as soon as Ruthven let him, whereupon Ruthven had called Greta and requested a house call. "I don't really like the look of him," he said now, standing in the doorway with uncharacteristic awkwardness. "He was bleeding a little—the wound's in his left shoulder. I cleaned it up and put a dressing on, but it was still sort of oozing. Which isn't like us."

"No," Greta agreed, "it's not. It's possible that lunar sensitives and draculines respond differently to tissue trauma, but even so, I would have expected him to have mostly finished healing already. You were right to call me."

"Do you need anything?" he asked, still standing in the doorway as Greta pulled over a chair and sat down beside the sofa.

"Possibly more coffee. Go on, Ruthven. I've got this; go and finish your unkind letter to the editor."

When he had gone she tucked back her hair and leaned over to examine her patient. He took up the entire length of the sofa, head pillowed on one armrest and one narrow foot resting on the other, half-exposed where the blankets had fallen away. She did a bit of rough calculation and guessed he must be at least six inches taller than Ruthven, possibly more.

His hair was tangled, streaky-grey, worn dramatically long— that was aging-rock-frontman hair if Greta had ever seen it, but nothing *else* about him seemed to fit with the Jagger aesthetic. An old-fashioned face, almost Puritan: long, narrow nose, deeply hooded eyes under intense eyebrows, thin mouth bracketed with habitual lines of disapproval.

Or pain, she thought. *That could be pain.*

The shifting of a log in the fireplace behind Greta made her jump a little, and she regathered the wandering edges of her concentration. With a nasty little flicker of surprise she noticed that there was a faint sheen of sweat on Varney's visible skin. That *really* wasn't right.

"Sir Francis?" she said, gently, and leaned over to touch his shoulder through the blankets—and a moment later had retreated halfway across the room, heart racing: Varney had gone from uneasy sleep to *sitting up and snarling viciously* in less than a second.

It was not unheard-of for Greta's patients to threaten her, especially when they were in considerable pain, and on the whole she probably should have thought this out a little better. She'd only got a glimpse before her own instincts had kicked in and got her the hell out of range of those teeth, but it would be a while before she could forget that pattern of dentition, or those mad tin-colored eyes.

He covered his face with his hands, shoulders slumping, and instead of menace was now giving off an air of intense embarrassment.

Greta came back over to the sofa. "I'm sorry," she said, tentatively, "I didn't mean to startle you—"

"I most devoutly apologize," he said, without taking his hands away. "I do *try* not to do that, but I am not quite at my best just now—forgive me, I don't believe we have been introduced."

He was looking at her from behind his fingers, and the eyes really *were* metallic. Even partly hidden she could see the room's reflection in his irises. She wondered if that was a peculiarity of his species, or an individual phenomenon.

"It's all right," she said, and sat down on the edge of the sofa, judging that he wasn't actually about to tear her throat out just at the moment. "My name's Greta. I'm a doctor; Ruthven called me to come and take a look at you."

When Varney finally took his hands away from his face, pushing the damp silvering hair back, his color was frankly terrible. He *was* sweating. That was not something she'd ever seen in sanguivores under any circumstance.

"A doctor?" he asked, blinking at her. "Are you sure?"

She was spared having to answer that. A moment later he squeezed his eyes shut, very faint color coming and going high on each cheek. "I really am sorry," he said. "What a remarkably stupid question. It's just—I tend to think of doctors as looking rather different than you."

"I left my pinstripe trousers and pocket-watch at home," she said drily. "But I've got my black bag, if that helps. Ruthven said you'd been hurt—attacked by somebody with a knife. May I take a look?"

He glanced up at her and then away again, and nodded once, leaning back against the sofa cushions, and Greta reached into her bag for the exam gloves.

The wound was in his left shoulder, as Ruthven had said, about two and a half inches south of the collarbone. It wasn't large—she had seen much nastier injuries from street fights, although in rather different species—but it was undoubtedly the *strangest* wound she'd ever come across.

"What made this?" she asked, looking closer, her gloved fingers careful on his skin. Varney hissed and turned his face away, and she could feel a thrumming tension under her touch. "I've never seen anything like it. The wound is...*cross*-shaped."

It was. Instead of just the narrow entry mark of a knife, or the bruised puncture of something clumsier, Varney's wound appeared to have been made by something flanged. Not just two but four sharp edges, leaving a hole shaped like an X—or a cross.

"It was a spike," he said, between his teeth. "I didn't get a very good look at it. They had—broken into my flat, with garlic. Garlic was everywhere. Smeared on the walls, scattered all over the floor. I was—taken by surprise, and the fumes—I could hardly see or breathe."

"I'm not surprised," said Greta, sitting up. "It's extremely nasty stuff. Are you having any chest pain or trouble breathing now?"

A lot of the organic compounds in *Allium sativum* triggered a severe allergic response in vampires, varying in intensity based on amount and type of exposure. This wasn't garlic shock, or not *just* garlic shock, though. He was definitely running a fever, and the hole in his shoulder should have healed to a shiny pink memory within an hour or so after it happened. Right now it was purple-black and...oozing.

"No," Varney said, "just—the wound is, ah, really rather painful." He sounded apologetic. "As I said, I didn't get a close look at the spike, but it was short and pointed like a rondel dagger, with a round pommel. There were three people there, I don't know if they all had knives, but...well, as it turned out, all they needed was one."

This was so very much not her division. "Did—do you have any idea why they attacked you?" Or why they'd broken into his flat and poisoned it with garlic. That was a pretty specialized tactic, after all. Greta shivered in sudden unease.

"They were chanting, or...reciting something," he said, his odd eyes drifting shut. "I couldn't make out much of it, just that it sounded sort of ecclesiastical."

He had a remarkably beautiful voice, she noticed. The rest of him wasn't tremendously prepossessing, particularly those eyes, but his voice was *lovely*: sweet and warm and clear. It contrasted oddly with the actual content of what he was saying. "Something about... *unclean*," he continued, "*unclean* and wicked, *wickedness*, foulness, and... *demons*. Creatures of darkness."

He still had his eyes half-closed, and Greta frowned and bent over him again. "Sir Francis?"

"Hurts," he murmured, sounding very far away. "They were dressed... strangely."

She rested two fingers against the pulse in his throat: much too fast, and he couldn't have spiked *that* much in the minutes she had been with him, but he felt noticeably warmer to her touch. She reached into the bag for her thermometer and the BP cuff. "Strangely how?"

"Like... monks," he said, and blinked up at her, hazy and confused. "In... brown robes. With crosses round their necks. Like *monks*."

His eyes rolled back slightly, slipping closed, and he gave a little terrible sigh; when Greta took him by the shoulders and gave him a shake he did not rouse at all, head rolling limp against the cushions. *What the hell,* she thought, *what the actual hell is going on here, there's no way a wound like this should be affecting him so badly, this is—it looks like systemic inflammatory response but the garlic should have worn off by now, there's nothing to* cause *it, unless—*

Unless there had been something on the blade. Something *left behind.*

That flicker of visceral unease was much stronger now. She leaned closer, gently drawing apart the edges of the wound—the tissue was swollen, red, warmer than the surrounding skin—and was surprised to notice a faint but present smell. Not the characteristic smell of infection, but something sharper, almost metallic, with a sulfurous edge on it like silver tarnish. It was strangely familiar, but she couldn't seem to place it.

Greta was rather glad he was unconscious just at the moment, because what she was about to do would be quite remarkably painful. She stretched the wound open a little wider, wishing she had her penlight to get a better view, and he shifted a little, his breath catching; as he moved she caught a glimpse of something reflective half-obscured by dark blood. There *was* something still in there. Something that needed to come out right now.

"Ruthven," she called, sitting up. "Ruthven, I need you."

He emerged from the kitchen, looking anxious. "What is it?

"Get the green leather instrument case out of my bag," she said, "and put a pan of water on to boil. There's a foreign body in here I need to extract."

Without a word Ruthven took the instrument case and disappeared again. Greta turned her attention back to her patient, noticing for the first time that the pale skin of his chest was crisscrossed by old scarring—*very* old, she thought, looking at the silvery laddered marks of long-healed injuries. She had seen Ruthven without his shirt on, and he had a pretty good collection of scars from four centuries' worth of misadventure, but Varney put him to shame. *A lot of duels,* she thought. *A lot of…* lost *duels.*

Greta wondered how much of *Feast of Blood* was actually based on historical events. He had died at least once in the part of it that she remembered, and had spent a lot of time running away from various pitchfork-wielding mobs. None of *them* had been dressed up in monastic drag, as far as she knew, but they had certainly demonstrated the same intent as whoever had hurt Varney tonight.

A cold flicker of something close to fear slipped down her spine, and she turned abruptly to look over her shoulder at the empty room, pushing away a sudden and irrational sensation of being watched.

Don't be ridiculous, she told herself, *and do your damn job.*
She was a little grateful for the business of wrapping the BP cuff
around his arm, and less pleased by what it told her. Not critical,
but certainly a long way from what she considered normal for
sanguivores. She didn't know what was going on in there, but
she didn't like it one bit.

When Ruthven returned carrying a tea tray, she felt irration-
ally relieved to see him—and then had to raise an eyebrow at
the contents of the tray. Her probes and forceps and retractors
lay on a metal dish Greta recognized after a moment as the one
that normally went under the toast rack, dish and instruments
steaming gently from the boiling water—and beside them was
an empty basin with a clean tea towel draped over it. Everything
was very, very neat, as if he had done it many times before. As if
he'd had practice.

"Since when are *you* a scrub nurse?" she asked, nodding for
him to set the tray down. "I mean—thank you, this is exactly
what I need, I appreciate it, and if you could hold the light for
me I'd appreciate that even more."

"*De rien,*" said Ruthven, and went to fetch her penlight.
A few minutes later, Greta held her breath as she carefully, carefully withdrew her forceps from Varney's shoulder. Held between
the steel tips was a piece of something hard and angular, about
the size of a pea. That metallic, sharp smell was much stronger
now, much more noticeable.

She turned to the tray on the table beside her, dropped the
thing into the china basin with a little *rat-tat* sound, and straightened up. The wound was bleeding again; she pressed a gauze pad
over it. The blood looked *brighter* now, somehow, which made
no sense at all.

Ruthven clicked off the penlight, swallowing hard, and Greta looked up at him. "What *is* that thing?" he asked, nodding to the basin.

"I've no idea," she told him. "I'll have a look at it after I'm happier with him. He's pushing eighty-five degrees and his pulse rate is approaching low human baseline—"

Greta cut herself off and felt the vein in Varney's throat again. "That's strange," she said. "That's *very* strange. It's already coming down."

The beat was noticeably slower. She had another look at his blood pressure; this time the reading was much more reasonable. "I'll be damned. In a human I'd be seriously alarmed at that rapid a transient, but all bets are off with regard to hemodynamic stability in sanguivores. It's as if that thing, whatever it is, was directly responsible for the acute inflammatory reaction."

"And now that it's gone, he's starting to recover?"

"Something like that. *Don't* touch it," Greta said sharply, as Ruthven reached for the basin. "Don't even go near it. I have no idea what it would do to you, and I don't want to have two patients on my hands."

Ruthven backed away a few steps. "You're quite right," he said. "Greta, something about this smells peculiar."

"In more than one sense," she said, checking the gauze. The bleeding had almost stopped. "Did he tell you how it happened?"

"Not really. Just that he'd been jumped by several people armed with a strange kind of knife."

"Mm. A very strange kind of knife. I've never seen anything like this wound. He didn't mention that these people were dressed up like monks, or that they were reciting something about unclean creatures of darkness?"

"No," said Ruthven, flopping into a chair. "He neglected to share that tidbit with me. Monks?"

"So he said," Greta told him. "Robes and hoods, big crosses round their necks, the whole bit. Monks. And some kind of stabby weapon. Remind you of anything?"

"The Ripper," said Ruthven, slowly. "You think this has something to do with the murders?"

"I think it's one hell of a coincidence if it *doesn't*," Greta said. That feeling of unease hadn't gone away with Varney's physical improvement. It really was impossible to ignore. She'd been too busy with the immediate work at hand to consider the similarities before, but now she couldn't help thinking about it.

There had been a series of unsolved murders in London over the past month and a half. Eight people dead, all apparently the work of the same individual, all stabbed to death, all *found with a cheap plastic rosary stuffed into their mouths*. Six of the victims had been prostitutes. The killer had, inevitably, been nicknamed the Rosary Ripper.

The MO didn't exactly match how Varney had described his attack—multiple assailants, a strange-shaped knife—but it was way the hell too close for Greta's taste. "Unless whoever got Varney was a copycat," she said. "Or maybe there isn't just one Ripper. Maybe it's a group of people running around stabbing unsuspecting citizens."

"There was nothing on the news about the murders that mentioned weird-shaped wounds," Ruthven said. "Although I suppose the police might be keeping that to themselves."

The police had not apparently been able to do much of *anything* about the murders, and as one victim followed another with no end in sight the general confidence in Scotland Yard—never tremendously high—was plummeting. The entire city was both angry and frightened. Conspiracy theories abounded on the Internet, some less believable than others. This, however, was the first time Greta had heard anything about the Ripper branching out into *supernatural* victims. The garlic on the walls of Varney's flat bothered her a great deal.

Varney shifted a little, with a faint moan, and Greta returned her attention to her patient. There was visible improvement; his vitals were stabilizing, much more satisfactory than they had been before the extraction.

"He's beginning to come around," she said. "We should get him into a proper bed, but I think he's over the worst of this."

Ruthven didn't reply at once, and she looked over to see him tapping his fingers on the arm of his chair with a thoughtful expression. "What?" she asked.

"Nothing. Well, *maybe* nothing. I think I'll call Cranswell at the Museum, see if he can look a few things up for me. I will, however, wait until the morning is a little further advanced, because I am a kind man."

"What time *is* it?" Greta asked, stripping off her gloves.

"Getting on for six, I'm afraid."

"Jesus. I need to call in—there's no way I'm going to be able to do clinic hours today. Hopefully Anna or Nadezhda can take an extra shift if I do a bit of groveling."

"I have faith in your ability to grovel convincingly," Ruthven said. "Shall I go and make some more coffee?"

"Yes," she said. Both of them knew this wasn't over. "Yes, do precisely that thing, and you will earn my everlasting fealty."

"I earned your everlasting fealty last time I drove you to the airport," Ruthven said. "Or was it when I made you tiramisu a few weeks ago? I can't keep track."

He smiled, despite the line of worry still between his eyebrows, and Greta found herself smiling wearily in return.

CHAPTER 2

Neither Ruthven nor Greta noticed when something that had been watching them through the drawing room window for some time retreated, slipping away before the full light of dawn could discover it; nor were there any passersby there to watch as it crossed the road to the river and disappeared down the water stairs by the Submariners' Memorial.

In the early hours of that same Monday morning, the owner of a little corner grocery shop in Whitechapel came down to unlock the steel security grates over his display window and start preparing for the day. He had just rolled the grates up when he saw something in the street that at first he thought to be a stolen department store mannequin; on closer examination it turned out to be the body of a naked woman, her eyes nothing but raw red holes, with something pale spilling from her gaping mouth. He didn't look closely enough to make out that this was a cheap plastic rosary: as soon as he'd finished being sick, he stumbled back inside and rang the police. By the time most people were awake, it was plastered all over the newsfeeds: ripper strikes again! death toll rises to nine.

A few streets away from the grocer's shop and his unpleasant early morning discovery was the tiny office sign of Loders &

Lethbridge (Chartered Accountants), one floor up from Akbar Kebab and an establishment offering money transfer and check-cashing services. The Whitechapel Road accounting firm predated its neighbors by approximately forty years, but times were tight all over, and it had been deemed wise to move the offices upstairs and let the ground-floor space to other businesses. This meant that the entire atmosphere of the firm was permanently permeated with the smell of kebabs.

Fastitocalon, who had worked as a clerk for the firm for almost as long as it had been around, didn't really mind the grease and spice in the air, but he did object to taking it home with him in his clothes. He'd made the best of it by demanding of old Lethbridge that he be allowed to smoke in his office. This Lethbridge had grudgingly permitted, mostly because he enjoyed the occasional cigar himself—and perhaps on an unconscious level because he'd found that keeping "Mr. Frederick Vasse" more or less content seemed to be correlated with fewer boils on the back of his, Lethbridge's, neck.

Lethbridge was actually one of the more accommodating employers Fastitocalon had known in his time. It wasn't all that easy to find someone willing to hire a middle-aged and unprepossessing person with an oddly greyish complexion and a chronic cough, even if reassured that he wasn't actually contagious. Lethbridge had overlooked the physical shortcomings and hired him because of his uncanny gift for numbers, which had worked out in everyone's favor.

As a general rule Fastitocalon did his best not to read people's minds, partly out of basic good manners and partly for his own sake—most people's thoughts were not only banal but *loud*—but he knew perfectly well what Lethbridge thought of him. When he thought of Frederick Vasse at all.

Right now, for example, Lethbridge was thinking very clearly *if he can't stop that goddamn racket I'm sending him home for the day*. Fastitocalon's cough never really went away, but there were times when it was better and times when it was worse. He had run out of his prescription antitussives and kept meaning to call his doctor to get more of them, but hadn't gotten around to it; the cough had been bad for several days now, a miserable hack that hurt deep in his chest no matter how many awful blue menthol lozenges he went through.

The thought of going home was really rather appealing, even if his flat was currently on the chilly side, and when Lethbridge came into his office a few minutes later scowling intently he argued against it—but didn't argue very long.

Ruthven moved through the empty drawing room, picking up the debris of first aid supplies scattered on the floor around the sofa, the discarded gauze-pad and alcohol-wipe packaging looking oddly tawdry in the light of day. He was very much aware of the fact that he had not actually been *bored* for coming up on ten or eleven straight hours now, and that this was a profound relief.

It had become increasingly apparent to him over the past weeks that he had, yet again, run out of things to *do*, which was a perilous state of affairs. He had staved off ennui for a while this time by first renovating his house again and then by restoring an old Jaguar E-type, but the kitchen was as improved as it was going to get and the Jag was running better than new, and he had felt the soft, inexorable tides of boredom rolling in. It was November, the grey end of the year, and November always made him feel his age.

He had considered going up to Scotland, moping about a bit in more appropriate scenery. Going back to his roots. There were several extremely good reasons *not* to do this, but faced with the spectre of serious boredom Ruthven had begun to let himself imagine the muted melancholy colors of heather and gorse, the coolness of mist on his face, the somewhat excruciatingly romantic ruins of his ancestral pile. And sheep. There would be sheep, which went some way toward mitigating the Gothic atmosphere.

Technically Edmund St. James Ruthven was an earl, not a count, and he only sort of owned a ruined castle. There had been a great deal of unpleasantness at the beginning of the seventeenth century that had done funny things to the clan succession, and in any case he was also technically dead, which complicated matters. So: ruined castle, to which his claim was debatable, almost certainly featuring bats, but no wolves. Two out of three wasn't bad, even if the castle didn't overlook the Argeș.

Ruthven wasn't much of a traditionalist. He didn't even *own* a coffin, let alone sleep in one; there simply wasn't room to roll over, even in the newer, wider models, and anyway the mattresses were a complete joke and played merry hell with one's back.

He took the crumpled wrappers into the kitchen and disposed of them. Having seen Varney properly installed in one of the guest bedrooms, and been reassured that his condition—while serious—was stable, Ruthven had spent a couple of hours looking through his own not inconsiderable library. The peculiar nature of the weapon Varney had described didn't fit with anything that immediately came to mind, but something about the *idea* of it was familiar.

Now, having killed a few hours, he judged it late enough in the morning to call August Cranswell at the British Museum, hoping to catch him in the office rather than somewhere in the complicated warren of the conservation department. He was rather more relieved than he would have liked to admit when Cranswell picked up on the third ring, sounding distracted. "Hello?"

"August," Ruthven said. "Am I interrupting something?"

"No, no, no—well, yes, but it's okay. What's up?"

"I need your help with a bit of research. As usual."

"At your service, lordship," said Cranswell, a smile in his voice. "Also as usual. What's the topic this time?"

"Ceremonial daggers. To be more exact, ceremonial daggers dipped in something poisonous." Ruthven leaned against the kitchen counter, looking at the draining board by the sink: Greta's surgical instruments lay side by side on the stainless steel, once more boiled clean. It had been a long time since he'd been called upon to sterilize operating tools, not since the Second World War, in fact—but the memory was still vivid in his mind seventy-odd years later.

Cranswell's voice sharpened. "What kind of poison?"

"We don't know yet. But the dagger itself is extremely peculiar."

"You are not being even slightly reassuring," Cranswell said. "What happened?"

Ruthven sighed, removing his gaze from the probes and tweezers and directing it at the decorative tile work on the walls instead. He sketched out the events of the past night and morning as briefly as he could, feeling obscurely as if the details ought to be communicated in person, as if the phone line itself was vulnerable. "Varney is stable, at least," he concluded, "and all the...foreign material...has been removed and taken for proper analysis. Greta says he should recover, but nobody knows quite how long it'll take, and she pointed out the rather obvious similarities between this business and the Ripper cases. But the dagger is why I'm calling you."

"Wow," said Cranswell, sounding somewhat overwhelmed, and then rallied: "Tell me everything you can. I don't have our catalog of arms and armor memorized, but I can go and look."

"Varney didn't get a good look at it—he described it as a spike, or a short weapon like a rondel dagger. But the blade itself was cross-shaped. Like two individual blades intersecting at right angles. I have no idea how one would go about making such a thing."

"I've seen something like that, but it wasn't a knife," Cranswell told him. "Lawn sprinklers have spikes like that to anchor them in the ground. I'm guessing your friend didn't encounter a ritual lawn sprinkler stake, however."

"The likelihood is slim. But if you could look through the daggers you've got hidden away and see if anything even close to this exists in your catalog, I'd appreciate it—but mostly I want you to check the manuscript collection."

"Manuscripts," Cranswell repeated. "You think this thing might show up in one of them?"

"It's the monk costumes. I can't get the medieval warrior-monk orders out of my mind, you know, taking up arms in the service of some flavor or other of god. Varney said they went on a bit about unclean creatures of darkness and purification and so on, which is difficult to credit in the modern age, but then again this whole wretched business is somewhat unbelievable."

"I'll have a look," said Cranswell. "If we have anything it'll be in storage; none of the manuscripts on display are likely to have anything useful to offer, but I'll check."

"Thank you. I...do know you're busy," Ruthven said, wryly. "I appreciate it."

"I could kind of use a break right now, actually. I'll call you this afternoon if I find anything, okay?"

"Splendid," he said. "If you aren't doing anything tonight and feel like being social, come over. I'll make you dinner in partial recompense for your time."

Cranswell chuckled. "Done," he said. "Any opportunity to avoid eating my own cooking, you know. Okay, I'll go see what we've got."

"Thank you," Ruthven said again, meaning it. He set the phone back in its cradle, feeling somewhat guilty at having dragged another person into this business but mostly relieved to have Cranswell's assistance and his access to a staggering number of primary sources.

Greta rubbed at the hollows of her temples, leaning against the lab bench and watching her ex-boyfriend twiddle knobs on his microscope. "Well?" she said.

"Well what?" Twiddle, twiddle. "How do you expect me to do any sort of analysis if you keep interrupting me to say 'well'? In fact I can't make out anything useful in this. Just looks like a sharp piece of silvery metal to me. I'll have to run it through the GC-MS." Harry sounded interested.

She came forward; after a moment he moved to let her have a look down the scope. As he'd said, it wasn't much use: a triangular fragment of white metal, presumably the tip of some kind of blade, with a weird greyish coating on bits of it. The coating was what worried Greta. Other than metal and blood, it had smelled sulfur-sharp and *familiar*, as if she'd been around that scent some time before, but she couldn't place it. And Varney's reaction to whatever it was had indicated a fairly complicated inflammatory response.

"*Can* you?" she asked. "Last time I had to get some spectrometry done I had to wait ages for my samples to be processed, there was a queue of several labs ahead of me, and anyway it must cost something awful."

"Maybe at King's College you'd have to wait, but this is the Royal London," Harry told her with a smirk. "As it happens we don't have a queue for the mass spec just at the moment and this is weird enough to be interesting, so I'm willing to take it on."

"You're magnificent," said Greta, straightening up. "Completely *magnifique*."

Harry laughed. "You didn't get any sleep at all, did you? I can tell. Go away and let me get on with my work. I'll ring you as soon as I get any results out of this mess."

She nodded, stifling another yawn, and collected her vast and untidy handbag. "Right. I'll be in touch, Harry, and thanks. I really do appreciate it."

He was already packing up the sample to prepare it for the gas chromatograph–mass spectrometer, and just nodded— the same annoyingly distracted little nod she remembered without love from the time they'd spent together. Greta shoved her hands into her pockets and headed out of the laboratory, making a conscious effort to think about something—anything—else.

Greta's personal life was practically nonexistent, given the demands of her career, and in any case it had been a losing proposition trying to date someone completely outside the world she worked in. She had had a handful of relationships in her adult life, none of them lasting more than a few months and all of them largely unsatisfactory. It was difficult to keep coming up with new and inventive cover stories for her day job, for one thing, and while she defaulted to *I run a private clinic for special-needs patients* and relied on doctor-patient confidentiality to avoid having to discuss what it was she actually did, Greta found the effort of it exhausting. She had allowed Harry to think that the nature of her clinic tended toward the discreet treatment of diseases one simply did not talk about, but dinner-table *how was your day* conversations had been a daily minefield to negotiate, and the benefits of being involved with someone had simply not measured up.

He was a useful acquaintance, however, and Greta had from time to time presumed on that acquaintance to get some lab work done—and been very, very glad that Harry didn't ask questions, particularly those starting with "why."

She made her way out of the lab building without paying much attention to her surroundings until she was outside again, looking up at the façade.

The original structure of the Royal London Hospital wasn't a particularly prepossessing building, made out of yellow-brown brick with some cursory pilasters stuck on the front in a stab at classical gravitas. Over the years new bits had been built on here and there, including a vast series of rectangular additions clad in blue glass that contrasted very oddly with the Georgian design of the original building. It was ugly but it was also clearly thriving, busy, and not relying on optimism and duct tape to keep going.

Her own clinic in Harley Street was about as spartan as you could get, and the only reason she was located in that particular hallowed realm at all was that her father had owned the property outright and left it entirely to her on his death, along with just about enough to pay the taxes. These days her neighbors were mostly other specialist clinics rather than the personal offices of famous and/or knighted medical men, but she was still very conscious of her own comparative unimportance. Premises in London's historic medical VIP area were a bit exhausting to live up to, especially when she couldn't afford to keep the place looking quite as glossy as the rest of the street, despite the protective illusion wards on the door. What money she could spare after expenses and upkeep went toward helping her more disadvantaged patients with necessities.

Greta let herself entertain a thoroughly idiotic fancy of building some modern blue glass boxes on the roof of the property to create a solarium for her mummy patients, and shook her head. Harry was right. She needed sleep.

She had called her friend Nadezhda Serenskaya early that morning to see if she could possibly take Greta's office hours for the day; Nadezhda, who was a witch and thus well acquainted with London's supernatural community, and Anna Volkov, a part-rusalka nurse practitioner, regularly stepped in to help Greta out, but generally with more notice. Now she took out her phone again and dialed the clinic.

It rang three times before Nadezhda came on the line, and Greta knew it would have gone to voice mail if she was with a patient, but there was still a stab of guilt at having to make her friends do the receptionist part of her job as well as the actual doctoring.

"Greta," Nadezhda said, sounding unruffled. "What's up?"

"Hey, Dez. At the moment, not a lot." She couldn't suppress a yawn. "Thanks again for stepping in on zero notice. How's it been so far?"

"Hush, you know I *like* the work, I'm glad to help. Pretty quiet, some walk-ins but mostly I'm amusing myself tidying up your sample cabinets and dusting your office, which is hilariously disorganized. Are you okay? What's going on?"

"I'm fine," she said. She could picture Dez bustling and had to smile. "I just didn't get any sleep last night—house call, and a bad one; it's something I've never seen before. I think we're out of the woods, but I'm waiting on test results."

"Which are going to take forever," said Nadezhda. "So you ought to go home and get some damn sleep while you can manage it. Don't worry about the clinic, everything's under control, and Anna says she can take tomorrow and the day after if you need them, I've called her already."

There was absolutely nothing in that statement that should make Greta want to cry, but much like Ruthven's latte art it tightened her throat nonetheless. She didn't *deserve* friends like these. "Thank you," she said, and was relieved to hear that her voice sounded entirely ordinary. "I'll...find something to eat, and then yeah, okay, I will go home for a little while. Thanks, Dez." What she really wanted to do was hurry back to Ruthven's to see how Varney was doing, but she knew perfectly well that Ruthven would call her if there was any change.

"No worries. You call me if you need anything, all right?"

"I will," she told the phone, and "Good-bye," and swallowed hard. This was fatigue and low blood sugar. Nadezhda was right: food first, and *then* rest.

With a sigh Greta turned and started off along Whitechapel Road. There was a fairly decent pub just a block away, the Blind Beggar, which ought to be able to provide her with some lunch; then perhaps she might actually have a chance to drive home and get some sleep.